INTO SEETHING DARKNESS

INTO SEETHING DARKNESS

LONDON TO CAIRO TRILOGY:
BOOK II

ALEX DAVID

This is a work of fiction
Into Seething Darkness Copyright© Alex David 2020

First paperback edition 2020

Cover by Alex David

ISBN: 9798609319807

Author's Note:

This is a work of fiction. Names, characters, places, and incidents either are the product of the author's imagination or are used fictitiously, and any resemblance to actual persons, living or dead, events, or locales is entirely coincidental.

Imprint: Independently published

PROLOGUE

DUST GRINDS OUR post down.

"Dirty little beasts!" Toc grumbles.

"What are you on about?" I ask.

"Rats," Toc snaps, bits of fine yellow sand caking at his mouth.

Releasing my chinstrap, I stare at Toc, my eyes smarting with the effort. "Our entire camp is covered in dust. Most of the tents have already collapsed because of gusts of wind. And when I go outside to tighten the ropes holding down our own tent, sparks fly from under my fingers. And you talk of *rats?*"

"Sparks? Jack, did you say sparks?"

"Sparks." The word rides on my exhaled breath. I am drained. Drained and scared, because as soon as the sandstorm passes, we will be face to face with the German Afrika Korps, Rommel's troops.

"Electrical charges carried by dust particles generate sparks. But, damn it, the least I could hope for in a dust storm is relief from those abominable rats!"

"Abominable rats?" I croak.

Close by, our tent mate, Moss, the one with the pet monkey, Bandar, mumbles, "There he goes again. Our very own Byronic Corsair."

"Lord Byron's Corsair?" I glance at Toc. "Now that you mentioned it, Moss…"

Toc certainly has some characteristics of Byron's Lord Conrad. Toc is intelligent, dark and sunburnt, and of noble birth, and when he aims, he shoots to kill with something of a raging devilry. But we all have that, I suppose. After all, we must win this war. We must protect our island, our empire.

We must stop the Nazis.

But then I recall that Byron's Lord Conrad is of moderate height. I turn to Moss and say, "No, Toc's too tall."

"What?" Moss asks.

"Toc's too tall."

Moss stares in bewilderment while Toc comes close, squinting through his mask of yellowish dust, blood, and cordite, then rubbing his face on his sleeve angrily. "Are you going to discuss poetry right now, or are you merely doing it to criticize my form of speech?"

"No. You cannot help it. What with your education and upbringing!" I drop onto my cot with exhaustion.

Toc settles down next to me and whispers, "Jack, are you holding it against me?"

"I don't understand."

"Are you holding my education and upbringing against me?"

"No, of course not. How could I? But why aren't you an officer? People of your class usually are! With people like me as their faithful batman. Why are you in a lowly regiment, and a corporal, in the middle of the desert in North Africa?"

"Does it matter?" Toc asks.

"Of course it matters!"

And just before Toc's face clamps up, he blurts, sotto voce, "Well, it won't matter in a couple of hours."

And so we wait out the storm in silence. Well, not entirely in silence. We neither of us speak, but the hissing wind outside hurtles sand at our tent. And the hiss is maddening.

At three in the morning, just hours into the first day of July of 1942, the storm abates and is immediately followed by the crump of Axis artillery.

"Let the battle begin!" Toc explodes in boyish insanity and passes rum all round and that's the last that I see of Toc's face as we set to buffet the onslaught of the enemy vanguard.

#

Running in a ditch towards our anti-tank guns, my lungs fit to burst, I bend my knees and cover my head. Something like thirty German Stukas dive in relays over my head.

"I'm still alive," I hurl cheek at the last disappearing bomber.

But as I lift my head, my position is bleak.

Smoke and licking flames hide the enemy tanks much like the salvo and its unholy din drown out the eldritch screech of Rommel's infantry.

The tanks are right before me, I know. And my senses reel with the smell of blood and explosives, vomit, sweat, and feces, and with the burning pain in my eyes from dust and smoke and a myriad of chemicals of warfare. And each time I take a step, the shelling starts up again.

Finally, I sprint forward and almost make it to my box when the ground shakes under my feet.

For a moment, I feel nothing and hear nothing, until rough hands shake me and a harsh voice calls, "Johnson, get up!"

Now, my body throbs with pain.

"Johnson!"

Pinned in a minefield in North Africa, somewhere between hell and delirium, Sergeant is shouting, his mouth gnashing insults barely an inch from my ear. "Get the hell up! Damn it, man, off your arse and on your feet!"

Confused, I stumble into a crouch and shuffle behind Sergeant. We reach our position and, as if automated, I follow the command and set the guns to the firing range.

"Where's Toc?" I ask but Sergeant is already gone. "I can't do it by myself!"

Out of the wall of dust, a giant of a man appears and in his Yorkshire accent offers his help. He calls out, "Pull!" and I pull as he thrusts the canister in and then the machine shoots, taking potshots into the wall of smoke, into the Afrika Korps and toward their hated artillery, the 88mm anti-tank guns.

My giant picks up the next canister, and I hope that their gun hasn't had the chance to speak because when the solid shots of the 88 do not hit a target, they go bouncing along the desert floor like a skipping stone on a placid lake, that is, until they find something or someone to hit, annihilating whatever or whoever is in their path.

Hours later, a tank appears behind us.

As I stare into the main gun, I am certain that this is it.

This is the end.

But out of the thick screen of smoke and dust, men jump out. They have the same accent as the giant by my side and call out, happy to find their comrade. They offer to relieve our position.

In the distance, bombs fall now from above but they are a little different. Tonight, they explode higher up then cascade down, the burning bits of metal aglow, twinkling through the haze.

Blinking hard, I recollect Sergeant's speech. We are the Eighth Army. We must defend this stretch of desert, the last barrier between the enemy and the Suez Canal, the lynchpin of the British Empire. If we fail, the consequences are unthinkable. And in my tumble of thoughts, I want to ask, *what of Malta?* And then again the sense of wonderment grips me - *I am still alive!*

The Yorkshire giant and I head to Sergeant's dugout in the sand, to get our next orders. Before I drop down to my knees with exhaustion, a hand reaches to steady me when I sway. It's not the Yorkshireman, I know. He has already joined another gunner and I cannot but wonder at his level of energy.

"Jack."

"Toc! It's you! What're you doing here?"

"Jack, I used to go hunting. I used to go hunting with my father on our estate. Do you know what I think? We are bombed, and we cannot do a thing about it. Like those ducks attracted to the decoys my father used!"

"What?"

"Ducks," he rasps.

"Toc, don't speak. I'll get some water." I can sense that something is wrong with Toc. There is a gash on Toc's face, a dark stain spreading rapidly.

"And what about all those promised reinforcements? Where are they?"

"We need better guns and tanks. We're no match to the 88."

Toc croaks, "We need hunting tricks. Why not stage dummy encampments with tanks, carriers, lorries, antitank guns, the lot? Let the Jerries strafe dummies, not us."

CHAPTER 1

Saturday 30 May 1942
CAIRO, EGYPT

"FARAJ, WILL YOU help me?" Elliot Westbrook wiped his brow and leveled his cobalt eyes at Faraj.

Sitting at an alcove in his sprawling café, the Egyptian Jewish businessman looked at his young English friend, an indulgent, avuncular smile lighting up his plump face. "Elliot, *mon ami*, of course. Did you lose much at the races again?"

"I never lose."

"No?"

"It's not money, Faraj!" Elliot waved his hand in a suave dismissal that matched his well-modulated accent.

"Well?"

"I need an accomplice." Elliot's dusky curls bounced on his forehead, a shiver of electric excitement coursing through him.

"Accomplice?" Faraj's brown eyes flew open and his fingers scratched his rough, salt-and-pepper stubble.

"*Aywah*. And a strategist."

Faraj's dimples reappeared in his cheeks and a deep gurgle surfaced. "An accomplice and a strategist? What would you have me do, my English Effendi?" Then, struck by some horrific realization he exclaimed, "Nothing related to shooting or killing. I cannot abide by that! I am not a coward, mind you."

"No, Faraj, I ask for nothing of the sort!"

"No, not a coward! But I cannot bear the sight of all those beautiful, young men carried to Cairo with half their bodies gone," Faraj continued, his eyes shut and his palms clapped on his face, a mask of sorrow. "The last time your Eighth Army retreated, I saw the boys piled high in lorries. The sun beat down on them, and there was blood everywhere and missing body parts! What is happening to humanity?"

"Humanity?" Elliot snorted.

Faraj waited patiently.

"It's nothing to do with war."

"Good."

5

"Faraj, imagine a night club like no other here in Cairo! A reputable establishment with superb cabaret and excellent service. Some card rooms, for select gamblers. And all clean and aboveboard."

"Yes? But it will be hard to find a good building for such a club at a fair price now."

"There is such a building, a rare gem, and that's the very reason I'm here. I need you."

"Eh?"

"It's a rare beauty of a building. And I need an idea, a trick, to get it for a decent price and right away!" Elliot proceeded to describe the structure and its location, and he even disclosed the name of the structure's owner and her agent.

"A club! At a fair rate and *tout de suite*! Here? In Cairo?"

"Precisely! So, here I am."

"Yes, here you are!" Faraj drawled in Cairene Arabic. "A fine English gentleman! Young and wealthy! A handsome effendi! The son to Cairo's most prominent politician! Popular and well known throughout Cairo! And although you are not your father's first born, you are next in line while James, the heir, is risking life and limb, galavanting in the Western Desert with the Eighth Army as a surgeon, or so we think."

"Faraj!"

"No, no, this will not do!" Faraj held up his hand and counted on his thick fingers. "Your good looks, your youth, your wealth, and your nationality and social status will have to be altered. That's first!"

"And second?" Elliot's eyes flashed with mischief.

Another appreciative chuckle came out. And Elliot marveled at Faraj's laughter, at its peculiar accent. "Why, we'll need a grand illusion."

"On par with Aziza the Beast?"

"Jest if you please, my effendi, but Aziza was a mistress of strategy. You get yourself a disguise. While I'll think on it, *mon ami*. Visit me later." The utterance was sealed with an oriental hand wave, some French words of farewell, and a wistful glance at the backgammon tables. Suddenly, Faraj shot a quick sentiment of concern, "But what would your mother say?"

"Mother will learn to accept me as I am."

Faraj sighed. "I do not wish to upset Lady Westbrook."

"You won't. But I certainly will, one way or another. I always do! And, since you'd mentioned your concern for James, Faraj, my brother is a surgeon. What could possibly happen to him? Get slapped on the arse by one of his pretty nurses?" Elliot's mouth then stretched into a smile as he rose. *"Au revoir, mon ami!"*

#

The hazy afternoon foretold of another dust storm. In the café, Faraj's new ceiling fans rotated on. Moistened sheets added humidity and discomfort to the heat the same way the loud wireless, broadcasting Umm Kulthum ululating over her symphony of violins and tambourines, added to the noise in the café.

"Jamal, see that *salaud*?"

Jamal nodded. "Yes, Effendi."

"Throw him out. We don't serve the likes of him here."

Jamal, inured to such acidic requests from his master, bowed his head and walked toward the antique, monocled French interloper who creaked into the shop shouting curses in French and demanding service, ridiculing natives and shooting sharp words and glances at servers and customers alike, abusing indiscriminately, complete with adequate Arabic translation of the spicier insults for everyone's benefit.

"And how do you listen to such noise. I cannot call it music. Hellcat's meow!"

"It's Umm Kulthum, *salaud*!" Chin up, and with firm steps, Jamal approached the Frenchman. Jamal would have had doubts if the man were younger, more virile. But the specimen before him was gray and hunched, and dressed in the height of fashion of the previous century. In fluent French, Jamal dismissed the intruder, his insults echoed by gleeful cries from the patrons.

Though the Frenchman fell silent, he did not turn to leave. Instead, his cobalt blue eyes rested shrewdly on the Egyptian. "Call your employer. Call Faraj Effendi," he rasped in fluent Arabic.

The stranger stood his ground until Faraj presented himself. Then the Frenchman looked up and smiled a wolfish grin straight into the brown eyes of his old friend, the proprietor.

"Mon Dieu!" Faraj's hand shot to his heart and with his second *"Mon Dieu,"* Faraj pulled the Frenchman into an embrace and into his office in the back of the sprawling shop, chuckling and murmuring, "You devil," all the while. "You had me. I congratulate you! Part one is indeed complete." Faraj slapped Elliot's back.

"Good enough to order Jamal to chuck me out? And with *such* language!"

"Certainly! You had me thoroughly fooled, my friend. Hellcat's meow? My music? I play Umm Kulthum! I play Egypt's best female soloist!"

"And a very fine diva she is. While enjoying the performance and playing backgammon, have you had a chance to think of step two?"

7

Faraj's only reply was one of his deep chuckles. It was some time before he spoke since his spasms of mirth rolled into barks of laugher.

"Do I amuse you, Faraj?"

"*Mon Dieu!*" Faraj finally squeaked. "And are you, Elliot Effendi, familiar with the *woman* who owns your little *gem*?"

"Some old Levantine," Elliot replied, feeling piqued. What was so amusing?

Again, Faraj choked into laughter.

"Faraj."

Wiping his eyes, Faraj managed, "I have made some inquiries. Old Levantine does not begin to describe what you are up against, my friend. But, you will succeed. Thanks to that outrageous outfit of yours, too! And little did you know!"

"What do you mean?"

With Herculean effort, Faraj brought his paroxysm under control. "Your Levantine is none other than," he paused. "None other than Madame Sukey!"

"I've never heard of her."

"No, you wouldn't."

"Well?"

"Madame Sukey is a rapacious widow in her late fifties. Very greedy and is known to have a penchant for the French."

"Good God, I can see where this is going."

"Yes, after her husband died and maybe even before, she had a string of French lovers. There was an English beau. She loves a good bargain and negotiating is her *raison d'être*. Do you want me to go on? Are you still interested in the club?"

Elliot did not answer right away. "The location is perfect, Faraj. The structure is sound. Open floor plan. A large hall facing the main thoroughfare. There are a number of back rooms, well appointed and with strong walls and tall ceilings."

"I see."

"It's a chance of a lifetime."

"She is no beauty, and her halitosis is a death wish," Faraj warned, but his warbling voice undid the funereal tones he endeavored to summon.

Elliot kept still.

"This is what we will do. You will be the wooing lover and I the rascally businessman ready to buy her out of a rundown, dilapidated property that would bring her nothing but trouble."

"Faraj, how do I exit the wooing stage and enter nightclub ownership?"

"I make such a low, almost insulting, offer, you are obliged to make a better one. Still low, mind you, but better, a fair market offer. All in the name of love."

"And she is in her fifties?"

"Fifties? Yes, old, for you, and with bad breath," Faraj clinched his argument, his face aglow, outshining his dimples.

#

"Look here, Faraj, you did not tell me about all the chins. Halitosis, yes, but not the chin or its subordinates!" Elliot remonstrated as he burst upon his friend mere hours after their last interview.

Boiling in a dinner jacket and tolerating civilities with Cairene high society, Elliot had taken tea with his mother at Shepheard's hotel. As a general rule, he avoided such outings since his mother insisted on formal wear despite the immeasurable heat. But, Faraj's man informed Elliot that Madame Sukey often took tea at the famous hotel.

Observing Madame Sukey in the company of a wealthy octogenarian on the terrace, had stupefied Elliot. Madame and her courtier were laughing energetically and all Madame's chins, to Elliot's horror, quivered. Madame had two girls in attendance, and one of the girls held a fan and used it to fan her mistress.

Elliot had felt that he was transported to some grotesque dimension of Pharaonic times. As he rushed back to Faraj's shop, his mind reeled at the prospect of courting such a hefty creature with bizarre attendants and insalubrious habits.

"Elliot, any woman next to the beautiful and elegant Lady Westbrook is a cow," Faraj dismissed Elliot's concerns regarding Madame Sukey's looks. "Your mother's exceptional beauty alters your perception of other women. Are you sure that your Madame Sukey was that repulsive? And," a smile stretched across Faraj's face, "does it matter?"

After a pregnant moment, Elliot choked, "No, of course not. It's the club that I want and nothing would stop me. Not even those folds of flesh under the chin. But it'd have been nice to know."

"I hear that she is tall," Faraj commented.

"Very tall. For a woman. You know Faraj, you might have the right of it. After all, I was having tea with Mother and indeed Mother does alter one's view of the rest of the female population."

"Lady Westbrook dazzles."

Elliot agreed distractedly. "Faraj, what do we do next?"

"We will need to have you properly introduced to Madame Sukey. Do you know anyone who might be able to help you with introductions?"

"No one that I can think of."

"Your mother would recoil from such a creature."

9

"She did just that this very afternoon!"

"It has to be someone who goes between the two worlds, between English high society and the Cairene society," Faraj mused.

"My father? Or even my kid brother, William?"

"William? Really?"

"William's a doctor, isn't he? He's in contact with all sorts!"

Faraj corrected Elliot, "James is a surgeon, yes, but William is a medic, an assistant in a military hospital here in Cairo. William himself explained to me that his experience working with the rescue units during the Blitz in London opens up a wider range of responsibilities but he does not have the proper credentials like James."

Elliot lifted his shoulders and jutted out his chin. "Same thing as I see it. You should hear some of the things William does! He says little, but the few bits that he lets slip are enough to get my spine tingling. And every now and then, I walk in on him when he's patching someone up, or chopping something off. So much blood and organs, veins and sutures, fluids and such horrid smells…"

"No more, Elliot. You know my sentiments on blood and all that. William is a brave man," Faraj raised his palm. "As is James. Let us leave it at that! *Laisse tomber!*"

"Still, I'll ask William. He comes in contact with many Cairene personalities. You'd be surprised at the ghoulish delight the privileged class takes in visiting a hospital!"

Faraj doubted that William would be able to make the introduction. And he had a notion that Elliot's father, a diplomat, would be reluctant to bring Elliot into the company of such a woman, despite her unimaginable wealth.

Madame had married a landlord who had purchased one district after another and when he died, he had left it all to his relict.

Faraj would have to find the solution himself. He was prepared to do so! He liked his friend and enjoyed his company. He had known Elliot and his brothers, James and William, for many years now. The three boys erupted into his shop one winter and had been popping in and out regularly ever since, bringing with them effervescent cheerfulness and challenges. They had been intrigued by his stories of Aziza the Beast, a grand Cairene mob heiress, and Elliot had even gone as far as searching for Aziza's offspring and came upon a beautiful woman who had to be the mob heiress' granddaughter.

Faraj smiled to himself.

He wanted to help Elliot. So how to go about it? He knew many people in government and he knew many people in business and merging the two together was something that he could do.

"I can imagine a meeting in the afternoon between Madame and you. Maybe in the gardens! We'll ask Jamal to continue to follow Madame. Study her movements!"

"Before we go any further, Faraj, you must give me a name. You seem to be confident in the authenticity of my disguise, but what the devil should I go by. What name?"

"Some sort of an 'Armand' or 'André'?"

"No, no, sounds like an arse!"

Faraj smiled and suggested, "Dominique?"

"Sounds like a buffoon!"

"Then Leclerc!"

"Faraj, did you get the idea for the name from General Philippe Leclerc?"

Raising his thick eyebrows, Faraj pulled a face. "And what if I did? Leclerc then?"

Elliot consented with an unbecoming grunt.

#

Later that day, help came from unexpected quarters, at least unexpected by Faraj.

"Do you happen to know a Madame Sukey?" Elliot, not entirely ready to dismiss possible help from either William or his father, approached William as his younger brother walked into the drawing room still in his hospital garb, mysterious stains darkening, patchwork like, his outer layer.

William's hand reached for the whiskey decanter. He directed his unblinking pale blue stare at Elliot. Then he poured himself a generous measure, tossed it off neat, and asked, "Madame Sukey with the dragon breath?"

"Faraj called it halitosis. Come now, you're a doctor, you know she can't help it!"

William raised his hand. "I am not a doctor. But you're in the right. Describing a person by the ghastly smell emanating from her mouth is rather low. So, the Madame Sukey who I met is often in the French ward, with her servants laden with goods for our patients. She runs lascivious eyes over the soldiers' bodies. She caresses their cheeks with her red talons. Sometimes she brings a glass of wine to their chapped lips, she even goes as far as shaving the lads, too, or playing cards, as noisy and as carefree as any of the boys. And, no, I have no idea where she gets the

11

wine. Maybe black market or maybe her dead husband had bottles stored somewhere. And even though she is a widow, she never wears black when she visits our hospital. Never! It is always some bright shade of crimson and gold. She makes it a point to keep a flowing chatter of flattery and flirtatious remarks, with occasional comments on the weather and food and wine." ·

Elliot had turned pale at the description of the widow. He had been hoping that Faraj was indulging in exaggerated details when he had last described Madame Sukey. But William's disclosures would be accurate all right. His younger brother rarely used melodramatics.

"When will she next visit your hospital?"

"She is a regular ghoul. Besides the French, she likes one of the doctors, oh, and some of the taller Australians."

"Is the doctor French or Australian?"

"Neither! He's English. And rather short. But she's a valetudinarian of lascivious habits."

"You cannot be serious, William."

"I know. It does not add up but there you have it. She is concerned with her health and so plagues the nurses and doctors alike with an ever changing catalogue of ailments and medical concerns yet willingly engages in intimate relationships. Sure she washes her hands frequently but she never covers her face when someone's coughing. And she's unperturbed at the sight of blood. She is an enigma with innumerable contradictions. But, look here Elliot, Madame Sukey is generous and good hearted, there's no doubt about that. Our hospital staff welcome her visits with open arms! Except for Mrs. Wright."

"The nurse you work with?"

"She might be jealous of Madame, but I can't tell. By the way, why the sudden interest in such a creature?"

"A hypochondriac and a lecher," Elliot rasped.

"Doesn't lecher apply to a man?"

"All right, a hypochondriac and a libertine."

"Yes. And the bad breath, you know, but we won't mention that. But do tell. Why the sudden interest in Madame Sukey? Oh, by the way, she is rather mature, too. Did you know that? Does Mother know about your interest in Madame?"

"I want to buy her club," Elliot stared at William wondering why William was taking such care at describing Madame Sukey and then pointedly asking about Mother. "When will Madame Sukey visit you? And when she does, will you be able to telephone me?"

12

William held Elliot's steady gaze. "Buy a club? What sort of a club?"

"Entertainment and such."

"And such? What precisely would 'and such' entail?" William was beginning to doubt whether he should assist his brother in purchasing a club, and from such a woman!

Elliot lit a cigarette.

"Look here, Elliot, is this another scheme you and Faraj have concocted to capture the attention of the granddaughter of Aziza the Beast? Because if there ever existed such a paragon of beauty and cunning and femininity…"

"She does exist! I've met her!"

"Yes. You met her under rather mysterious and dubious circumstances and then gallivanted to some hellhole in Northern Egypt only to be captured by local police on spurious grounds and narrowly escaped after a series of explosions rocked the prison while you swam to safety, returning home smelling of death and looking haggard a day before Christmas Eve!"

As William threw words around, retelling Elliot's fictional search for a woman he was deeply infatuated with, he never noticed the pain etched into Elliot's seemingly passive face.

"So, you mean to tell me that it is not a scheme to find Aziza the Beast's granddaughter?" William pressed on.

"Far from it!" replied Elliot with energy, happy that, for a change, he could give an honest answer to William. "I want a club and Madame has a fine structure that is for let. I want to buy it, though, and I want to buy it without delay. And, I want a fair price!"

"I will phone you then as soon as I spot her. But what would Mother say?"

"Mother?"

"Elliot, your reputation is deteriorating!"

"Deteriorating?"

"First, you blow up a dormitory…" William began and held up his index finger foretelling an inventory of misdemeanors.

"*We* blew up the dormitory. It was a joint effort!"

"Fine. We blow up the dormitory. We get sent down."

"Expelled!" Elliot laughed.

"Then we pick up a tutor and *you* manage to eliminate the tutor…"

"William, we were expelled so Father shipped us to Egypt to live with Grandfather. Grandfather then saddled us with a tutor. Both of us managed to eliminate the tutor by the simple initiative of delivering him into Faraj's able hands! That adventure was as much your doing as mine."

"Well, yes, Elliot. So it was. We did drag the poor man into Faraj's coffeeshop and hoped that Faraj would keep him busy while we explored the suks, but Faraj took it farther and introduced the fellow to the very person that turned out to be our estimable tutor's love match."

"A dwarf from Aswan!"

"Love match, Elliot."

"Never mind!"

"But while I returned to England for private tutoring and to pursue medical studies, you remained here, carefree..."

"Carefree? Grandfather was a slave driver. His library alone would baffle any scholar. Then, the old rascal dragged me as far north as Lebanon and Syria and as far West as Benghazi on diplomatic errands. Besides, I was day and night harangued by that linguist whom he had employed for my erudition."

"It was your own fault for letting it slip that you have incredible memory!"

"Hush, don't remind me. Or Father!"

"Well, you cannot help it. What else was Grandfather to do but put your skills to use?"

"I wanted to explore the city. Cairo has so much to offer. I didn't ask to be his translator!"

William leveled a knowing look at his older brother, refraining from listing what Cairo had to offer and the dangers and diseases that came along with it. "Despite your efforts to feature as the half-wit of the family, or a Casanova, Grandfather recognized your genius, and kept you out of the suk."

"I was his translator!" Elliot howled.

"Pity Grandfather died before this war broke out."

"Yes, he would have made an excellent High Commissioner."

"But, Elliot, about this idea of yours, your club, I mean. You must admit that even though your schooling has been eccentric to say the least, it does not entitle you to own and run a club. Besides, are you not working at GHQ? When will you have time to do it all?"

"I have time to spare for a club, and I will have a majordomo to help me run it. You need not worry about my time. But I doubt that that is what is troubling you."

"How will you contrive? How will you convince Mother to allow you to stray from your social obligation and what is expected of a man in your position? A club, Elliot?"

"But you forget, I am not the eldest son and James is a surgeon. A surgeon! Most unsuitable."

William broke into a fit of unmanly giggles as Elliot mimicked their mother's complaint of 'not suitable!' He relented, "Elliot, all right. I will telephone you when I next see Madame Sukey. But if Mother hears of it, she'll be incensed!"

"Father won't like it either, you know."

"No, neither will particularly like it. But will you, Elliot? Will you like it enough?"

"Very much."

"And your fiancée, Louisa Baker?"

"What about my fiancée?"

"Will she like her future husband dangling himself at the tap?"

"William, don't let it bother you. Yes, I am engaged to be married to Louisa. But I cannot marry her until James returns, at least on a furlough. Louisa knows that! She cannot expect me to hold a wedding ceremony when my brother is out in the desert, patching up the Eighth Army!"

"Must you marry her? What about your attentions to Aziza's granddaughter?"

Elliot clicked his tongue. "William, will you phone me when Madame is visiting your Humpty Dumpties?"

"Yes, of course," William agreed, rather contrite. He did not mean to ask such blunt, personal questions of Elliot and felt a trifle chastened for letting his curiosity and concern for Elliot get the better of him.

15

CHAPTER 2

An excerpt from Jack Johnson's Notes
Sunday 31 May 1942
THE CAULDRON, NORTH AFRICA

A FREE FRENCH Brigade is defending an Ottoman fortress called Bir Hakeim against Axis forces. The French resist simply to delay an attack on Tobruk, purchasing, with their own blood, a few days for the rest of the Eighth to retreat to the Gazala Line, and for the garrison in Tobruk to ready itself for a siege.

But Bir Hakeim, a Libyan Desert oasis southwest of Tobruk, is about to fall into enemy hands.

"What an odd sort of plan," Toc comments, and rests his head on his knees as the rest of his body sinks against the pillbox wall, trying to take as little space as possible.

"Are the French taking random potshots?" I ask.

Sergeant is listening to incoming communications, calling out sporadic sentences for me to write down. Eventually, Sergeant silences our remarks. "We'll be falling back to the Gazala Line." His gravely voice scratches my conscience. "There're defense boxes along the Line." Sergeant's voice is gaining cheer we none of us feel. "Did you take it all down, Johnson? Jolly good. Now, wire back to Division HQ, destroy the notes, and then drive over the escarpment and deliver these orders to the next pillbox. Verbally, Johnson, verbally! Don't drive round with anything written down!" Then he launches into an abusive litany of the state of our communication lines, and concludes with, "Why I can't have *someone*, *anyone*, from Royal Signals is absolutely beyond me! Johnson, have you wired yet?"

#

After delivering the depressing news, we head back.

Suddenly, Toc shouts, "Aircraft!"

He shakes my arm, yanking on it, as he thrusts his door open and hurtles himself out the lorry, rolling into a nearby ditch.

We remain in the ditch for hours.

As night falls, the blood that covers Toc's leg sends chills down my spine and cools Toc, who is already weakened with loss of blood.

Cold, thirsty, and hungry, we wait. It is only thanks to Toc's excellent eyesight that we are alive, because as we jumped into the ditch, a lone Stuka dive-bombed us, peppering our lorry, then flying away with a final gift, an incendiary bomb that blew up our lorry.

Toc removes the stained vest wrapped round a bit of metal embedded in his thigh.

"No," I say, louder than intended. "I used up all our water to cool off the hot metal in your leg. Keep it wrapped. Flies and sand will get into it and infect the wound."

Toc places a finger to his lips.

With the horrendous noise of the aircraft and the explosion, my hearing falters. So, silent and cold, we await dawn. We plan to leave our ditch with the first light of day and hopefully catch a ride with a roving desert patrol, preferably Allied, though, feeling Toc's convulsive shivers I wonder if I have it in me to surrender, for Toc's sake. He needs medical attention, fast.

When brilliant light floods the horizon, I squint into the rising sun. Suddenly, I feel some vibration then notice a moving vehicle. I shift, ready to step out.

"No, Jack."

Of course, I cannot hear his words but I watch his lips as he pulls me back and it is rather easy to decipher. "Jerries."

"How can you tell they're German?" I shout.

"Jerries."

With the thought that the slow moving lorry is an Axis vehicle, I find that we are not yet so desperate.

I have no wish to surrender.

Glancing at the lorry again, I turn to Toc.

But Toc has fainted.

With another agonized glance over the ditch, I make up my mind. Removing my vest from Toc's leg, I extend the filthy fabric out of the ditch and wave.

A bullet whizzes by.

I quickly draw back. I must get at least some water for Toc.

"Out!" The command is delivered in English. "Come out!" The accent is off.

I peek out, again waving my vest.

A group of unkempt, extremely hairy and sunburnt blond men jump out of a lorry that has no roof nor windscreen. They watch as I crawl ignominiously out. They are leathery and with the desert skin sores one gets when exposed to the sun and dust.

"Name?"

"Private Johnson," I croak.

"Alone?" Their bayonets are extended, ready to eliminate me the instant I displease them.

"Look, who are you?" I strain to stand up.

"Alone?"

"No."

Toc will never forgive me. I know his sentiment about surrender.

As soon as I say 'no,' I see the trigger fingers and stances change to give battle. So I hurriedly explain. "My friend's injured. He needs water and a doctor."

"Just two then?"

"Yes."

"Where?"

"Look, who are you?"

My question, as before, is ignored and one of the hairy men circles round me then peeks into the ditch.

"Bruno! Look here," he says in accented English then bursts into speech in a language that I have never heard before. It is not German. It is not Italian.

"South Africa?" Relief cracks my voice.

The butt of a Bayonet strikes me. Dark emptiness takes over my senses. There is a lingering thought in my head, a hope, that as I die I will see Toc floating to heaven by my side. I feel euphoric because somehow there is nothing better than the prospect of floating heavenward with Toc, except of course for both of us to remain alive.

CHAPTER 3

An excerpt from Jack Johnson's Notes
Monday 01 June 1942
CAIRO, EGYPT

"I wonder why he does that."

"Does what, Jack? And who?" Toc asks, confused but not caring much.

Toc's leg must be throbbing with pain and the bit of morphia tablet the ambulance driver gave him only makes him hazy. But the pain is there, I can see it etched across his countenance by the cracks in his facial mask of fine dust, machinery grease, and runnels of blood and sweat.

I explain, "Sergeant seems to find fault with my hearing rather mercurially."

"Mercurially, Jack? You're still shouting."

"I can hear you all right. But still, Sergeant's decision to send me to Cairo for hearing check-up coincides with some urgent medical need of yours!"

A ghost of a smile flicks across Toc's face. "You're my nursemaid."

The ambulance lurches, and Toc lets out an involuntary cry.

"What's my pay then?" I ask.

"This," he replies then delivers a rather hard punch to my shoulder.

"Didn't think you'd have it in you, in your condition!"

"Didn't think that I would have to pay my friend," Toc rejoins as he closes his eyes. "Take a peek in the looking glass, Jack."

"Why?"

"What did they do to your face? Broke your fine, Roman nose, did they? Ruined your good looks. Was it really necessary?"

"I suppose so. I am intimidating, don't you think?"

"Intimidating? You must be joking."

"What?" I ask.

"Baby food advertisement."

"Shut up."

We rattle across the desert until we end up in Cairo, back with William Westbrook, his homely apostle, Mrs. Wright, and his noisy Australian entourage.

#

"Don't they have their own hospital in Heliopolis or somewhere?" Toc complains as he pokes at his dressing and grimaces. "Why is it always Australians with Westbrook? Can't they send them to their hospitals?"

"Overflowing, dear, like all other hospitals all over the world," chides Mrs. Wright.

"Will Madame Sukey visit us?"

"I'm sure she'll visit *you*. She's partial to the saturnine and dark look."

"What?" Toc squawks.

"Saturnine? More like suffering great pain," I quip.

"Shut up!"

"Now, you settle down. The doctor will be here shortly to check up on you."

After I see Mrs. Wright's skirt trail out the door, I ask Toc, "Madame Sukey?"

"Well, damn it, is it too much to ask for some wine? She often brings wine with her."

"Toc, you cannot be serious."

"I like her!"

"I do too."

"Do you?"

"Yes, but not because of her wine," I say.

"Her caresses?"

"No, of course not! She amuses me, and she *cares*. About us, I mean, about the *troops*."

"She helped me shave last time I was here."

"Look here Toc, are you expecting your father to visit you?"

"Oh, no, no. He cannot know about another injury. Remember last time? He ordered a private ward as if it were as simple as a private parlor or ballroom to commandeer at a hotel or some such place. He has such old fashioned notions about how one must behave and what is due to one's name and status ... Well, you were here. You saw how he went about it."

"I never saw your father. I've heard of his visit, though." I lower my eyes, recalling my family back home. Four of us, crowded in a tenement, and all depending upon the construction industry that fluctuated with the tides of time, politics, and now war. Would my mother and younger brother evacuate to the countryside? I have not heard from them for some time now. Father must be busy with debris removal and reconstruction. But I quickly tuck away thoughts of family. Better focus on the *now*.

"Toc, you're lucky to have him."

"I know Jack, I know. But one must rebel at some point, and this is my little rebellion. Not too bad of me, don't you think?"

"I can't say."

"What did Sergeant say about the hairy beasts who delivered us to him? My memory is foggy."

"You drifted in and out of consciousness."

"I remember thinking that I was in hell with a bunch of singed albino apes," Toc whispers.

"Gives a whole new meaning to the term 'ape-leader,' don't you think?"

Toc gives a faint snort. "I am not a dead, unwed woman who has not fulfilled her duty to marry and bear children!"

"Is that what it means? Damn, I've heard the term somewhere..."

"And never bothered to learn its meaning?"

"Why bother? I have you, Toc."

"Back to the apes, Johnson, if you please."

"Your vision didn't fail you. We were in the ditch, all night. At sunrise, I saw a lorry. You pulled me back thinking that the Panzerarmee was approaching. And no wonder because that South African patrol unit drove a German lorry. They were South Africans, and they mistook us for, well, they mistook me for a German spy and you, oh, Toc, they had you as my Italian accomplice!"

Staring at me with dawning disbelief, Toc shapes his lips to ask, "Why?" but instead he takes a deep breath and begins a proper inquiry, "But what had led them to believe that we were a German spy and his Italian accomplice?"

"Your coloring," I choke into laughter.

"Nonsense!"

"It's true!"

"I have blue eyes!"

"Still, your skin and hair color ... dark."

"And the spy bit?" Toc persists.

"They have been investigating sources of information leaking out of Cairo. Rommel seems to have an uncanny ability to anticipate our attacks and in his communications he refers to the 'Good Source,' the cheeky bastard!"

"Makes sense, but why search the vast desert? If they'll find any such creature letting information pass into enemy hands, it'd be someone in Cairo."

"Sergeant didn't go into details. As soon as the South Africans dumped us at his feet, he growled something about Neanderthals and complained about incompetent idiots. I passed out shortly after I heard the South Africans apologize for their error."

"Are we the Neanderthals or the idiots?"

"The idiots, I'm afraid."

"So here we are, Sergeant's idiots, delivering orders, getting strafed, then to top it all, we get picked up as some common German spies."

"Ah, a German spy and his Italian accomplice!"

"Shut up!" Toc grins.

"Toc, it's not going to be easy here, in Cairo. I want to do my bit! What will I write home about? I want to be *there*, on the front."

"With Sergeant and his troupe of flies?"

"Will Bandar be all right?"

"Of course he will. He's with Moss."

"Rommel's Panzerarmee is advancing, 88mm anti-tank monstrosities at the ready, annihilating one defense box after another. And here we are, idly waiting for some doctor to poke me in the ears or flip you over to redress your thigh."

"And all the while, eagerly awaiting a visit from Madame Sukey! Well phrased, Jack."

CHAPTER 4

Tuesday 02 June 1942
CAIRO, EGYPT

CARNAGE ALONG THE Gazala Line!

The orders were to fight to the last bullet or to the last man. So a steady flow of wounded poured into military hospitals.

"Westbrook, we'll get more convoys within hours now. Get your men ready!" the matron boomed then marched to alert the next ward.

"They're not going to make it. They'll go under, too," an immature voice drifted into William's ears.

"What?" William lifted his eyes to the orderly who was leaning over him, holding the pan a bit too close to William's face while he finished up his work with a catheter.

"The Free French in Bir Hakeim."

"Yes, well, let's hope they make it. The British 150th Brigade defended the Cauldron to the bitter end, if you will, and here we are. Hold it steady, lad, can't have all *that* sloshing about and so close to my face, too. It is infected, you know. Have they showed you how to dispose of it yet?"

"Sorry." Confused, the orderly departed.

William got up and stretched his back, heading to the hallway.

Working with the rescue units in London during the Blitz had won William respect among the hospital staff. He was pale and often sombre and not much older than his orderlies, yet they respected him and obeyed his merest request.

"Westbrook." Standing with folded arms across her chest, Mrs. Wright gave the approaching William a quizzical look. "Well, well, she's all out of Frenchmen!"

"What's that?" William noticed Mrs. Wright's eyes swivel to the Australian ward.

"Madame Sukey."

"What about her?"

"She's with the Australians," the nurse tittered at William's shoulder.

"None of that now," William whispered. "We need Madame Sukey. The desert's on fire again, so we'll soon be very much glad of Sukey's wine and chocolates. Besides, the patients love her shenanigans. They joke and laugh together. It's like going to the opera or to the play, and it helps them with their pain and loneliness. Well, you know," his speech trailed off, half hearted, noticing the sobering effect of his homily on Mrs. Wright's worried, pinched face.

Mrs. Wright was not beautiful at all, but her compassion and her friendly demeanor won her many admirers.

"How's Charles?" he asked, in brisk, cheerful tones. "Is your husband all right?"

"Busy. Running from regiment to regiment, sermonizing."

"He helps the men with their worries and concerns. The conditions are bad enough, but retreating destroyed their morale. And I doubt that the casualties they are taking make it any easier."

"Charles says that the men of the Eighth Army... oh," she broke off. "I'm so sorry."

"About what?"

"I said the Eighth Army, like a reporter. But you know how it is, I get tired of hearing the ubiquitous '*they*' and so I wanted to be precise."

"That's refreshing." William smiled.

"Well, they're afraid to form close friendships. So, they are, in a way, isolated. And they have been away from home for so long."

"Your husband is a man of rare good sense, you know. I've seen him with the troops."

William's compliment to her husband brightened Mrs. Wright's face. "Thank you. Well, I better go. I've more cots to prepare before...they come..." Her last words fell out of her mouth.

Another convoy of ambulances was scheduled for later that day from the Western Desert. More wounded, more men who needed help, and possibly some would get help but all too late. And that was the hardest to bear, the feeling of impotence.

Walking to reception, William asked the secretary to phone his home. "Ask for Mr. Elliot Westbrook."

"Would you like to talk to him, Mr. Westbrook, or should I pass on a message?"

"A message, if you please. Tell him that I have his cake." He blushed.

"Have his cake, Mr. Westbrook?" repeated the secretary in her Cockney accent. She had heard high praise of the pale man, but now she doubted his sanity. What was he talking of cakes for?

William was wishing that he had never agreed to such a ridiculous code word. Cake? What on earth was Elliot thinking? At the time, Elliot simply explained that it was symbolic. But symbolic of what?

"It's symbolic," William threw his parroted words over his shoulder and walked away rather faster than was necessary, hoping that the secretary would not make a fuss.

#

"This is a nasty one, mate," the Australian said. Although spoken sotto voce, his words were echoed by the other patients peeking over William's shoulders, disgusted yet delighted at the mess before their eyes.

"Look here, do you mind?" William remonstrated, extending his arm to hold the wiry Australian away from his comrade.

The patient had a putrid gash running down his thigh. He was barely nineteen. He opened his mouth to curse but fainted from pain instead.

His mate rushed to support him. "Poor little devil," the friend croaked, fighting down nausea.

"Better pray he makes it. You promised his mother you'd bring him home safe!" another man advised. "What a stupid thing to do!"

"Enough of that," William snapped. "Prop him up and shut up."

Eager, muscular hands reached to the soldier and a chorus of cheers erupted when he opened his eyes, confused pools of brilliant blue.

Madame Sukey was close by, her eyes admiring the young man's muscular loins despite the blood and the evil discharge and its foul smell.

"*Bonjour, bonjour!* Well, where is he?" A loud French-accented voice echoed in the hall.

A stooped monocled Frenchman sporting an outrageous gray mustache worthy of the last decade or maybe century materialized. His lapels flapped just under his chin and yellowing lace cuff peeked out of his dusty sleeves.

William stared.

"My patient, where is he?"

The pregnant moment of silence was finally punctuated with a resigned, "Here. Right here, Doctor." William relished the look on the Frenchman's face as the old man noticed the thigh, white-yellowish pus oozing out.

"We've just about finished with the maggots!" The patient's friend pointed to another dirty pan by his feet, waving about the soiled forceps.

Recoiling, the Frenchman brought his handkerchief to his mouth, a wave of nausea overpowering his acting skills.

William turned to Madame. "Madame Sukey, if you'd be so kind and show the good doctor out. His patient is in good hands, and the doctor could use a cup of tea. He's had a long night. It's going to be hellish here soon enough. We're expecting another convoy. I'll leave the introductions to you, Madame."

"But of course, dear. Delighted," Madame Sukey chortled, pinched William's cheek and drew her hand through the French doctor's arm, leading him, triumphant, to the cafeteria.

CHAPTER 5

An excerpt from Jack Johnson's Notes
Tuesday 02 June 1942
CAIRO, EGYPT

"WHO'S THE CHARLATAN dallying with Madame?" Toc asks wrathfully.

"I don't know. But what an act! She cannot even drink her tea!" I observe.

"Windmill arms gesticulating and bragging. Damn the fellow!"

"French? Does she understand a word he's saying?"

"He's interlarding modern French into the conversation," Toc interjects. "An old man would speak differently. I told you, didn't I, my mother was French. This idiot is an impostor. A devilish good one because look at the beatific expression on Madame's face!"

"Not French at all? Are you sure?" I keep Toc talking because he does not like to mention his mother. He lost her to diphtheria.

"He is not French. He slips into fluid, almost native, French now and then but somehow it's inconsistent. I can't quite understand why he does that."

"What?" I ask.

"Why would he try to appear less French?"

Staring at Madame's companion, I say, "And he cannot possibly be a doctor! His conversation is gibberish. I've been to hospital before and helped out too. I've heard the talk, and none of what this buffoon is saying is making any sense."

"Jack, are you upset?"

I am upset that Madame Sukey is in company with such an odd companion. "Look here, I didn't care much for her caresses while I was laid up, but she was kind. She meant well. She is very generous, and she helped the hospital staff when they ran out of disinfectants. She knew where get supplies when there were none in Cairo. And she sent in a company of servants to help, you saw them, the seriously dark and large ones with herculean strength. Cleaned up my ward in no time! Then she sat down to a round of cards."

"My memory is vague. I was in another ward. Doped. Still, I hate to see her gulled by an ass," Toc hisses.

"She's no harpy! She loves men, and that's a fact, but so do other old hags and yet few visit hospitals. Fewer yet donate goods!"

Toc grins. "She's keen on exotic disinfectants."

"Damn, it was sage and garlic dominating the last batch."

"Suspended in vinegar. Half my ward nearly gagged on the fumes alone."

"Oh, so you remember that bit?"

"Garlic and vinegar can penetrate any fog! Jack, we better keep an eye on her. Here, they're leaving now."

"Can you walk?" I ask.

"Oh, I'll walk." Toc gives me one of his rare smiles that light up his sun-burnt face.

CHAPTER 6

Tuesday 02 June 1942
CAIRO, EGYPT

FROM UNDER BUSHY, gray brows, Elliot Westbrook ogled Madame Sukey. "You enchant me, Madame. But I have to ask, what are you doing in this English hospital? I am but arrived to town. It must be philanthropy that brings you into such a place?" he half asked, half commented.

"Dr. Leclerc…"

Elliot put a finger to her lips and whispered seductively, "Philippe, Madame. We are friends, are we not?"

Toc and Jack Johnson had followed the couple to the courtyard.

Toc bristled at the sound of Elliot's last utterance and repeated it with exaggerated accent.

"He's charming enough. But what does he want from Madame?" Jack wondered.

"Money, what else?"

"Toc, could it be?"

"It has to be! But Jack, I cannot go on. It's my leg. You follow them. I'll wait here."

Jack stared at Toc.

"Come back if they leave the gardens."

"All right," Jack agreed, leaving his friend on a bench. Then, Jack meandered close to Madame and her unlikely beau.

"I am to attend a dinner party tomorrow night," said Elliot. "I would that you could join me."

"I will consult my secretary about my social engagements, Philippe."

CHAPTER 7

GASPING FOR AIR, bracing my hands against the garden bench, I croak his name. "Toc!"

"Jack, where on earth have you been? It's been over an hour!"

"And would have been longer had Madame not alerted her Leclerc to his duties! I ran back. Damn this heat! But look here, Toc, I don't know that he wants her money, by God. The liberties he took with her, and in public too. His hands were all over, mouth going up and down her neck and, and … body! And the caresses! Breasts and thighs! And the old horror had the indecency to moan."

"On a bench, and in public?"

"Yes. Well, hidden by bushes, but still."

"Oh, Jack!"

"Oh, Jack indeed. What I had to endure! But I forget, that's not all."

"What?"

"Toc, this Leclerc, this so called Dr. Leclerc, leaves Madame and hails a taxi to a café in the old town."

"If he were a doctor, should he not have returned here straight away?"

"Yes!" I call out.

"Damn."

"And I got a good look at his hands. Not a single wrinkle. Long, firm, very much young and healthy hands! I have heard of young men like that, who enjoy older females."

"Enjoy? Older females? Jack, no, he is after her money!"

"How can you be so sure?" I ask.

"I'm not. But why did he not take her to a hotel room or back to his place or her house then if the passionate scene had progressed as far as you describe? No, we better get a taxi, and get to that café. I've rested long enough here on the bench," he adds as I look at him with concern. "I'm fine. Can you find this café?"

"Yes, of course. I've visited the shop before."

"Then there is not a moment to lose!"

#

The taxi dumps us outside a sprawling noisy café that is decorated with colorful woven rugs, or kilim, and is cooled with fans and moist sheets dancing like ghosts. The café has many alcoves with low tables and cushions except where the backgammon games are roaring with activity. Heavy tables and long benches and some thick chairs support the bottoms of the gamblers.

Inside, Dr. Leclerc is with the backgammon players, so we slide onto a nearby bench and order coffee.

A large man, the owner of the shop who goes by the name of Faraj, talks to the Frenchman. Both are so enthralled by their game that neither bothers to look up from the board as they discuss their business.

Dr. Leclerc, or whoever he is, is still wearing his Frenchman garb but is upright, and his voice is a young-man's voice now. He is talking to Faraj in a mixture of Arabic, English, and French. His English is British, well-educated and beautifully modulated, similar to Toc's, who grew up between Mayfair and his family's estate in Durham, and educated at Eton.

"Jack, no wonder his French sounded odd! It's Cairene French! Complete with the sort of speech patterns Cairene upper class uses!"

I stare at the now obviously disguised man. What is such a man doing playing backgammon with one Faraj, on such friendly terms, talking about a dinner party and Madame? And what club are they talking about? How did that man change his shape and form and class and nationality within seconds?

While thoughts run through my head, almost in a flash, Leclerc reverts to a Frenchman with a monocle, taking his affectionate leave of Faraj.

As we trail behind the impostor, I whisper, "Toc, this is the man England needs right now!"

Shifting his gaze to me, he replies, "If he has not already engaged himself to the enemy. It's possible, you know."

"Everything's possible, but if this man is English and not *otherwise* engaged, then he is the man we need here, in Cairo."

Toc's sweaty curls fall on his forehead as we stroll only paces behind Leclerc. "What a splendid fellow this chap is!" Toc's words are laced with awe.

"Not a charlatan after all?"

"A splendid charlatan."

I read quite a bit into this utterance because Toc himself is a splendid fellow, broad shouldered and well-spoken, a son to a long line of English peers. Well, almost. His mother was French.

"But what the devil does he want from Madame?"

31

"A cabaret, Toc, he wants a club. *Her* club."

"Nightclub?"

"I couldn't tell."

"They spoke of talking to Madame at a dinner party. Jack, normally my hearing is excellent only there was such an infernal noise at the shop, that caterwauling soloist one hears round town. Do they really have to play it at such great volume?"

"And what about the loud giant?" I ask.

"Oh, I know of him. He owns the café! And many other venues here in Cairo and Alexandria. He is no simpleton. He's not a politician either, just enjoys his wealth and privacy, hiding in this suk. He's a Jewish merchant. Rumor has it that he donates generously to the hospitals. But look here, Jack, we better follow Leclerc. We must find out more about him! First, to protect Madame Sukey, but I'd like to find out more about our dear Leclerc. And, can he help us? Because I will be damned if I agree to give sport to Axis Stukas!"

"Or the Messerschmitts!" I add darkly.

"We need new ideas, new strategies, and men who could pull it off here in the desert. I can't endure another retreat!"

"It seems like most of the resources are in England and Europe. But maybe that is just our perspective," I end gloomily.

"Would anyone even listen to our ideas?"

"Your father?"

"My father? Maybe," Toc grumbles.

"Could you walk into GHQ to find a sympathetic ear?"

"When I declared my intention to volunteer as a lowly soldier and work my way up the ranks, I caused a rift between us."

"But he's your father!"

"He wanted his son at university. Can you visualize me at a university?" Sulkily, Toc kicks a pebble with enviable skill. Even with a wounded leg, Toc is a natural athlete, a master at football. "I have to dine with him this evening, did I tell you?"

"Are you going to be all right?"

Toc musters a smile. "Yes, Nurse."

"You know, if I were you, I would delight in such an opportunity to eat delicious food without dust and chemicals and none of it out of a can or from the blistering steel roof of a tank."

"True. And I am expected to dress for dinner so that entails a nice, warm bath."

"Surrounded with comfort in your father's mansion, *and* without your favorite pets."

"Jack, are you calling rats pets?"

"I'm not going to call them abominable rats either! I'm not from Mayfair!"

"No, you come from a long line of Cornish smugglers who made it their habit to share living quarters with vermin."

"Shut up."

Away from Faraj's café, Leclerc's mincing steps gradually become steady, confident strides, heading directly toward the Ezbekieh gardens.

"Elliot!" a fair-complected man hails our quarry.

"Jack, it's our medic, Westbrook."

"He might recognize me."

We turn to face a shopwindow as Leclerc, or Elliot, briefly talks to the medic before slipping into a taxi together.

"Well, he is out of sight now. Where did they go?" Toc jerks his head this way and that but the medic and our mystery man are gone.

"At least we have his name," I say.

"Elliot, but Elliot what?"

CHAPTER 8

Tuesday evening 09 June 1942
CAIRO, EGYPT

TINKLING SOUNDS OF music drifted softly on the sultry night air. Madame Sukey held her glass of wine and looked into the eyes of the elderly Frenchman.

"They give much credit to the French General Koenig," Dr. Leclerc relayed to Madame.

"Oh, I know him. What a strong man he is! And his troops!"

"Did you know that they are no longer called Free French but Fighting French? Quite a fitting change, don't you think?" Elliot chose this topic of conversation since William had mentioned Madame's partiality to Frenchmen and because of his assumed nationality.

"*La France Combattante!*" breathed Madame Sukey. "You must be proud."

Dr. Leclerc raised his glass. "Of course, at the moment, that is all that they can do."

"What do you mean?"

"Well, our Fighting French were declared traitors by the Vichy government. General Koenig and his men were dispossessed of their property, titles, and civic rights. If captured by Vichy, they are traitors. Sport for the firing squad."

"How horrid!" Madame exclaimed.

"And now, they are in Bir Hakeim."

"But that's the front, no? An exposed ridge!"

"You are aware of desert topography?"

"Oh, I am a ghoul, I know! I follow the reports, and I do pay attention when the boys talk about the desert. Bless them, the things they have to endure!"

"Just so," agreed Leclerc with bitter tones. But before Leclerc could continue in such an unromantic vein, Faraj walked onto the balcony.

Waving his arms, Faraj urged his friends to dance. After all, his dinner party turned out to be more than just a lovely gathering. He chuckled as he spoke and ran appreciative eyes over Madame Sukey. "You look breathtaking, Madame," he murmured as she glided by him on the surprisingly firm arm of her Dr. Leclerc.

"Oh, Faraj," she warbled, sizing up his massive form.

Noticing this, Faraj gave a gurgle of satisfaction. He was sure that he could help his friend now.

What an odd trio we must present to the world, thought Elliot in amusement. But when he led her off the dance floor, Elliot was alerted to Madame Sukey's roving eyes.

Elliot engaged Madame in conversation, asking her about her homeland and when she had first come to Cairo. He knew that his questions were bold, but his kisses to her hands and French mutterings of flattery should cover up his gauche investigation.

"I am not from Syria at all. Not Lebanon, either. I know what they say about me. They call me Levantine, but I assure you that I am not. I prefer to be known as Levantine. That's a fact!"

"But why?"

She cast him a dubious glance then lowered her voice. "I am from an oasis near the Qattara Depression. I am from Siwa."

"Siwa?" Shocked, Leclerc stared.

Madame Sukey's lips twisted. "So, you appreciate why I prefer to continue the masquerade of a Levantine?"

Siwa! Elliot thought about and then tried to forget what he had seen last time he'd visited that desert oasis. "It is such a place that one cannot really believe it exits outside fiction!"

"It exists, and well I know it!"

"The building style is ant-heap like. As soon as a house crumbles down, another gets built right on top of it."

"You think of architecture?" Madame's eyebrow, darkened with kohl, shot up.

"And the women! Are they really all…"

"I am not, but many are," Madame Sukey admitted. "The men have long enjoyed each other's company, and Siwan women are quite forgotten."

Elliot cleared his throat. Madame's frank revelations disarmed him. "What I have always failed to understand is the women's hair! Why do they apply so much grease? And the scarlet robes? What is the significance of that?"

"Oh, so you have been there, have you?" Madame fixed him with a steady stare, searching for a hint of his true sentiment on Siwa.

Dr. Leclerc lowered his head. "Forgive me, Madame, for referring to such matters in your company, but, yes, I have visited Siwa."

"And did you also pay your two whole Egyptian pounds for a girl?" Her question was hurled at his bowed head.

Dr. Leclerc straightened. "Never," he growled. "We delivered quinine pills to the villagers. All I got were mosquito bites. My face swelled. You are a lucky woman to have escaped. Why don't you have an accent though?"

Faraj had been observing Elliot and Madame. He noted the rather somber expression on their faces. This would never do, he thought, and quickly formed a new plan. He had already found a hole in his original scheme. What would happen during the purchase of the club? Legally, Elliot could not transfer funds to gain ownership under a false name! He would have to buy the club for Elliot after all.

"Madame Sukey, allow me," Faraj towered over the couple, displaying a bottle of wine as Jamal set a chair for his master. "I will join you."

Like a magician in a conjuring act, Faraj summoned all his charm. The threesome enjoyed the wine, and Faraj's more amusing *on-dits* kept them chuckling until Faraj turned his attention to the entertainment he had planned for the night.

"You want something from me, I can tell," Madame Sukey confided, her hand crushing Elliot's ancient sleeve. "You tell me that you delivered quinine pills to the Siwans. What else did you do? What took you there? Is it the truth? I can tell that you have been to Siwa but what of your motives?"

"I went to Siwa late in 1941. I have friends who received alarming reports of disease and ill-treatment of women, girls I should say, because some of the ones we saw had not reached puberty yet." He paused, recalling the appalling scenes. He pulled out a silver chain.

Madame Sukey's eyes glittered. She reached for the silver chain and its pendant. "What beautiful jewelry they make, no? You purchased this?"

"A gift. From a friend."

"So, I ask you again, what would you wish from me?" she breathed in his ear and Elliot turned slightly to bestow a light kiss on her cheek. "I will give it to you, child."

"Child?"

"You are no old Dr. Leclerc. I had my suspicions," she admitted and brought Elliot's unlined hand into the light, turning it this way and that. "And Faraj confirmed. You did not think that he had sent you to take a look at the choking Jamal for no good reason?"

"I should have known. Jamal never chokes."

"Faraj was kind. And he told me some of the work you do throughout Egypt but he never told me your name and what you desire. He left it to you to disclose."

Elliot could do nothing but stare for a few moments. He had been holding one of Faraj's roses in his hand and methodically removing the thorns from the stem.

He reached to clasp Madame's hand, the rose now between their palms. With dogged resoluteness he decided to be honest. "There is a woman… I want to impress her and to that end I do what I do. So, there is little kindness to anything that I do. I go sometimes with and sometimes without Faraj to villages in the north of Egypt or even as far as Siwa to deliver what little medicine and modern commodities I can collect. It's wartime. There are limitations on medicine and general hygienic items that are available to us, the commoners, or to the military for that matter!"

Madame nodded in appreciation. "Rationing, they call it! Puh!"

"And wanting to impress this woman also puts me in mind of purchasing a nightclub."

"Oh!"

"Yes, you have a building I want to buy. Your agent has it for let. But I wish to buy the structure."

"Oh!"

"Actually, you have several buildings. I want only one. The one that I want to buy, and for a fair price, is in Clot Bey."

"Clot Bey?" she asked, surprised. "A club in a wicked slum?"

Clot Bey enjoyed an immoral reputation for more than a century. During the Great War, Australian soldiers swarmed its streets and brothels, throwing furniture out of every window!

"That's right."

"But look at us," she suddenly tittered. "We are becoming serious again! How could we be so cruel to disappoint our host?"

Elliot turned, spotting Faraj escorting a gorgeous woman. Beaming with delight, Faraj appeared carefree.

"Faraj is a sight to behold in his sharkskin suit," Madame Sukey breathed.

Elliot rarely saw Faraj in anything but a white linen robe and sometimes a white turban, and unkempt thick head of hair greying here and there. "It's from America. Faraj whispered that much to me when I complimented him on his suit earlier. You must admit, from America or not, it's his fantastic body that makes the suit stand out."

"Yes, large body and thick head of hair," agreed Madame. "And who is the beauty?"

"The Aphrodite?"

The woman by Faraj's side was a beauty in an impeccable silk suit that clung to her shapely figure, honey caramel hair piled high, a halo to her rosy complexion.

"Does that make Faraj Zeus? Am I getting my Greeks mixed up?"

"No, your Greek mythology is in order, Madame, only I am certain that Faraj would reject the role of Zeus. Aphrodite was his daughter, you see, at least in one of the accounts. And, Faraj would not appreciate figuring as Zeus in this melodrama, or any other for that matter. He's too good natured and so very well liked. He's not at all the sort who would lunge lightning at mortals."

"He is an amicable man. A peaceful man. Still, who is the English girl?"

"I've never met her before," Elliot turned his gaze away from the couple and stared at Madame. "English?"

"Her coloring … her stance."

Was Madame Sukey interested in Faraj? Or in the woman? She was from Siwa. No, no, Madame loved men far too much to be seeking feminine liaison.

Holding the beauty's hand, Faraj walked to a great hall in his sprawling stone mansion.

"I expect that she is somehow related to tonight's entertainment," commented Elliot, making an effort to appear uninterested.

Soon the guests who were seated rose to follow other guests into the hall. Largely English, the crowd, representing Cairo's wealthier merchants and politicians strained to hear Faraj's introduction.

Faraj spoke softly, welcoming the beauty and the four musicians on stage, all four wearing funereal suits and severe expressions. Finally, Faraj's hands stretched up. "Lady Jane!" he announced, then stepped down.

First, the haunting violin crept forward, timid but seductive, and then the piano joined until Jane began to sing and it was at that moment that the guests forgot to notice anything else about the music besides the bewitching voice that filled the air and carried them home, longing for love and peace in green fields and soft rolling hills.

Madame Sukey heard an intake of breath as Elliot, overcome by the vision and her enchanting voice, betrayed his interest in Lady Jane on stage. Madame was sensitive enough to sip her champagne in contented silence. She watched not the singer but her patron, Faraj. He was a magnificent man, and she wondered what attracted Faraj to Elliot and vice versa. How was it that a Jewish businessman in his fifties was a close friend with a young and handsome man, a talented rogue of a gentleman? She kept darting glances at Elliot, too, who, although still disguised as Leclerc, no longer kept up the mannerism of a stooped doctor, at least, not throughout the performance. But she marveled at his transformation when Elliot returned to enacting his part as soon as Faraj joined them, much later, accompanied by Lady Jane.

#

"I was never more amused," she teased Elliot later, afterward Faraj walked away.

"How so?" Elliot asked.

"You!" she replied.

"Me? Madame Sukey, do I amuse you?"

"Your antics when Faraj and Lady Jane joined us! Elliot, how could you touch that lovely little girl in that odious, or should I say lecherous, manner? She was, well, she…"

"Loved it, I'm sure!"

"Loved it? Elliot, you naughty boy! To her, you were an old man!"

"Oh!"

"Now, if she were aware of your true identity, I'm quite sure she would have enjoyed every minute of it, as I did the other afternoon. But she had no idea who you were except for what Faraj supplied as an introduction: Dr. Leclerc, a Parisian doctor, a dear, *old* friend!"

Elliot grinned as Madame Sukey's rolling amusement filled the night air in their secluded balcony. He raised Madame's hand to his lips and kissed it. "I'd better escort you home, Madame, it's late."

CHAPTER 9

An excerpt from Jack Johnson's Notes
Tuesday morning 09 June 1942
CAIRO, EGYPT

"JACK, WAKE UP!" Toc's curls hang above me. His face is lit up with a bright grin that smells of tea and marmalade.

"Too early!"

"Jack, wake up!"

"Bedbugs and creaking bed kept me up."

Ignoring my complaint, Toc shakes me, exclaiming with all the jubilation of a boy in a sweetshop, "Jack, our chap, our Elliot!"

"Damn him."

"He's the son of Sir Niles. Niles Westbrook!"

"Wh-what?" I stutter, hoping that I am still asleep and that as soon as this bit of dream is over I will again fall into deep, dreamless rest.

"Jack, Westbrook is our man!"

I rub my eyes.

"Jack?"

"I'm here."

"You look awfully confused. Jack, do you recall Madame Sukey and her Frenchman?"

"What?"

"Recollect that we trailed the Frenchman. We ascertained that he was pretending to be an old doctor. Do you recall that we thought him to be an Englishman of superior education and some rank?"

"Toc, I'm sleepy not dim witted!"

"You seemed confused."

"I need sleep. There's no need for you to rehash Madame's affair! It only happened yesterday."

"Of course not, Jack, only do wake up."

"Yes."

"Last night, at my father's dinner party. I sat next to the Big Man. General Sir Claude Auchinleck!"

"The Auk himself?"

"Commander-in-Chief in the Middle East and our Acting Eighth Army Commander!"

"Toc, I am awe struck."

"But I figured it out. First, our mystery man gets hailed by William Westbrook as Elliot even though he was wearing his hideous disguise. Also, Elliot met Madame Sukey in hospital. So, again, there's some connection to William Westbrook. Then, the Auk pointed out Sir Niles, Niles Westbrook, at the dinner table. With a few exceptions, Sir Niles actually resembles Elliot. Lastly, I heard that Sir Niles has three sons: James, Elliot, and William. So that's it!"

"Brilliant. But what of the Auk?" I ask.

"I spoke to him about our idea of decoys. I also pointed out that a man like Elliot Westbrook is useful. The Auk promised to have a word with Elliot's own father, Sir Niles! Also, he gave me his word that he's working on tricks to fool Jerry. Can you believe our luck?"

"What else did you tell the Auk?"

"Jack, I told him all that we know of Elliot Westbrook and how he managed to playact enough to deceive Madame. Then I explained that I was not regaling him with amusing tales for entertainment only but that my friend, Jack Johnson, and I had a notion to set up decoys in the desert and bring mischief to the enemy. Then, the Auk mentioned a man called Clarke, Dudley Clarke, and said that now that they got him out of women's clothing, whatever that means, he's back in Cairo, and should be made aware of someone like Elliot Westbrook."

"Who the bloody hell is Clarke?"

"Language, Jack," Toc admonishes.

"Well, who's Clarke?"

"A genius in Intelligence playing tricks on Axis' informants. But Jack, here's what the Auk knew about Elliot. He grew up in England but was educated by a succession of unusual tutors in Egypt because his public school dormitory went up in flames after he and his younger brother, William Westbrook, experimented with explosives."

"William Westbrook? Our medic?"

"The very same!" Toc confirms.

"So, Westbrook's not a saint after all! I feel a lot better now," I say, grinning.

"Jack, do you know what else he said? And mind you, I was never so shocked to hear such a high ranking general speak to a nobody like me…"

"You are not a nobody!" I interject. "Your father is…"

"Socially, no, but, in military terms, you know, I'm a nobody."

"Well?"

"The Auk acknowledged that, here in Cairo, Elliot would be of great use in recruiting militia men, aside from his knowledge of the area and his fluency in languages."

"Toc, look here, how's your leg today? My hearing is back to normal, but how is your leg? Did our galavanting all over Cairo yesterday damage it in any way? The dressing still on?"

"Never mind that now, Nurse. I can sit and drive just fine which is what we will be doing for the foreseeable! You know how Sergeant loves to molly coddle us!"

"You."

"Eh?"

"You, Toc. Sergeant molly coddles you!"

Toc gives me a despairing look. Then he says in serious urgent voice, "I've got my paperwork from hospital this morning."

"Are you allowed to head back?"

"Oh, yes! Today!"

"But you have not heard my news," I say.

"What news? Oh, yes. Carousing. How was it?"

"Carousing? No, Toc, I met two men who do extraordinary things in the desert. In fact, I've made up my mind. Will you join me? Will your father and his connections at GHQ help us?"

Toc stares at me.

"It's a couple of blokes from Australia. I ran into them outside the cinema. We hit it off, and then they disclosed something rather interesting. They belong to a secret unit."

"And they blabbered it all out to you?"

Ignoring Toc's acidic remark, I say, "Long Range Desert Group."

"It's not a secret unit," Toc asserts.

"LRDG now collaborates with David Stirling's L-detachment, SAS brigade. SAS stands for Special Air Service. They strike enemy air fields. They sneak up on them in the dead of night, plant explosives, and leave the enemy in utter confusion as they disappear into the desert. But the two blokes that I talked to, they do other things, too. They go on reconnaissance tours behind enemy lines. They report back enemy strength, machinery, vehicles. If possible, they sabotage communication lines or petrol dumps."

Toc lowers his eyelids. "Who described the Long Range Desert Group as 'piracy on the high desert,' do you recall?"

"Don't know. But it's not piracy." I am rather piqued. Toc is casting back to think of a quotation. "It's not piracy!"

"No. It's lunacy. Most of the North African Desert war up until such units sprouted into being was along the coastal stretch of road along the Mediterranean … But, I'm in!" Toc is thoughtful. "It's not what we are trained for, but I'd much rather raid enemy airfields than be strafed in my own pillbox! But, Jack, this is rather odd, don't you think? If the two Australians just met you, how is it that they confided in you? Were they inebriated beyond reason?"

"There was little alcohol involved in our chance meeting. And, I must call it chance because I'm related to the tall one, Bill Tate. Toc, I ran into a cousin from Australia here in Cairo! Tate's my cousin on my maternal side."

Ignoring all the rest, Toc focuses on one detail. "What do you mean 'the tall one'? You are not exactly short yourself, so what does it make him?"

"In his boots?"

"In anything!"

"Over six six."

"And such a giant of a man can survive on a cup of water a day, or whatever it is that they allot themselves?"

"Tate's still alive, isn't he?"

Toc considers his next words, then asks, "Jack, how do we find them and take part?"

"Bill, I mean Tate, my cousin, promised to talk to Sergeant about reassigning us."

"And I'll pop into GHQ and see my father before we leave. We'll need *persuasion* on our side."

"Toc, would *he* let you join the LRDG?"

Toc's gaze rests on me as his shoulders move into a boyish shrug.

Tuesday Early Afternoon 09 JUNE 1942
WESTERN DESERT

As we turn off the main road onto desert tracks, the lurching and jostling become almost unbearable for Toc. His lips disappear into a thin line under his massive eye-shields. The orange mask of caked dust on his face cracks when he shifts in his seat.

Desert tracks are bumpy, and the sand hides the rock ledges underneath. With more and more transportation activity, the sand becomes finer and turns into dust that appears to behave like liquid. This diabolical fine dust rises up like a column then becomes a bow-wave at the wheels of our lorry as we speed onward through a mist of fine particles that are slow to disperse, leaving us in poor visibility conditions for some time.

Now the shimmering heat haze of mid day blurs our progress across the desert as we finally drive into less traveled areas. We press on. Ahead, the shifting desert sands are a vision of the end of the earth.

Finally, Toc declares, "Nearly there."

And I see our regiment, well, not much of it, just the bits that peek out of the pillbox.

#

In the late afternoon, when Toc and I enter the shadowy pillbox, we hear a whispered question, "Any rum?"

"Moss?"

"Yes. Any rum?" he replies, with the echoing chatter of Bandar.

"Rum and other supplies. Gather up the gang. It's in a crate at the back," Toc answers, and Moss quietly summons first the monkey then additional help to carry and enjoy the rum.

I backtrack to help Moss but as I squint into bright light, I see columns of sand approaching.

"Jack?"

"A storm's coming," I say.

"Better talk to Sergeant first. Leave the unloading to Moss. We best have a chat with Sergeant. You know how he loves to hear news of Cairo," Toc advises.

"What, get him in an affable mood before we…"

"That's the general idea, yes."

"I hope he'll reassign us to the LRDG," I whisper.

Scanning the horizon from a rather extensive dugout, Sergeant barks at someone who is frantically trying to write down the commands and remember his "yes, Sirs."

I am relieved it is not I by Sergeant's side, straining to hear his words.

And then Sergeant's deep resonant voice reaches us, loud and clear and dreamlike. "How's my Lady?" Sergeant refers to Cairo as a *lady* and we none of us have the heart to remind him the nature of his lady, a trollop, by all accounts.

"Lively," Toc grunts, then begins to regale Sergeant with an interesting *on-dit* he must have picked up at his father's dinner party.

"I want to hear more, but better get to your tent, Johnson. Go get ready for the storm," Sergeant rasps, avoiding mentioning Toc because he can never get over the fact that Toc appeared at his section with the appellation of Toc and nothing more, and higher ups had instructed him to accept Toc. But Sergeant is an admirable man and does not hold it against Toc, neither does he make a fuss, he only avoids using Toc's name.

#

Toc and I are in what has become our desert uniform, a pair of boots, short woolen socks, khaki drill pants, and a string holding two identity disks round the neck and bouncing on our bare chests, and on our heads a wide brimmed hat turned down all the way round.

Tightening anchors, Toc crawls round our tent on his hands and knees. His bare back is deep chestnut brown and his body is sinewy. His dusty, messy hair falls heavily over his forehead. What a stark difference to his looks in town, to his well-tailored suit, the polished shoes he wore, and his slicked hair when he went to the dinner party at his father's Mena mansion!

I avoid looking at his leg. His shorts cover up his recent thigh wound. But, below the shorts, wholly exposed to sun and dust, a scar of badly healing skin disfigures his lower leg. Earlier in the summer, Toc's leg got a piece of shrapnel embedded into the calf muscle. The surgeon removed the bits of metal but medics that Toc consults on a regular basis because of recurring pain are not quite sure that every single bit of metal was indeed removed.

When the dust storm abates, Sergeant summons us to his dugout.

"Sir, what have we missed?" I ask.

"While you two galavanted in the streets of Cairo," and Sergeant says Cairo with silky tones of affection, "we've been enjoying low bombing raids. And I've a notion that we'll soon see more of it. Ah, yes, here they come. Go on, see for yourselves!"

The setting sun illuminates a lonely lorry plodding across a ridge. A low rumble resounds, then the lorry goes up in flames and the ack-ack shells slice through the evening air.

"Jack," Toc utters in disgust just before his mouth meets the sand and I fall next to him. "Sergeant's predictions are dead on."

"Damned aerial shelling that'll more than likely go on for hours."

"Over here," Sergeant calls from the bowls of his dugout.

We scuttle close and when Toc pulls blankets over us, something like an entire army of mice is disturbed. And the mice begin their running to and fro, dancing like mad all over us. Sergeant and several other men laugh, accustomed to the dancing mice and the fleas.

But how is it that we find their hectic, helter-skelter goings-on amusing? Are we not doing the same thing? Only we are hiding from a far worse enemy that swoops and dives in the sky, pouring death down on us.

#

"When did this horror arrive at our box?" Sergeant points to a lorry, its driver strewn over the wheel, blood draining out the side door, pooling into a dark stain on the sand.

Toc strides over to remove the driver.

As Toc performs the ghastly ritual of laying down the dead and writing his name and rank, I remain rooted to the spot.

"Johnson, give him a hand!" Sergeant barks then walks to a battered communications lorry, shouting at the mechanics to hurry up.

"Toc, your hands are shaking," I say.

Toc's palm rests over the driver's face, closing his eyes.

"Who's he?"

"Moss."

"What?"

"Not our Moss. Not from our regiment. Did Moss have a relative?" Toc asks.

I pull Toc by the arm. "Shovels are over at the back of that lorry," I point out to a charred lorry, tipped over and smokey. "Let's get them."

"No."

"No?"

"We cannot bury him right here. We'll have to take him elsewhere. General retreat is imminent."

"Imminent, Toc?"

"About to…"

"I bloody well know what *imminent* means!"

"Jack…"

"But why you should choose such a word in the middle of the desert is beyond me!"

"Well, how else would you have phrased it?" He then gives a bad imitation of my accent, using foul language after every word almost as if speaking in code, an offensive, wrathful, indecent code.

"Sod off!" I push him.

Toc retaliates, and we are both wresting on the ground when a howl of despair jerks us apart.

And it is Moss.

And Bandar is screaming in fear, because Moss just saw the dead driver and is on all four, shouting and howling in unearthly despair.

Sergeant grabs hold of Moss, ignoring the frantic monkey clawing at his head. Sergeant shouts and men show up with tarpaulin to wrap the dead and transfer him to an equipment carrier.

The dead Moss will be buried in Alamein.

#

Thursday-Friday 11-13 June 1942
WESTERN DESERT

"Koenig is without stores, without reinforcements," Toc calls out.

"Without hope!"

"Don't be so coarse, Jack!" Toc snaps. "He's reporting that he can do no more. Sir, he was ordered to come out." Toc backs away from the communication radio, directing his dark stare at Sergeant. "He has his orders. Sir, about us?"

"We hold our position for now. We stay on the Gazala Line."

After yesterday's shelling, Toc and I both show signs of fatigue and shock. Toc is ineffectively hiding the pain in his leg and I am having trouble with my hearing on and off.

"Bad job you two'll do representing the 50th in the Long Range Desert Group! But for now, since Royal Corps of Signals hasn't sent a communication engineer, you can receive and deliver messages along our stretch of the Gazala Line."

So Toc and I follow the horrific tale of the Fighting French in Bir Hakeim through radio communications, running to and fro with odd jobs.

Although Koenig is told to come out, it is not the Fighting French style. The French hang on through the 12th somehow. Then, that night, they set course north-east and actually fight their way out! They leave behind them, on the ridge, the most badly wounded men to wreck the remaining arms and cover their comrades' retreat.

It is blood-curdling news.

Toc is staring into the desert, not blinking, just staring. I join him, wishing silently that I will do my best when my time comes, that my bowels will not turn to water or my knees to jelly.

The next day, Koenig and his men come out safe inside British lines after a bayonet and rifle skirmish with the enemy.

"What a sight awaits the Axis soldiers taking over that ridge at Bir Hakeim!" Toc says.

"Probably similar to what the Roman soldiers saw once they broke into Masada!" grates one of the religious chaps.

An uproar of "Come off it!" hails him.

"Masada was a fortress on a plateau in the Judean Desert put under Roman siege just miles away from the Dead Sea!" he rejoins.

"Come off it."

"The besieged Jewish zealots killed one another rather than be taken prisoner by Roman warriors. No one escaped!" religious chap continues sermonizing.

"Koenig isn't doing that!"

But I cannot help but agree with the religious man because what Koenig left on that ridge is nothing more than shattered scraps of humanity.

Sergeant is sombre, staying out of the ensuing argument in the communication box.

The capture of Bir Hakeim is a devastating blow to the Allied defense line.

"Damn that fellow. Rommel has just cut the Gazala Line in half with a fat wedge in our line of defenses!" Sergeant rumbles sotto voce. "Now the Panzerarmee can get supplies and equipment. They will launch an attack anytime now."

A disaster by all accounts.

Sergeant glances at me. "Johnson! Scouting duty, now! Both of you! Load up a radio. See if the road's clear. We'll be retreating anytime now."

Our hopes to drive back to Alexandria and join Tate's LRDG are dashed.

#

Friday Afternoon 12 June 1942
WESTERN DESERT

A cloud of billowing dust along the Capuzzo track, a desert road that runs from Fort Capuzzo to El Adem near the Egyptian-Libyan border wire, covers our tracks.

Suddenly, Toc signals to switch the engine off. He cocks his head and cups his ear. "Do you hear that?"

I shake my head.

"Get off the road. Now! Switch her back on and drive off the road, quickly now, quickly!" Toc shouts, alarm and fear reshaping his features.

Pushing the clutch in, I rapidly switch gears, swerving toward a jebel.

"Mines?" I shout.

"More than likely."

"Damn!"

Shifting mercilessly the grinding gears, I press down hard on the gas pedal.

"Park behind the hill."

"Park?" I ask.

"Yes. Get Sergeant on the radio, can you?"

Like a nightmare shaping out of a column of dust, a procession of Axis lorries and equipment carriers loaded with 88mm guns materializes, complete with the squealing tanks in the rear. The machinery charges down the same strip of track we have just driven off.

"Tell him it's no ordinary dust storm heading eastward on the Capuzzo track. And then, Jack, we better take ourselves off before the aircraft arrive. Otherwise, we'll be sitting targets."

Sergeant's voice crackles on the radio, then he is silent as I shout and warn him of enemy strength.

Throwing caution to the wind, Toc and I jump back into the lorry and I drive as fast and as far as I can, away from the horrifying Panzer cavalcade.

Saturday 13 June 1942
WESTERN DESERT

Thighs quivering with muscle fatigue, I stoop to enter the bunker.

"Johnson," Sergeant summons me then places a finger to his lips. He is by the radio dispatch.

Toc's head appears at the entrance. Then he hobbles into the dark bunker.

"Rommel cut between two British brigades," Sergeant shoots out.

"Our warnings came too late," I say gloomily.

Sergeant nods.

"With or without our warning," Toc growls, "British forces have to run headlong into the 88mm anti-tank barrage."

I stare at him.

"Damn the fellow," Sergeant spits out the words with heat, condemning the German Field Commander. "Annihilating our tanks," Sergeant rasps then adds the necessary curses. "And how the hell does he know our plans and movements?"

One after another, British squadrons report heavy losses. More men join us in the bunker. Moss, the monkey Bandar wrapped round his neck and head, brings with him a bottle of rum.

Bandar leaps into my hands, chattering.

"Sergeant?" Moss hands him the bottle.

"Moss?"

"Sir, I've been saving it. But…"

Despite Bandar's cheerful dances, the atmosphere remains tense. Moss has yet to sober up from his latest debauch, after kneeling by his brother's dead body.

I step outside for some fresh air and to let Bandar throw sand around. Screwing up my eyes against the glare, I feel a sharp stab of pain where Toc landed a heavy blow two days before.

"Immediate retreat!"

I look back.

Toc's lips move to shape the painful intelligence, then he kicks a Jerrycan.

The news falls about my ears. And with black dismay, a lump forms in my throat.

The Eighth has worked and fought hard. Great men have fallen in the battles over this stretch of desert we must now leave behind. And it's not just the loss of men and heavy work but the loss of equipment and supplies. Whatever we cannot carry away with us will have to be destroyed lest it falls to enemy hands.

"Ritchie's orders are to abandon the Gazala Line," Toc repeats the Deputy Commander's orders.

"Why abandon Gazala?" I ask.

"Tobruk will seal itself. Hopefully, it'll hold for at least a month. Forces are to fall back and re-form along the Egyptian frontier, then counterattack," Toc explains.

One after the other, faces crumpled, men file out of the bunker to pack up while Bandar is still gleefully busy covering my boots with sand.

#

Our 3-ton lorries creak and rumble as we zigzag across the wadis. We have split up into small brigades and Sergeant admits that we are lost, possibly behind newly forming enemy lines.

Eventually, we find a strategic escarpment to hide under and entrench, overseeing bits of the road from behind an odd geologic formation.

Sergeant is urging us to move faster and pile high the sand bags to erect a makeshift pillbox. We bring in our heavy guns, bury them in the sand, then pile more sandbags and stretch netting and tarpaulin with the occasional sprig, hoping that from above we resemble nothing more than another sparsely vegetated jebel. Moss and Bandar are sweeping our tracks, blurring the lines in the sand.

When darkness wraps round us like a deadly blanket, we can only see bright flashes of some piece of equipment bursting up in flames in the distance. It is our darkest night yet with ghastly sounds, the screaming and the shelling, the cracks and claps of metal bursting and exploding on the hills beyond.

At dawn, after a fitful night's sleep, Stukas arrive and pour fire.

"How did they find us?" I wonder.

"Will they strafe us until we're nothing more than a charred sieve?" Toc shouts, and then my hearing falters, and I just stare at his moving lips.

I shake my head.

Toc realizes that my ears are acting up. He pulls me close, crouching lower by our machine-guns, waiting, waiting. We have a signal. As soon as Toc hears Sergeant's command, he nudges me and I know it's time to fire, so I load the canister and Toc pulls and the machine lurches releasing its deadly shell, then recoils back. Toc stays close and nudges me, and we fire like a creature in a freak show.

But still the bombs fall.

The crump is unearthly. Flames leap up, devouring the desert shrubs. Shellfire demolishes one tank after another. Even one of our own lorries blows up into bits and a flash of memory of the last lorry that went up in flames, under Stuka shelling, hits me, and I wonder in stupefied amazement while I load another canister how many bodies Toc will find this time? Will there be anything remaining of their faces? Will he need to shut their eyes?

51

CHAPTER 10

Friday morning 12 June 1942
CAIRO, EGYPT

SOMETHING HAD HAPPENED to him since meeting Madame Sukey.
What appeared at first to be a business pursuit shook Elliot to the core.

Here was a woman who enjoyed one of Cairo's most scandalous reputations,
but almost as a Shakespearean Puck.

Madame helped British troops, assisting the Allied Forces, in ways that few
people could believe. A valetudinarian herself, Madame Sukey was naturally
attracted to military hospitals that popped up round Cairo. True, she consulted the
doctors on private matters but would always leave behind mountains of treats like
chocolates, oranges, bottles of wine, decks of cards and stationary, and cigarettes.
And she visited the wounded, sympathetic and entertaining. She even went on
desert expeditions with a troop of servants to deliver fresh fruit and meat to the
men. Some of her people went to abandoned battlefields dressed in rags, looking
for all the world like the lost souls of Hades, collecting soldiers' personal items
such as diaries or photos, items important enough for humanity. She would then
deliver the belongings to charities to sort through and send back home to the
families any items that could be identified. With her connections in America, she
was able to import the impossible, donating such desired items among the troops.
But more often than not, she procured basic commodities from local Egyptian
suppliers.

"I cannot take this offer!" Elliot exclaimed, waving a stack of papers before
Faraj.

"What's this?" Faraj tore his eyes from his backgammon board.

"See for yourself, Faraj."

"Madame Sukey's business agent delivered it?"

"Today," Elliot replied.

Faraj put an arm round his friend and hurried him to the back of the shop. "But
it is what you wanted!"

"You never told me about her charities!"

"I never knew." Faraj's hands and sleeves fluttered. "I learned more about
Madame from you, my friend! And thanks to you, I am now in the company of a
magnificent woman." Then he added in caressing tones, "What a lady! What a
benevolent soul! And from Siwa, you say? Well, well, the Siwa women aren't always

treated right, rarely cared for in anyway. She deserves praise. I will see to that from now on. So, Elliot, why not accept Madame's offer?"

"How can I?" Elliot closed his eyes as he threw himself on the divan, his fingers still clutching the papers from Madame's agents.

"Price is too low?"

"Paltry!" Elliot shot.

"Your noble conscience is smarting?"

"Faraj…"

"Buy the club. Turn it around quickly and entertain the troops properly. It would please her! She cares for the troops. She wants England to win. There is something that she is certainly keeping from us. Why the desire to help the Allies? Why go to such great lengths? But it does not matter. Now, you owe her a cabaret where men can go to and enjoy shows and drinks without the hustling prostitutes or the prying pickpockets, without the venereal diseases and unreasonable prices. Elliot, you can have music, dancing, and even conjuring acts and all in good taste. Hire talented performers!"

"Cards?" Elliot asked.

"Card games? You can invite only the few upper class gamblers that you know can well-afford the risks and enjoy the game. That, you can keep separate. Behind the stage, tucked away."

"Faraj, you're certainly convincing!"

"Look at me!" he boasted and swept his arm in a show of grandeur.

"You've the right of it. But what shall I call the club?"

Scratching his silvery stubble, Faraj gurgled. "The name has to be cheeky!"

"Cheeky?"

"Why, yes. It all started as an impulsive purchase with a cheeky plan to trick a rapacious widow. Only things turned out better than expected. We found a friend and a charming, noble creature instead who has given you *un cadeau*!"

"A gift? I suppose you're right."

"Elliot, buy that building, set a crew to work on it and bring it round so that before the summer ends, you have a cabaret to be proud of, a profitable cabaret, *mon ami*."

After a moment of silence, Elliot said, "*Monnayeur*."

Faraj kept almond-shaped brown eyes on Elliot. Weighting Elliot's utterance for some time, he nodded in approbation. "*Monnayeur*. One Who Coins Money! A forger?!" Finally, Faraj's deep chuckle filled the air.

"Cheeky?"

"Cheeky!"

"You'll give me Lady Jane?" Elliot's sudden request had him puzzled, too.

"Lady Jane?" Faraj's voice cracked. "*Mon ami*, you'd like Lady Jane to sing at your club?"

"Not exactly."

"Elliot, what do you want of Lady Jane?"

\#

Friday afternoon 12 June 1942
CAIRO, EGYPT

"William! You look exhausted!"

"Elliot? Oh, I am!" William entered his father's study, sinking into the nearest armchair, his rumpled fair head plopped on his unsteady knees.

"I'll call on Fatima. She can bully Cook into giving you tea," Elliot offered.

"I'd rather be left alone."

Elliot's dimples appeared. "Left alone? Really? What, have you already looked into the stables? Salomé isn't there, you know."

"Leave me."

It was fortunate for William that his father walked in just then. Catching sight of Mrs. Judd, the housekeeper, in the hall, Sir Niles demanded tea. "Promptly! And without any of Cook's carryings on!" he instructed, then complained, "Damn Cook! Braying complaints at any passerby!"

"A pity we do not have a dungeon for him to practice his art there." Head still resting on his knees, William growled his wishes.

"William, how can you call the load of dung we get at table *art*?"

"But you yourself have been to some of London's modern galleries, have you not?"

Elliot grinned. William's words were inconsequential. He grinned because his brother had snapped out of his ill humor and whatever plagued him was ousted by the thought of Cook in a damp, dark dungeon. And Elliot had a fairly good idea of what was troubling William. The Eighth Army was returning in bits and pieces to Alexandria and Cairo.

"Any news, Father?" Elliot asked and William raised his head expectantly.

Sir Niles thought that the wan face of his youngest son reflected the anxiety crippling GHQ. "Nothing to signify! British public morale is low, so our ambassador is calling for a remodeling project at his estate."

"That's grand!" barked Elliot. "Anyone walking by and noticing the crew painting that sprawling estate by the Nile would have no doubt that we, the British, are here to stay!"

"That's the general idea. William, is something the matter? You're hunched over!"

"Exhausted, that's all."

Sir Niles glanced at Elliot.

"Carnage," Elliot uttered and left the study.

Sir Niles leaned close to William. "How is Madame Sukey?"

"She has not failed us yet. Thank you, Father, for putting in a good word on her behalf at GHQ. It's let her keep on visiting our patients. And we need an angel like her."

Sir Niles' voice cracked, "An angel?"

"Not all angels are cherubic with seraphic smiles lighting up their innocent faces and adorned with golden wings that flap behind."

Sir Niles, appreciating William's comment, recalled just how far Madame Sukey was from a cherubic angel. He had met her while visiting William. Tall and imposing in a crimson silk dress of excellent tailoring, she directed a crew of swarthy servants, distributing sweetmeats, walnuts, and dates, and other such well-loved Cairene delicacies. At the time, however, Sir Niles doubted the reception of such items by the patients. To his surprise, the men enjoyed the attention even more than the sugary Turkish Delight. The men made sure to thank Madame, partaking the treats in her presence.

"Her servants mend sheets and help out with patients' personal hygiene. Just last week she delivered bars of soap and fresh towels! And then there is the added benefit of her company."

"Her presence is a benefit? How odd! The men do not mind her habit of ogling them?"

"Far from it, Father. They think it's a lark! They even enjoy it when she helps them shave, chattering and laughing like school boys. She helps them escape reality."

"It's wonderful, is it not, how a single person can affect the lives of so many?"

William was unsure whether his father was commending Madame Sukey's admirable efforts to improve conditions and morale or whether Sir Niles was referring to a different person.

#

Sunday afternoon 14 June 1942

55

"Father?" Elliot's features reflected in Sir Nile's mirror.

Turning round to face Elliot, Sir Niles asked, "Anything the matter?".

"Where's Mother?"

"She's with Lady Lampson."

"The Ambassador's wife?" Elliot asked.

"The same."

"What are they scheming now? Another delightful ball? I certainly hope not. Mother would expect me to attend in formal evening wear and that would be disastrous."

"Disastrous?"

"Tailor."

"Still afraid of that devil? But you're not a child anymore."

"No, I am not a child. And so it's worse now. Damn the fellow."

"Well, I can put your mind at ease about the tailor. Is he really that bad?"
Elliot nodded.

"Your mother and Lady Lampson are organizing care packets for the wounded."

"Excellent," Elliot said and Sir Niles wondered about that word his son often used. Excellent? What was excellent? The care packets? The fact that finally his wife was taking interest in the war? Or, that Elliot had found him on his own, alone in his study, staring gloomily into the mirror above the mantle?

"Care packets," Sir Niles repeated.

"They would do well to consult Madame Sukey."

"Madame Sukey? Elliot, what do you know of Madame Sukey?"

"Quite a lot, as it happens."

Sir Niles' features softened. "She is marvelous, is she not?"

"Father, I would call that an unexpected, or rather uncharacteristic, comment, especially coming from you."

"Normally, you would be in the right. However, since my son is now in business with the woman, I made it my business to investigate. William too helped me understand Madame a bit better."

"And? What did you learn?"

"Quite a lot, as it happens," Sir Niles said.

"Father?"

"She is certainly not what she appears to be. Native to Siwa, yes. She married a stupendously wealthy man. Marriage to said wealthy man was actually what the vulgar tongue would refer to as a 'love match.' So, when Sukey Effendi was attacked by bandits on one of his business expeditions up the Nile, British troops stationed in Aswan came to Sukey's rescue. The Sukeys vowed to reciprocate. Although Sukey has long been dead, the widow, Madame Sukey, continues the tradition. Her motives are sincere, and her generosity - legal and, for the most part, proper. Though I have not found out why she goes by the name Madame Sukey. She is not French!'"

Stunned, Elliot stood still.

"Surprised, Elliot?"

"Why, yes!"

"Well, I am not. You seem to choose your friends well. And on that note, where are you off to? You are going somewhere, are you not? Where?"

"Desert."

Sir Niles stared.

"Bill Tate asked for my help. Recci work."

"Recci?"

"Reconnaissance."

"Where precisely will you be reconnoitering?"

"Along the coast," Elliot replied.

"Churchill's insisting that Tobruk must hold against Axis attack. The Eighth is throwing everything it can into a line of defenses in front of Tobruk from the coast to Acroma!" Sir Niles knew that the latest command from Auchinleck to Ritchie had been 'Tobruk must hold,' a reflection of the British Prime Minister's sentiment. He also knew how little prepared the Army was for such a massive defense effort. "I am reluctant to let you venture into the desert, Elliot, because of the uncertain outcome of hostilities."

"It's a short day trip to check out the roads and what available lorries we could scrape together. We also want to examine watering holes. There are rumors that some of the fresh water sources have been contaminated."

"No doubt that they have been contaminated. Although, I cannot say by whom."

"May I go then?"

"Tobruk is in grave peril. No, I misspoke. The troops in and around Tobruk are in grave peril. I cannot be certain how long they'll hold. Norrie is presently holding the defense line, but with little resources. Tobruk once again will fall under siege and into enemy hands. And it may be a matter of days or weeks, or," and here he inhaled, "hours."

"Father, will Tobruk fall within hours?"

"It is possible."

"Damn. The Australians had held it last time at such a dear price. What if it fell back into German hands?"

"Tobruk will fall. We don't know when. I wonder what defenses it has left? Would Norrie hold, or would he withdraw, leaving Tobruk defenseless?"

"And I wish we knew for certain that James is not trapped somewhere in there, in Tobruk, or outside its fortifications."

#

Tuesday morning 16 June 1942
ALEXANDRIA, EGYPT

The desert road stretched before Elliot and Tate.

"I cannot bear looking at it any more," Elliot spat then hopped out of the slow moving, specially fitted Canadian Chevrolet lorry.

Leaning over the scrub at the side of the road, Elliot heaved as his breakfast gushed out in sharp spurts. Dizzy and weak, he stumbled.

"You all right?" Tate asked.

"It was that last lorry."

"The bloody one? Isn't there a better way to transport our wounded? Do they really need to lie on top of each other?"

"And the cherry on top was that amputee."

"Poor fellow was delirious. Singing songs! Let's hope William sets him aright."

"William," Elliot croaked. "Tate, how does he do it? I walked in on him once, he was draining someone's puss into a basin, and his patients were watching him, helping him extract maggots!"

"Maggots?"

"Puss and maggots and some witty remarks that make for an altogether pretty bad show, for me at least."

"But that's how he does it. Wit and hilarity and the conviction that he's helping 'em."

"Not all of them. Many die!" Elliot grumbled.

"And those are the hardest moments for him. But what of the mothers? The families that receive that awful letter from the King?" And here Tate growled in fake British accent, *"The Queen and I offer you our heartfelt sympathy in your great sorrow..."* Swarms of flies came and went, attracted to Tate's sores and blisters.

"Let's press on," Elliot said. "We have our own work!"

Tate punched the air, switched the engine on, and let the lorry lurch forward.

Studying the seemingly undisturbed desert, Elliot noticed a gazelle sucking dew from scraggly shrubs and then, upon hearing the approaching lorry, taking off in a panic.

When they arrived at the dusty barracks just outside Alexandria, Elliot asked, "What will be left of this desert once the campaign is over? Both sides are amassing troops and equipment such as has never been seen here before."

"The sand will obliterate any traces of anything soon enough. A while back, we camped near the coast, close to Sidi Barrani. A sandstorm passed by in the afternoon and by morning we could barely locate one another. Getting up with a sheet wrapped round him, Sullivan looked like a ghoul!"

"And you're still his friend?"

"Not sure that I looked any better, worse, for I was recovering from a blow to the head and the sand stuck to the blood."

"I can believe that!" Elliot replied.

"You know, Elliot, Sullivan has a slight advantage over us."

Elliot tilted his head. "How so?"

"His eyes."

"Sullivan's eyes are pale!"

"True, but have you noticed his eyelashes?"

"Not particularly."

"They're thick, keep the dust out of the eyes. His eyes are squinty or slanted down, too, so drainage is better."

"Superior evolution. And here he is!"

Out of an office constructed of corrugated metal, emerged an athletically built man, slanted pale blue eyes and a wide grin under a shock of sandy hair.

"Over here!" Tom Sullivan hailed them, shading his freckly face from the glaring sunshine. "Have you brought us a lorry?"

"You have to see it to believe it."

When Sullivan clapped eyes on the new, specially fitted Chevrolet he whistled in admiration. "Your work, Elliot?"

"It took me an entire afternoon to finagle consent from GHQ. It's newly arrived from Canada, no windscreen, no doors, no roof, and with super sized radiator and condenser, and your desert tires complete the job. Where're you heading off to today?"

"Kabrit. SAS camp," Sulliavn answered.

"Wish that I could join you, but I must return to Cairo. As soon as I get your man in charge here to sign off on receipt of one fantastic Canadian lorry!"

"Any other miracles coming our way?"

"I'm working on it," Elliot promised then saluted a farewell.

Elliot entered the officers' barracks, took care of paperwork, then quickly approached the driver assigned to drive him back.

The driver, runnels of sweat trickling down his dusty cheeks and dripping on the rosary beads resting between his busy fingers, was leaning against an extremely dirty lorry.

"What's this?" Elliot kicked the machine. "It's caked with mud!"

"A Jerry piece of shit!" replied the driver.

"Can it get me to Cairo?"

"One can only hope," the lugubrious driver replied, concern rather than cheek adding an edge to his words, explaining his ill humor. "I wouldn't dream of cleaning it up, though, Sir. German insignia, you know."

"I don't care about the dust," Elliot began but the driver interjected.

"Oh, but you would. You would if one of our aircraft were up above!"

"Why?"

"Dust hides the markings on this machine."

"Jerry?"

The driver grunted in affirmation.

"Just get me to Cairo, quickly."

Louisa had invited him to a dinner party at her father's mansion. Elliot hated the scenes Louisa had put him through whenever he was late. And he was going to be late this time.

#

Fumes of cleaner assailing his nostrils, Elliot blinked at the diminutive woman.

"Effendi?" The startled scrubbing woman straightened up. She had just gathered up her bits and pieces when the doorknob turned and the door flung open.

"Good evening."

"Effendi, good day. I am finished here."

Elliot surveyed his Gezira flat. He had a bedroom, a kitchen, and his own private bath. "Excellent." But before he thanked her, he smiled. "Now you can help me get ready."

"Get ready?"

"There's not a moment to lose. I need help scrubbing off all this dust. Draw up a bath. You'll have to scrub hard."

She shook her head in resignation but drew a mirror before Elliot. "It will cost you extra!" she rasped gutturally as her finger indicated Elliot's windblown appearance.

Later, sitting bolt upright in the tub, Elliot drawled, "You know, I can deduct *piastres* from your exorbitant charge for the scrubbing of my person. I never knew a woman to be so merciless!"

"I walk out if you do not pay!" she replied as she yanked on his ears and, with a cleaning rag and abrasive soap solution, scrubbed his neck and shoulders. "You English!"

"I do need some skin left on my body."

"You English." Then a litany of men's shortcomings commenced while strong arms handled his exhausted body with unforgiving vigor. But she was thorough, and when the ordeal was over, even Elliot could not tell that he had been anywhere near sand that day. She polished his evening shoes and ironed his tie. For the first time since the war broke out, Elliot felt that he actually made an effort to appear the gentleman that he was.

#

Late Tuesday evening 16 June 1942
CAIRO, EGYPT

Confidence sprang from his gleaming shoes, straight tie, and pomaded hair that parted on the side and let a dramatic curl fall over one thick, dark eyebrow. Sitting at the seemingly endless dinner table at the Bakers' mansion, Elliot went for inane conversation topics. "Pity I cannot have a walking stick, you know, one of those old fashioned ones with polished silver, encrusted with diamonds."

"You could if you would only join the army and return with a leg injury."

"But my dear Louisa, you are well aware of my pacifist sentiment, are you not?" Elliot asked, twirling a white feather between his fingers. "Only this afternoon one of Mother's old things handed me a white feather."

"I thought they only did it during the last war."

"No. Some feel the need to shame pacifists with this symbol of cowardice even now."

"But just think, Elliot, if you returned with an injury, everyone in society would dote on you."

"And you? Would you dote on me? With a leg injury? What, would you have me as an amputee?"

"I am to marry you."

Elliot kept his irritation at Louisa's suggestion that he join the army in check and began to demolish the generous portion on his dinner plate.

What were Louisa's motives to have a husband in the army? She had made such a suggestion to him earlier in the year. He never mentioned to her that he *had* joined the army and *was* working closely with intelligence officers in Cairo GHQ. So far, he obliquely referred to loitering about GHQ on any given day at his leisure and without the slightest commitment because of his anti-war views. In fact, Elliot let such rumors circulate throughout Cairo and as a result he had several white feathers added to his growing collection.

"You eat quite an awful lot."

Elliot replied with mischievous intentions, "Louisa, haven't you had the pleasure of sampling our Cook's creations?"

"Of course!"

"And what did you think of it?" Elliot asked.

"Delightful!"

"Delightful? What, no cramping? No running or vomiting?"

"Elliot!"

"Louisa, our Cook is easily offended. And, at the slightest perceived offense, he takes his ill humor out on me, or on William, depending on which one of us disagreed with him."

"Impossible!" Louisa gave a dismissive wave.

"I don't know how he does it, the cur, but there you have it. So, you have been warned."

"You have the wildest sense of imagination. If this were true, your cook would be out of a job."

"Not he. The cockroach! He gets out of any scrape."

"The cockroach?"

"Cook."

"Elliot, you beast, how can you be so uncouth?! Talk of something else. Here's Tilda coming to tell you how handsome you are tonight."

"I'm always handsome," Elliot shot back while wondering who was Tilda. Had he met her?

Louisa rolled her eyes and tittered, "Silly, are you tight again?"

"Tight? Not yet. This is my first glass of wine. Doesn't your father have anything stronger?"

"Beast! Elliot, of course he does. In the library," Louisa cooed right before her giggling friend accosted the couple.

And as Elliot stared smilingly into the ugly teeth of Tilda, his mind ran through the possibility of extricating himself and going on a tour of the Bakers' mansion.

He needed hard evidence that his fiancée and her father were in communication with the enemy. He hoped to come upon correspondence or any such documentation that would be enough to fling the Baker female out of his life and leave the field open for one magnificent singing Aphrodite.

"Ladies, you must excuse me."

"But, Elliot," protested Louisa.

With characteristic insouciance, he bent to kiss her cheek, "I must commune with nature."

#

Elliot briskly walked along the Bakers' hallways, darting in and out of rooms, cursing the popularity of such sprawling construction and damning his search as an excursion into the ogre's den. He was instructed to be careful, inconspicuous. The Bakers' had powerful political friends and the case against both father and daughter had to be ironclad.

Finally, Elliot managed to locate a locked door. Recollecting a rough floor plan of the mansion that he had studied when he took on the job, he thought that this was where a question mark indicated a possible office, locked and unavailable to general staff. With bated breath and while listening to sounds of approach, Elliot fiddled with the lock, enthusiasm and hope bubbling inside him.

CHAPTER 11

Wednesday afternoon 17 June 1942
CAIRO, EGYPT

"INSUFFERABLE NOISE," ELLIOT grumbled, knowing full well that his temper was due to frustration: the failure at the Bakers' mansion last night and this morning's disappointment.

The divan gave under his weight and Elliot strained to block out the piano and his memory of last night's foundering. He had been about to enter a room at the Bakers' grand house. The room was out of the way, and its door was locked. It appeared to be an office yet with a rather modern but simple locking mechanism. To his dismay, before he could open the door, Elliot was spotted by the yellow-toothed Tilda, an ugly and rather manish specimen holding the title of dear friend of Louisa. Tilda had been on the hunt for Elliot. Was she really only chiding him simply because Louisa wanted to dance with her fiancé? Or was she sent to spy on him?

"But you're fond of pianos." William's pragmatic voice reached Elliot's jaundiced ears.

"Not this one."

Elliot found the cheery tune grating. He struggled with the haunting sights on the road to Alexandria the previous day. Having had to leave the Bakers' dinner party empty handed, his failure gnawed at his conscience. He wanted to thwart the Bakers' pro-Nazi activities. He wanted the Eighth to crush the Axis in the desert, charge Europe, and end the horror.

Sir Niles had asked Elliot to stay close to home, which infuriated his sense of freedom and made it impossible to join Tate and Sullivan. Elliot groaned.

The fan groaned, too, as incoming electricity faltered.

A string of threats and foul language escaped Elliot's lips in a fit of ill humor.

William handed him a drink. "Ignore the piano. You'll do yourself a mischief and your rough language is not ingratiating you with me right now."

Elliot, recalling the amputee, blood-soaked dressings and drips of the stuff running down the heap of men below, closed his eyes and forced some civility into his speech. But he could only produce a complaint. "Cairo's a raging inferno."

"Will Father arrive shortly? He has been at GHQ for days now!"

"And you've been in hospital for ages. By the way, where do you sleep when you're away? At Mrs. Wright's?"

"I've a cot." William's reply was curt. William had no intention of talking about Mrs. Wright, nor where he slept.

"I know it's been hot and dry, but sandstorms usually assail us in the spring, not now."

"Khamsin and Nazis," William said.

"What's worse? Infinitesimal bits of sand hurtled at your face, your car, your house? Suffocating dust that smothers you in your sleep? Or the Nazis?" Elliot asked.

"There's no comparison between the two."

Elliot could scarcely imagine William's experience in England. A year earlier, during the Blitz, his younger brother had remained in London to join the rescue teams. Whatever medical skills he had not picked up in the lecture hall, William learned on the job. William, Elliot thought bitterly, would know all about bombs dropping on a town. "Right then, let us begin to cover the windows. Who will assist us? Ali?"

William stood silent.

"Maybe that lovely girl could lend a hand."

"I bought black fabric to tack over the window frames. We mustn't let any light out during an air raid. Blackouts confuse the enemy. Pilots can't pinpoint populated areas."

"All right, but the staff need not know this great bit of detail. It is more likely that a sandstorm would hit us. An air raid is an unfamiliar evil, whereas khamsin is feared throughout Egypt. Besides, we should also get some soap for everyone."

"Soap?" William asked.

"It's difficult to wash sand out of one's arse."

William's pale eyes surveyed Elliot. Why was his brother resorting to ribald language and crass remarks while trying to cheer him up? Still, William appreciated Elliot's efforts and so his lips twitched upward.

"Well, William, I am ready when you are."

"I'll call Salomé."

"Good. I prefer her over Ali. Now that he has grown up, he struts his machismo! Don't know how Cook hasn't sent him packing," Elliot said.

Although William wanted to ask a few questions about Ali, he suggested, "Perhaps we should wait for Father to return from HQ?"

"What for?"

"He'll have news of enemy advance. All this preparation might be in vain."

"If it is not Nazi bombers, then it is sandstorms! We need to get this business done and over with and, besides, there's no telling when Father will return. He's been gone for days."

"Why?"

"He's burning sensitive papers. Come William, there's not a moment to lose. And we cannot expect the piano to stop plinking. The world is at war, and Mother plays her piano, or tennis, or goes to the play or to the opera. Call on that lovely girl for help. I'm damned if I'll be a finely outlined target for bombers."

#

"Troops are evacuating Alexandria and setting up reinforcements by the Delta." Elliot noticed William glancing at Salomé. Was his brother trying to shield her from knowledge that indeed the enemy was within a day's drive from Cairo?

"How did you come by this information?"

"I drove to Alexandria," Elliot replied.

"Oh?"

"And on the road, I saw equipment carriers loaded with wounded men who looked rather apathetic. They were so hot and tired that pain and bleeding probably played a small role in their long list of discomforts!"

"Long list of discomforts?"

"Well? What of it?" Elliot barked.

"That's an understatement."

"It's all the same. Words." Elliot felt a trifle chastened as his heavy tidings spilled out of his mouth, a fiend regaling children with scary fairytales. He shifted his gaze to Salomé.

Salomé, a mute servant who had appeared in December of the previous year, was watching Elliot and William with widened eyes, straining to listen and understand their war talk. She came to the estate as a shadow to Sir Niles who handed the girl over to the housekeeper, breaking his own decree that prohibited hiring new staff. But the girl was never really assigned any specific duties on the estate. Mrs. Judd and Cook, both, seemed to ignore the silent waif.

William had named the girl Salomé. Why? What did William know of the biblical Salomé? Had he ever read that story? Unless William came across the story at school, Elliot doubted that his brother read much. William was not one to busy himself with religion nor was he literary, having always favored the sciences. Did William come across Oscar Wylde's play, then?

Elliot watched the girl's hands. Her fingers were thin, but dexterous. Her hazel eyes dominated the aperture of the veil she wore. The veil often frayed, so much so that it came on and off at alarming speed and at inopportune moments.

Sensing Elliot's gaze, Salomé moved close to William. She tapped William's shoulder and looked at the fabric. William and Salomé seemed to understand each other with little need for conversation. And when William's eyes rested on the svelte figure of the girl, his gaze softened, a trace of a smile flitting across his lips.

"Get on my shoulders," William said. "You can reach the topmost windows."

"These are over eleven feet high!" Elliot called in alarm. "And there's a great number of these window panes. She'll have to stand up. Can she do it?"

"I'll stand on a chair." William drew a heavy wooden dining chair.

"You can't! William, it's unstable."

"You're here for support."

"Yes, all right, but leave the chair out all the same."

With a roll of tape between her teeth and the cloth wrapped round her neck and shoulders, Salomé held onto William in shocking familiarity. She put her feet on his thighs and moved onto his shoulders, her thin hands reluctant to move from William's shoulders and face and did so after a barely noticeable caress.

Elliot held his breath. It was such an unsteady position. The girl was balancing on William, her whole body in front of a pane of glass, with nothing to hold her back.

Suddenly, his presentiment came true.

Salomé tried to steady herself, when her body tilted forward, towards the window.

Elliot pounced and balanced Salomé in time. Biting his lips, his arms extended up, holding Salomé as she regained her balance. He watched Salomé pull and stretch the tape across the window panes. Then Elliot's gaze travelled to his brother's face.

William winked, trying to ease the tension, while echoes of piano music and shouts from the kitchen filled the void.

"William!" the sudden booming voice made William gasp. "Put her down!"

"Father?" William choked.

Sir Niles' wrath continued. "Haven't we a ladder? Can't Ali do this job?"

Startled, Elliot looked at William then at his father as he tightened his grip on the girl.

Noticing his son's dark curls beyond William's lighter, messy crop, Sir Niles called in agitation, "Elliot? I expect you to behave sensibly, and here I am walking

67

into a street circus. And a fine circus this is! A troupe of tumblers under my own roof!"

Elliot's hands gripped Salomé harder.

William, eyes downcast, stood still, barely breathing.

And in the silence that fell, Sir Niles' faint utterance of "buffoonery" gave vent to his feelings while Salomé kept on uncoiling, stretching, and ripping the tape.

Salomé knocked on the window.

"Finished?" William's head tilted up then his eyes leveled with Elliot's.

As Elliot moved closer, Salomé dismounted into his arms. "Light as a feather!"

"No wonder! Cook barely feeds *us*! I cannot imagine what our staff eats. Is dinner ready yet? What is that old horror up to now? Damn the fellow. What's he shouting about?" And on that sour grievance, Sir Niles turned and marched to the noisy kitchen.

"Never saw him in such a temper. Have you?"

"Must be the strain of the army's retreat," William whispered. "Is he really going to the kitchen?"

"I doubt it."

Salomé pointed to the cloth, still draped over her shoulders.

"Right, the dark fabric. Mother won't like it. It's hideous. Here girl, get on my shoulders. I'm stronger."

"But smelly…ah, ouch!"

Elliot jabbed William's arm and tripped him.

But Salomé flung the fabric over Elliot's head as he settled on William's abdomen. "William, I can't breathe!"

"Get off me."

"I'm off!" But as Salomé let go of him, Elliot picked her up and bolted through the grand hall, carrying her pressed against his chest.

"Elliot?"

Elliot ran to the irrigation canals, hoping to have a good splash in the deeper water.

"Elliot, stop!"

And while William urged him to stop, a soft cry came out of the girl.

Elliot put Salomé down and smiled as he adjusted her veil that was coming undone. His hands on her shoulders, he asked, "Did you say something?" He knew very well that the girl had not uttered a sound since her arrival at the estate and was now rather excited to hear her, hoping that she would explain her presence.

"She does not speak, Elliot. Dinner will be served soon. We'd better go."

Elliot turned to the house, pensive. Who was the girl? Why did she not speak? And did the sound he had heard come out of her throat or some squeaky, chirpy bird in the reeds?

CHAPTER 12

An excerpt from Jack Johnson's Notes
Sunday 14 June 1942
WESTERN DESERT

WE ARE THWARTED.

Oaths ride on the desert dust as we obey orders to destroy priceless stores of fuel, food, and ammunition, the very commodities we have struggled for so long to accumulate and deliver to posts up the desert escarpments.

Moss and Bandar walk by, and I catch Moss handing Bandar a date along with a homily on money and effort the retreat is costing the British Eighth Army. "And besides, it's a miserable job."

Bandar in his turn chatters.

And again Moss explains, "But of course we must keep it from the enemy. Not that the Jerries would care for our bully beef, but they'd love to have our oil stores and our water tanks." And all this is said in a dry monotonous voice, punctuated by Bandar's ceaseless chitter.

"Jack, how are the South Africans coping?" Toc's voice is unsteady with nerves.

"Most of them are getting through. Ten thousand of them were ordered into Tobruk. Rommel wants to take over those cliffs above the coastal road because, if they get their guns up there, then it's all over for anyone trying to use that tarmac track."

"They're sealing up Tobruk."

"Toc, what of us? And our 50th division? The coastal road can hold only one division at a time! What about us?"

Sotto voce, Toc asks, "And what of poor Moss? He's losing it, you know. *Bomb-happy.*"

"At least he has Bandar. What will I have when I go bomb-happy?"

Toc's lips part to let out a screech. He scratches and dances, chittering and screeching in a fair imitation of Bandar.

"Shove off," I collapse with laughter.

Sergeant walks over. "Johnson!"

"Sir."

He casts a fulminating glare at Toc. "Communication lines are disrupted. We'll follow yesterday's order from Lieutenant-General Neil Ritchie. Let the men know."

#

With truculent discontent, we withdraw farther from our Gazala Line boxes. We form mixed columns and charge into the Italians southward then eastward avoiding German forces but leaving the Italians rather in a state of chaotic confusion, because they never expected such pugnacious visitors as us!

Driving toward Fort Maddelena on the Egyptian side, we ride in the back of an equipment carrier with our regiment. But there are few of us left.

"Aircraft!" comes the dreaded shout.

I jump out, onto the dusty desert road, my knees and palms coming in contact with rough scrub and I am heedless of scorpions or snakes. There are Messerschmitts overhead that open fire, and little spurts of sand remind me to hide, dig into the sand and keep still, make myself invisible to the enemy above.

When the Messerschmitts depart, the din in my head pins me to the ground, confused, and still tightly clasping Toc's booted heel.

Toc gets to his hands and knees and looks at me, his head tucked in, his chin to his chest. "Johnson, I'd like the use of my foot now!" He pulls away and crawls backward to my side. "What would Elliot Westbrook say?"

My forehead pressed into his arm, I whisper, "A lucky escape."

"Lucky indeed, because otherwise we would find ourselves in the clutches of his brother, William Westbrook! That bossy, pale medic. Every time I open my eyes to gaze up at him, I think the angel of death is hovering above."

"Toc," I groan.

"I know, Johnson, I know. He's a good enough fellow. One of the best actually so I won't make bad jokes, not now." He pulls me into an embrace, and rocks me, humming The Noble Duke of York nursery rhyme.

"Poor stupid bastards."

"Language, Jack," Toc says, half-heartedly.

"I feel sorry for them, you know, that's all. Marching up, down, up, for no good reason."

"It's Flanders."

"What?" I ask.

"The Flanders campaign. The Duke and his men were actually running away from French troops. They never suspected the French would attack in the rain."

"What?"

"Duke of York made his men retreat during the Flanders' campaign."

Eventually, we pile into the remaining lorries after we remove the three who never really had a chance.

The bodies are laid in an orderly line off to the side of the road.

We remove their red identity disks and leave the green ones on the bodies. Normally, we would bury them and plant a makeshift cross with the soldier's name by each grave, but not now. The hard substrate makes digging quickly impossible. And the Axis bombers will soon return.

We must find shelter, fast.

But Toc goes over to each of the bodies and runs his palm over their faces, making sure their eyes are shut. One of the men split his skull and the image is ghastly. So, Toc strips. He wraps the messy remains in his shirt and vest and straightens the rest of the body, lining him up with his fallen comrades. Toc then diligently copies down names and ranks from the green disks, oblivious to the grisly aspect of his actions.

Shirtless and silent, Toc returns, stuffing his lists into his shorts pocket and I notice for the first time that my friend's right shoulder is stooped. I am surprised because, to me, Toc represents a superior man. His physique is athletic and his education is classical and well rounded, but there is something rugged about him, too. He is often ready for the sort of warfare the desert demands, testing stamina, requiring stealth and then standing up to rigorous action. Adding his enviable linguistic abilities, I am amazed that Intelligence have not pounced on such a paragon yet.

#
Tuesday 16 June 1942
WESTERN DESERT

Still retreating, gas masks on our faces, we clear the road to Bomba and Derna. We head in the direction of Bir Hakeim where the Fighting French bravely defended the ridge until a few days ago.

"What are you doing?" Toc takes his mask off. His dirty face, a sombre visage of dust and oil, turns to me.

"Can't neglect my journal!"

"Let's see then." He reads:

"*It is 16 June 1942 and all British positions west of Tobruk have fallen or are falling.*" He pauses. "Not a very cheery entry! What should I scrawl next for you?" he asks, his pencil hovering over the page.

"*The gates of Tobruk slammed, and the town is under siege!*"

"Jack!"

"Damn, how is it that I am saddled with this business of recording events? I'm not very good at it, am I?"

72

"Appalling. And you have a tendency for the dramatics, too."

"Was it your doing, Toc? I'd much rather stand by my gun. That's what I trained for! Not writing and communicating! I am not a bleeding minstrel!"

"Can you sing and dance?"

"Shut up."

"But you and I are recovering from shock!"

"I congratulate you on your perspicacity, damn you."

"Perspicacity?" Toc asks.

I look away.

"Jack?"

"What is it?" I return my gaze to him.

Toc's jaw is clenched. "I hate retreating."

I cannot let my friend down. "It'll come about. It has to because I can't be a minstrel for much longer."

Toc clicks his tongue.

"Look, Jerry is advancing. Yes. However, the farther Jerry gets from his supply ports, the weaker he becomes."

"I know, Jack."

"And although we're retreating, we're also getting closer to our main supply lines."

"You're in the right, Jack. Besides the Americans are joining us soon," Toc says, a little more cheerful. "And, which is far more to the point, they'll bring tanks."

"I believe it," our driver speaks loudly. "If Toc says so, then I believe it."

The truth is that Toc has become some sort of a demigod for our driver. Toc's discourse in erudite tones and his heroics defending our position do not go unnoticed by the men and one after another they fall before his charms. I cannot blame them. But for me, it's not his air and speech, neither is it his keen senses and quick actions on the battlefield. I admire him because I cannot ask for a better friend, loyal and kind. War is hell, but not such a bad hell for me.

I have Toc.

#

Wednesday-Sunday 17-21 June 1942
WESTERN DESERT

As our diminished cavalcade is nearing the Egyptian frontier, my journal entries are grimmer.

73

"Between 17th and 18th of June, Rommel isolates Tobruk. With insufficient help from the Royal Air Force and one line of defense after another crumbling under the heavy anti-tank, anti aircraft barrage, Tobruk is left to defend itself.

On 21 June 1942, Tobruk falls."

It is during the uncertain days between the 18th and 19th of June while our division is reassembled at Bir el Thalata that I remind Toc of the LRDG.

"Sergeant will refuse our reassignment at the moment. He can't let two of his men go, not now that so few of us are left," Toc explains.

CHAPTER 13

Saturday 20 June 1942
CAIRO, EGYPT

"ELLIOT!" FARAJ'S EYES scanned the tradesmen at their work. "June is almost over and here you are! The owner of Monnayeur's!"

But since Elliot's smile was less intense than usual, Faraj gave him a knowing look. Faraj suspected that Elliot was not interested in the club as a means for generating wealth. "You chose an interesting location, Elliot," he commented. "Clot Bey is usually frequented by the laymen, the whores, and the druggies. No?"

"I particularly sought this place out in this particular district," admitted Elliot. "And I intend Monnayeur's to thrive as a cabaret. Nothing dirty. No dope. And, I've cards and roulette tables. GHQ's staff has already succumbed to the ennui of Cairene clubs. Monnayeur's fills in the void admirably."

"But Clot Bey?"

"Does it not amuse you to watch society men traipsing into such a disreputable district?"

"Cheeky boy! Will I be an invited guest?"

"You're my honored guest!" Elliot embraced his friend. Relief and happiness washed over him as Elliot had just realized how much Faraj's approval had meant to him.

#
Monday 22 JUNE 1942
CAIRO, EGYPT

"Tobruk's in German hands." Settling heavily into a leather chair in his study, Sir Niles' words rankled. "Again."

"What will you have?" Elliot asked.

"I'm due back at GHQ. I wanted to talk to you."

Elliot walked to the sidebar, filled up his whiskey glass then tossed it off neat.

"Elliot, William must remain in Cairo. His duties in hospital dictate so. And so it falls to you to take your mother to Palestine. Ideally, I would like her to leave to South Africa, get a passage to the Cape but that's out of my hands, and I doubt she would agree to be so far apart."

"Why not ask her first? Mother would want to stay. After all, she grew up in India during turbulent times. She's fearless. A blonde Amazon."

Sir Niles grunted. "I've never heard of her being called that! She certainly does not have the figure of an Amazon, neither the coloring."

"It's only you and James who insist on treating her as if she were made of delicate porcelain, a china-doll."

"The thin girl can accompany her."

"Father, my advice is that you talk to Mother first." Elliot was noncommittal, hiding his surprise at his father's suggestion to send Salomé away. He deftly avoided mentioning that his mother ignored the thin servant. "Mother has been talking of a gala at the ambassador's villa. But she really is awaiting news from James. She feels that while she remains here in Egypt, she is somehow closer to him. What is it between them? First Born Son and his Mother?"

"They do seem to get on famously!" Sir Niles smiled at his wife's relationship with James. "Somehow, they understand each other."

"Well, I understand neither one."

"Still, I wish you to take your mother to Palestine, Elliot."

"If I must escort Mother, I will do so. But, I'll return on the next train."

"Return?"

"Monnayeur's! Have you forgotten?"

"Not that nonsense, Elliot! What on earth possessed you to purchase such a place and to freely admit that it is yours, too. Have you thought of the consequences? Socially?"

"Father, there's also the other business. My, ah, wedding."

"I dislike both."

CHAPTER 14

An excerpt from Jack Johnson's Notes
Friday 26 June 1942
WESTERN DESERT

A FLUID AND bloody battle rages on the cliffs of Matruth between the New Zealanders and the 90th Light German Infantry.

"Astonishing," Moss murmurs as he passes his field glasses round, Bandar trying to snatch the glasses every time they change hands.

Surrounded by German anti-tanks, and with little ammunition and few men, we are in no position to help the New Zealanders. We are tucked into an escarpment, hidden.

"Freyberg certainly trained his people well. Their bayonet charge is superb," Toc observes.

A grin cracks the caked grease and dust on my face. "Maoris! Haka war dance!"

"It's their haka that instills such fear in the Jerries that they're reluctant to stand their ground!"

"Look, Maoris are charging down the cliffs with their war cries."

"Is that paint on their faces?"

"Paint and bayonets," I exclaim in awe. "And the Jerries scamper off."

"I wouldn't want to face those Maoris for anything in the world!" Toc spits his words, exhausted and dusty. He crawls back into what might be called a cave, but it's only a crack or fissure in the rock face. I follow him and am amazed at the silence inside.

"Jack, this is agony." His eyes are raised to mine, and I put my arm on his shoulder.

"I know. You never fully recovered. And the unsanitary conditions here just make it worse. It can't be easy having a swarm of flies attacking your flesh at all hours and mice and rats nibbling at you when you try to sleep. And that stupid bastard, our fucken' orderly, scrubbing your desert sores with a metal bristle brush, can't but make things worse."

"Orderly? Not a doctor?"

"No. Can't you sleep a bit?"

"Sleep? I never pursue forlorn hopes, my dear Jack. I've given up sleep. No, it's not the physical discomfort. It's not knowing what's coming our way."

"Toc, Johnson!" Moss suddenly blocks the light entering the cave. "We're moving out."

"What?"

"The armored division made it through the minefield and is backing up our magnificent Maoris. Sergeant reckons we can slip away. No formal orders beyond retreat."

"How far back?" Toc asks.

"The orders are still the same."

"Alamein line?"

"Yes," Moss confirms.

The Alamein line is a ridge, a natural defense line between the Mediterranean coast and the Qattara Depression.

"Bandar?" Toc looks up.

"Here," Moss fishes out the monkey from a satchel slung over his shoulder.

Without another word, Toc rushes to grab his kitbag and hurtles himself into a lorry. Moss and I follow after passing the word round, Bandar clutching to Moss, chittering.

The mood is sombre because the Maoris' battle is a last stand in a rout, and we are unable to help in any way.

Our original order to travel in echelon formation, three columns abreast, one hundred yards apart, fifty yards behind each vehicle is impossible. After the Battle of the Gazala Line, and the consequent skirmishes, there is little left of our battalion and it is a similar story for the rest of the Eighth. From ten thousand men, we are down to tens, and with little equipment, so that instead of traveling like ships at sea, we retreat like ghosts at Sheol, in a wide wadi, hiding in shadows.

Withdrawing is hard on all of us, but Toc takes offense at the idea, and he is prickly. Toc and I walk alongside our transport, heavy equipment clanking on our thighs, rubbing up against sores and wounds. We prefer to march because it is a bone shaking journey on the lorry plodding along the uneven wadi bed. Toc's head swivels this way and that, taking in the wadi's steep walls. Teeth clenched, he chafes at our slow progress.

"Expecting the worst?" I ask, keeping my steps in pace with his.

"Expecting an 88 to glare down at me."

Toc's uneasy glances up the wadi walls are not unjustified. But as the sun sinks, the wadi is in deep shadows so Toc walks on, silent, under the cover of imperfect light

Earlier, our lorry had bogged down in the shifting sands and the effort to extricate the machine has left us wrung out.

As soon as we reach flatter and harder ground, Sergeant shouts, "Hop on, Johnson!"

We jump onto the lorry, gripping the metal bars, flapping tarpaulin slapping our faces.

Presently, the lorry gets stuck again. Toc and I jump off, ready to dig it out.

But like a truant dog, Toc remains still, and sniffs the air. He raises his finger to his lips.

The smile that is forming on my face is wiped off and I rush to the front wheel of the lorry, quietly opening the door and signaling for silence. I wave for Sergeant and his driver to come out. Sergeant waves to other comrades, gathering all into a crack in the wadi wall.

"What is it?" Sergeant rasps.

Toc points above us. "Sir, I caught a glint of reflected sunlight and smelled cooking fire. With any luck, it's Jerry!" his words slice their way out from between his teeth.

"Luck?" Sergeant eyes him with utmost dismay.

Luck, to most, would be us stumbling upon another British camp or any Allied forces, as we have little of our machinery or artillery left. We are not down to the last bullet, but nearly so. Our company, halted and utterly exposed at the bottom of the wadi, stands as a monument.

Sergeant casts another glance at the remaining men at his disposal and at the machinery. Our last engagement has been a costly carnage as we came under heavy enemy fire. But crossing the wadi with possible enemy fire above is suicidal. "All right, you two, crawl out for a recci. Wait, where's that damned monkey? Is he going to give us away?"

"Inebriated," comes Moss' gravelly response.

"Does that animal drink all our rum?" Sergeant asks acidly.

"Sergeant, Sir."

Toc's urgent whisper summons Sergeant to his senses as he commands me to crawl out and investigate. "If Axis, stay where you are and make no sound. We'll join you."

"Sir, I'll accompany Jack," Toc announces.

"Jack?"

"Johnson, Sir."

Our intense physical training pays off. Toc and I climb up the wadi wall, with slow, light steps that disturb little.

"We are in luck." Toc's utterance is barely audible, though imbued with strong emotion. He crouches down, looking at me then at Sergeant's pugnacious face peeping out of the wadi wall where he is huddled with the rest of the men. Toc gives a nod and an inviting hand wave.

Sergeant acknowledges him.

What happens next is something out of a nightmare.

Without a sound, Sergeant leads us to the Axis camp which appears to be no more than four tents, machinery, some Volkswagen Kübelwagens, and light artillery. There is a lorry that bears all the insignia of the New Zealanders but the rest of the equipment is decidedly German as is the insignia on the uniform the men wear. The voices that carry across the desert sands are Germanic.

We fall back on our training.

Grenades fly out of our hands in the prone position on the rocky terrain, almost instantaneously shifting to our Bren guns, setting our trigger fingers to work.

We have caught the camp off guard and are soon staring at pitted remains within minutes. Waiting for the dust to settle, his Bren gun still aimed at the camp, Sergeant keeps us in the prone position.

But there is no movement.

By my side, I feel Toc's body give a shudder and then a howl of rage bursts out of him. Toc stands up and releases another grenade and is thrown off balance. He lands on somebody behind him but it does not phase him as he springs up, his gun at the ready. I am by his side, gun raised and looking for any movement that might threaten my friend as I wonder when his temporary madness will be over because it has to be madness, I have never heard Toc shout and act recklessly before today. He is shooting and reciting names that he's been writing down, the names of our fallen comrades that are scribbled down on pieces of paper that he keeps in his shorts pocket. I am astounded as I hear him pronounce the rather formidable names of some Indian soldiers or the outlandish Maori names just as easily as the English or Australian names, their identification numbers, of course, follow.

Sergeant crawls to us then rises to his feet. His freckly, thick hand is now resting on Toc's back but Toc is still shooting, his ammunition about to fail him and Sergeant lets him have his way, his hand still pressed against Toc's back in an avuncular position between Toc's wide shoulders. Moss and the remnants of our section rise up and approach Toc. Together with Sergeant, guns raised, we point at the perforated camp, still afraid to let our guard down but rather reluctant to pour fire and waste precious ammunition. Toc is doing it for us.

#

Tuesday 30 June 1942
EL ALAMEIN, EGYPT

A ridge and a barren marker across the desert with a railway station close to the sea, el Alamein Line is now the Eighth Army's line of defense 150 miles from Cairo, 60 miles from Alexandria. The Eighth has been digging trenches and laying wires and mines, and pulling sunshade netting over dugouts and pillboxes.

We must hold onto the el Alamein Line no matter what! It is a solitary barrier that separates the enemy from the Delta, the cities of Alexandria and Cairo, the Suez Canal, the safe flying zones over the region, general commodities supplied by the fertile delta region, and the expansive oil fields of the Middle East.

Vanguard of the enemy arrives on the last day of June 1942.

Although we are commanded to give the enemy hell, Mother Nature receives similar orders: A dust storm assails us.

When the storm finally subsides, a light rain of dust, fine cement-like dust, is falling. Across the horizon, columns of dust, like roaming desert giants, appear.

Staring blindly, my eyes are swollen and will likely remain so for the next few days. My mouth is full of dust.

"Dust and heat," Toc, standing behind me, reminds me of our conditions.

"And your rats."

Toc snorts with laughter then spits dust out of his mouth, muttering as he chokes. Half naked, we head into the tent where we finally give in to hysterical laughter much to the consternation of our tent mates.

"Three or four more months of this heat to go, then the temperatures will drop," I remind Toc.

"If you survive the next day."

When night blankets us in utter darkness, I trudge heavily into bed, checking that the paraffin can at the bottom of each bed leg is in place. I have no intention of sharing my bed with a scorpion. Rats and mice, fleas and flies, even bedbugs, I can handle those but the scorpions instill in me ungodly fear.

Shortly after I shut my eyes, I am fast asleep.

"*Wot* the bloody 'ell was that?" A giant Yorkshireman jumps out of his bunk, his booming deep voice wakes us into startled reality of Shire shouting and curses and flying bedsheets.

"Bandar? Bandar? Where are you?" Moss whispers urgently while the Yorkshire giant continues to swear, demanding to know what has just landed on him.

The man joined us only this evening. In the confusion of retreat and entrenching, he was separated from his unit before the dust storm.

"Rats!" I call out and try to get back to sleep but Moss continues to call for Bandar. So I leave my bed and, arms extended forward, feel my way round, searching for a bundle of fur.

"Who's Bandar? You daft or *summat* or 'ave you gone mad? Wot the 'ell jumped on my face?" the Yorkshireman booms. "And it's no rats!"

"I can't find my monkey!" Moss is exasperated.

"MONKEY??" From the sound of the his voice, some form of an apoplectic attack is not far. "*Wot* monkey? D'you 'ave a monkey?"

"I do, but I can't see a thing! It's the dust and it's so dark. Bandar?" Moss' voice is scratchy, worried.

In the brief silence of stupefied realization, Bandar gives a terrific shriek.

"Here he is." I hear Toc's calm well-bred accents then his athletic steps approach Moss. As Toc hands over the monkey, Bandar makes his happy sounds. "Bandar came from Cairo, from the bazaar. You know, you can pretty much buy anything in that city," Toc explains casually then introduces himself since we never had the opportunity before falling in sheer exhaustion on our cots, asleep within minutes. "I'm Toc and Bandar is the mischievous monkey. Moss bought him, curse the fellow, and over there is Jack, Jack Johnson."

We grumble sleepily our 'pleased to make your acquaintance' and 'good night' in appalling lack of sincerity and I head back into my bed but the Yorkshire lad, Turner, has not had his last word.

"You keep that damned animal of yours in your own bed. And next time you share your tent with a stranger, warn him of your penchant for beasts."

I recognize Toc's groan as one of pending hilarity, but somehow he keeps it subdued and I am relieved.

Our Yorkshire companion cannot possibly withstand such levity just now. Turner is one of the last three surviving lads of his regiment.

CHAPTER 15

Tuesday 30 June 1942
CAIRO, EGYPT

"WELL, WHAT IS it, Elliot?"

Bits of plaster escaped the mantle after Elliot had slammed the door shut behind him.

"Father, what do you mean by telephoning the Auk and asking him to put a stop to my project with the Bakers?"

"Come close."

Elliot crossed his father's study in quick, angry steps, his hands thrust into the pockets of his trousers.

And, before Elliot could bark out another word, barely above a whisper, Sir Niles explained, "Code 11 is the American code to transmit reports back to US government. Are you familiar with it?"

"I'm familiar with codes, yes, but I fail to see how you talking about an American Code 11 justifies *your* interference with *my* project."

"It's compromised."

"My project is compromised?"

"The Code is compromised."

Ice filled Elliot's veins. There would be far reaching consequences to a compromised code during war, especially if there had been *loose talk*. "Is that how Tobruk fell within days? Is that why our paratroopers were shot down one after another in North Africa, and air raids continue to fail?"

"Possibly. Probably. Yes."

"That's how Rommel knows what equipment we have. Our movements, our plans, our weakest flank…"

"Yes. Or I should say that the compromised code is one of our leaks. There's certainly been a lot of *loose talk* and *funning* over the radio waves, and at the clubs."

Silence hung between father and son.

"My boy, there's no need to torture yourself with Louisa's company any longer. Much less to saddle yourself with a butter toothed brown cow with no deportment and such an acidic voice that grates on my nerves."

"That bad?"

"Worse."

Sir Nile's laconic *worse* brought a brief twitch to Elliot's lips. "No, no. It is torture and mainly because I do not and cannot like her, how could I? But there is more to my project. Father, I managed to obtain the names, the contacts, Baker approached with demands for cotton and supplies that the Axis forces require. Mr. Baker has been threatening and bullying farmers and manufacturers throughout the Arab world. His daughter aids him. She must! Her Arabic is fluent, a fact she cleverly concealed from me for some time and only let slip by accident during one of the soirées at their mansion when I came upon her giving instructions to her housekeeper in fluid Cairene Arabic, complete with a heady set of oaths to match! She could be the go-between. At any rate, the lists, I found in her bedroom."

A groan escaped Sir Niles' throat. Then he inclined his head, accepting that abandoning Elliot's engagement to Louisa Baker was indeed premature. "She's taken a fancy to you."

"I cannot rely on that."

"How do you mean?" Sir Niles wondered.

"I must be careful at all times in her company. In fact, I'm now in the habit of carrying a pistol when I'm with her. She may have taken a fancy to me, but I doubt that. She might be interested in getting closer to you, to your contacts in Cairo perhaps. Why else would one of the wealthiest girls in Cairo agree to marry me within months and during a world war, too? And I must add without any demure."

"Demure?"

"How is she able to deceive herself that I, the son of Sir Niles, would marry a merchant's daughter? We are socially above her, and we are prosperous. True, I purchased a club and am running it as a show of 'devil may care' or 'social status be damned,' but she cannot fool herself that someone of our class would marry someone like her. She is not stunningly beautiful nor has she any special talent. She has money but our family has not fallen on hard times. We don't need to ally our family name with money! I know that I'm being blunt, but I am worried, Father."

"Elliot, she must have read too many of those damned paperback *romances*! They give the women *such* outlandish ideas."

"Perhaps. But the more obvious, more dangerous, possibility is that she's obeying orders from Berlin. Which is more than likely since I don't see such as Louisa relaxing at home with a paperback romance! Do you?"

#

With his hands across his chest and his back to a window, Elliot watched the stage at Monnayeur's. "No, I didn't get Umm Kulthum for tonight, but then I wouldn't be catering to that kind of crowd."

"No matter." Faraj grinned. "*Mon ami*, you have the best dancers in Cairo. Just look at them." Faraj ran appreciative eyes over the voluptuous women who popped on stage to check in with the musicians. "Magnificent! Bravo!" Faraj exclaimed as the dancers rehearsed difficult moves with sabers balancing on their heads. "*Yah chabibi!* You will do well. Get yourself burly giants as bouncers, and you eject on sight any trouble maker, and you are a success. You will do very well!" Faraj declared, patting Elliot's broad shoulders. He showered a few more compliments and blessings after casting approving glances at a diminutive dancer who stopped dancing now and then to admonish her drummer to play faster.

After Faraj left, Elliot walked outside and hailed a taxi, heading back to his parent's estate. William had asked him to look into the rehabilitation project of the ditch network on their estate. Although Elliot had found the project farcical, his father had also asked for his help, explaining that Ali needed a rigorous occupation. "Ali is kept on as a stable boy. However, you and William rarely go riding. Ali has too much time on his hands. He wanders into cafés and into the hands of nationalist gangs, an easy prey. The gangs make good use of discontented youths. They manipulate the young. And we cannot risk Ali turning against us. He's privy to too much information."

#

Pulling on his neck tie later that evening, Elliot wished that he had washed after his fatiguing work on the estate. He had enjoyed himself immensely, calling out orders, running and jumping along the web of irrigation canals, and pulling and pushing weeds and pipes and turnout gates. There was something gratifying in physical work. But as the evening progressed and the heat hung heavy at Monnayeur's, Elliot was itchy, bits of seed-heads irritated his neck.

Walking out of the gambling rooms, heading to his table during the violin interlude on stage, Elliot saw two servicemen enter.

"Maskelyn!" A young man, wreathed in smiles, immediately hailed the tall, thin man. "Jasper!"

Jasper Maskelyn, slightly stooped and with a thin mustache, looked pleased. "Courtney! What a surprise to see you here! Didn't I last see you in '41, in Helwan? The Royal Engineers, wasn't it?" Turning to his short companion, Maskelyn said, "Bobby, here's a master engineer!"

Pressed between Maskelyn and Courtney, Bobby could only stare into their larynx.

"Bobby's part of our troupe. Enviable skills at cards!"

"How do you do it, Maskelyn? A troupe of experts at your fingertips! Never thought that it could happen in the army," Courtney said.

"That's high praise coming from a craftsman such as yourself. You assembled desert mirages and half of the *other* Port of Alexandria."

"And how one manufactures a mirage is something I would dearly love to know," Elliot approached the threesome, extending his hand. "Westbrook."

The men, clearly well aware of the name Westbrook in Cairo, eagerly introduced themselves.

Elliot ordered a round of drinks, inviting the three to his table that crouched low, in front of the stage and close to the wide open windows overlooking the thoroughfare.

"I gather that you are *conjurers*?" Elliot began.

"Magicians, conjurers, illusionists. My Magic Gang."

"Army morale is important as much as any other military element. Probably the most important," Elliot observed. "Which is why I invite you to perform here at my club."

"Much obliged, Westbrook. Honored! I would dearly love to accept. But duty calls. We're on our way back to Helwan, you see, back to our barracks. We are army men at the moment. But I daresay, I'll accept your offer if I'm sacked!" Maskelyn winked.

Elliot turned his head, disappointed. He would have like to have access to someone like Maskelyn long enough to get tips on desert camouflage but also to perform at his club and maybe even take his troupe to visit some of his brother's invalids. Both William and Madame Sukey would be gratified. Startled at his thoughts, at his wanting to please Madame Sukey, Elliot made his apologies for having to leave so soon to attend to club matters.

Nevertheless, Elliot was inspired.

Illusions could swing the balance in the desert because resources were thinly stretched. Illusions of exaggerated strength could certainly alter enemy's strategy.

As Elliot observed his clients, some slipping behind the curtains into the card rooms, his mind turned to the running of the club, switching his gaze to the performance on stage.

There were three of them on stage, three deep bosomed swarthy young and agile dancers. And with every twist and turn of the music, their bodies moved in wave-like uniformity, matching each other, challenging. Undulating curves danced, chests rising and falling, popping out then retreating, spraying patrons with tantalizing bits of scent and sweat as the drummers stroked, beating, caressing the drums on and on. Meanwhile, his incredible dancers controlled their abdomen, breasts, and thighs. And as the music sped up, so did the dancers' ringed toes, shooting quivers up their bodies, jingling the golden coins, jingling all round, heaving and thrusting smooth mounds of skin.

Monnayeur's was an overnight success with quality acts and luxurious ambiance. Men could drink lukewarm beer anywhere but here they enjoyed efficiency and quality while tranced by the seductive shows.

Now on stage remained a single dancer. An idyl in Arcadia. A saber resting on her head, just above her elaborate headband of sparkling stones and pearls. No other instrument accompanied her steps except for the rolling drum, rolling slowly, slower, then speeding up the beat, and faster, and the chatter of her finger cymbals that added golden glow to the dance and its music. Her hip circles spellbinding the audience, legs apart, glittering bra barely concealing the wonders of silky skin that shuddered underneath, a glorious tassel its only boon companion. The dancer's skirt, a lush affair of strings of silk and beads, split open as she thrust her leg out, oil on her thighs glistening.

When the tempo sped up, faster like a racing heart beat, the dancer's pelvis juddered. She arched her back, her arms stretched before her, letting bracelets of gold and silver arm bands jingle and shine while her breasts faced the ceiling, saber still miraculously over her forehead. Sweat shone on her stomach, little beads that escaped from under her bosom that threatened to spill out of her dazzling brassier of sequin and pearl, lace and silk.

At the climax, the dancer's painted lips curved slightly upward, satisfied.

And just then, in a flutter of scarves and shawls, chinking golden coins, entered more dancers and the accompanying instruments, bringing forth the great tumult of snapped eroticism. The violinists joined the dancers on stage and donned a curtain of respectability.

#

Returning before two in the morning, a rather early hour for Elliot, he sought the chink in the double doors of his father's study. Elliot, like a moth, was drawn to the light. He wanted to consult with Sir Niles about Maskelyn. He walked in and firmly shut the door.

"Churchill's in Washington," his father commented dryly, not raising his eyes from the pile of papers before him.

Leaning against the windowsill, gazing at his father's bent bald head, Elliot caught the flicker of hope in Sir Niles' utterance, so he took a chance. "Churchill in

America? Excellent. Will he get more tanks, more aircraft, more guns and those American jeeps?"

"Possibly."

"Good, but what of tactics?"

"Elliot, not now." Sir Niles was well aware of his son's approval of the level-headed command of Auchinleck. However changes were about to take place in the chain of command. "Auchinleck has done a marvelous job."

"A marvelous job indeed considering that his movements, equipment, and force were known to the enemy. The Good Source!"

"Churchill took the information about Code 11 to Washington. One can only hope that the Americans will stop using that code immediately."

"Father, what is this rumor of a purge in the upper ranks?"

Sir Niles braced himself.

"Father, I know it's a promotion for the Auk to go to India. His wife's been in India for some time now. However, the Eighth needs him. The enemy vanguard, German 90th Light Infantry, is approaching the Line. It's the end of the month! And from what I recollect, the troops were ordered to fight fire with fire."

"Auchinleck himself is at the front now."

"So he must stay. Finish off Rommel!"

Sir Niles nodded but closed the discussion by downing his drink and exiting his study.

"This entire house is completely mad!" Frustrated, Elliot pressed his forehead to the window, staring at the moonlit grounds.

Two figures dragged a bundle. Ali and Salomé! The girl stumbled and fell. Ali grabbed her arm and roughly pulled her up, pushed her aside and thrust the sack onto his back. The girl, recovering her ground, put her hands on the sack from behind, pushing it upward, wanting to help.

What were those two doing up so late? What was in the sack?

Elliot admired the girl for wishing to help, despite Ali's rough treatment.

"Elliot," Sir Niles burst back into the study and jerked him out of his abstraction. "Come with me to HQ."

"What, now?"

"Now."

CHAPTER 16

An excerpt from Jack Johnson's Notes
Wednesday 01 July 1942
EL ALAMEIN

THE AIR IS thick with shell-dust, smoke, putrid burning oil, and bits of debris. Any empty can that is lifted by the wind, disappears into the impenetrable dust cloud. Somehow, the bombardment makes the desert more ferocious.

A mighty roar kicks up more scraps of burning metal and the heatwave slaps savagely at my face. I stare into the smokey veil with something approaching despair.

"Toc!" I call, again and again, until a rough hand lands on my shoulder, and it is Sergeant pulling me close then down to the ground, and soon he leads me into a dugout behind a tank.

Long fingers close round my wrist. "I'm right here, Jack," Toc speaks, pulling the rest of me to him, trampling others, some from our regiment and others from other units altogether. But our close friendship is acknowledged and is looked upon with sorrowful benevolence. The men move aside and make room. Toc and I are the youngest in the regiment and the older men have long refrained from forming close ties, because in such conditions friendships do not last. One or both of the friends often die or get shipped away for convalescence, they had once warned us. "Don't be daft, Jack. Toc's not going to last more than a week," they had joked. Although why they assume that Toc will not last, I cannot imagine. He is an athlete and his vision is of higher order.

I try to talk but what's the use? The uproar drowns out even Sergeant's ceaseless flow of barbaric imprecations and commands.

We join another section and anyone who can still function has to operate the antitank guns. Toc and I are on a Vickers water-cooled machine-gun.

"What do you make of our field of fire?" Toc shouts into my ear as the German mortars fall.

"Two hundred yards?" I shout.

"Not nearly enough…" Toc's words are drowned in the crump.

In gloomy agreement, I fire once more over the ridge where a German 88mm gun seems to be speaking.

And that is when Toc and I are thrust off the Vickers.

When I open my eyes, a hunk of metal bursts into flames in the air above me, then lands not a yard away from Toc's inert body.

A jolt of terror galvanizes me. The pain that grips every inch of my body vanishes as I scream, "Toc!"

But Toc is not moving.

There's a whistle overhead. A flash in the smokey sky heading away from us! Our shells! Seconds later, the crump is over on enemy lines, as flames leap to the sky and light up the desert. Then a black column rises.

'*Right on Target,*' Toc would have yelled.

But Toc is silent.

The earth shudders.

Cold fear claws at me as I crawl to Toc on the hard sandy ground with its unfriendly scrub.

Oblivious to the heatwave that is sweeping over us and the earth-shattering explosions nearby, I shout, "Toc?" because as I do so I feel less scared, a little less alone in hell.

CHAPTER 17

Wednesday 01 July 1942
CAIRO, EGYPT

"THE BATTLE IS underway at el Alamein. Finally! Our troops have been raring to settle the score, ever since June's retreat," the raw faced, fastidiously dressed officer remarked.

Elliot stared.

"It's maddening, really. This swinging pendulum type of war over the desert. But this time, this time, it'll be better," the officer worked himself up. "Besides wearing out Axis soldiers, we've some tricks!"

"Is that so?" Elliot's response was delivered like a benign, rehearsed social nicety.

The officer shuffled papers on his overloaded desk. Then, recalling his manners, he extended his arm. "I'm Crumper."

"Westbrook." The laconic reply was unfriendly, truculent. "So, why am I here?"

"Westbrook, you know Maskelyn."

"Maskelyn? Magic Gang Maskelyn?" Elliot was surprised to hear the illusionist's name.

"Is he an acquaintance of yours?"

"Maskelyn visited my club last night."

"Did you talk to him?"

"I tried to recruit him! Tuesday nights."

"Why not Saturdays?"

"You must be mad! Saturdays feature Soad, the best, most talented dancer in Egypt. Tuesdays, however, are different."

Forgetting formality, Crumper admitted, "Monnayeur's *is* a fantastic club. And one is *not* besieged by painted whores, cajoling one to buy too many drinks."

"Can't blame the prostitutes."

"Do they collect a percentage from the sales? And why do they leave one desperately sick, and alone, in a filthy alley somewhere in Cairo?"

Elliot glared at Crumper. "How the hell should I know? What d'you take me for? A whore?"

"You have a clean club, Westbrook."

"This is all convivial, but I'd like to know why I'm here."

"Certainly."

"An illusionist, Jasper Maskelyn was involved with war-time trickery besides the Magic Gang," Elliot volunteered.

"And more," Crumper allowed.

"There were rumors of projects involving mirrors and reflectors to hide the Suez Canal, of disguising or re-creating another port of Alexandria, something less real for the Axis bombers to sport with. Am I on the right track?"

The officer bowed his head.

Losing patience, Elliot thrust words at Crumper. "Look, I didn't show up here uninvited. You summoned me. What is it all about? I am tired. I do run a nightclub and my work is at night," Elliot stressed the word 'night' twice, staring hard at the officer.

"We wanted to discuss some ideas, to get your opinion. Opinion, mind you, so no heroics. No venturing forth on your own."

"Who is '*we*?' What do you mean '*on my own*,' Crumper?"

"We know of your prison blow up in December!"

Elliot cracked with laughter. "I was wondering when this bit of intelligence was going to make it to HQ. Does my father know about it?"

"He does," a deep voice replied.

"Theatrical," Elliot grumbled.

Sir Niles, removing his hat, nodded a greeting then swiveled his gaze to his son.

"And you were not pining for any descendant of Aziza the Beast as you convinced your brother."

The officer looked confused.

"William knew better than to believe me, but you raised him well and so he is too well-bred to call me a liar," Elliot rejoined, then, raised his voice, "Why am I here? Why not let me go to sleep if you are only going to plague me with riddles? I haven't the head for this right now!"

The officer took a step back, surprised at Elliot's temper and his unchecked words to his father, a distinguished politician.

"You and thousands of other men are not getting any sleep at the moment. The sooner we can prostrate the enemy the better, for everyone's sake. So, without enacting any scenes for the edification of our young officer here, we'll discuss simple, unexpected ways of delivering unpleasantries to Rommel's troops. You are here, Elliot, because for years your eccentric grandfather took you to the Western Desert to cavort with natives."

"Cavort? We went on diplomatic, sometimes medical, missions."

"Well, you have knowledge of the Western Desert such as few Englishmen have."

Although Elliot was well aware of a profound number of men of various nationalities who were intimately familiar with the region, he held back the snappy retort that sprang to his lips.

"Your thoughts, Elliot."

Reluctantly, Elliot propelled ideas into the dark office, across the messy desk. Over an hour he spoke, and Elliot's ill humor lingered as his suggestions were met with reluctance. Finally, his fist tightening into a ball, Elliot asked in strained tones, "Why not women?"

"Don't be absurd!"

"I am not!"

"Because it is unthinkable. Let me tell you about the Senussi tribe in the caves..." Crumper began.

"I know about the Senussi tribe that was violated by the Nazis! The bastards drag women away then return them in shreds after they..."

"Elliot!" Sir Niles snapped.

"Well, what of it then?" Elliot barked.

"That's why I won't have women involved in this particular operation. And, Westbrook, I'm not after anything flamboyant," Crumper growled.

"Not flamboyant? But where's the fun in that?" A seraphic smile transformed Elliot's face.

Crumper was disappointed yet reluctant to deliver his intended sharp rejoinder.

Sir Niles however had his say. "Fun? The troops out there just might find your flippant remark offensive."

Elliot cast his gaze down, fully aware of his crassness. "Yes. Of course. How could I?"

"We dabbled in reflective lights. Yes. We are working on set-ups of tanks in the desert that are not tanks and lorries that are not lorries."

"Not exactly tanks, not exactly lorries?"

"Undercover machinery," Crumper explained. "Lorries that give the impression of exaggerated concentration of tanks, and tanks that appear to be just another procession of lorries plodding through the desert."

"Are the threatening setups to draw enemy fire away? Nudging them toward the less-threatening setups, and so catch the Krauts unaware?"

"Just so."

"Elliot, we called you here because Churchill is keen on non-traditional missions. Rommel's troops have advanced far into the desert, closer to the Egyptian border. They are away from their supply port. And their communication lines are stretched for miles. There're Special Forces in the Eighth Army operating behind enemy lines, sabotaging radio and supply lines. We need to buy time for our troops to entrench and reinforce. We have the advantage of being nearer to our supply port and our pool of resources is at our fingertips."

"A half-day's drive isn't precisely one's fingertips!"

Crumper was getting to his real reason for summoning Elliot. "Elliot, you have friends in the LRDG. Tate and Sullivan?"

"I do, but can you change their assignment?"

Sir Niles watched Crumper give a slight nod.

Elliot recalled Faraj's tales of Aziza the Beast, the mob boss who ruled the slums of Cairo. Aziza and her women assistants would scare shop owners into paying protection fees, to keep their shops safe from thieves. Aziza used simple tricks, not just fear, but subtle machinations. "Subtle," he blurted. "Look here, from what I understand, the troops already have loose stools. So why not add cramps and blinding pain? A touch of the fever? Nothing extraordinary to suggest an enemy agent's hand in the matter."

"They already suffer from Gyppy Tummy," Crumper grumbled. "We all do."

"Bilharzia disease?" Elliot mused. "It's a fluke that thrives in stagnant water and fastens itself to reeds. It penetrates the human skin and needs not an open sore or abrasion to enter the blood stream. A laboratory assistant can collect samples and find a way to release the goods in any oasis we project the Germans or Italians to come across. Sick troops can't fight, not effectively."

"We can work with that," Crumper agreed.

"When my Grandfather was alive, we tracked nomadic tribes. Our medics immunized the Bedouins. A rather difficult task, because no matter what tribe we approached, no matter the proximity to a city, the lot of them would scream bloody hell at the sight of an eye ointment tube or a syringe."

"How does that help us?" Crumper asked.

"I've intimate insight into the lives of the Bedu. Assemble a group of men and women to train to move as the Bedu does. A roaming Bedouin tribe could inflict quite a bit of damage by simply coming in contact with enemy troops. Serve the enemy a cup of coffee that has some strains of influenza on it, and nature does the rest."

"I dare not ask for more men from our troops."

94

"Crumper, what have you been doing so far? Perhaps we can build on an existing operation?" Sir Niles asked. "We three are a task force, by the way."

Eyeing Sir Niles then glancing at the impish Elliot, the officer wrestled with how much information he should divulge. "We have a team working on scrambling radio waves with the idea of broadcasting false messages. Others work on ways to 'convince' enemy soldiers not to fight, like pamphlets promising fair treatment if captured. Some suggested that we let go of a number of hostages, ones who had been treated lightly at our hands, let them spread the word that after all, surrender is not as bad as fighting to the end."

"It's all very well. However, I still believe that we should take advantage of the Axis army's distance from its supply lines. Food and drink are now scarce. Petrol supplies diminish and equipment grinds to a halt the further an army gets from port. Let us take advantage of that. Besides, have you thought of the pure factor of physical exhaustion? Regular bombing raids applied day and night. Nothing too wasteful, just overhead noise. Constant fear on top of sleep deprivation," Elliot continued.

"Excellent suggestions," Sir Niles commented dryly and Elliot glared at him, piqued that his father would not discuss such ideas at home, in the privacy of his study. Why have this interloping officer between them?

"We have to repeatedly offer enemy troops insults, at least we can effect a delay in their progress and plans. Don't you agree? Stalling them may just tilt the balance. If I could buy our boys a few precious hours of rest and time to regroup and collect whatever ammunition they might need, lay mines or entrench, I would do it, wouldn't you?"

Crumper looked defiant, ready to shout at Elliot, '*and what the devil do you think we have been working on all these years?*' Instead, Crumper said, "But here, there was something else that I had called you in for." He glanced at Sir Niles. "Sir Niles, you must be rather busy."

Smiling at the abrupt dismissal of such a personage as he, Sir Niles admitted, "I am." Then he left the room, firmly shutting the door behind him after assuring his son that he would bring his ideas to Auchinleck's attention.

"Look here Westbrook, what's this rumor I hear about you and Ms. Baker?"

"What rumor?"

"Are you not engaged to be married?"

"What's it to you?"

"I'd like to know *when* you'll marry her."

Elliot lifted his shoulders and gazed up at the ceiling then searched for a cigarette to light.

"The Bakers are beneath you, don't you agree?"

"Socially? Good heavens, Crumper, you sound like Mother."

"Louisa is in trade, you know."

"What a snob!"

"Am I to understand then that you are engaged to Ms. Baker but have not settled on a date for the wedding?"

Elliot drew on his cigarette. "Crumper, look here, this is rather personal."

"The betrothal announcement was in the paper."

"Back in December of last year, yes. Right now, the less said about it the better."

"Why?"

"I am not such a callous idiot as you might believe me to be. My brother, James, is out there with the Eighth Army, or somewhere, we really have no clue. He refuses to write, damn him. I can't have a wedding at the moment!"

"Humbug!"

"What?"

"Liechester told me of your project."

"What project?"

"Westbrook, as we both know, the Bakers have been under surveillance. You are part of that effort. And so you must proceed with the wedding, missing older brother or not. Things are moving too slow."

Elliot was taken aback by the sudden authority in the officer's tone. "Look here, who the devil do you think you are?"

"Cairo swarms with intrigue. Spies pop in and out of every balcony and from every country!"

"Yes, and so I repeat, who are you?"

"We have good reason to believe that Mr. Baker and Ms. Baker are in Cairo to report back to Berlin. The father, through his wide web of Cairene and Alexandrian connections, has been useful to Berlin, providing rather accurate information to the Panzerarmee, and something more: Supplies! As the girl's husband, your intimacy, your proximity would allow us to bring them both before justice. And the sooner the better. We have a war to win."

Elliot was finally checked. He had no intention of actually marrying the creature. She was pretty enough but not at all to his taste, not at all the thing. And to his horror, he had every reason to believe that she was indeed a spy, a Nazi collaborator. He had proposed to her as a means to get close to her and her father and obtain admittance to their residence. Evidence pointed to their involvement with the enemy. He had reported all that he could ferret out back to GHQ. But never to this officer. He was rather shocked that his activities were so casually discussed.

"I took over for Liechester when he was transferred to London," Crumper remarked, noting Elliot's expression.

"Transferred to London? When?"

"Yesterday. A letter. For you."

"From Liechester?"

"Yes."

"You should have mentioned that from the start. It seemed like a farce to me to be talking to some raw-faced recruit."

Crumper grinned. "A fresh recruit? I admit, my looks are deceptive."

"How old are you? Eighteen?"

"I use my appearance to my advantage, though I cannot say that it won your trust. Well, not today."

"You were fortunate that my father came in and I simply followed his lead."

"Westbrook," Crumper leaned forward, his speech throbbing with urgency. "I must move things faster. Bring this matter to a close. Marry the girl. Make what arrangements you can to keep a close eye on her and that reprehensible father of hers! They are motivated by greed. His businesses have been failing as of late yet his lifestyle is lavish."

"I've already provided evidence that Baker gets foreign funding. He is paid mostly in cash but earnings that he reports are below his expenditures. His life-style for many years now has been above his means yet he has few debts!"

"But what is *Louisa's* part in all this? I would hate to get the father and leave the daughter out of it if she is indeed a party to his schemes. And she must be!"

"True. But, Crumper, it is rather a lot to ask of a chap, don't you think? I mean, we are talking about marriage, engagement is one thing, almost as bad. A wedding! And then living with the creature is a bit much!"

"An unfortunate circumstance. Rarely before did we have to deal with women taking part, and such a part, in espionage. Her involvement, and I am certain that she is involved, is a complicated matter. There must be pecuniary reasons and maybe something beyond that. Although why she agreed to your engagement, I cannot quite tell."

"I'm not a hunchback!"

"No, of course not. But does she really believe that you want her for a wife? Why?"

"Look here, this is absurd! Are you from intelligence or not? Has it escaped your notice that I'm a prize on the old marriage market?"

"But that's not what I mean at all! I expected that you would meet with a rebuff, partially because I cannot see Lady Westbrook ever accepting such as Louisa. But mainly because I suspect Louisa to be involved with a man in Berlin."

"I suspected that she might have hoped to obtain information from me. Or from Father?"

"Possibly. Wedding settlements too pose an interesting twist."

"I wonder how much information our lawyers will be able to draw from the Bakers."

"Westbrook?"

"Crumper?"

"I am curious. Did you not find our meeting rather odd?"

"I am hoping to grill my father about that!"

"I wanted to get the measure of you."

"What? Damn you, man, you had me talking all night when there's a major offensive for your own amusement?"

"If I am to work with you, I need to know you."

After a brief moment of silence, Elliot promised, "Crumper, I'll do what I can. I won't fail you. But I doubt my mother will like it."

"I'll leave breaking the news to Lady Westbrook to you."

"Then I'll set a date with Louisa. I'll have Father talk to Mother."

CHAPTER 18

An excerpt from Jack Johnson's Notes
Wednesday 01 July 1942
EL ALAMEIN

AIR ESCAPING MY lungs in short bursts. Deadly ice is coursing through my veins as my lips part wide and I scream, "Toc!"

"For God's sake, don't touch him!" Sergeant shouts. "Can you hear me?" His fingers clasp my chin strap, and he forces me to face him. "Johnson?"

"Yes, Sir," I cry out, a painful roar.

"Don't touch!"

For a moment, I wonder whether Sergeant will give me a B or C card or some such punishment, excluding me from the next engagement.

But what does it matter now? Fear grips me again, then the breathless, excruciating pain takes hold of my chest.

Toc is motionless. His body is strewn on the desert floor, a dark pool spreading under his abdomen.

"I'll radio for a stretcher. Stay by his side. Don't move him, Johnson, don't move him!" is Sergeant's sharp command, and he is off.

As I bring my face close to Toc's and run my hands from his head to his feet, some faint flicker of hope leaps up inside me. Toc is intact, except for a sharp bit of metal that has lodged itself into his abdomen.

#

The thunderous barrage has turned into silence. My ears ache, but I am able to pick up snatches of conversation.

"Do you think we'll have time to brew up?" A question drifts to me.

"Jerries must be exhausted too," I hear someone say with a mouthful of food then the murmured response and request to brew up tea.

There's a lump in my throat as I help the stretcher-bearer lift Toc onto a stretcher.

Toc is taking shallow breaths, unconscious.

Now the stretcher-bearer and the Bren-gun carrier driver work efficiently to pile Toc onto the carrier with careful movements. I watch and am grateful to them for not trying to cheer me up. The bearer collects two more men from our own regiment and the driver is already switching the engine on, not at all reacting to the blood that drips down all over the equipment.

"I am going with you," I declare.

"May as well," Sergeant's voice whooshes by from behind, startling me. He has a mug of tea in one hand and a flask in the other.

The driver shrugs, pulling his sleeve across his face and asks Sergeant to sign his logbook.

"Someone needs to hold them proper. Lord knows the terrain is rough enough and the jostling is more lethal than the wound," Sergeant adds. "Be off with you, Johnson. Get your ears checked out. Driver, anyone says otherwise, send them to me."

Immediately, the Bren-gun carrier heads to a jebel covered in cacti behind which a cavalcade of ambulances is waiting. Then, after offloading its cargo, the carrier returns back to the front, plowing through the wall of shell-dust and disappearing from sight.

As we await ambulatory transport, I look at Toc, pain wrenching my gut. I am afraid to lose my best friend. Around me, the wounded lie supine, their eyes either shut or looking heavenward in apathetic, glazed stares. Some are delirious, some are bomb-happy, and in their midst, I walk about, numb with worry.

"Moss? Is that you?" I pass a filthy man. He is on his back and clasping a leash.

Bandar, stretched out, is sleeping across Moss' thighs, his fur and the man's thighs are covered in dark, sticky fluid.

"Take him, Jack," Moss says on a sob. "Take him. I received one too many, Johnson."

"Is Bandar *well-to-go*?"

"*In-his-cups*," Moss replies, following my lead and mimicking Toc's frequent use of antiquated idioms for drunkenness when Bandar over indulges. A flitting smile flashes across Moss' face as he closes his eyes.

I scoop up the monkey and slide him inside my uniform, cringing at the feel of wet fur.

The ambulance Toc and I transfer into is headed to Cairo. It's always the Cairene British military hospital for Toc, I realize.

We jostle across the desert, salt marshes on either side. Suddenly, I notice a company of Indians, huddling round their commanding officer. Are they the rearguard? Will they be blowing up equipment so Krauts won't get their hands on it?

"What was it like out there?" the driver asks.

"They were coming at us, full force."

"Damn."

"And their anti-tanks wiped us out, in some places. Then the RAF picked up a sort of rhythm, flying overhead and bombing with speed and frequency we had not observed before. Made my Sergeant smile, if you can believe that!"

"The New Zealanders and South Africans gave the German infantry hell, but I had quite a cargo to take away! They paid a heavy toll. They were in bits and pieces, if you understand my meaning." His voice loses some of its gusto.

"Oh, I understand."

CHAPTER 19

Wednesday 01 July 1942
CAIRO, EGYPT

"ELLIOT, *BONJOUR!*" FARAJ'S teeth caught a shaft of sinking afternoon light.

Elliot leaned to kiss the seated Faraj, a habit he had acquired years ago in his youth. "Are you well?"

"Well enough, but I wish you had not asked me to introduce her to you."

"Lady Jane?"

Faraj gave a wry smile.

"Am I so very bad?"

"Bad? Oh, no, *mon ami!* None better! But I'd half formed hopes for her," Faraj snorted. "Vanity. When I saw her standing next to you at my dinner party, I realized just what a great fool I am."

"But I was dressed as Dr. Leclerc!"

Faraj gave a Cairene shrug.

"Faraj? Do you mean to tell me…"

"Yes," he croaked. "I had hoped. An old man's folly though. A whim! But you may have her, if it is what she wishes. You will make her happy. But what of Baker's daughter?"

Surprised, for he never believed Faraj to be interested in any young women before or any women for that matter, except for one beautiful but obese Luna, Elliot appreciated what his friend was giving up for him.

Apparently content with Elliot's silence as an answer, Faraj promised, "I will visit your club. Soon. I collect compliments galore, *mon ami!* I am like a proud father!" He shifted his gaze to Jamal.

Jamal leaned close and intimated barely above a whisper, "Madame Sukey is here."

With a brief, *"pardonne-moi,"* Faraj, eyes sparkling, moved to greet Madame.

Still seated, Elliot marveled at Faraj's bulk maneuvering to the front of his coffeeshop, at his agility of body and of emotions.

"Madame Sukey," Faraj boomed. "It is a rare pleasure to see a lady in this hovel. And how lovely you look today, too."

"Faraj," she breathed, her voice throbbing, as she sashayed ahead of her attendants.

"Welcome. Come into my office. We will all be more comfortable there." Then Faraj gave some short sharp instructions to Jamal, who abandoned all chores to attend to his master and Madame. "*Mon ami*, join us." Faraj summoned Elliot.

Elliot looked on as Madame Sukey and her entourage were swept with grand gestures into the private realm of Faraj. Madame Sukey often had two girls in attendance and they were rarely the same two girls! Did she have a collection of such girls stowed away somewhere? Or perhaps Madame Sukey was rather a difficult mistress, quick to dismiss her help. He had heard of such employers although he had never observed such treatment on his parents' estates. In fact, his parents retained their help almost to a fault. With an inward grimace, Elliot recalled Cook, a horrid lecher and a mean tyrant who was more inclined to stew trouble, gleefully fueling strife and squabbles over trifles, than perform any cookery.

Ensconced in Faraj's sanctum, Madame Sukey beamed at Elliot. "My dear boy."

"How do you do, Madame?"

"I am well. Very well."

As Elliot made a polite reply, he noted that Faraj was indeed a most generous host and Jamal, an efficient servant, had the side tables quickly laden with hot tea and sugary cakes, trays of dried fruit and nuts and the ubiquitous Turkish Delight. The center table was surrounded by comfortable sofas and divans and was nearly hidden by an assortment of fresh fruit.

"Faraj tells me that your club is called *Monnayeur's*."

"And that Monnayeur's is getting rave reviews!" Faraj chuckled with delight.

"Elliot, I am happy. That is precisely my wish for the place, or any place that I own or owned for that matter!"

Elliot inclined his head. "And you Madame? Any new projects?"

Pride and content in her eyes, Madame turned to the Jewish businessman, "Faraj, you haven't told him?"

"Not I!" Faraj opened his eyes wide, holding his hand to his heart.

"You may have noticed my attendants."

Elliot glanced at Madame's girls, not quite sure what to say. They were both wiry and rather dark-complected and had an air of being suspicious of anyone who was not their Madame Sukey, she who was held in their eyes as a goddess.

"Well, we have been busy."

"Shopping," Faraj quipped.

"American aphorism! Oh, you naughty man!" Madame flashed a roguish grin.

Elliot began forming some ideas about his two friends! And relief that Faraj was not going to pine for Jane widened Elliot's smile.

"Shopping is not how I would describe it. Faraj joined my efforts. Together, we amassed charitable funds to patiently extract girls from Siwa who need help. We bring them here, to Cairo, where we're building a seminary."

Elliot's face lit up.

"Siwa is just the beginning! We hope to reach many remote oases where females are often mistreated and misused," Faraj added.

"Girls are misused here in Cairo and in Alexandria. Once rescued from the oases, where do the girls go and who takes care of them?" Elliot asked, his interest aroused.

"There is a great war going on all around the world. But I have my own private war," Madame admitted, resting her fingers with their red nail polish on Elliot's knee. "I am committed to the ones that I rescue!"

Elliot bent his head and kissed her hands, one at a time and looked into her eyes. "I take part in your war, and a few others, too."

"I know, my dear boy." Her eyes shone with emotion. She put her palms to his cheeks and kissed him deeply. "I know."

Elliot marveled at the effect Madame Sukey had on his life and, above all, how her halitosis did not bother him at all.

"Faraj told me about you and your upbringing and about your grandfather. And I am acquainted with your brother. How is William doing in hospital?" Madame asked.

"Persevering."

Noting that the thread of conversation was drifting into the realm of the sick and dying, Faraj intervened, "Have I ever told you how Elliot and William blew themselves out of a prestigious English public school? Eton, was it?"

"Will that explosion forever shadow my life? Yes, we got sent down but we were soon saddled with some eccentric tutors. One in particular, my grandfather's choice, was *such* a specimen, oh, what a martinet."

Faraj chuckled. He had met the brothers when they were sent to their grandparents' estate in Cairo, accompanied by an impossible tutor. "He had the deportment of a dance master with a pencil thin mustache and greasy black hair and manicured long nails that he never held back from the boys' cheeks. It's one thing to have a lady's caressing finger at your face and another to have your tutor treat you like a naughty schoolgirl. Throw in maths drills into the bargain, and you have an unpleasant situation."

"Faraj! How can you? William and I brought him over here so you'd cure him of his appalling manners but instead you encouraged him!"

104

"Eventually, I did help you get rid of him. I introduced him to the dwarf!" Madame Sukey cackled. "A dwarf?"

"The boys did not enjoy mathematics. And I knew of a dwarf who was lonely. Forgive me, Madame Sukey, but I am afraid that I played cupid, for everyone's benefit. The tutor found his life's *bon ami*, and the boys were then free to roam Cairo. Spending most of their time here in my shop. Everyone was happy!"

"And what of the boys' education?" asked Madame Sukey, who apparently held education high on her list of necessities for the young.

"Grandfather had a magnificent library. In the afternoon, when it was too warm, we read. James devoured indigestible anatomy lessons on his own and I bullied William to read out loud. I detest opening books and reading on my own. Now William reads medical textbooks to one of our maids! Poor lass."

"That thin one you told me about?" Faraj asked, his tone rather severe and unamused. "It won't do to have the Effendi fall in love with a servant. Elliot, you must watch over him. He has a soft heart. And Lady Westbrook will be disappointed."

"Oh, no, William is not in love with a maid. Besides he wouldn't dare read medical textbooks to the girl of his dreams! A man in love reads poetry, Byron, Robert Browning." Elliot omitted that Salomé was not a servant. It was not for him to tell. He was certain that Salomé was European, and that his father and the Spaniard Marcello had something to do with Salomé's residence at the estate.

The conversation returned to Madame Sukey's projects. Elliot offered to help, but advised to postpone drives to the desert until after el Alamein was secured and the enemy driven away from the border. He spoke with so much conviction that the Eighth would triumph, that Madame Sukey and Faraj exchanged glances.

When Madame Sukey and Faraj were left alone, Faraj confided, "Madame, my dearest lady, you are too clever a lady to let my Elliot fool you."

"How do you mean?"

"Elliot likes to be considered the foolish, mischievous boor of his family. He is not. True, both his brothers are well educated. James, the oldest, is an army surgeon. William, the youngest, well you know, he is a medic here in Cairo, and before he showed up unexpected in Cairo after the Blitz, he ran round London with the emergency rescue units. But, Elliot is the genius of the family and doing his best to hide that fact. His education was unconventional, but few are my acquaintances who could boast of similar linguistic abilities. He has a clever scientific mind too and knows almost as much as his brothers when it comes to medicine although I doubt that he will ever be able to look at a bleeding man and not vomit. Elliot has read extensively and his memory is such that it takes one glance at a page for him to retain information. He even dances well and that is not simple. Not those intricate English dances with countless steps. I should know, I tried! Endless spinning and steps, *Allah Karim*!"

"Faraj!" Madame Sukey chortled.

"I waltz beautifully, though," he twinkled at Madame. He was finding her more and more enchanting. "I admire you, Madame. Your generosity. Your warmth. I never expected to fall for anyone, not at my advanced age."

"Faraj!" Madame Sukey beamed, and her eyes shone.

#

Arcadia! Jasmine flowers and woven baskets on lush kilim. Suddenly, Soad materialized out of the smoke. Then the drum thumped and boomed, *boom chuck boom chuck*, and the dancer's hips began to move ever so dramatically to the beat. And as the violins flared up, so did Soad's entire body, quivering and writhing, one foot or the other rarely touching the floor, undulating her abdomen and chest with her hips swimming before Elliot's eyes.

And as Elliot watched his dancer misbehave on stage, one of his stratagems solidified. "The Roaming Bedu," he whispered. An excellent theme for a show, but also an excellent piece of subterfuge.

How could he offer offense to the enemy? Dance into a camp and introduce strains of influenza? But who would dance?

Then his thoughts went to Lady Jane. Would she be delighted to do her bit for her country? Would she accompany him to the desert, pretending to be a Bedu, ready to face enemy soldiers?

Elliot had already lined up a scientist who had been collecting the blood drained out of turkeys and other birds to create strains of influenza, a special 'gift' for any enemy camp they could deliver it to. Elliot hated the thought, but better sick with a touch of catarrh than bullets, shrapnel, or mines.

Bill Tate and Tom Sullivan were already involved in unconventional projects, and, so, he would only add a bit of flare. A dancing Bedu troupe offering coffee to enemy soldiers and so introducing influenza. Would it work? Would they have to dance? Probably not. And certainly not in glittery bras! But, dancing lessons would not hurt. Authenticity in illusions counts for much.

Tate and Sullivan were, oddly enough, in Cairo, on leave. In lightning speed, Elliot decided to summon them to his flat, along with Soad, his top dancer for belly dancing lessons. It would be interesting to see whether his plan could work. And training the men in belly dancing would allow for flexible strategic planning.

"I've been through rigorous commando drills. I jumped out of moving lorries. Hours on the parade ground and doing impossible drills in the desert and I earned these wings for paratroop training. But, this, this is beyond me!" Tate exclaimed as one hand pointed to the insignia on his sleeve and the other massaged his aching back. "Moving, undulating like that is harmful for such as I. I'm a big man!"

"You know, Westbrook, this *is* taking friendship a bit too far," agreed the boyishly cheerful Sullivan, his slanted, pale blue eyes twinkling from under thick sandy lashes.

"Well, talk to Crumper. The joker won't let me recruit women," grumbled Elliot, barely above a whisper, massaging his own lower back and casting darkling glances at their dance instructor.

Tate objected in rough tones. "Elliot, you cannot be serious. The thought of having a woman in the hands of the Krauts!"

"The Italians have red lorries that are traveling brothels, can you believe that!"

Elliot kept silent. History was strewn with tales of brutality toward women during war, regardless of race or nationality.

Soad, their instructor, finished wiping sweat from her face at Elliot's sink, then sashayed over to Elliot, smiling in understanding, a cloud of rose water wafting by. "In pain?" she asked in Arabic but immediately switched to show off her American-accented poor English. "Effendi, I show you what to do. Okay?" She reached for Elliot's back and pressed hard. She pointed out pressure points to ease his strained muscles.

"Certainly not women!" agreed Sullivan.

"We'll talk of it later." Elliot refused to discuss plans while Soad was within earshot.

"Soad, Sullivan and Tate need more lessons."

"Effendi, you need lessons too. You asked me to teach you the belly dance, yes? You must practice. Okay? Everyday!" she instructed then slapped Elliot's bottom.

Her employer commented, "I was rather shocked the first time you did this, Soad."

"It helps you move, Effendi," rejoined the irrepressible dancer with jovial banter.

"A Jack Collins will help *me* move," growled Tate.

The dancer turned her brown eyes on him. "But you asked me to teach you! Why? Because you English boys want to play a trick on your friend! So, practice."

107

She drew Sullivan to her. With a series of hip motions, she made Tate and Elliot want to escape and leave the two alone.

Instead, Elliot announced, "Sullivan isn't English!" then dashed to his kitchen to get a Jack Collins before Tate got to it.

Soad was one of his dancers at the club. She agreed to help Elliot and his friends learn belly dancing for a practical joke. "We have a wonderful prank planned for our friend. We want to pop out on him and dance. And we need to be convincing," Elliot had explained.

The dancer had laughed at first then agreed for the sheer delight in seeing her employer bow down to her commands, and such commands!

Returning from the kitchen, and well lubricated, Elliot watched the dancer reluctantly detach herself from the freckly Australian.

She reached into a bulging sack.

Apprehensively, Elliot peeked at Soad from behind his drink. Soad had already produced such horrors from the sack in the form of glittery belts that bristled with chinking brassy coins for the men to wear. What next?

"Tambourine, Effendi. You play the tambourine!"

"Can't I play the tambourine while Sullivan and Elliot dance?"

"Tate, you will dance and do the tambourine too," Soad decided and pressed the drum into Tate's palms. "Big hands." She stared in admiration at the tambourine, made minuscule, in Tate's hands, then touched Tate's long, thick fingers. In brisk motions, she had the gramophone blasting metallic chinks and ululating howls throbbing with eastern emotion. Soad then moved back to Sullivan and slipped her cymbals on his fingers, her motions, like caresses on Sullivan's rough index, almost indecently intimate, and at odds with the harsh chaos crashing out of the gramophone.

#

Thursday 02 July 1942
CAIRO, EGYPT

Waking up in his Gezira flat, Elliot stared into Tate's countenance. "What? Where am I?"

"Sullivan and I have to push off, mate. We'll come back in a day or two. Tea is on the table. Though why I brewed tea for you is beyond me. You deserve a whipping, Westbrook!"

"what?"

"You deserve a proper whipping for your dancing idea. I can barely walk. What would the men say?"

"What men?"

"Men in our unit! Wake up, Westbrook, wake up, mate! Tea's ready." And with his last announcement, Tate turned, rapidly catching up with Sullivan at the door.

"Tate! Where's Soad?" Elliot called out, hoping his friend had not left yet.

"She took off last night!" shouted Tate, regretting his choice of words. Then he shut the door with finality, leaving Elliot to recover.

Elliot and the two Australians drank deeply the night before, hoping that alcohol would help them relax enough to be able to gyrate and then ease the pain of gyrating and pelvic thrusting and leg twitching, bending and chest shaking. And late into the night, Elliot had fallen sound asleep, a rare treat. Now, he was groggy and out of sorts, aware of countless achy muscles in his buttocks, abdomen, and thighs.

Walking stiffly toward Faraj's café, Elliot's fingers played with a key in his pocket. Faraj had invited him to his inner sanctum, his office, that looked more like a bordello than an office.

Sweat runnels already making a mark on his face and shirt, Elliot was swearing terribly under his breath. Booming music of flutes and violins and the ululating diva whose voice caterwauled to the rise and fall of the sharp concert reverberated in his ears from a nearby shop. Not for the first time, Elliot wondered at what great, loud volume such music was played and the trance-like effect it had on its listeners.

"Peace at last!" Elliot flung the door open. Within a few hurried steps, he sank into a plush sofa that embraced his achy body.

When he next opened his eyes, he stared at a pair of long legs that stretched out of a skirt and ended in a pair of lovely strappy sandals, red nail polish on shapely toenails, with the letter V painted with conviction.

"Elliot, *mon ami*, you are awake now and I wanted you to meet my Lady Jane. But, I forget, you have already met at my dinner party." Faraj exerted himself to use proper English. The effort had cost him much.

Up in a flash, Elliot clasped Jane's hand. The two had eyes only for each other.

Faraj hesitated. Lady Jane's welfare was now his concern. Was it appropriate for Elliot to take such interest in his friend's daughter?

"Have we met?" Jane asked, her nose crinkling in puzzlement. "My dear Faraj, are you sure?" Jane turned to Faraj with such warmth that Elliot instinctively stole a glance at her face then at Faraj's.

Faraj realized his solecism. Lady Jane had met Dr. Leclerc! Faraj backtracked, "Well, maybe not."

"We have met, true, at Faraj's dinner party. Only we have not met properly. I was Leclerc."

Faraj breathed a sigh of relief.

"Dr. Leclerc?" Jane exclaimed. "That old horror who ogled and groped me while mumbling poetry into my poor ear? You?"

"I was keeping in character and some of the quotes were from Lord Byron's Corsair. Don't you know your poetry?"

A short snort escaped Lady Jane, then she broke into laughter.

Elliot grinned while Faraj fidgeted, contemplating when it would be best to leave the two to themselves. He had no intention of being *de trop*!

Lady Jane's mirth stemmed, at first, from amusement and then from relief. When the doctor had touched her and traced clever fingers along her neck and cheek, she, Lady Jane, actually felt a quiver of excitement and desire. She was now thoroughly relieved to know that her reaction was not to the touch of an antique roué but a handsome man. And with that realization, excitement and a degree of fear crept in. What did she know of this Elliot Westbrook? But relief that her body had not betrayed her after all lit up Jane's face and she smiled at Elliot.

Elliot felt his heartbeat quicken.

Finally, Jane choked out, "But, why?"

"Why?" Faraj was alarmed.

"Yes, why? Why the masquerade? And with such a costume and, oh, I can't!" Jane broke off again into fits of laughter, recalling the lecherous Leclerc in contrast to the upright specimen before her.

"I was wooing Madame Sukey," Elliot replied, immediately regretting his laconic explanation when Jane uttered, "Oh."

"No, no, Elliot was only trying to…" Faraj wanted to help but failed miserably.

Suddenly, Faraj viewed their ploy, which began as a cheeky challenge, as contemptible.

"We may as well come clean, Faraj, only I cannot let you take responsibility since it was all my doing." Elliot gestured to Jane to sit down. "I'll explain how I came to be a French doctor wooing Madame Sukey." And while Elliot was struggling to justify his actions, Faraj slipped away and summoned Jamal, ordering hot mint tea, coffee, and a selection of cakes. When he returned, Faraj heard Elliot bringing his explanation to an end with, "I had no idea, you see. Madame is an angel. Even my kid brother had no idea until he got to know her as her visits to hospital grew more frequent."

"Was William confused?" Jane asked.

"Why, yes! She does dote on the soldiers but is also inclined to corner doctors and discuss her own ailments, something that rather baffled William and he, and I, consequently formed a confused impression of Madame."

"But you bought the club nonetheless?"

"She would have it no other way," Faraj chimed in. "She is happy with Monnayeur's. It is a safe haven. The drinks are harmless, that is, free of added drugs or impurities, and the performances are fine. Such a club is rare."

"Oh, don't encourage him," Elliot hurried his words as he saw another question forming on Lady Jane's beautiful lips.

"Why not? I am proud of Monnayeur's!" Faraj declared.

Relaxed now that his deplorable plan was at least acknowledged and had not sent Lady Jane flying out with contempt, Elliot let Faraj talk.

Lady Jane watched the giant businessman with affection, grateful for his cheerful stories.

When Jamal came in with hushed intelligence, Faraj lit up. "Splendid! Where is she?"

The sound of bangles, the flash of a scarlet gown, and her scent heralded Madame's arrival.

Elliot froze, and so did Lady Jane, but not Faraj. With genuine pleasure, he leapt up, chuckling in delight and without any preemptive introduction, he regaled Madame with Elliot's and Lady Jane's meeting. "The shameful prank!"

Madame looked at Faraj with affection and then cast an amused look at the young people, standing now, ready to greet her properly but unable to do so while Faraj told his tale.

Finally, Faraj took Madame Sukey's hand in his and brought it to his lips. "But all is well now, is it not?"

"Now that I have friends like you, all is very well indeed," Madame Sukey chuckled as she approached Lady Jane. Clasping Lady Jane's hands with affection, Madame began to talk of her growing friendship with Faraj and Elliot, and of their help and support with her philanthropy.

"I must join too," Lady Jane exclaimed even before Madame's remaining words were out of her mouth. "Madame Sukey, you must let me help."

"We can go to my villa at once and you can see for yourself, dear child," Madame Sukey beamed.

"Ladies, I will join you," Faraj declared.

Elliot dropped his voice to ask, "Faraj? You? But you rarely leave your café."

"It's time I did, then."

#

Friday 03 July 1942
CAIRO, EGYPT

"A boat ride?"

"A boat ride! Elliot, you will do well following my advice," Faraj assured him.

"Does Lady Jane like boat rides?"

Faraj fell silent.

"Faraj, you are her guardian. You even picked out a fine villa for her near your own with a formidable companion. But do you know what Lady Jane likes? Her tastes? Preferences?"

The large Jewish businessman paused, summoning his wits. "Helping people."

"Helping people?" Elliot asked.

"She likes to help. Like Madame Sukey. Both have all the comforts they need or want. Both want for nothing. They are generous souls."

"I was hoping for a simpler answer like 'Lady Jane likes dancing or French scent,' if you get my meaning."

"She took ballet years ago. A little darling in a tutu!"

"So, you have known her for a long time?"

"Her father and I were close. Anyway, I suggest you take her on a boat ride, by moonlight."

"Then what, pretend to drown so she'd leap into the water and rescue me? Pulling me ashore and resuscitating my drowned soul?"

"Well, there's an idea!" Faraj breathed.

"No, Faraj, this won't do!"

"Why do you want to take her on a boat ride?"

"I don't. You suggested the boat."

"I mean, why do you want to...you know, to entertain her?"

"Who wouldn't?"

"Elliot," Faraj growled.

"She enchants me." Elliot felt like a school boy having to confess a great secret.

"And your intentions?"

"I'm engaged to Louisa Baker."

Faraj regarded Elliot.

112

"I only want Lady Jane's company. I will not betray your trust, Faraj." But as he made his promise, Elliot felt a weight in the pit of his stomach. He knew that he wanted Lady Jane. He felt battered, too. His conversation with Faraj bordered on the farcical. One moment Faraj advised him on a romantic boat ride by moonlight in the Nile and the next his dear friend was asking what Elliot's intentions were like an outraged Victorian uncle.

To Elliot's relief, Faraj finally said in soft tones. "*Mon ami*, do not say that. I trust you. And Lady Jane will make her choice, whatever it might be. I cannot choose for her but if I could, it would be you, but not as an already engaged man. I have my suspicions about your engagement, so I keep silent."

"What suspicions?"

"Elliot, you are not a man in love, at least, not with *Louisa*. Now, will you attend Madame's dinner party tonight?"

"I'd love to, but is it not odd to dine in such pomp and style when the Eighth is facing the Africa Korps at el Alamein?"

"Let the indomitable Eighth do its job, you do yours."

CHAPTER 20

Friday 03 July 1942
CAIRO, EGYPT

CITY LIGHTS BLURRED as Elliot's car thundered across Cairo.

"But this is not the way back to my villa, Elliot. Where are you taking me?"

"My flat."

Lady Jane tensed.

"For a talk. A talk about...war."

Lady Jane stared ahead.

Before his resolve abandoned him, Elliot launched into an explanation of his various plans to assist the advance of the Eighth Army in the desert. He wanted to remove some of the obstacles the Allies had to face. He had been struck with one of them being of particular use. He explained that while special forces, like the SAS and the LRDG, blew up aircraft, communication lines, miscellaneous vehicles, and supply dumps, he reckoned that the Africa Korps needed a lesson in tropical diseases to keep their heads down. He laid out his idea of introducing flu-like strains into enemy camps and letting nature do the rest. "So," he concluded, "I thought of you."

"Of me, Mr. Westbrook?"

"Mr. Westbrook? Wasn't I Elliot only moments ago?"

"Elliot, yes. But, that was before I learned of your designs on me."

"I misspoke. I thought of your talents. I was sure that you would be delighted to help."

"Delighted?" Jane's eyes opened wide in shock.

"Are you...not delighted to have an opportunity to do your bit?"

Jane waited as Elliot negotiated the thickening traffic. Swearing, he exclaimed, "It's nearing midnight, there's a hellish battle raging in the desert, but Cairo's unmoved! The streets are swarming with drunks! Damn them."

Jane snorted and Elliot turned to look at her. He ached to kiss her.

Recollecting his project, he wrenched his attention back to his driving. "So, what say you? Will you help a couple of gangly Australians and an English amateur dance into Italian and German camps to serve up a charm of powerful trouble? Nothing lethal, mind you. I cannot bear the sight and smell of blood."

"But, your younger brother is a medic."

"To my mother's horror, both my brothers are in the medical field. I am not."

"Oh."

"Will you help?" he asked but did not expect an answer since they were parked and he had already engaged the arm brake.

Lady Jane was absorbed in thought. Was she really visiting a man's flat alone and at night? And what about his ideas? She looked at the enormous clock hanging somberly on Elliot's wall.

"Elliot, it's one in the morning."

"I have coffee, or tea. What would you have?"

"Coffee. No, nothing at all. Madame Sukey's style overwhelms me in every way. I half expected her table or servants to collapse under the weight of the dishes tonight and so much wine. Elliot, did you really…? Did you and Madame Sukey…?"

"Make love? No."

"I…I did not mean to ask that."

"No, just…" he began then, made desperate by the knot of desire snarling inside, he found himself at Lady Jane's side, his hands on her shoulders then sliding to her neck and jaw, cupping her face. Soon, his deft fingers found the offending clasp that kept her glorious tresses in a chignon and pulled it out, letting her hair tumble down as his lips caressed her mouth, gently, softly.

"Lady Jane," he breathed and found himself in desperate need for her when her hands fluttered to his chest then slid up his back, lips yielding, her body pressing against his strong frame.

Saturday 04 July 1942
CAIRO, EGYPT

With the first shaft of light, Elliot's hands explored Lady Jane's curves. Waking up lazily was not his style, so he drew a bath. Carrying Jane in his arms, smiling, he said, "Good morning." The slippery soap fell into the warm water and Elliot was letting water trickle down Jane's back from a decanter as he traced gentle kisses along her exposed neck and down to her breasts. He was savoring every curve, every bit of his Lady Jane. He had always been carefully patient and attentive with women ever since his first, a young widow with doubtful morals, cried in bitter disappointment at his greedy, crass treatment. He had made it up to her and had been perfecting the art of pleasuring a woman. But this was different. Tracing his lips over Lady Jane's shoulder, Elliot's only conscious thought was *mine* and the relentless urge to savor and relish.

115

His gentle hands stroked her then Elliot steadied himself, wrapped his arms round Jane and carried her out of the tub, swaddled in a thick cotton towel. "I won't have you slip out of my hands," he murmured into her damp neck. His metal frame bed creaking under his knee, he lowered Jane into the cool sheets, covering her mouth with his.

His movements were gentle, caressing, holding back his need for this wonderful woman. He ran his tongue between her thighs and as Jane moaned he was suddenly aware of noises coming from the kitchen, running water and brisk opening and shutting of cabinets.

Wondering who could be intruding his flat, and in broad daylight, he signaled Jane to wait and with his finger to his lips stressed the need for silence.

Elliot crept to the bedroom door wanting to peek into the kitchen when the door was suddenly flung open and a cheerful metallic voice rang out a song then broke into a shout of terror.

"Effendi!"

His scrubbing woman stood stock-still, a kitchen towel and a broom in her hand and her mouth gaping open. Before her stood her master, naked and wet, and clasping a slick little semi automatic. She followed her initial exclamations with bleats of shock and surprise but her eyes kept roving over his form until he collected himself and shut the door in her face. "Out!" he cried.

"Effendi!"

"Go away!"

"But, my pay!"

"Not today, tomorrow!" he shouted back.

The front door slammed in a temper and from behind him Elliot could pick out restrained giggles, muffled by his pillow.

"I say, what is so funny about all this? Didn't you see how she stared at me? What damnable effrontery!"

At his last words, Jane's giggles turned to laughter.

"Are you laughing at me?" Elliot asked, still standing transfixed to the spot, completely naked with droplets of bathwater rolling gently off his brown curls.

"Elliot!" she choked. "The look in her eyes! And you, standing there more than a foot taller than her little self, exposed to the world! And the gun…"

The front door opened again. Firm and brisk footsteps approached the bedroom door. "Effendi?"

"Yes?"

"Tomorrow is no good. I need my pay today. Today is the day I clean for you and you pay or leave money for me. Today."

"Oh, the devil take you!" he shouted acidly. He reached for his trousers and fished out piasters from his pocket. He opened the door and thrust the money into the woman's small palm. "Wait," he said, contrite. "Here's extra…for the shock. You weren't to know that I'd be here."

"Thank you, Effendi," the scrubbing woman's face brightened and she bowed slightly at the sight of so much money. She hurried out, showering her master with flowery blessings and raptures of good will and prayers for stamina.

#

Elliot handed Jane a steaming dish of tea. "So, back to my question, does the war effort not concern you?"

She paused. "My younger brother is training in Aldershot. I often worry, where would they send him from there?"

"Is he still at Aldershot?"

She nodded.

"I heard some atrocious things. Did you know that they have the redcaps lined up as the new recruits are marched onto the boats?"

"Redcaps? Do you mean military police?"

"Military police, yes," Elliot replied.

"Why?"

"They line up military police just in case anyone has any second thoughts, any *misgiving!*" Elliot hated using such subtle methods to coax his Jane to throw herself behind enemy lines. But here he was and, with magic words of fear and shock, he was breaking her defenses and persuading this amazing woman to go disguised as a dancer into Axis camps. "What if it were in your power to cause a delay? Maybe even a painful and embarrassing blow to the very blokes who if they survive the desert might return to Europe and face your brother in just a few more weeks?"

Her silence encouraged Elliot.

"A delay could mean so much for the Eighth right now. We expect the Americans to join us here in the desert - full force. And any slight humiliation we could offer Rommel would certainly rattle their pride. More troops, more tanks, more ammunition, and possible success means diminished enemy resources. Though by God, they have the advantage. They have free labor."

"Free labor?"

"They have prisoners. Children, women, and men work day and night in Nazi mines and factories all throughout German occupied Europe - mining, manufacturing, sewing uniforms, all for free because they are *prisoners*. They are declared criminals because of their religion, their nationality or political views, even their preference for sexual partners make them all fair game. Prisoners working to produce the massive Nazi war machine, all for free and with little expense because they do not get paid, not in clothes, not in meals, not really. Heat isn't provided. What more, any valuables, yes, including gold teeth, are extracted out of them. Bank accounts, priceless art or jewelry, or whatever carries any value whatsoever goes into Nazi hands. Europe has many Jews, Gypsies, Jehova's Witnesses, Catholics, homosexuals, communists, even the mentally ill or any other such bunch the Germans can tag as criminals, strip them of their rights and property, and put into work camps. Well, the *lucky* ones go to work camps. Others are eliminated outright."

Jane closed her eyes, the words too horrible to withstand.

"Will you help me?"

"But Elliot, I am trained in ballet and voice, not the sort of entertainment that one expects in the desert."

"Courage, you have. Because here you are, all alone in Cairo, and you are here with me in my flat," he gave her a wolfish smile.

"Faraj takes good care of me, and my father wished it."

"You were not afraid of me last night."

"No," she admitted. What was she to say, that she had wanted to be close to him ever since she'd first met him?

"Soad will give you as many lessons as you need to alter your dancing skills. You have more than the basics, that's obvious. But you could imitate her and with proper coverage and a proper Bedu entourage you'll be perfectly safe. Give enough time for our chaps to do some nice bit of damage while the enemy is inattentive."

"All right," she agreed on a whisper.

Smiling, he brought his mouth to her, kissing her lips and then playing gently along her jawline down to her throat. "Now I need your help with something else."

Elliot knew that his plans were audacious and far-fetched but if they worked, if he were successful, the Eighth would have fewer enemy soldiers to deal with, more delays, buying time enough for the extra equipment and supplies to arrive to the desert from America.

#

Arcadia, Elliot thought much later that day, had a lot to answer for! The dazzling dancer on his elaborately set-up stage kept the eyes of the crowd focused on her performance while a trickle of powerful and wealthy Cairene personages entered the back room. They had probably tired of the racecourse, mused Elliot, and of the cricket matches, and were drawn to the secretive and exclusive nature of his tables and the strong drinks. Madame Sukey's connections kept his club well stocked. Madame never abandoned him and in her way continued to be his guardian angel, or perhaps his dragon? Her contacts helped him stock up on some of the best wines and liquors in Cairo.

A deep, resonant Australian voice shook Elliot out of his reverie. He wrenched his eyes away from Soad balancing her sword on her anatomy, and acknowledged his friends, Tate and Sullivan.

Bill Tate's gigantic boots approached Elliot and the tall man was soon towering over the table while Tom Sullivan sidled to the tap first, joining them moments later with drinks.

"Where is she?" Tate's voice sounded impatient as the metallic music ceased and a drumroll introduced a subtle, almost haunting piano piece.

Tate was uneasy. As soon as Elliot had introduced the idea, it displeased him. Why get a woman involved with their missions? Dragging a woman into such a nightmare was unconscionable.

Elliot indicated the stage.

A woman with caramel golden hair moved to the center. Her voice was silky, the kind that soothed and filled one up with yearning.

Sullivan's mouth dropped in disbelief. "Her? The goddess on stage?"

Tate and Sullivan exchanged confused looks but soon strayed back to the stage as if by magnetic pull, watching the woman singing a love song, behind her the pianist and violinist charming the audience. And then, as soon as the initial shock was over, the darkling stares fell on Elliot.

"You're mad!" Tate spat.

"Absolutely not!"

"She'll join us shortly, just after the next number. Talk to her."

"I'm leaving. You're a madman, Westbrook!" Tate stormed out.

"She's extraordinary, Elliot. Tate and I disagree that a woman is necessary for our mission. In fact, we were quite certain that you too would change your mind," Sullivan explained, trying to catch a glimpse of his friend. "I better get Tate to calm down. He's in a temper, you know."

"It's not easy to imagine her out in the desert in rags. But her appearance need not deter you from recruiting her. Certainly, it is up to the two of you. I need you and so does she."

119

Sullivan had no idea what Elliot meant, but he was relieved to find Elliot by his side when he stepped out of the club to search for Tate.

#

Another one of Cairo's fleet of derelict cabs slewed round the corner and down the street, an eldritch screech leaving behind it surprised faces that froze as a spicy Australian imprecation rode the cab's exhaust trail.

Jane watched three men arguing incoherently about what one can do and cannot do and how it was all bloody nonsense and worse. Then Jane approached the threesome with head held high and firm, unfeminine steps.

Elliot had offered to drive her home, but she refused. "Will you introduce me to your Australian boys from the roguish Long Range Division."

"We're not boys," Sullivan threw at the beauty, in a rare show of obstinance.

"Nor rogues for that matter!" Tate growled but then softened his tones and clasped both Lady Jane's hands in his. "Your voice is magic."

"Thank you."

"Fantastic," Sullivan agreed.

"And who are you? Bill Tate or Tom Sullivan?" she smiled at the man with the slanted blue eyes. "I'm Jane, you know."

"Lady Jane," grumbled Elliot.

"Sullivan," he summoned a smile. He was rather in awe of her and upset with Elliot. "You are magic, I mean, your voice is..."

"We should probably get to a more private place."

"And more salubrious. The smell of sewage!" Lady Jane twinkled at the wall of muscle that was Tate.

"See?" he turned to Elliot, triumphant. Tate had been pacing the street in agitation, working out his feelings and drafting arguments to deliver to Elliot. He liked Elliot and had no intention of telling his friend that he was an idiot and that his idea of dragging a woman along on their expeditions was folly. But the maniac had to be stopped somehow!

"She's teasing you, Tate," Elliot replied cooly.

"Beg pardon, Lady Jane, but I cannot stomach the idea. I've been sick with worry and how do I tell my friend that he's an ass and that his idea is rubbish?"

"But, Tate, it is brilliant! Don't you see? They will fall for the charade."

Her voice reached his ears but Tate was in doubt. "How is it that you agree to this scheme? It's sheer madness."

"My brother is in Aldershot."

No one spoke until Tate asked, "Conscription?"

"No. He was a student at the time. He chose to go to Aldershot. I wanted him to accompany me to Egypt. I wanted him to talk to our father's friend, our guardian, Faraj, and then decide."

"Has he left to the front?"

Jane lowered her gaze. "I can't tell. We quarreled, and so he ignores my letters. Maybe he has already left to the front. I asked him to consult with Faraj, before enlisting."

Tate remembered his own sister. Throughout their childhood, she had plagued him and his friends, trying to join their play battles and later hunting trips. And when war broke out, she threatened to enlist, too.

In the utter silence of defeat, Tate offered his hand to Jane. "I hope that I do not live to regret this."

Sullivan cast uneasy glances about, then commented, "Better find a quieter place to discuss the next few days."

Later that evening, Lady Jane heard, "*Recci.*" She tilted her head.

"Tate means, reconnaissance." Elliot uttered his words in his silkiest accent as his gramophone, blasting jazz, was propped by the front door of his flat. A simple measure against anyone eavesdropping while the Australians and Lady Jane were drinking tea at his kitchen table.

"You can join us on this week's water treatment mission."

"Elliot, what good would that do?"

"She'll get to see the desert, the front, or at least bits of it, and then she can decide for herself. You forget, she is not familiar with the smells. She might faint dead on sight. And all your worries and arguments are unnecessary."

"My arguments are unnecessary because the desert is no place for a woman, any woman, pretty or ugly!"

"I agree with Tate, but it is Lady Jane's choice." The idea of women in the army was foreign to Sullivan as well as horrifying when recollecting the conditions and dangers that awaited them behind enemy lines. Although their mission for that week was a simple one, it would deposit them behind enemy lines, or maybe it was classified as no man's land since the Germans had not driven over it yet and the British Army retreated east of it, to el Alamein.

"We head to a watering hole between el Alamein and the Coast. Our job is to collect water samples. The Eighth had already retreated past that mud puddle," Tate explained.

121

"Our scientists want to experiment with it. Turn it into a non-potable pool, to deny the enemy the luxury of fresh water until the next heavy flash flood," Sullivan added.

"Still, I'll continue my lessons with Soad," Tate volunteered. "In case Lady Jane changes her mind. Which is my dearest wish!"

#

Sunday 05 July 1942
CAIRO, EGYPT

"Sassy, Elliot, sassy!" commanded Soad, the devoted dance instructor, in her harsh accented voice. She spoke an odd mixture of Arabic and American English, resorting to English when commanding Elliot to do mischievous things.

"It's no use!" complained Sullivan. "My hips were never meant to move in such a way. I can sassy it from here to eternity and never will I look like you!"

"Follow the tambourine. Listen to it. Feel it," Soad breathed into Sullivan's ear who looked like he had other plans for his hips and the pretty, diminutive dancer.

"Thrust forward, pull back, slowly then fast, and faster," Soad explained and demonstrated her moves barely an inch away from Sullivan.

"Belly dancing is not for such as us," Elliot announced after hours of making the attempt at bending over and wriggling under cover of itchy goat-wool robes. "And the robes are a definite hindrance. My skin is raw!"

"But they cover up your unmentionables and hairy legs!" snorted Sullivan.

"I'm leaving." Tate escaped hastily after a parting shot at Elliot. "Watching the two of you, and laughing at you, would do me an injury."

"Bugger off," Elliot had shouted at Tate then quickly apologized to the amused dancer.

Elliot was hating Rommel more and more as his bottom was smacked once again and the demand for "sassy" echoed about.

Sullivan collapsed, exhausted and humiliated on the floor. But Soad returned to Sullivan. Long, dark hair whipping his face, she helped Sullivan up, her body at his back. Hands on his hips, her breasts pressed against his back and her lips close to his ear, she throbbed, "Move with me." Hips thrust forward, she guided him in endless circles. Sullivan went along at first but soon he began to respond to the woman and her hands that were getting lower and lower and closer to his uncooperative parts and the firm breasts pulsating in seductive push pull rhythm.

122

"Now, work on the shoulders." Her hands snaked up his chest and moved to his shoulders, hips still circling clockwise, counterclockwise, while Sullivan was grinding his teeth.

"I need a break," Elliot muttered and, with a fair imitation of the Australian 'cheerio,' ran to the closest club where he had no doubt Tate had been carousing while he and Sullivan labored with pelvic circles.

The hot, humid air held onto the cigar and cigarette smoke as much as the bar held to the din of noisy soldiers, drinking themselves to delirium while on leave.

Tate was talking in rapid Australian accented English and receiving witty answers in the lilting brogue of his Scottish companion.

When Elliot approached him, Tate turned an amused look at Elliot then snorted with laughter.

"That's right. Take your time about it." Elliot paused, feeling a wave of inexplicable shame wash over him. He was beginning to back out the door when Tate slid a bottle into his hand.

Looking at the label, Elliot's voice cracked with pleasure. "Talisker?"

"Break the seal, mate."

"Where did you get this?" Elliot asked.

"My mother!" announced the Scott, pride and alcohol shining in his eyes.

"Bless her."

"But what of Sullivan?" Tate asked.

"Sullivan?" Recalling the blissful expression on his friend's boyish face, Elliot was sure that Sullivan would welcome a break from the lessons. "Sullivan is well. Very well indeed."

CHAPTER 21

Saturday 04 July 1942
CAIRO, EGYPT

STARING AT WILLIAM, dark circles under her eyes, Mrs. Wright settled into an aluminum chair William had pulled out for her.

"Tea?"

"Please."

"Fourth day of July. And, I picked up a flurry of good news." William's lips curved up a bit. "As of just a few hours ago, the Eighth continues to hold el Alamein."

She sighed with relief.

"Alexandria and Cairo are safe for now. The Eighth is set to give battle. Morale is high, and the troops are in better shape than those of the enemy. The Germans hoped to open up their supply port in Tobruk. However, they haven't achieved that yet."

Mrs. Wright's tone was sober as her eyes scanned the cots that were stretched outside the cafeteria. "Auchinleck at least would not throw his Eighth Army to the wolves. He wants to keep the Eighth in 'being,' and he declared that his army is much more valuable to him than the whole of the desert! Is he disobeying orders?"

"Probably." William grinned.

"Did he really refuse to fall back as far as the Canal?"

"He did. And so he managed to surprise his superiors."

"Does it make sense?"

"What? To line the troops at Alamein?" William asked. "It does. El Alamein is a defense line stretching from the sea at the north end and the impassable Qattara Depression in the south. The Germans would have to go through a chain of defenses to get to Alexandria. They'd rather not circumvent the Line. Even though it is possible to go through the rugged terrain, it is difficult and slow work with heavy equipment. And the best bit is this: The Rats of Tobruk are now on the Line, too."

Mrs. Wright's eyes glowed. Earlier in the war, her husband, the vicar, had been in Tobruk with the 9th Division, tormented under siege with the rest of the Australians, the Rats of Tobruk.

"They're tired of garrison life. And they're very much ready to fight."

"I am grateful, Westbrook."

"Grateful? Why?"

"You bring me good news. And the tea is most excellent. By the way, the tea, it's sweet. Where did you get sugar?"

"Do you really want to know?" A grin altered his wan features, revealing his youth.

"Westbrook, where's the sugar from?"

"Madame Sukey!"

"Oh, how could you!"

William simply smiled his charming smile that lit up his face.

"I almost forgot. Westbrook, that *aristocrat* wants to talk to you."

"What aristocrat? And why do you say it like that? Is it a crime to be highborn?"

Mrs. Wright clicked her tongue in annoyance. "He goes by the name Toc. No last name, no proper Christian name. Just Toc!"

"Toc? I remember him."

"Yes, and I say 'it' like 'that' because back in May, his father, Lord M., marched in here demanding a private ward for his son, threatened to bring in a specialist surgeon."

"Poor fellow. Was Toc embarrassed?"

"Yes."

"And Madame Sukey? Did she take a liking to him?"

"Of course. He's dark, handsome, and strong. I just hope that his father keeps away. Do go and see him."

"Do you know what he wants?" William asked.

"No idea. And do tell his friend that I have his monkey."

Was Mrs. Wright jesting? "*Monkey?*"

"Bandar. He came in covered in blood and other things. Dead drunk, too."

#

Saturday 04 July 1942
CAIRO, EGYPT

"So, you're back!" Upon entering our ward, the pale medic heads straight for Toc. He casts a glance at me and says, "And with Johnson, too."

"Bandar?" I ask. "What did you do with him?"

"Monkey? He's with Mrs. Wright. Why did you ask for me?"

"Toc wanted to see you," I reply, my thumb angled at Toc.

"What can I do for you?" William Westbrook asks as his hand shoots up, checking the plasma next to Toc's bed.

125

Toc lifts his dark eyes and almost growls at the medic, "Westbrook, get me out of here! Back out to the front!"

William smirks. "First class?"

Toc stares in silence.

"I'll see what I can do, but look here, give yourself a chance to recover."

"I'm well enough."

"Have you run into my brother by any chance? James Westbrook, army surgeon."

"I get my surgeries done here!" Toc lifts a tired arm and sweeps it across the ward as a grand gesture of pomp.

"James Westbrook?" I ask. Although my hearing is back, my head has been aching. The doctor has written it up as shock and prescribed quiet time for recovery.

"Doctor James Westbrook. Tall, fair fellow. Have you seen or heard anything?" the medic repeats.

"Isn't he the chap with the LRDG?" I say then regret my blurting out this information. If Westbrook is unaware of his brother's whereabouts, perhaps it is not my place to enlighten him.

"Long Range Desert Group?" What little color Westbrook has, leaves him in a rush. "Are you sure?"

"Of course not. I really don't know. The name sounded familiar, but I can't be certain."

"Steady on." Toc rises and nearly falls backward from the effort and also because he is still attached to the plasma.

Westbrook adjusts Toc's tubes with slow contemplative motions. "Toc, give me a couple more days, and I'll see what I can do. In the meantime, rest and rehydrate."

"Is Madame Sukey around?"

"She'll pop in soon. But, get some rest," he replies then exits our ward.

I lean close to my friend. "Toc, you cannot rush back *there* like that."

"I will. The Jerries are digging in. They are laying minefields all round their positions. We must attack, quickly and swiftly, before they get to lay more minefields and get more supplies."

I doubt that Toc is well enough to walk out the hospital, much less hold up a gun. Glancing at his face, I notice his thick dark lashes shut and cast a shadow on his cheeks. Sleep is recuperative, I rally, and fall asleep myself.

#

126

Tuesday 14 July 1942
CAIRO, EGYPT

Toc's sweat-stained sheets are finally replaced with fresh ones, and I breath a sigh of relief as William Westbrook informs me that Toc's fever has broken.

"Johnson, shrapnel wounds almost always end up infected. The fever is his body's reaction, his fight against infection. He'll soon be better."

I stay close to Toc's bed as the orderly and Westbrook administer to Toc.

Westbrook explains Toc's condition, urging me to be patient and to stop swearing.

"Could you read to him?" Westbrook asks as he hands me a paperback.

"Read to him? You mad? He's asleep, sweating and twitching and mumbling. I can't read to him! What's the point?"

Westbrook's smile is wan and yet he holds out the book. "Read out loud. It'll do you both good."

"What is this book?"

"Madame Sukey's choice."

"The Forsyte Saga?" I am dismayed.

"Well, yes."

"Look, you have not answered my question yet. What's going on out there? At Alamein?" I ask.

"We have good days and bad days. Johnson, it's offensive defense type of engagement at the moment. The Jerries attack, and our Eighth holds them off. Eighth's holding on while gathering supplies. More troops are joining the Eighth, too. We're growing stronger." Westbrook levels his eyes at mine. "Read."

"So, it's the *Forsyte Saga* for Toc." I open the worn paperback, grateful that Madame Sukey avoided the popular but erotic *Lady Chatterley's Lover*. When I read, I notice the other boys in the ward tilt their heads, listening. So, I read on, and my voice is loud and clear.

CHAPTER 22

Monday 06 July 1942
DESERT, EGYPT

"MY LADY JANE. We're going to examine a particular oasis today, reconnoiter, and possibly, contaminate a source of drinking water Rommel has been planning to use."

"Does Rommel intend to use the water? How do you know that? And what of the locals who rely on it?"

"Intelligence," Elliot gave a noncommittal shrug. "They provide us with instructions and directions. And as for locals, they've left a while back. Can't have their goats caught in crossfire! We have decent intelligence reports on the area. The RAF flies over this stretch regularly, and some LRDG men monitor conditions here."

"Only some?"

"There're units that are sabotaging communication lines and fuel dumps along the coast because LRDG is also collaborating with the SAS, David Stirling's L-Detachment brigade."

"SAS?" Jane asks.

"Special Air Service."

"What air service do they provide?"

"None. It's all a bit of a prank. David Stirling needed a name for his newly formed commandos and Dudley Clarke, you know, the chap responsible for so many spells of misdirection…"

"The man who came up with fictitious special forces units then leaked the information to the Germans and had British actors parade round Cairo in uniform of units that do not even exist?"

"That's it! SAS was one of those fictitious special forces units but is now very much in being and a unit to be reckoned with. Initially they planned to parachute into the desert. But because their first excursion entailed jumping out of aircraft during a severe storm, the operation ended tragically. Almost half the unit was wiped out." Elliot paused. "As a result of that horrible experience, the SAS, a unit of parachuting and commando saboteurs, now has the LRDG's escort. So, you see, the LRDG, originally a reconnaissance unit, has become a more versatile unit. That's why we get Tate and Sullivan. You and I are the reconnaissance experts while Tate and Sullivan are the navigation and sabotage experts. HQ gave me hell about *you* joining us!"

As Elliot and Jane headed further into the desert, they saw processions of guns, RAF wagons, recovery vehicles, armored cars, and lorries crammed with tired men, pressed bonnet to tailboard, all crawling eastward over a hundred miles in length. Heading to Cairo, soldiers slept on top of one another, their rides bouncing and jostling, yet they slept while the vehicles proceeded slowly.

"I don't understand," Elliot said. "The battle is at Alamein. Where are *they* going?"

"The road to the front is clear, Elliot. Is your information correct? Can we reach this oasis before the enemy does?"

"We have to drive behind enemy lines to reach our puddle. Tate and Sullivan won't fail us. Take a look over there," he jerked his head to a round jebel.

Two dark figures danced on a lorry. Tattered long robes and headdress covering their heads and faces, the Bedouin's shouts were a concoction of Australian greetings and profanities and drinking songs. Then an RAF bomber thundered overhead, drowning the songs and the chatter of Sullivan's cymbals.

"What cheek!" Jane raised her hands to wave.

Elliot's cobalt eyes fixed Jane with a steady gaze. "Are you ready?"

"I am!" Jane gave a sample of her recent lessons with Soad, ululating and dancing in the most shocking and provocative manner, making Elliot doubt the sanity of his plans. After all, he wanted to marry Lady Jane and promptly, as soon as the sour business with the Bakers was done and over with!

#

Shimmering in the sunlight, the oasis gave the appearance of a marvelous watering hole.

But as the four approached it, they recoiled from the stench.

"Pooh! Smells like death itself," Sullivan exclaimed.

"Looks terrible," Tate said.

"Why are there so many bloating carcasses of gazelle and jerboa by the side of the pool?" Lady Jane asked.

"The area is a deathtrap already." Sullivan looked dismayed.

"Looks like our work is done for us," Tate concluded.

Elliot pulled the camera equipment. "I'll photograph this nasty mud puddle. And when I return to HQ, I'll demand an explanation. Can't HQ give us more accurate more up to date information?"

Tate stood guard.

Staying close to the boyishly effervescent Sullivan, Jane assisted him with drawing samples.

"What do you think, Lady Jane? Should I dump this in?"

"Bilharzia?"

"Bilharzia is a worm that enters the human bloodstream through the skin. So I am told by our scientist." Sullivan opened and dumped the contents of his vial, then carefully replaced it in the well-lined case from which it was extracted.

"Lovely," Jane and Sullivan exchanged worried looks, glancing at their hands.

"We have gloves on our hands," Sullivan said.

"Let's hope Rommel does not," she rejoined and the two snorted with giggles until they saw Tate waving, urgently summoning Elliot.

"Already?" Elliot complained.

"A cloud of dust," Tate pointed out.

"One of our vehicles?"

"I can't be certain. Ever since that confounded Gazala Gallop, when we fell back to the Gazala Line, with each army driving each other's vehicles, I can never trust my eyes. Many mistakes were made, on both sides!"

"Best be off."

#

Tuesday 07 July 1942
CAIRO, EGYPT

Thrusting the flimsy door open, Elliot pushed his shoulder in, marching into his Gezira flat with Jane in his arms.

An Asian man down the hall stared, unabashed, at the happy couple.

"What a scoundrel you are!" exclaimed Jane as Elliot kicked the door shut and dropped her on her feet.

"Because I would not let you dirty your feet on the unholy grounds of Gezira?"

"People do stare so."

"Let them. Curse them. Do you care?"

Jane was not given the opportunity to answer because Elliot pulled her to him and let his lips gently rub against hers. He ran his fingers along her slender arms up to her shoulders and neck and deepened his kisses. Jane gave an unexpected moan and Elliot suddenly found her irresistible, his searching lips moving away from her mouth.

"But we must wash this yellow dust off first. Can't have you looking like a ghoul in a haunting."

And once again, Jane found herself in Elliot's strong arms and in the bathtub.

#

Saturday 11 July 1942
CAIRO, EGYPT

"Elliot?" a voice reached Elliot from the dark courtyard.

"William, what is it?"

Elliot noticed his kid brother struggling to his feet, walking slowly into the shaft of light cast by the kitchen back door.

"Don't doctors change at hospital? How come you always appear so ragged?"

"I can't be bothered. Besides," William's face lit up for a second as he explained, "the smell and the stains keep many of the tram passengers away and the taxi drivers are very obliging to go faster."

"Taxi drivers? Why?"

"Either they want to be rid of the smell or maybe they think I'm actually a doctor. I don't know!"

"Well, you do smell. What would Mother say?"

William's lips stretched wide and a soft chuckle shook him.

"It's good that you're home."

"Elliot, Cook's been acting up."

"What else is new?"

"No, it's different this time, and you should attend to it. Cook found Louisa in the house. Mother was out, you were out, I was out, and father…"

"Was out. William, what's happened?" Elliot could barely conceal his alarm.

"Cook heard noises. How he, the cockroach, heard noises I cannot imagine, but he did. So he went to investigate. Elliot, Cook found Louisa trying to open Father's study door."

"Why?"

"No idea. Cook explained that she was leaning on the door. He assumed she was trying to push it open or working on the lock."

"Did she have a key?"

"Cook couldn't tell. He asked her to come to the sitting room and have tea, assuming that Lady Westbrook had extended an invitation."

"Did Mother extend an invitation?"

"Not according to Mother. So, Cook's in a rage. Of course, it's only so that our housekeeper…"

"What's he done to Mrs. Judd?" Elliot growled.

131

"Put a damper on it, Elliot. Cook's putting on a show so he could justly scold Mrs. Judd," William sighed. "You know how Cook loves to make a scene and to shout and yell."

"Damn the fellow!"

"What I want to know is this: *When* is dinner?"

Elliot laughed and clapped his brother on the shoulder. "So, that's why you're out here. You walked into the kitchen, tired and hungry, got a proper scolding from Cook even though all this nonsense with Louisa must have taken place hours ago and he and Mother have already sorted it all out. You slunk out to brood on a bench in a dark, dusty courtyard. I see it all now. Come, I'll drive you to the club. We'll get food there. Although," Elliot paused, looking at William's disheveled facade, and sighed, "William, you do look a fright."

Elliot wanted to appear nonchalant about discovering that his fiancée tried to enter his father's study, and so he kept a light banter while William leaned his head against the window, giving him half-hearted answers. Elliot was determined to take this bit of information to Crumper and ask for better locks to be put on Sir Niles' study.

After a solid meal, Elliot drove William home then took off at great speed to Crumper's flat.

But Crumper was not in his flat.

Elliot raced to HQ where he found Crumper struggling between glee and anger and worry, his crisp uniform in contrast with the bristles on his face.

"What's happened?"

Crumper pulled the young man inside his office and shut the door. He moved close to Elliot. Bringing his lips to Elliot's ear, he disclosed, "9th Australian Division overran Signal Company 621."

His whisper felt like an assault on Elliot's ear. What on earth was happening?

"What's Signal Company 621?"

Quietly, Crumper explained, "Signal Company 621 is Rommel's eyes and ears in the desert. German intelligence officers have been listening in, deciphering our communications, and relaying everything to Rommel."

Now Elliot understood why Crumper stayed captive all day and night at GHQ.

"When did that happen? Recently, I take it." Elliot pointed to Crumper's face. Crumper scratched his whiskers. "A day ago."

"Well, here's my news," Elliot whispered. "Our cook caught Baker trying to enter my father's locked study."

Crumper looked confused. "What would your baker need with a study? And doesn't your cook do the baking at your estate?"

"Louisa Baker. Louisa Baker tried to force her way into Sir Niles' study. We were all out, and she had not been invited."

"Did she manage to go inside?"

"Damn. You know, Crumper, I haven't the slightest idea. I better talk to Cook myself."

"We better see to it. That study door must be secured, and properly. I'll send men out there with locks. And inform your father. I doubt that he keeps anything useful there. Still..."

But when Sir Niles finally heard of Cook's heroics, a smile lit his face. Amused, he said, "I've kept the deplorable creature on staff for years, and it has finally paid off. Mind you, I've always known him to be loyal, but the raw vegetables, stringy meat drowning in heavy sauce, and wriggling fish he serves us at table under the pretense of delicacies does seem a bit much."

Elliot's acrid rejoinder came to his lips but remained unspoken. His father was pleased with Cook, especially since Louisa was stopped before she could enter the study. She was served tea and quickly dispatched, all seemingly proper. So there was no need to point out Cook's history of abusive behavior to the rest of the staff and often his refusal to serve meals to Elliot or his brothers throughout the day, holding that he cooked according to schedule and that the boys must avail themselves at mealtime. But what was Cook doing following Louisa? Was Cook yet another person to monitor?

"Of course, it was rather intuitive of your mother to let Cook know that we rarely expect company and certainly no one uninvited should be entertained here at the estate," Sir Niles elucidated as if reading his son's thoughts.

"So, Cook simply followed noises he'd heard?"

"After letting Louisa in, Mrs. Judd ran to the kitchen to complain that although affianced to Mr. Westbrook, Louisa was not an invited guest while none of the family were present. It was rather suspicious. She then asked Cook to watch over the girl."

"Hence, his ill-humor and Mrs. Judd's subsequent plight," Elliot remarked dryly.

"Plight?"

"William said she was in tears when he came home, and he had to soothe her. Father, why do we have such needy help? And why would Louisa want to have tea by herself?"

133

"Maybe she was thirsty," Sir Niles grunted then asked, "So, you know of Company 621?"

"Yes."

"The Auk is calling for a series of offensives right away, while Rommel is temporarily deaf and blind without his decrypting capabilities."

CHAPTER 23

An excerpt from Jack Johnson's Notes
Thursday 23 July 1942
EL ALAMEIN, EGYPT

"*YALLAH*, DIG! DIG!"

Bandar clings to my neck, making sounds that irritate the men.

"Does that monkey have to be here?" Underhill asks.

"He gets lonely in his cage. We agreed, did we not, that I'll keep him caged only when it's too dangerous for him to roam."

"Look round you. D'you call any of this safe?" cackles Underhill, a comrade who up until now has been mild and inoffensive.

Toc is not the only one affected by the retreat and the subsequent offensives that end in a nightly routine of digging in and entrenching.

"That's enough, Underhill," Toc gives a low growl, and his body undergoes a transformation, like a dog ready to tackle.

Toc and I rejoined our regiment only two days ago in el Alamein. But Toc continues to be rash, and is often involved in brawls which leave him with the commanding officer's secretary inside a pile of rusting corrugated metal we call 'the office.' Toc brashly tells me that it is still better than the treatment he received in school. "They don't thrash or cane me!" And I wonder at him, at his choices.

"What Bandar needs now is physical activity. We all do," I say, trying to deflect the tension building up between Toc and Underhill.

"Monkey doesn't play football, does he?"

"Doesn't wield a pickaxe either, damn him," comes a comment from further down the trench.

Toc grabs a handful of gravel and tosses it over the trench, Bandar shrieks and leaps off of me, trying to catch the last bit of cascading gravel then he scuttles from clump to clump in noisy delight.

"Well, digging is completed and monkey troubles over, what's next?" Toc asks.

"Guns," comes the inevitable order.

Bandar leaps on Toc's shoulders. And such is the charm of both Toc and the monkey that our comrades are rarely offended by their ill humor. Almost after every fist fight, Toc gets pats on the back, as if the men commiserate with his frustration at having to accept the order to entrench. Bandar, too, might get a sharp reprimand from one of the men but an instant later the same man would allow the monkey to climb on his head or rest across his shoulders, almost as an indulgence after a scolding.

Hot and tired, we set to cleaning the guns after digging a pit for them. Clutching rags, we attend to the springs and feeding clips.

For the past two days, Sergeant has been keeping Toc and me on guard duty.

Sensing our uneasiness, and missing Moss, Bandar has become irritable and often shouts and shrieks while gripping my neck or abusing the little teddy bear that one of the RAF boys brought him. The teddy bear was a kind thought, but Bandar so ill-treats the poor old toy that it now has but a loose button for an eye and stuffing coming out of its seams in unlikely places.

"I'm finished," Toc croaks. "Jack?"

"Yes?" My voice is muffled by the mechanism between my face and Toc's.

"Bandar has been allowed too much freedom. Too much leisure. We should train him to be useful."

"What? Teach him to clean the guns?"

"No, of course not. Train Bandar to come and go on command."

"Could Bandar deliver cigarettes and drinks?" Underhill suggests.

Popping my head out and wiping my forehead on the greasy rag, I agree, "Brilliant. But he'll drink whatever has alcohol in it."

"Why did we have to dig yet another trench? Aren't there enough?"

"A defense line. Damn Rommel," I growl.

"It's the last one before Alexandria and Cairo, the Canal, and the oil fields."

"It's something to do," Underhill grunts.

Looking grave, Toc chimes in. "No, Underhill, this is crucial. We entrench here because to our north is the Mediterranean Sea. Tanks don't swim. The Qattara Depression is to our south. So far, it's impassable by tank because of its geology, salt pan of shifting sands."

"Not the fact that it looks like the end of the earth and is 200 feet below sea level and hot as hell?" I ask, lightening the mood.

"Armor cannot drive over the Qattara. Not yet. So, we must hold Alamein. It's lined with belts of barbed wire and mines. Now, we ready the anti-tank guns," Toc finishes his lecture.

"Don't be such a prig," Underhill says.

"Shut up."

#

Later that day, as part of the Auk's entourage, a thin man emerges out of a Willys jeep, pulling his goggles off and unwinding his scarves, shaking the fine yellow dust off with fastidious care.

Toc stiffens. Then in a slouch, he disappears into the dark recesses of the trench. His back against the trench wall, he asks to join in a game of cards. He is refused, of course. The boys have been playing for some time now, and even the Auk's arrival is trivial to them. After all, the Auk would want to see the commanding officers.

Bandar jumps off my neck and scuttles to Toc, and for a brief moment Toc finds solace in minding Bandar.

"Toc, why are you here?"

"Too hot to stand out there just to catch a glimpse of the Auk," he replies.

"Oh, that's right. You've already met him. And the man in the scarves and goggles, who's he?"

"They are all swaddled in scarves."

"As soon as you saw that particular man, you took off."

"Leave me," he says darkly.

"What?"

Toc rarely speaks unkindly.

"Come," I summon Bandar and walk outside.

Sergeant is now standing and talking to the Auk, gesticulating with his hand, probably asking for additional ammunition. And every now and then Sergeant's gaze shifts for an instant to the fastidious man in the scarves and goggles. True, the Auk and his entourage all have similar garb but his is somewhat more elaborate and he carries it with a bit of an air, not a soldier, I know, because the Auk stands and talks and breathes like a soldier, a life-long soldier, and this man is nothing like him.

"Who's the jackass with the dance-master deportment?" Grave Scottish brogue reaches my ear, and I suddenly face a handsome man, slightly older than I, wearing the decorated uniform of a lieutenant of the Black Guard.

"The Auk is here, Sir," I answer.

"Well, of course he is. But who's the jackass with the scarves still on his shoulders? What's he searching or looking for? Has he paid any attention to the Auk or to your Sergeant?"

And I understand what he means. The 'jackass,' his chest protruding, rear sticking out, and that mustache, has been idly scanning the troops! "I'm trying to endeavor that myself, Sir."

"Why?"

"Why?"

The polite Scottish accent drifts to me. "Does he interest you?"

"Like you said so yourself, Sir, he's different."

"Let's find out then." The Scottish voice and its appealing visage melt away and suddenly appear by the *jackass*'s side.

Nearly choking with surprise, I watch the Scottish Lieutenant introduces himself, almost like a highland chieftain might do in a Walter Scott novel. And it is only a strong sense of decorum that holds me from bursting out laughing at the farcical buffoonery of the introduction and the stern reception it receives. The two men exchange words, apparently pleased to have met despite the odd beginning. Then within minutes the Scottish voice is behind me, barely above a whisper, asking me whether I know of an aristocrat's son in our lines.

Unable to conceal the truth yet reluctant to give Toc's identity away, I tilt my head.

"Well, where is he, laddie?"

Twisting my neck back so I can catch a glimpse of the Lieutenant, I stare into his blue eyes.

"Your friend, then?" he says easily, with a trace of a smirk. None of the older men approve of close friendship. He, too, must have been through rough battles and have lost many of his comrades and is now turned weary of the basic human need for a friend. For it leaves one in a desert of pain and hurt when the friend is shot or blown to bits or killed by tank fire. "I won't say anymore. However, let him know that his father is here and wants a word with him."

"Yes, Sir." I feel his hand clapping my shoulder and then he walks away. I doubt that I will ever forget those intelligent blue eyes, groomed mustache, sunburned straight nose, and kind grin with the soothing brogue of Scotland.

Holding onto Bandar, I watch the Auk inspecting maps and looking out with his field glasses and talking to his entourage, most men at least two or three inches shorter.

Should I go to Toc?

Inevitably, our comrades will learn of Toc's lineage, but I try to postpone Toc's moment of exposure for a while longer. Shifting my weight, scratching Bandar to shush his chittering, I linger a while then walk to the trenches.

But Toc is not in his foxhole.

Bandar still in my arms, my legs carry me to the cemetery, a field with makeshift white crosses.

And there is Toc, shirtless and noisy, playing football. His black hair curling at the nape of his neck from perspiration and his pressed-fiber identity disks, flung across his back now, bounce up and down as he runs and jumps and kicks.

I remove my shirt and let Bandar settle into it, repeating the command 'stay' because none of the lads appreciate it when Bandar darts into the field and snatches the ball.

When I join the group, I am by Toc's side, as usual. The men are used to us playing football on the same team and doing pretty much everything we can together. They are used to the fact that Sergeant never addresses Toc but calls on me and Toc is expected to follow. Sergeant can never bring himself to pronounce 'Toc,' says he can't be bothered and that Johnson is proper and easier on the mouth. Toc only grins at comments like that and meekly obeys orders. Well, most of Sergeant's orders. Toc rarely cuts his hair. My fair hair is often shaven but his dark mop is left to fall into his eyes. "Disgraceful," Sergeant growls into his face and Toc nods and agrees but stays away from the barber.

"Toc?"

"Yes?"

"Your father's here to see you."

"I know. Here, Johnson, cover Underhill, will you?" he says and runs as if on wings to the other side of the field and I know that he wants me to get the ball from Underhill, somehow, and kick it over to him, across a thick defense line. We have practiced that move so many times before that my body moves with little conscious effort. The game goes on until, exhausted, every one of us is out of breath and sweaty and more than willing to take a break because of the heat. Even at repose, the sun scorches us while the flies stick to our sweat and buzz.

"Will you go?" I ask.

"I don't know."

"Afraid?"

"Of course not. Johnson, what do you take me for?"

Then a loud whistle summons us to the parade ground.

After a game of football, the sweat and the flies are intolerable, especially since I never had a chance to wash up. Standing in the parade ground, I listen to the Auk's encouraging words in agony, blinking sweat out of my eyes.

It is while the Auk speaks, that I realize that we are heading into battle.

Afterwards, we amble to the mess and join a group of men eating biscuits and jam. Featured on the menu is what we refer to as butter, but is really some form of congealed fat, perhaps margarine if we are lucky. The men pass round the biscuits and jam and most are reluctant to touch the butter.

A pale and dusty man has just arrived. He is rather ravenous from the way he stuffs his mouth with biscuits. His neighbor passes him the jam and, after he thanks him, he asks for '*wagenschmiere.*'

The word is barely out of the newcomer's mouth when Toc leaps up and, in a flash, pins the pale man to the ground.

"Jack, your gun, your gun!" Toc shouts.

On my feet the instant Toc shouts, I look round for any weapon. I have no gun, of course, I am not an officer, but there is always some sort of a weapon leaning up on a wall. Rather careless, but as it proves to be this time, useful. And, within seconds of Toc's command, I train a bayonet on the struggling pale soldier.

"What's this?"

"Someone, get Sergeant. Now!" Toc commands.

I am hardly breathing, keeping the bayonet leveled at the pale soldier as I suddenly wonder, what is going on?

I am so used to reacting with unquestioning speed to Toc's directives that I act without hesitation, without a second thought. But why am I standing pointing a bayonet at a fellow soldier? What has he done? Or, who is he that Toc is straddling him so roughly on the ground, in a tight hold. And the pale soldier is fighting back, giving it his all!

Heavy footfalls sound close to the mess and Sergeant is standing at the entrance.

"What is this? Johnson, what the hell's the meaning of this? Put that thing down."

"No, Sir," Toc objects. "I can't hold him down any longer, Sir."

And at that brief moment, the pale man overcomes Toc and throws him off his back with a heavy facer, but I am ready. The cold end of the bayonet is immediately pressed against the soldier's cheek.

"Stand still!" I shout. I want to check on Toc, but I press the bayonet deeper into the man.

Sergeant restrains the pale soldier and calls for reinforcement. "Turner, hold him. Gibson get that fellow off the ground, pick him up quickly! Now, Johnson, what's the meaning of all this?"

"I don't know, Sir."

"Well, what happened man? Why are you pointing that bayonet at him?" he asks, giving the pale soldier a shake.

"We came for biscuits and jam, Sir, Toc and I. This chap joined us, stuffed his face with biscuits."

"Food fight, Johnson?" Sergeant barks.

"Well, no Sir. He got jam," I continue, bayonet still pressed hard into the soldier's cheek. "Then he asked for that butter."

"No, he didn't. He asked me to pass the *Wagenschmiere*." It is the pale soldier's neighbor, Guy Gibson, speaking and my face grows cold when he delivers his next words. "Sir, Toc's still out cold, Sir."

Toc is face down.

"His head bumped the wall, Sir, and he isn't moving, Sir."

I throw an agonized look at Toc's inert body, and as the bayonet drifts slightly, the pale soldier lashes out with all his might. But there are more of us, so he is quickly kicked into a more subdued state.

"Gibson, *that* needs to be kept with a guard until we find out who the hell he is. Call the MP. Johnson?"

"Yes, Sir?"

"You get your friend some medical help and fast. The boy's father is here…that's all I need right now." Then Sergeant mumbles, incoherently, "A delegation of highly powerful Members of Parliament touring with Auchinleck … why the devil bring them to me? Visiting dignitaries … Take them to the pyramids, or Mena House, for Heaven's Sake. Damn it, Gibson, why haven't you left already? Get this filth out of here."

#

Nighttime Thursday 23 July 1942
EL ALAMEIN, EGYPT

The day's last shafts of sunlight sneak into our tent.

"Toc?"

"Johnson?"

"Johnson? Why is it Johnson all of a sudden?"

"Well, it's your name is it not?"

"You were the first to do away with surnames. You very well know why. Unwilling to be dehumanized. Well, never mind that now. Toc, why did you not go with him?"

"Do you take me for a coward?"

"I don't. Of course not. How could I?"

141

"Then why wonder that I stayed when my father urged me to leave to South Africa, to the Cape?"

"Because he is your father."

"My duty is to my country. Anyway, what did they do with that German?"

"Removed him to Alexandria. They want to find out how he got into our camp and who sent him, I mean, they want to find out the specific unit he is attached to," I say, propping myself up on the cot. "Sergeant's still in shock." A short giggle escapes me but Toc is grim. "First he had that Han on his hands then when you were not coming to and some idiot went to get your father…And your father raised hell demanding that you leave at once and join him on the next steamer to the Cape…Sergeant howled that it wasn't a village schoolroom."

Toc is running his hand through his hair.

"Toc?"

"Do you have Bandar?"

"He's here. The wretch!"

At last, Toc grins. "The parade ground! Oh, what a perfect ending to a queer day!"

"I can't believe he did it. Can you?"

"The wretch!" Toc repeats my words.

"And right in front of the Auk! That little brown devil takes a piss on the parade ground then returns to me to nestle on my shoulder!"

"Confirming your relationship!"

"What a day. Hold on, what relationship?"

"You're a good boy, Bandar!" Toc's caressing voice acts as a whistle to a hound and Bandar leaves my cot and squeaks his way to Toc's. "But I still wish that you were a cat. A fat kitchen cat! A good hunter to hunt the abominable rats!"

#

After a restless night with rats and Bandar's antics, Toc blearily walks to the mess hall, a dug-out pit under nettings stretched between several lorries.

Following Toc inside, I am anxious. I wonder what today will bring. How will the men treat Toc now that they are well aware of his true identity, the only son to a prominent politician and an aristocrat? Will they tease him? Will they treat him with diffidence? Toc would find diffidence distasteful and teasing fatiguing.

But Toc's aristocratic lineage is soon forgotten. At first our comrades stare then they continue with their routine, tea and liquified bully beef and biscuits and jam. And I realize that of course our comrades let Toc be. They are marvelous lads and, having fought by Toc's side, they value his worth as a man and as a soldier. And

142

they honor him for joining their ranks and, above all, for sussing out an enemy who could have killed them in their sleep. They honor him by treating him as they have always done, and continue to call him Toc. Well, Sergeant will never utter that appellation, but Toc is used to that.

CHAPTER 24

Thursday 30 July 1942
CAIRO, EGYPT

"ELLIOT, HOW WONDERFUL! You *are* back." Floating down the stairs, his mother, her arms extended forward, reached for him in a plea. "Elliot, Sir Niles is away." Her golden hair cascaded beautifully down her back.

Elliot rarely saw his mother's hair unpinned. "Still?"

"You must settle the dispute!"

Staring in bewilderment, for never before had his mother greeted him with such enthusiasm and certainly never to settle a dispute, Elliot was stunned. "Dispute?"

"Cook," she began when a shriek and a roar resounded at the end of the hall. She pressed her hand to her forehead and moaned, "Not again."

"Who's caterwauling?" Elliot shouted, springing toward the din.

And to Elliot's amazement, Cook was backed into a corner of the vestibule, roaring and clutching his pate like a lunatic, facing a chambermaid holding an ugly, fat cat in her hand with a dead mouse hanging out of the cat's jaws.

In fluid Egyptian Arabic, the maid explained that she hated rats and had sent for her family's cherished mouser extraordinaire. "Effendi," she shrieked, lifting the cat up and down like a pump handle. "He is very good. Look at him."

Elliot eyed the ugly feline with appreciation. "He's the fattest puss I had ever laid eyes on. Yes, he looks like a good mouser. Tell me, can your cat's legs actually support his weight?"

"Effendi?"

"Never-mind."

"We live by the river," the maid's voice trailed off as she finally realized her blunder. She really should have left her family pet at home. Showing him off, as fat as he was, only meant that her family had rats! "And Cook detests cats," she added, quietly.

"Vermin!" the lunatic shouted again. "Animals belong outside!"

"And rats?" Some impish delight drove Elliot to interject an inflammatory remark and he almost chided himself for the pleasure he got from watching Cook going into a near apoplectic rage.

Meanwhile, Elliot's mother uttered, "Oh, dear." She looked every which way except at Cook, Elliot, and the chambermaid, her thin hands clasping and unclasping. "Such an unpleasant scene," she murmured while Cook howled.

Taking pity on the maid, and his mother, Elliot held his arm up. "Silence."

Cook continued to roar but the maid upturned her brown eyes with admiration to Elliot.

"Are there rats in the kitchen?"

The maid nodded miserably as Cook screamed, "RATS?! There are none! Not in MY kitchens!"

"You, take your cat back home."

"Rats," the maid's lips moved.

"I'll call experts to eliminate rats from the kitchen," Elliot nudged the maid, adding in an undertone, "shame we can't get rid of the other type of vermin in the kitchen as easily," and threw an admonishing look at his mother.

"Cook stays," Lady Westbrook insisted quietly, but Cook heard her and, bestowing a sycophantic grin, bowed and scuttled to the kitchen.

CHAPTER 25

An excerpt from Jack Johnson's Notes
Friday 31 July 1942
WESTERN DESERT

STARING AT THE empty sky, I draw a shuddering breath. Last night, we rammed into the Italians, full force. The night before that, we pumped fire into the Germans and before that into both Italians *and* Germans and now, as daylight takes control over the desert, all of us just want to crawl to bed, all of us except Toc. He, alone, is in our tent battling rats.

"Is he done yet?" Turner complains, his massive shoulders are hunched with exhaustion.

"No. He'll let us know when the rats are gone," I reply to Turner's inquiry.

Turner grumbles in his Yorkshire slang and stalks off.

I loosen the chinstrap of my helmet, leaning against supply barrels that are covered in netting over top.

Bandar is restless in my arms.

"Want to play with the ball?"

Excited chittering tells me that I must fetch the ball and play with the animal.

Bandar's demeanor immediately brightens when I toss the ball to him. He chatters happily. Back and forth we go in our secluded area surrounded by supply barrels until Toc's head appears through the netting.

"Well, there might be one or two left but, on the whole, I'm pretty sure that they're gone."

Bandar leaps to Toc's shoulders.

Toc turns to me and asks, bewildered, "How does this monkey stay cheerful and friendly after all that's been going on?"

"No idea. How did you recover from your fit?"

"What fit?"

"When you pretty much drained all our ammunition into the German camp. I expected Sergeant to lecture you on husbanding ammunition."

"A fit? No, I was evening the score." Toc waves the notebook where he keeps track of anyone strafed to death or blown up in the minefields, any soldier that he recognizes or that still has identity disks on. Some do not have disks or are unidentifiable, so Toc writes in Latin *non idem*.

"Toc," I start but think better of it. How can I tell him that the score cannot be made even because the world is cruel, unforgiving, and rarely fair? But I am too tired.

I slog into the boiling tent that reeks of blood and cordite. Stripping, the dull ache in my muscles floors me, and I soon fall sleep.

Growls and roars from my comrades, Toc, of course, in the lead, jerk me out of slumber.

"What's it this time?"

I make out from the uproar that the Auk ordered an end to the offensive operations. He wants to gather supplies and materials and men, strengthen the Eighth Army and then launch a major counter-offensive. And in the midst of their disappointment or relief or both I find myself wondering about Toc, eliminating one rat at a time then reaching out to Bandar with warmth and love and then Toc at the battlefield firing the Vickers machine-gun or picking up a Bren gun as easily as if he's picked up a holdall.

CHAPTER 26

Saturday 01 August 1942
CAIRO, EGYPT

From the breakfast room, he heard, "Elliot!"

"Father?"

"Where are you off to?"

Elliot stared mulishly.

"Have you forgotten? Prime Minister's visit."

"When?" Elliot croaked.

"It will be sometime after the fifth."

"Then I should be back by then."

"Where are you going?"

"I'll be back by the fifth, Father!" Elliot promised, bounding down the stairs.

But as the sandy miles stretched ahead of him, Elliot realized the foolishness of promising to return before the 5th of August.

The front line was close to Cairo, but vehicles often ran into difficulties. Tate and Sullivan navigated the sand dunes like sailors out at sea but Elliot, now jostling behind them in his new Willys jeep, wondered not for the first time just what to do once he returned to Cairo.

As the tawny wasteland before him rolled by, Elliot considered how to find evidence against his fiancée and his future father-in-law. He knew enough about their misdeeds to turn his stomach. With his help, British Intelligence gathered that Mr. Baker was purchasing vast quantities of cotton and grain. Mr. Baker was even arranging for deliveries to reach the Axis army in the Western Desert. But how, and who was the contact? And what role was Louisa playing?

Were the Bakers involved with information gathering? Espionage?

He shuddered at the thought of having to live with Louisa. But he was not the only one shuddering. Tate and Sullivan lurched forward as their lorry once again stalled.

"This is bad," Tate growled gravely, his glass scanning the horizon as his lips vanished into a thin disappointed line. "Hardly any cover out here. And to think that we're just a few miles away from the rendezvous point."

"I'll look into it." Sullivan was soon stretched under the lorry, hands in the chassis.

Quickly pulling out netting and burlap, Elliot covered both vehicles. Eyes blinking out dust, he spotted some shrubs which he dispatched and threaded into the netting for better coverage. But as Elliot bent over the windshield to attach the camouflage, he noticed a rising cloud and increasing noise coming over a jebel.

"Tate?"

Tate flung off his field glasses.

Then, almost instantly, Tate and Sullivan had their Bren guns ready as they fell to the prone position, watching the approaching cloud.

Squinting into the shimmering heat haze, Elliot's eyes focused on the menacing undulation of heat and dust. He could feel Sullivan tensing up, ready to fire.

Three lorries roared across the jebel and plunged down almost recklessly toward them. Two of the lorries had a cleverly mounted Vickers machine-gun, remarkably similar to the contraption Tate and Sullivan had in their own lorry. A man in each of the two lorries stood behind the machine. The third lorry displayed the Red Cross markings.

Elliot and the Australians remained still until the lorries pulled up close, machine-guns glaring at them.

Elliot heard Tate boom a wrathful curse as Sullivan bellowed out a bawdy Australian drinking song. They were on their feet and running toward the newcomers.

The unknown visitors stayed unmoved, and so Elliot grabbed Sullivan's discarded Bren gun.

When the roar of the engines was silenced, Sullivan's song could be heard and it gathered volume and force as unfamiliar voices joined in. The men abandoned their Vickers, springing off the lorries to greet Tate and Sullivan.

Elliot scanned the ragged men. They were thin and sinewy, matted beards under an almost theatrical array of headdresses and scarves, made drab by the thick coating of dust. Their hands and lips were covered with desert sores. Their sunken eyes suddenly lit up to see Tate and Sullivan, then flicked, alert and ready, in his direction.

If ever a rugby team went on a prolonged hunger strike, then the men before him were it, thought Elliot as he sized up the impressively built yet gaunt figures. Then he noticed that not all of them were large lads. Besides Sullivan, there were at least two more who were lithe and of average height.

As Tate was making introductions, Sullivan hurried off with a shaggy individual to examine the broken-down Chevrolet lorry and two others went to Elliot's Willys jeep to unload supplies and precious water.

One of the men approached Elliot with languid, almost patrician, bearing. Bit by bit, the barely recognizable figure of his brother, James Westbrook, the Army field surgeon, materialized. He looked dreadfully dirty, scarred, and unkempt.

Now, it was Elliot who was doing the swearing.

"And I suppose that you find this amusing?"

"What?"

"Leaving us in the dark. Where were you? And what do you mean by writing such short letters? Father has been badgering people at HQ, hunting for your whereabouts and Mother..."

"How is Mother?"

"She's worried."

"But still *devastatingly radiant* as the tabloids report?"

"Do you get tabloids here? Look here, James, you can't do that!" Elliot had been thinking of his parents, their anxiety when few, short, noncommittal letters arrived so rarely.

But with silent, slow motions James led Elliot to glance at his passengers in the Red Cross lorry. "I need your help, as I will not be returning to Cairo to pay Mother a social call. Elliot, take them to hospital as fast as you can."

Elliot was surprised because for the first time since war began, he did not vomit at the sight of blood.

The patients were strapped to stretchers, delirious in morphia induced sleep, and their blood-soaked desert uniform was covered in dust and soot, axle grease and sweat.

"Elliot, as fast as you can!"

"William will take good care of them for you."

"God, no, not William."

Elliot's eyes flew to James'. "Why the hell not? Don't you trust the boy?"

Contempt distorting his dirty, hairy features, James spat, "Of course I do."

"William was trained with the best rescue units in London."

"And you think that I don't know that? He could probably do my job and better," admitted James. "He would not have let his comrades deteriorate like so. William follows the rules, you know."

"Well?"

"Look here," James pulled Elliot further away and confessed, "they're both badly wounded. One of the chaps has infected desert sores in addition to the wounds. Diphtheritic infection of the sores is, at this stage, fatal."

"Damn you," Elliot exclaimed with emotion.

They were wrapped in silence, two brothers in the desert, surrounded by noisy yet efficient and capable LRDG and SAS men, transferring the wounded and unloading and loading supplies.

Looking grave and woebegone, James croaked, "If I could spare him two letters to write to a grieving mother, I would. Wouldn't you? So, I ask this favor of you."

"And what would you have me say to Father?"

James stared.

"Any words of affection for Mother?"

"You have nothing to say to either because you never saw me here. The LRDG needs supplies, food and medical supplies. Get Father to squeeze more morphia tablets for the troops. Damn those clerks at GHQ branding us all Neanderthals, mistrusting us to properly administer those tablets! Some of us are also assisting Sterling's L-Detachment SAS men. All is well."

"All is well? And what of your facial disfigurement?"

"What?"

"Your scars." Trying to hide his worry and fear for his brother, Elliot drawled, "Your desert sores, are they diphtheritic as well?"

"No. Now look here Elliot, not a word of it to anyone."

Elliot's cobalt eyes darkened with anger as he leveled his stare at James.

Like the other men in his unit, James' eyes were sunken and dark shadows appeared underneath the yellow dust. Then James stretched his dry lips in a smile, reflecting the ghost of his youthful self.

Feeling rather chastened, Elliot's anger died and he simply nodded.

James wanted to protect his family from anxiety for his welfare. If only they knew…If only Mother knew!

"James."

"Looks like your lorry is running again. Be off with you! And remember," he lowered his voice as he removed his Red Cross arm band and put it on Elliot's arm. Then, thrusting his bearded chin toward the groaning, injured men now strapped in the back of Elliot's jeep, he said, "Watch over William!"

#

Sunday 09 August 1942
CAIRO, EGYPT

Four days earlier, Prime Minister Winston Churchill had visited the Eighth Army, galvanizing the boys with his 'V for Victory' salute and stirring speeches.

Lieutenant-General Bernard Montgomery was taking over command of the British Eighth Army after Lieutenant-General William Gott's plane crash-landed and, unable to escape, Gott was strafed by ME 109's.

At GHQ, the Auk was briefing Montgomery, and Sir Niles wanted to look in on the meeting. After all, he would have to work with Montgomery.

In the conference room, the brawny Auchinleck reviewed plans he had set forth, pointing to maps and studies.

Standing close and thus rather accentuating his slim stature as he stared at Auchinleck's medals, Montgomery was asking questions, his voice metallic.

Sir Niles remained by the door, listening and weighing the information when he heard a thump and a grunt in the hallway. He eased the door open then stared into cobalt eyes.

"Elliot!" he hissed.

"Father."

Sir Niles slid out.

"Over here." Elliot, unabashed, indicated an empty office, casting suspicious glances about.

Once inside the unoccupied office, Elliot whispered, "Father, I need jeeps."

Sir Niles looked at Elliot in puzzlement.

"I need those new American jeeps," he breathed, barely audible. "For my project with the LRDG."

Suddenly, they both swiveled their heads toward a shuffling sound.

"Cook's been arguing with Mrs. Judd again. Something to do with outrageous expenses," Elliot complained loudly.

"Not his lecherous goings-on with that chambermaid?"

"Outrageous expenses," Elliot repeated somberly, although his face almost cracked.

"What outrageous expenses?" Sir Niles wondered, and his voice rang with true bewilderment because he and his wife had decided not to entertain during war. His wife had agreed to the scheme simply because Cook had warned her that they were short on staff for such events. And Sir Niles was reluctant to have strangers enter his house. Cairo was swarming with spies and enemy agents. "Tell the scoundrel to see me tomorrow morning. His farcical nonsense is beginning to verge on the impossible!"

"Impossible?"

"Impossible to believe that I have him in my employ. Damn him! He's a terrible cook."

"He's appalling! Have you dined at Faraj's? The food is a poem!"

"How is Faraj? He's been a good friend to you. When did you meet him? When I first sent you to Egypt and your grandfather saddled you with that martinet of a tutor who ended us marrying a dwarf?"

"Why, yes! Faraj is the best of friends," Elliot admitted.

A trace of worry or envy appeared in Sir Niles' eyes.

"As is Madame Sukey."

"Madame Sukey? Not William's Madame!"

"The same!"

"Elliot," Sir Niles sighed. "How do you get yourself entangled with such persons? What would your mother say?"

"That was precisely what William asked when I begged him to introduce Madame to me!"

"Nonsense! You never beg, Elliot. You command people to do your bidding!"

"Steady on. I have a reputation to maintain."

"How many?" Sir Nile's voice dropped again.

"Two jeeps, at the very least. Morphia tablets too, lots of them."

"Morphia? See here, Elliot..."

"No, Father. Morphia tablets. LRDG and SAS both need more morphia tablets. Field dressings. More plasma. It's important."

"But what about more general supplies, or even ammunition? Why are you largely interested in medical supplies, Elliot? And how do you know about plasma? You?"

"Father, it's a family failing."

#

Monday 10 August 1942
CAIRO, EGYPT

Squinting into the harsh lamplight in the crowded Long Bar, Elliot dreaded joining his fiancée. He would rather do it with the numbing effects of alcohol because he knew that he would find Louisa Baker tittering with a group of silly females, parading themselves on the terrace of Shepheard's Hotel.

"At least she is pretty."

The sepulcher announcement so near his ear slapped Elliot's senses. "If you like that kind of look, I suppose that she is. But what is it about her giggles, Crumper? What am I to do?"

"I don't envy you," the officer remarked sotto voce as Elliot turned to look at him.

Crumper was in his twenties, and thus far exhibited remarkable sense, good common sense! He did not fall for Louisa Baker, she of the large breasts. True, her middle section was thick but one supposed it was so to support the bosom. Louisa's face had small features, if on the mousy side, a twitchy mouse because her eyes sometimes fluttered in affected spasms. Her dark brown hair was done up, professionally. Elliot wondered just how often she went to or summoned the hair dresser. And who was responsible for the shocking red fingernail and toenail polish?

"What else have you learned about her and her father?"

Crumper's eyes fixed on Elliot's face. "Beyond the unsavory connections and mysterious bank deposits?"

"Well?"

"There's been little surveillance. What little efforts were taken, they were taken by me. But my social rank prevents me from entering their circles, you know how it is."

"So that's where I come in. But what if I have to marry the creature?" Elliot asked.

"As I said before, you have to marry the creature and promptly! But the marriage will be short lived... As soon as we have solid evidence, we move in, and you need never see her again. We'll have a coverup story ready, and your name will not be tarnished, well, not much."

"Not tarnished? Not much?" Elliot repeated, a rueful smile easing his tension. "What damnable effrontery, Crumper. But I suppose you're right. Besides, it's negligible when my own brother is...Well, when William is elbow deep in blood in hospital. I suppose a little thing such as exchanging wedding vows is insignificant."

"Elliot, the Bakers are connected to Young Egypt, too."

A dark gloom settled on Elliot. "What a mess!" Now he would have to reckon with Young Egypt, a nationalist organization.

"What's a mess?" Crumper wondered.

"Ali, our stable boy, drinks coffee with a few members of Young Egypt, damn the boy. Now I have to keep an eye on him, too."

To Elliot's dismay, Crumper's next words confirmed that Elliot's vigilance was about to get harder. "There's a Syrian-born man, a former student of the University of Cairo. He's been gathering funds and support from businessmen and politicians who hold similar views advertised by the Nazis."

"Mahmud?" Elliot asked.

"That wog!" The officer uttered wog with all the dislike one holds for a despised disease.

"A relative of the Mufti, he is. I doubt that he'd appreciate you calling him wog, a rather derogatory term for natives, don't you think?" Elliot flashed Crumper a wicked grin.

"No, I don't. And you, Westbrook, would be more serious if you had an inkling of the man's vicious character. You get something on the Bakers, quickly. Marry the wench. It's necessary, you know, and get something that seals the case against her and her father. I want them both in front of a firing squad!"

"Steady on, Crumper!"

"As a husband, you won't need to wait for special invitation. Enter their mansion at will and without worrying about their security measures! But it's going to be rough. She has a hellish temper, I gathered that much from observing her interacting with her staff."

"Household staff?"

A smile stretched across the officer's face. "When Leicester approached you, you know, he had me apply for a housekeeping job at the Bakers' great mansion."

"Housekeeping?"

"You have no idea how uncomfortable it is for a chap to turn into a large-breasted woman! The heavy weight of the fake breasts! And I had to shave twice a day so no one would notice a trace of stubble! There was also the apron strings to tie properly and all this without smearing the makeup, that horrid, sticky face powder!"

"My dear Crumper, I am in awe!"

"You should be! Housekeeping is the devil's work. Keeping accounts and settling disputes, inspecting pots, and beds."

"What did you learn?"

"Besides household accounts and a bit of cookery?" Crumper's face lit up. "Did you ever wonder who provided the blueprints for the mansion?"

"You?"

"I did. I also confirmed information on the father and his frequent absences. Absences, I must add, that often coincide with his daughter's long absences. We also intercepted some deliveries of merchandise but unfortunately I was sacked all too soon. The confounded butler, damn the man, almost raped me. And even after enduring ruthless groping, I fell under Louisa's wrathful tongue-lashing. She sent me packing. And without a reference!"

"Damn…"

"There was also the indignity of the servants' hall and the internal battles there, much encouraged, I must add, by the mistress of the house, since divided camps can be easily conquered."

"Lovely, Crumper, I shall have a jolly good time with such a woman. When's Montgomery taking over?"

"The 18th of August."

"What of the mock setups, the phantom army on the south side of el Alamein?"

"Operation Bertram," Crumper revealed. "Let's hope that Rommel will fall for the ruse and send his troops north, to the coast, because that's where we'll be ready for him. Look here, Elliot, you better go talk to her," he said, shuddering when he uttered 'her.'

#

With remarkable sangfroid, Elliot sauntered onto the terrace of Shepheard's, approaching Louisa with arrogance etched into every movement of his erect figure, a cigarette dangling precariously between his lips.

"Elliot," Louisa called, waving her hands, breasts wiggling.

Elliot unapologetically stared at the large mounds, thinking about the comment Crumper had just made about being disguised as a deep-bosomed female on the Bakers' staff. Then his thoughts flicked to Cook and his ogling, lascivious manners. And the power that that creature held over the staff. He decided to try some of Cook's methods of 'courtship' on Louisa. She just might like such a lecher for a husband, he thought bitterly.

"My dear Louisa," he took his cigarette between his fingers and bent low to bestow a kiss, only his souring mood made him misbehave and instead of planting a chaste kiss on Louisa's cheek he covered her lips, neck and exposed bit of breast. There always was an exposed bit of breast, he realized.

An uproar of shrieks ensued and Louisa's friends came to her rescue. Slim, feminine hands pulled at him while other long slender painted fingers fluttered about.

"What's a chap to do when his fiancée is so delicious?"

"Beast, you can't do that," Louisa giggled, obviously pleased with the attention and the envious stares from her friends.

Elliot had never quite understood female friendship. It had always seemed to him to be tinged with malice and jealousy.

"Darling, I've had the most awful morning shopping with Tilda."

Who the devil was Tilda? Confused, Elliot decided to play up his attraction to Louisa, let her bask in its effects on her entourage. So he pulled Louisa to his lap.

Again came the shocked, yet envious, reaction of the other women.

And as Louisa carried on, regaling him with acidic remarks regarding Tilda's ineptitude, he ran lascivious hands on her body, vaguely aware that the same Tilda who was being brutally criticized, was staring, shocked, at Louisa.

But luck sometimes failed Elliot, and Mr. Baker suddenly materialized with a sour expression on his face. "Propriety, Elliot, propriety," Mr. Baker growled, pointedly staring at Elliot's roving hands that had settled on one of Louisa's breasts and thigh.

"My dear girl," Mr. Baker took Louisa's hand in his. "I regret this, but we must hurry."

Louisa never asked him why and never protested. Standing up, she simply waved in valediction and followed her father into a taxi.

"Wish I were Ali Baba!"

"Ali Baba?" giggled one of the girls. "Wasn't he the poor woodcutter who discovered a cave full of treasure?"

"Open Sesame!" Elliot replied with a smile that evinced a completely different meaning than his true intentions.

Again, the girls shrieked, misunderstanding the "Open Sesame" to be a ribald remark by an infatuated fiancé, never suspecting that Elliot simply wanted to be able to walk into Louisa's house to collect incriminating hard evidence.

#

Just before dinner that day, at his parents' estate, Elliot summoned William. "Do you know, William, I've just about had enough of our staff. There's that horrible Cook, caterwauling in the kitchen like it's his own private bedlam and the chambermaids ogling me and ridiculing Salomé."

"Ridiculing Salomé? Why?" William asked.

"The girl's helping Ali. They're working on the ditches, clearing debris and weeds and re-planting the gardens and orchards! I've been helping them. They need the help, too. By the way, we finished identifying dead and dying trees. Ali will give you our tally."

"But why are they ridiculing Salomé?"

"She's doing a man's job."

"Damn, I never thought of that."

"Nor did I."

"Well?" William inquired.

157

"It's our ugly Fatima, damn her. What a grotesque customer!"

"She can't help her looks."

"No, it's not that. She's rather cruel and malicious. I don't trust her."

"So what about Cook and the maids, what do you intend to do about them?"

"Do about them?"

"Elliot, I'm well aware that once you declare that you've had enough of someone, that someone better beware because mischief is forthcoming!"

Elliot chuckled. "And I'll have accomplices this time, too. You will help?"

"That depends!"

"Depends on what?"

"Tell me your plans, Elliot. Will our house get blown to bits?"

Elliot cast a hurt look at his brother. "I'll never live it down, will I? I overestimated the explosive powder and caused a bit of damage to our school. But, think, William, was it so very bad? After all, there were the *prefects* and the beatings, the prayers and the religious studies."

"Elliot, what do you have in mind for Cook?" William insisted. "I'll help because I cannot stand the creature, but what's your plan?"

"Oh, don't worry. Nothing explosive! A string of unpleasantries, that's what he'll be enjoying pretty soon. But first, there's the business with the maids."

"What about the maids?"

"They need to be put in their place."

"Elliot…"

"All you need to do is talk to me in their presence. Warn me not to continue with ditch work, with digging. Warn me of demons that lurk beneath the sandy pits of our estate! Can you handle such a conversation?"

"Easily!" William's lips parted. "Now that I recollect how often one maid or another reports my comings and goings to Mother … Never met with such a meddlesome lot!"

"You need your own flat. A private refuge!"

"I do. Though, at the moment, I come home to sleep and that's about all."

"Well, not just sleep. You certainly look into the stables often and not to go riding either!"

"Who else will be helping you?"

"Ali! But why are you changing the subject?"

"What will you have the boy do?" William asked, his forehead wrinkled.

"He's in charge of stage production."

"You never really liked him, Elliot. Why have him help you with such a prank?"

"He's growing on me," was Elliot's noncommittal response.

"All right, I'll help. Now, Elliot, tell me more about your work out here. You've certainly bronzed!"

"And don't I know it! That maid, the one who carries the washing sideways rather than over her head keeps sending smoldering glances at me but daggers at your little one."

"What?"

"Smoldering glances at me but daggers at Salomé," Elliot repeated. "Now, mind you, I enjoy smoldering glances from pretty ladies, but not from our staff, it's too fatiguing, and certainly not at the expense of Salomé. She's a hard worker."

"Why do they dislike Salomé?"

"No idea."

William looked worried.

"Jealousy, perhaps? Salomé works with me. She is certainly physically closer to me than any one of the maids and what a field of conjecture that opens up!"

"You think highly of yourself."

Elliot's grin disappeared. "You are often away, William. You do not hear what they say and do. I know my worth, but sometimes I cannot help but feel like a piece of meat in the maids' eyes. Especially the one I told you about, damn it what *is* her name?"

"Are you talking about Fatima again?"

"Oh, enough about her, curse her. I hate her already. How is it going for you in hospital?"

"Nightmarish."

"Well, at least you can have some sport scaring our staff!"

#

Tuesday 11 August 1942
CAIRO, EGYPT

Standing still in the courtyard with half the washing in her basket and the other half dancing in the wind, Fatima watched Elliot.

"Elliot Effendi!" Ali hailed him.

Elliot fixed Ali with a cold stare. Waking up to the cacophony outside, Elliot had not paused to nurse his throbbing headache. Instead, he came out to work, to shake off the pain. "What have you been up to, Ali?"

"Digging, Effendi."

Elliot looked at his watch. "It's almost noon. If I join you and Salomé, we'll work faster. I'll get my gramophone and jazz will give us speed and stamina."

"Jazz? Maybe Umm Kulthum, Elliot Effendi?"

"No, no, jazz."

"Lady Westbrook sometimes plays her piano."

"Yes, and I am certain that that is exactly how you end up in a café or two."

"Effendi?"

"Never-mind."

When Salomé approached the sweaty Elliot, he smiled. Elliot liked the mysterious, mute maid. "Hot, isn't it?" He removed his shirt, handing it to her to hang on a tree.

Somehow, the girl understood his wishes without any instructions other than a glance in the direction of the tree. But when Salomé returned, she stood close to him, not moving much, almost as if hiding.

Fatima's beady eyes watched Elliot. Her crooked mouth was busily gossiping. In fact, the wretched woman was now casting dark glances at the girl beside him. Then he noticed the jeering edge to the maids' buckshot tones.

"Are they mean to you? Do they hurt you?"

Salomé shook her head.

"Leave them, then. Get your shovel, girl, and dig sand out of this pit."

Watching the girl work, Elliot appreciated her quiet, enthusiastic company and was rather interested in his brother's attempts at befriending Salomé. How old was she? She seemed to be no older than a child, and often he wanted to ruffle her short hair and hand her a toy. But lately, she appeared more mature. Her figure was blurred by her robes, but Elliot had, on several occasions, glimpsed a shapely feminine body underneath. Sweat-soaked linen clung to the interesting parts of a woman's curvature, and there was the time he saw her bathing in the canal. Odd, he thought, why did she avoid the bath in the servants' quarters? Why did she trot far out to the canal with that donkey and a bucket to wash herself?

Later that day, Elliot bumped into his brother climbing up the stairs. "William!"

"Elliot?"

"You're home. Excellent. Do you remember our plan?"

"I do," William replied thoughtfully.

"Well, it's time. Wait until the maids, that particular one, are making the beds. Storm into my room, then warn me not to dig. And make sure you speak Arabic!"

"Arabic?"

"They wouldn't care. They'll be eavesdropping and too enthralled by your warning!"

Pushing aside a strand of hair, William said, "Fatima's there now."

Following his brother's gaze, Elliot observed the women move to and fro in his room. "Well, well, well," growled Elliot, a wicked gleam in his eyes and a curled lip his only trace of animation. And as if electrified, he sprang to his room with William right beside him.

Noisily changing bedsheets, Fatima was instructing her counterpart on how to do it better. But as Elliot and William entered, the maids fell silent, eagerly attending to Elliot's and William's staged conversation, never once wondering why the two brothers were chatting in Egyptian Arabic!

"Elliot, you disregard my warning. Stop digging, my brother."

"It's a tall tale."

"It has been awakened. How else would you justify what happened to you?"

"Think nothing of it. A simple accident!"

"You nearly died!" William howled in guttural staccato.

The maids were certainly paying attention.

"I merely slipped."

William persisted and clarified what had supposedly happened. "The demon nearly devoured you. You heard its shrieks as you dug deeper. Father said that this estate was built on a sacred burial ground of royal pet monkeys."

Pet monkeys? Damn the boy! Elliot knew that he was about to burst into peals of laughter. Why did William choose blasted *pet monkeys?* Of all things! "Nonsense," Elliot cast over his shoulder and stormed out, coughing and choking, with tears in his eyes.

William remained behind.

The two maids were dumbfounded and terrified, holding white bedsheets between them.

"A demon attacked my brother because he opened up burial grounds," William explained to them, clicking his tongue in disapproval. "Jinn will get him. Digging into the sand is risky!"

Elliot was a genius at contriving devious schemes. As it was, he had tapped into deep-rooted superstition, manipulating a gossip network to his advantage. And he was patient.

Over the course of the next week, maids spotted *afreet*.

Whispers of terrifying visions were rife. "It glowed in the dark...It looked like a monkey."

161

Over breakfast, when he spoke to William about his latest success, Elliot explained that he used sheets and torchlight while Ali produced eery sound effects.

"All it now requires is a thistle-eating ass."

"Shakespeare," grunted Elliot.

"And some other nonsensical beings that frighten people out of their wits," William continued in admiration.

"For a charm of powerful trouble, let it brew and bubble. Father does it too, you know."

"What?"

"He recites Shakespeare at me. And often either Puck or Macbeth's three witches!"

"When will you get them?" William asked.

"Who?"

"Elliot, I'm talking about Fatima."

"Well, right now!"

Standing outside, Fatima regaled her companions with her latest encounter with Elliot's demon.

Having noticed their agitation, Elliot howled.

The maids jumped, frightened.

A brief moment of silence ensued then frenetic exclamations filled the air.

"It is He."

"He sounds like that."

"Help!"

Behind bushes, Elliot stripped naked and dipped himself in the water flowing in the ditch, then rolled in mud and sand.

Already uneasy about the ditch work and the menace of a jinn popping out of the ground, the maids saw what they had been led to believe.

Elliot ran from the bushes toward the cultivated land, howling and yowling. His sand-covered body pantomimed a dance, haka-like, while shouting curses.

There was not much for it but to run, so the maids flew into the kitchen, into the arms of the horrible cook, for people often turn to the biggest bully when scared.

Cook indeed tried to look brave, but he too shuddered at the thought of a demon on the estate and vowed to ask his master for another pay raise while the rest of the staff plunged into a flurry of superstitious preparations, most of which involved garlic and spitting.

#

Wednesday 12 August 1942
CAIRO, EGYPT

Elliot was uneasy about Louisa Baker. His project was going much too slowly.

"You look lovely today," Elliot said, pulling a chair out for Louisa.

Although Shepheard's hotel was crowded, there was always room for the Westbrooks. Sir Niles' prominent position in Cairene politics opened doors, and tables, for his sons.

Dimpling, Louisa basked in his compliment.

Elliot wanted to charm Louisa into good humor, good enough to invite him to her father's mansion. The old man was so crusty and private and insisted on formal invitations.

But while his mind was busy with conjectures, Louisa amused Elliot with the latest *on dit* about his brother, William, and a nurse from hospital.

"Elliot, it is not at all the thing!" she chided. "You must talk to him and explain how things stand. She's married, after all, and to a vicar, no less!"

"Louisa, do you expect me to talk to William about his illicit love affairs?"

"She is a married woman."

"And where did you hear of it? I trust that you did not repeat it all over town." Elliot eyed Louisa with a slight grin. He was controlling his temper, conscious all the while of his duty, of his mission. How was he to get invited to the Bakers' villa?

Elliot watched Louisa's lips move, still talking about his brother and that married nurse. "I'll see what I can do." He winked at her, his fingers caressing her cheek. "You need not worry about William. But I'll talk to him," he added, noticing her lips shaping up to give battle. "Now, what are your plans for later this week?"

"Oh, I almost forgot!" she exclaimed. "Father is holding a formal dinner party. And I am to invite you, Elliot."

Elliot grinned.

"Aren't you pleased?"

"Delighted, my dear."

"I will get an invitation sent out to you. So, where do we go dancing tonight?"

"Tara," he replied.

Elliot's social calendar overflowed with invitations to exclusive parties. His ownership of Monnayeur's only added to his social cachet. So when he needed to hold a treat out for Louisa, he found it to be an easy task. And Louisa, in turn, went into raptures. She was wealthy but unpopular and often found herself excluded from upper class events.

"Come kiss me and we part," he pulled her to him. Farewell over, Elliot then thrust her away.

#

Friday 14 August 1942
WESTERN DESERT

The jeep sped on, with Elliot's foot heavy on the pedal. He wanted to put as much distance as possible between him and the Panzerarmee that was only a few miles away.

Sullivan, Tate, Elliot, and Lady Jane had just completed another quick mission. The Eighth had left behind watering stations, and it was up to Tate and Sullivan to take care that the water would bring little relief if not something much worse for enemy troops. So, Tate contacted Elliot and the four had piled into two brand new jeeps and hurtled themselves across the dunes and into no man's land.

Along the way, Elliot made frequent stops to photograph conditions of the land the Eighth had left behind. There were still valuables to be picked up or destroyed before they fell into Axis hands.

On their return, Tate and Sullivan turned northeastward, closer to Alamein while Elliot and Jane swerved onto the Cairo road.

Tate watched Elliot and Jane disappear behind a cloud of dust. "I just can't believe this!" he spat.

Sitting by his side, quiet and worried, Sullivan agreed with Tate's sentiment.

Neither of them approved of Elliot's choice to include Lady Jane.

"His reasoning makes sense but in such a cold, calculating way! And I don't want to see Lady Jane come to harm. It goes against every proper feeling. Don't you agree?"

Sullivan nodded, blanching at the thought of one of his sisters running such a risk.

#

"That's unfortunate." Elliot shrugged out of the straps and scarves, then sprang out of the jeep. "Puncture. Rear, left."

Jane picked up her field glasses and stood up. She looked almost boyish.

Elliot, pulling and tugging at the spare tire strapped to the jeep, finally contrived to wrench it loose. He then turned to the ruined tire. "Tire's ripped to shreds."

Jane grinned. She was not sure why, but the rueful look on Elliot's face reminded her of a boy who had just realized what a mess he had landed himself in. "Will it take long? We have a spare, I see. And I can keep watch."

"Will you sing for me?"

She wondered what song would come to his mind. "Anything in particular?"

"You Go to My Head."

Her field glasses trained on the horizon, and with a smile flitting across her lips, Jane began to sing.

As the setting sun flung long shadows on the desert sand, Elliot became aware that Jane had stopped singing.

Jane scanned the empty desert, methodically. Enemy patrol vehicles were never too far away.

"What a sunset!" Elliot approached Jane, flinching at the banality of his statement. Had he actually run out of flirtatious remarks?

Jane turned to him. "You're finished with that tire! I'm happy. Punctures out here always make me nervous."

Elliot drew her close. How rare it was to hear a woman say that she was happy!

"Jane," he breathed and his arms moved to encircle her. He pressed his lips to hers. Her body clung to him and in a wave of desire he ran his hands up her back to her hair and was removing her scarves, then her shirt, lowering her onto the desert sand. His tongue met with sandy skin, but it was Jane's skin and her special scent called to him. His kisses grew deeper and more searching and his hands were running over her flat stomach then unclasping her undergarments. She moved toward him, unhesitating. Her short gasps urged him on and he was lost in her, not caring should an army descend upon him.

On their way back to Cairo, Elliot made a request. "Will you permit me to introduce you to my brother?"

"Elliot?"

"Will you go with me to Monnayeur's and meet my brother? My younger brother, William. James, my older brother is somewhere in the desert, with the Eighth. James' a field surgeon. But William is here in Cairo. Will you allow me to introduce you to him?"

"But he cannot know."

"No, he cannot know how much I love you, my Lady Jane. But it is important for me that at least my kid brother would meet you and you him. He is not such a bad fellow."

"Pale and exhausted is how Sullivan described William," Jane revealed.

Elliot stared in silence then commented, "I'll have to do something about it."

"About what?"

"Can't have a pale virgin for a brother, now, can I?"

"Sullivan had said pale and exhausted not pale and virginal! Elliot, how could you be so coarse?"

"I have to look out for him."

"When?"

Looking at Jane again, Elliot's face was a mask of confusion.

"When would you like me to meet your brother?"

"How about Monday night?"

Jane leaned back and nodded in agreement and Elliot ached to console her with information, with an explanation why he was still engaged to Louisa when his own feelings for Jane were so strong. He knew that Jane understood that his engagement could not be broken while the war continued and his own hints were enough to help Jane accept their clandestine affair. But how much Lady Jane knew and for how long she would agree to meet him in his flat in Gezira or go on dangerous forays into the desert, only a few miles from the front, flirting with the Panzerarmee and the minefields, he could not guess.

#

Monday 17 August 1942
CAIRO, EGYPT

Watching William disappear to the unkept area of their estate by the canal tributary, Elliot examined his wristwatch. He determined to give the lad a quarter of an hour to contemplate.

As he trampled through the reeds, Elliot marveled at William's disregard of insect-induced discomfort. With repeated oaths, Elliot massacred mosquitoes on his face and hands.

When Elliot startled William out of his reverie, he drawled, hiding his irritation as William grimaced at him, "Watching the fellahin again?"

"Leave me."

Casting a bored glance at the fields far away, Elliot said, "You know, William, the fellahin are not a sight to behold. Laborers of the fields are morbidly unhealthy."

"True," William replied with laconic simplicity.

"William, I've been looking for you. It's been donkey's years since you joined me in Monnayeur's." Elliot plopped himself down on the reeds by William's side.

"You'll ruin your suit, you know."

"I don't mind. Will you help me tonight?"

"Do you need my help?"

"It's been a busy week."

"And Louisa?"

For a moment, Elliot wondered about William's obsession with propriety. James had mentioned that William followed the rules, but this was taking it too far! "I need to work, and my work is at Monnayeur's."

"Work? Monnayeur's is your own club."

"Precisely! I must supervise my people. Who would run the place?"

"You cannot call it work. You go there dressed in the latest fashion."

"Well, I cannot go there looking a fright."

"And you strut about surrounded with beauties."

"A man needs his ornaments."

"Elliot, you watch dancing women and play cards all night then drive home for breakfast!"

"I get hungry at sunrise. What do you expect, William, that I work all night and skip a fine English breakfast?"

"You know what I mean."

Elliot began to sing and dance and all he got in reply from William was an emphatic, "No, no."

"You're my alibi. Dance?" He extended his hand.

"Why not?"

And to Elliot's delight, William got up. But, instead of dancing, his brother dropped a wet mud ball in Elliot's palm, sprinting back to the house, like a carefree child on holiday.

Triumphant, Elliot stabbed the air with his muddy fist.

#

"Here he comes, damn the fellow, why is he late?"

As William entered the club, a couple of amputees hailed him. His unkempt hair flapped as he turned his head to smile at the men, his fingers immediately adjusting his collar and necktie.

"And look at him marching in like royalty, his humpty-dumpties paying homage to him."

"Elliot, are you jealous?"

"Of course I am. I wish that I could help the boys, too."

Lady Jane smiled at her handsome companion. "But you do."

William was before them now, and Elliot shot his inquiry, "What took you so long?"

"Car problems. Aren't you going to introduce me?"

"Right you are."

Artificial niceties exchanged, then Elliot explained that Lady Jane wished to sing at Monnayeur's. Elliot caught the look of surprise on Jane's face when he rushed to explain, "While I dash off to take care of something, Mr. Westbrook will show you round. Talk about schedule, too."

"Schedule?" William asked, looking baffled.

"Why not?" Elliot flashed a smile and walked out. He was suddenly hit with a bewildering sense of love and longing for Lady Jane. William would pick up on Elliot's emotions. In a flash, Elliot decided to risk everything and take a taxi to Louisa Baker's house, try to sneak in, and to collect evidence to put an end to the charade. He felt wrung out. Keeping his Lady Jane a secret from his family, from William in particular, was hard on him. So, he harnessed his courage and hailed a cab.

Lady Jane looked at William. How could she put him at ease?

Looking everywhere but at Lady Jane, William led her to Elliot's table in the cabaret hall. He then fixed his gaze on the belly dancer on stage and allowed his thoughts to race. Where was Elliot? Who was the gorgeous woman by his side? And what was he doing at a cabaret when his body demanded sleep?

And while William and Lady Jane were heroically watching the show on stage, Elliot approached the Bakers' mansion. He refused to wait for another promised dinner party. He would go in and look into that mysterious room he had come upon previously. It was risky, jeopardizing the entire operation if caught. His superiors had been careful building up an iron clad case against Mr. Baker, but the extent of Luisa's involvement was still not known. So Elliot was prepared to break in. What if no one was home? And if Mr. Baker or his daughter were home, if he were challenged, then he could pretend to be inebriated.

A spark of hope rose to his throat when Elliot noticed that the mansion was sparsely lit. He picked up his pace. His hand was on the door handle of the wrought iron gate leading into the mansion's grounds and front door when he caught sight of them.

Standing on the veranda, Louisa and her father were holding champagne flutes, chatting with an elderly couple.

From the dark shrubbery, Elliot made out that the relationship was rather intimate or at least of long standing and that the elderly couple was either Cairene or Levantine - Their motions betraying their origins.

"Why Elliot, is it really you?"

"Westbrook? What?" echoed Louisa's father, alarmed. "I say, if you were not my daughter's fiancé, I'd have you locked up! Skulking in the shrubbery like that. It won't do, Mr. Westbrook, it won't do!"

"Oh, Father, do let him join us," Louisa urged, theatrically.

Elliot, rather than find himself pressed to join the Bakers, decided to act out a drunken scene. He did it so well, with all the aplomb of a man blind drunk, singing and hollering, declaring his undying love for Louisa in rather warm terms, that Mr. Baker announced that enough was enough and that he was calling the police.

With the panache reserved for the intoxicated, Elliot slipped into the Bakers' guests' car, switched the engine on and drove off. Just as he entered the more crowded area of the city, he abandoned the car after a quick search for anything interesting. Quickly, he then hailed a taxi into the teeming, if disreputable, Birket Street. When he entered his club, William and Lady Jane were talking, his brother watching Jane somewhat confused and, as Soad's cymbals began to chink on stage, Elliot was behind Lady Jane and commenting, off handedly, "She's the best in Cairo. She's the real thing, not like a painted Hollywood girl just shaking a leg and bending over. She is the real thing, the best belly dancer in Cairo."

Throwing him a bewildered look, William replied, "She just danced with a sword balanced on her breasts. She has to be the best. And what with all that mythological set up on stage, I half expected a cobra to pop out of the basket over there or a tiger to leap over her head."

"Oh, good suggestions!"

"I wasn't aware that I made any."

"Well, it's late." Elliot turned to Lady Jane. "Why don't you follow me? This young chap will take you home tonight."

"Joseph? Joseph is not young," commented William in Arabic then, switching to English, turned to introduce Joseph to Lady Jane. "Our former groom. Joseph once took care of anything that walked on our estate. But he has recently retired."

Joseph smiled at Lady Jane then nodded at William and crooned, "Master William, good to have you here."

"Good to see you, Joseph. How have you been?"

Joseph gave the appropriate reply.

"I am glad that my brother has you in his employ, because I do have some questions about the health of Nick Bottom, the old donkey in the stables. Do you remember him?"

"I do," replied Joseph darkly.

"I'll talk to you later then," William's words came out in a rush as he noticed that Elliot was anxious to depart.

"You have a donkey? Named Nick Bottom? Shakespeare's ass?" Lady Jane asked.

"I do."

"Why? I mean, why do you have a donkey and why name a donkey Bottom?"

"Because he's an ass!" boomed Elliot, pleased with his quip.

"Lady Jane, I have a donkey because Elliot and I found it tangled in wires and Joseph here, and a stable boy called Ali, helped heal his lesions. He was mistreated and misused by tourists. So he's a misused ass," William halted. "Hang on. Do you understand Arabic?"

"One must. There's all that infatuation with the orient or should I say the East, or Middle East, nowadays."

"I see."

Elliot, who seemed to be rather in a hurry, blurted out a gruff farewell, "Lady Jane, stop by again," as he handed her over to Joseph and his immaculately clean car.

"Elliot, where were you?"

"How did it go? Are you all right?" And noticing William's pallor, Elliot said, "Come."

Too tired to object, William followed, pausing long enough to ask, "Elliot? Where do you find the time for all this?"

#

Elliot twitched the curtain. "William's by the hot tub."

"Do you think it wise that you brought him here, to a bathhouse?" asked the woman by his side in upper class Cairene dialect.

"I cannot have a pale virgin for a brother. I have to look out for him."

"It's all very well for you, Elliot, to make such dashing remarks, but is it really wise to set your brother up with a... well, with a hostess?"

"She'll treat him gently. Whoever she is. Do you recognize her?" Elliot asked.

"I can't tell yet, her back is to me." The woman crinkled her nose in distaste. "And the drink? What was in it?"

"Some liquid opiate to help him relax, you need not worry. William handles much worse in hospital."

"Yes, he handles the stuff, but he does not touch it. He does not abuse drugs like that."

170

"Look here, it's not abuse. This is a bathhouse, not exactly a brothel. No one is forced into anything here!" Elliot snapped.

Elliot and the woman stared at each other, each trying to impress their point of view on the other. Then the woman smiled, her head tilted slightly. "Oh, what's the use! I have never been in the habit of disagreeing with you, my friend."

"Aziza, I won't have you meekly acquiesce!"

"I shan't."

"Well?"

"Oh, look! It's Daliah with William. Good. She'll amuse him a bit then send him home safely. He won't come to harm."

Admiration sparkled in Elliot's eyes. "Thank you for helping me set this up for William. He needs it, you know. He works in that hospital day and night, and it can't be easy."

"No. But he is doing his bit."

"Let me just dunk the boy into the water because it looks like otherwise he'll be there all night sitting and grinning like the village idiot!"

Gently, Elliot eased his brother into the warm water, fully clothed, and set him on a step, William's chest and shoulders exposed.

Elliot laughed, ruffled William's hair, and marched his friend, Aziza, to the bar.

"I hope he likes it."

"He must!"

Aziza laughed her melodious laugh.

"It's been a long time since I heard you laugh," Elliot remarked. "Not since we blew up that prison."

"And that hideous, hatchet-faced nationalist in it! Oh, I am glad he's gone!"

Elliot's shout of laughter broke the tension between the two. "We made a mess of it, didn't we?"

"That devil's gone. We wanted to extricate an alarmingly powerful nationalist from prison in Luxor and bring him to British HQ for proper questioning. Well, instead, we eliminated him."

"I am certain that he was in communication with the enemy. Why else would he rise to power and popularity so fast?"

"It was a botched affair, but I don't regret it!"

"And how do you fare now that I am gone and you do both our work in the desert?" Elliot asked.

"Fairly well. But you are not gone. Only busy elsewhere."

"It's good of you to agree to take over my project in upper Egypt."

"Of course. But Elliot, I profit from it, as you are well aware."

"Profit or not, you provide people with much needed vaccines and proper medicine, not some crack witchcraft, or hobgoblin brew!"

"Hobgoblin brew?"

"Shakespearean nonsense," Elliot mumbled.

"Do you know, I have a mind to see what I can do further up the Nile, striking farther into the desert. I want to enlarge my market of modern medicine."

"Why not? There are humanitarian organizations here in Cairo and in Alexandria that will finance such missions. And who knows, you might just stumble upon an enemy spy or two and send me a word."

Aziza chuckled. "You would like that, Elliot. I can see you making haste to upper Egypt in an American jeep, engine revving at impossible speed, desert goggles on your face and scarves muffling you from the sand and sun, ready to arrest a naughty Jerry!"

"That bad?" Elliot leveled his blue gaze at Aziza's dark, almond-shaped eyes. "Are you mocking me?"

"No, not you." Her tone became serious. "Elliot, you will alert me to possible dangers?"

"If I learn of anything suspicious in upper Egypt, you'll be the first to know."

"And I'll do the same."

Aziza and Elliot allowed time to slip by when Elliot recalled his obligation to his brother. He bid Aziza farewell and collected the now sleepy William and brought him home, noting as he sped across Cairo that Aziza judged at least his driving correctly.

#

Tuesday 18 August 1942
CAIRO, EGYPT

"Dinner parties in Cairo should be reserved for winter," Elliot's acidic remark slapped William out of his abstraction.

William turned to watch Elliot pace his bedchamber. "Your face's smeared with mud."

"No time to wash up properly. I've only just arrived. And it is not dirt or mud, it's vomit, my vomit, and road soot. Have a look at my shoes!"

"You saw blood. Where?"

172

"Everywhere..." Elliot replied off handedly, his arm moving in a vague direction.

"You really must get used to the sight of blood, Elliot."

"I can't help it."

"For now, you better get the vomit scrubbed off. Call on Mrs. Judd. She'd know what to do. You cannot go looking like this! Where the hell have you been?"

"Are you watching her again?"

"Watching her? Elliot, what are you talking about?"

"Salomé! Your eyes are constantly in the direction of the stables. This is a splendid room to view the stables. I'm surprised that you have not dislodged me yet."

The frown lines suddenly disappeared from his face, and William smirked. "But I will. As soon as you marry Louisa! Mother informed me that you will be moving into the guesthouse."

"Yes."

"What about privacy? Your flat is splendid."

"My flat is a splendid hideout for me. It's mine. Anyway, Louisa is already planning a lovely villa in Ma'adi. She's working with an architect when she isn't bullying the wedding planner."

"Wedding planner?"

"She has hired some long-nosed female to arrange the wedding, the guest list, the flower arrangements, and other such nonsense."

"It's not nonsense to Louisa."

"No. Only last week she spent a fortune on something or other, maybe the wedding dress? Took her ages just to pick up the thing, whatever it was! Can you imagine the nightmare her fitters had to go through?"

"No." After a short silence, William asked, "Elliot, do *you* prefer to live here?"

"At least for the moment. This gorgeous estate is convenient. It's not too far from GHQ which is where I have been known to lollop about since war broke out."

William doubted that his brother shirked his duty but helped him maintain the fiction by saying casually, "So, I'll have this room, and the magnificent view of the stables. Only I'll first have it whitewashed. Some new furnishing is in order. Don't you think?"

"I don't. Look here William, you haven't mentioned hospital. How are things there?"

"Why, miserable! Convoy after convoy! We have many sitting up cases, but the real devil is heat exhaustion, sunstroke, and enteric cases. We've several malaria patients, too, besides those with influenza. One boy came in with a sharp rusty bit of metal embedded into his abdomen. It was a miracle that he was actually immunized for tetanus! A brilliant stroke of luck. He must be… well how should I put it? He spoke well, like an Etonian."

"Educated at Eton?"

"I should think so. He's the son of a Lord M., but there he was, a private in an infantry regiment with his apostle, a lowly private who goes by the horrible name of Jack Johnson. Do you know what the nurses called fleas from the trenches during the Great War? Jack Johnsons!"

"Jack Johnson?"

"Yes. Jack Johnsons, or JJ's, were fleas."

"Not the German 15 cm artillery shells? The ones with the black smoke?"

"For being such a carefree young man, wholly devoted to carousing and mischief about town, you certainly exhibit a remarkable knowledge of military terms. Elliot, how do you come by the information?"

"I read," Elliot replied, his lips stretching to a grin. "Poetry!"

#

Tinkling sounds of music drifted onto the balcony, and Elliot momentarily lost focus, recalling the last time Lady Jane sang "You Go to My Head." He had been repairing a punctured tire in the desert.

"What are you thinking about?" Louisa's reedy voice ripped his silky memory.

"You," Elliot replied, smiling into Louisa's eyes, wondering all the while when had he become such a hardened liar, a rogue!

"Looking so thoughtful? I hope they were pleasant thoughts."

He was about to utter his, 'you look lovely tonight,' compliment then recollected that he had used the very same gambit only a few days prior and fell back on, "You enchant me."

"Elliot," she breathed and leaned close.

Elliot and Louisa were on one of the Bakers' stone balconies. Dinner was over, and a band played softly while servers came and went, offering French champagne to the guests. How did the Bakers manage to procure such rare treats? And why they had invited what seemed to be the entire upper class or very wealthy members of the Anglo Egyptian society?

Elliot pulled Louisa into his arms and closed his eyes, conjuring up thoughts of Jane all the while, his lips lightly teasing her. His hand caressed her back as his mouth explored her jawline and neck. Louisa breathed heavily, responding to his caresses, whispering his name as her skirt rose over her leg, and his hand explored and rubbed her thigh, then upward.

Louisa pressed against his exploring hand until short sharp gasps of pleasure came out of her mouth, Elliot silencing her with deep kisses.

Suddenly, Elliot became still and placed a hand over Louisa's mouth. He listened to the sound of approaching steps. "We can't stay here."

"What?" she asked stupidly, staring at him in confusion.

"Take me to your bedroom. Someone's coming."

In silence, Louisa walked past stone corridors and up several short flights of steps. Elliot followed, his mind clear as he focused on the direction and number of steps Louisa was leading him through. "What a labyrinth!" he commented, sotto voce. He was grateful for Crumper who had provided a rather detailed plan of the estate, which was built in the oriental style probably a century earlier and was remodeled and improved upon once the Bakers had taken up residency.

"Not far now. Just remember, the third door past the blue balcony on the second landing," Louisa, her hand holding on to him with thin fingers tightly clasping his wrist, simpered. She opened a set of double doors that revealed a grand room with a dark square bed.

Elliot had a vision of the iron maiden.

The bed was flanked by two tall French windows that led to narrow, stone balconies on either side of the bed with ornate iron balustrades.

Immediately, before Louisa distracted him, Elliot gave the room a cursory glance, searching for any sign of a desk or cabinet or any hint of documents, in view or hidden.

But all too soon, Louisa drew his face down.

"Wait. Nature calls."

"Oh."

"And I would rather use the guests' lavatory, please."

"Will you find your way back here?"

"Nothing will keep me away from you."

Walking unobserved, Elliot slipped into Mr. Baker's study. His heart thumping and thundering, Elliot wondered how much time he had and whether anyone would walk in on him.

Scanning the desk and peeking into a top drawer, Elliot began to sweat. Suddenly, his eye caught a flash of white under a thick volume. With shaky hands, he lifted the book and peeked at the bundle of papers.

Foreign fund transfer slips.

Elliot felt his heart leap out of his chest. Where was his camera? Why had he never thought to bring it along? He had just enough time to scan bank information and the contact name when he suddenly heard brisk footsteps.

#

Elliot eyed the Desert Military Intelligence Officer with disfavor.

"Crumper, there *has* to be a way out of this!"

"Why the sudden reluctance? Lady Jane's on your mind?"

"What?" Elliot was unaware that Crumper knew of his relationship with Lady Jane.

"The show must go on. And it has to be convincing. Can't have too many rumors about your womanizing about town either."

Elliot felt like a sulky child being told to eat his vegetables.

"The mansion is guarded, day and night, like a fortress."

"Not so much the grounds."

"No. The house itself is guarded. Haven't you noticed? *Somehow* there is always *someone* behind you. We have not gathered enough information. You have been helpful in supplying names of her father's contacts and fund transfers but what is *Louisa's* part? I want to prove her guilt, because I just know that *she* is behind all this."

"Even as her husband, I cannot watch her day and night."

"No, you cannot, but her husband could have a close look at her activities and finances. I have engaged a group of solicitors and lawyers to help you with pre-wedding arrangements. You won't be left in a financial crisis and the facade of propriety and legal dealings will be convincing."

"Crumper, you better provide some extra watch dogs on our estate then because that's where I intend to live with Louisa. But I won't have my family at risk. Her father is in touch with Berlin, and when either her role or my role is discovered and there is hell to pay, I can't have enemy agents running loose in my mother's house."

"Elliot, look here, why are you crying off?"

Elliot shrugged.

But all along, Elliot was worried. How would his Jane take the news of his wedding? She did not rejoice to hear that he was already an engaged man, but accepted the fact. He went so far as to hint that his engagement was a part of the war effort.

"War effort?" Jane's voice had been wary.

"I cannot say more. You must accept me as I am for now. It will be of short duration. I dare not explain because you and I chose to work for the War Office, in a classified manner, so to speak. What if you're caught? It is a possibility."

"I know. I have made up my mind to join you on your desert forays."

"And will you stay with me? Will you be mine once this war is over?"

"Yours?"

"As my wife, of course."

She had then nodded solemnly and Elliot, elated, drew her into his arms. "Lovely Lady Jane." His fingers brushed away strands of hair and his lips found her cheeks. There had been salty tears. He had kissed the tears away. Then his lips slid to her mouth, and once again he rejoiced at his good fortune at having found such a woman to love. Her touch, her lips, reassured him that he was loved and, most importantly, trusted. She joined him on his assignments. And, she understood that he had his duty, his other mission, to carry out. He was a lucky man!

CHAPTER 27

An excerpt from Jack Johnson's Notes
Sunday 30 August 1942
ALAM HALFA

"PROPER HEAVENLY ADMINISTRATION!" shouts Sergeant. He is genuinely in high spirits, his sunburnt features softening.

Above us, RAF bombers are heading northward. They have spotted heavy concentration of enemy vehicles. And while the Royal Navy is dropping flare after flare to illuminate the desert, our bombers offer repetitive offense to the enemy.

But RAF bombs are not going to stop Rommel from making his final attempt to push and break through the el Alamein Line. Rommel orders his troops to plow forward, and by mid day his troops are through deep British minefields and are heading to Alam Halfa pass under continuous fire from British tanks.

\#

Tuesday 01 September 1942
BATTLE OF ALAM HALFA

Our convoy slogs through Rommel's Devil's gardens, a rather elaborate network of explosive devices. We travel in single file. We are to relieve an Australian position on a jebel.

Suddenly, the ground shakes. A wall of fire and dust erupts as a lorry up ahead hits a mine.

Besides the heat wave that comes my way, an accompanying din instills fear like nothing else in the world. The feeling of everything falling from under my feet hits me along with the knowledge that more comrades are now either maimed or gone so Toc will be adding more names to the list in his pocket.

Toc's mouth moves.

"I can't hear." But then, horrified, I recognize one word.

"Aircraft!"

Together, we jump out of the lorry, forgetting to pray that we do not land on a mine.

When the enemy planes maneuver a turn-around in the sky, we cover each other with sand, blending into the desert. We lie still, breathing smoke and dust, hands over our ears.

The attack goes on for hours.

My arms are stiff when the hell is over. Ears still ringing, I follow Toc.

Crawling about, looking for Sergeant and survivors, Toc ends up staring at body parts.

There is a hand with a wedding band on it and another arm with a watch still strapped to the pulpy wrist. Recognizing both, Toc pulls out his tattered notebook to record the names, repeating them and their rank like an invocation.

I want to put an arm on his busy hand, writing and scratching out names, but I dare not. I want to say, "Don't," but I am silent.

Toc has taken it upon himself to keep track of the dead and injured. This is his catharsis. This is how he is coping with the horrors smoldering at our feet.

Finally, at nightfall, our dwindled convoy drifts into the empty desert of soft rolling sand mounds. Our lorry has a puncture. The other lorries and equipment carrier in our convoy halt. Some men start a fire in a tin can full of benzine and brew up tea.

"I've driven through this area before. There are sizable jebels just ahead," the driver turns to Toc.

"Does Sergeant know anything about this area?"

"Not sure, but I'll let him know," the driver volunteers. "If no one else is using those jebels for cover, then we should."

"Jack, I hope that Sergeant tells us to head for cover. It's too late to drive back. And I'm certain that we are lost. Our navigator is gone. Did you know that?"

"I saw the wedding band." I tighten the lug nuts of the replacement tire because the mechanic, a new recruit, is stupidly staring at Toc, astonished at his refined accent.

When the driver returns, he gestures for us to hop on. The mechanic squeezes himself between us while the driver pushes down on the gas pedal, heading straight to the hilly area ahead, fear of mines clean forgotten.

We travel less than a mile when Toc commands, "Stop!"

The other vehicles in our convoy stop, too, and Sergeant pops out and stares. Burned tanks to our left, and it is grim.

"Eighth Army, American-made M3 Grants, charred," the driver chokes.

"That's the trouble with the Grants," Sergeant speaks, his bitter words claw themselves across the darkening desert. "The silhouette makes these American tanks a splendid target. At ten feet tall… They're too slow."

A figure darts out at a dead run toward one of the Grants.

"Toc!" My shout rips the desert air.

Toc sprints to the Grants.

As Toc climbs up one of the tanks and opens up the lid, I am only several paces away but the smell reaches me. Toc is off balance when I get to the tank and scale up. He is holding himself just above the rim but my hurried climb and shouts send us both inside.

Warm fluid covers my face, and I vaguely register it as vomit but how? Whose? Toc's body gives an almighty shudder and his howl of pain shakes me out of my stupor. I wrap my arms round him and shove him upward. Still retching and shuddering and screaming when he can, Toc tumbles down the great big tank and I follow his descent, eyes shut, my body heaving in revulsion.

"Johnson?" Sergeant calls then he barks orders and a deluge of water comes down on my head. "Why on earth did you go in there?"

Sergeant's profanities are directed at Toc who is trying to explain that he wanted to look for the identity disks of the men inside. "There were six of them, Sir, I could tell by the number of eyes, six matching pairs, not that they were all together…had to do some searching…"

But Sergeant walks on. Shouting and cursing, ordering us to move out, making a commotion, as if his racket might put things to right again.

I am wet and cold and shivering, and I wonder if Toc managed to get a look at those disks. What would Toc add to his notebook? And does he need a new notebook now?

Camping at the foothills of the dark jebels, Toc and I are given extra rations of rum and lime juice. Sergeant indicates that we need to wash up properly, but a growl from the quartermaster that, "Water's scarce," has Sergeant command, "roll in the sand then."

Throughout the night, Bandar crawls from one sleeping bag to the next. At least two men cry out when Bandar's little fingers prod them.

When Toc's calm voice calls the monkey back to him, I suspect that the monkey is not keen on Toc's scent and is likely to wander off again.

"Did you sleep at all last night?" I ask Toc at the breakfast mess.

"As soon as my eyes shut, I saw them staring."

Burying my face in my tea, I avoid admitting that the dead eyeballs haunt me still. And the smell of death is everywhere.

"You naughty boy!" Toc exclaims.

For an instant, I wonder what have I done wrong when I realize that Toc is chiding Bandar, who is groggy but chirps happily enough, asking for biscuits.

CHAPTER 28

Saturday 05 September 1942
CAIRO, EGYPT

AT SUCH AN early hour, Elliot expected to park his car, enter his family home through the kitchen back door, then go to sleep. But as he mounted the steps, his sharp hearing caught sounds from the gardens. His hand pulled the door open to let light out. Then he looked again at the gardens.

The shaft of light that poured out of the open door fell upon William kissing and caressing Salomé. She was on his lap, and William's hands were on the interesting bits of Salomé's anatomy, exploring her passionately with single minded determination.

"William!" Elliot called William away before it was too late.

But what if it was already too late? He hoped that William had better sense than that. The maid was not a maid. She was a refugee. It was obvious from the start. Father had brought her soon after news of an attack on American Hawaii reached Cairo. Then, an odd looking Spaniard had appeared for Christmas dinner asking to see the girl. Elliot had overheard the exchange between the two men and had noticed William keeping to the shadows. Then, in February, the girl had been snatched away during a political riot. William and Ali soon rescued her. William had looked after the girl, bringing her back to life, as his father had put it, and now, what was that brother of his doing to the girl? Another wrathful cry, "William!" escaped Elliot's throat.

"Coming." William tore himself from Salomé.

Elliot and William both liked to use that kitchen entrance. No one was expected to open the door for them and sometimes, especially after hours, there were treats to enjoy.

It smelled promising tonight. The scent of fresh baked cake wafted in the air.

Elliot's eyes lit up when he noticed the warm cake nestled on a golden edged plate. He tore a chunk of cake, cramming it into his mouth.

"The cake! How could you?" William protested.

Elliot's mouth was full of cake. He worked the sweet and sticky mess and even tried to swallow before he confronted William's behavior with Salomé with a rejoinder, "And, you, William, how could you?"

"What do you mean?"

"Don't be the ogre that pounces on the maidens of the village! Salomé has been through enough."

# #

Monday 07 September 1942
CAIRO, EGYPT

Wafting into hospital, trailing scent fumes and crimson skirts, Madame Sukey smiled at the roar of cheers.

The patients propped themselves up, eager to talk to Madame, share letters and photographs from home, or play cards with her.

William marveled at the men, at their ease with such a mature woman. They were not at all put out when she eyed their thighs or watched their lips move.

"Any news today?" William approached Madame.

"Westbrook! How good to see you." Madame cast a roguishly admiring glance at William's face, his sensuous lips, and his neck. "You are about to have a bit of a break. Monty wants to hold his line at Alam el Halfa. No offensive operations for a while!"

"Madame Sukey! How do you do it? How do you get your information?"

"Oh, I have my sources," she replied, secretive and somehow cheeky.

"Will you stay for tea?"

"With you?"

"Would the cafeteria be all right? I'm afraid I can't stay away for too long, or I would have offered to take you to Shepheard's for tea."

"I came to visit you and the boys. I brought cakes, biscuits, and tea leaves, nice and fresh. Cafeteria's just fine."

"Excellent. I'm starved. Cook has been cross, so we get swill and slops!"

Madame Sukey grinned. "I remember now. Elliot did complain about a nave in the kitchen."

"Well, Elliot savaged his cake."

"Where has Elliot been by the way?"

"Elliot? He comes and goes. And usually returns filthy and smelly like a camel's arse."

"That is smelly!" agreed Madame with aplomb.

"I am so sorry!"

"My dear Westbrook, do not stand on ceremony with me. Let us have tea. It'll do you a world of good." She turned round and called, "I'll be back in a moment!" to the disappointed rumble.

The men called her back, inviting Madame to play cards, then chiding William for whisking her away so soon.

CHAPTER 29

An excerpt from Jack Johnson's Notes
Saturday 12 September 1942
WESTERN DESERT

"I HAD HOPED, Jack, that rathole digging and trench sleeping were over. But Sergeant must send us on petty errands. And alone, don't you think?"

"Isn't it a rule to travel out here in groups, at least two vehicles, in case…"

"In case? What could possibly happen that hasn't already happened to us?" Toc reaches for the shovel, eyeing it with disfavor. Then, after he glares at the patch of scrub beneath his feet and examines the blisters on his palms, he strikes the ground and digs steadily on.

"Dig deep, I don't want a tank to crush me."

"Of course," Toc drawls.

Suddenly, there is movement along the horizon.

"Quickly, to the trench!"

A lorry pulls up close, a giant Star of David painted on its side. Then three middle aged men pop out speaking in what sounds like German.

"Toc, what do you make of this?"

"Yiddish," he whispers.

"Gibberish?"

"No, Yiddish, Jewish language. Sounds like German but isn't."

"Not Germans?"

"Not sure. No of course not, look at that star. A Jerry wouldn't dare drive *that* lorry! Come out, Jack."

One of the men notices us and is taken aback.

"Hello," Toc hails him, raising a hand in a friendly salute.

The three soldiers look at each other, no doubt wondering whether we are friends or foes.

"Private Toc, and this is Jack, Private Johnson. How do you do?"

Again the Germanic barrage assails us. Then one of the soldiers extends his hand and introduces himself and his comrades in English.

"Will you join us in celebrating our New Year's Eve?"

"New Year's Eve?"

"The Jewish New Year begins this evening," Private Mosenson explains. "Join us? We were headed to our base camp but got lost. The sun is setting, so we celebrate now."

Behind him, his comrades are laying out a field blanket and a box with jars of jam and crackers, some oranges and dried fruit packets.

"Normally we eat honey, apples, pomegranates, cake, and fish but the jam will do," Mosenson continues.

"So is there a special ceremony?" Toc is actually intrigued, ready to stay and learn more about this ritual of welcoming some other religion's New Year.

"We pray. We sing and we eat. And we usually drink some wine but tonight we have jam and water."

"But why fish, by the way?" Toc, as he often does, recollects one inconsequential fact and inquires about it.

"A symbol of abundance."

Two of them laugh, quietly.

"Their grandmother used to eat the head of the fish, and they can never forget that. For children, watching a fish head eaten is an unforgettable sight."

"They are brothers?"

Mosenson nods.

"In the same regiment?"

"No. We got special permission to get together to celebrate our New Year."

"Well, happy new year!" Toc grins and pulls a flask from his belt. "It's my emergency rum."

Ever since Toc learned of how I 'irrigated' his shrapnel injury and how he lost consciousness in the ditch from blood loss, he has been following his father's instructions, carrying rum with him. "Mix the rum with the jam. Pretend it's wine." His smile is so genuine that Mosenson and his friends again invite us to join their meal and afterward they help us dig our hole in the ground then drive off into the darkness.

"So, we've made friends in the newly formed Jewish Palestine Regiment of the British Army," Toc concludes.

Somehow, the ceremony, the singing, and the meager meal blanket us in warmth and peace, if only for an hour.

#

Sunday 13 September 1942
WESTERN DESERT

185

"You're back."

"Yes, Sir."

"And?"

After Toc and I give our report to Sergeant, I drive our lorry to the mechanics' area, to clean out the gearbox.

Although it is just past ten in the morning, conditions in the field are scorching hot.

Stripping to my shorts, my back bare with identity disks at my neck, I stare at the lorry and wonder how any machine can operate with such a coating of sand.

There is a mechanic who has been popping in and out of lorries and jeeps like a jack in the box, switching engines on and off, muttering a litany of complaints about the inoperable field service vehicles.

He is close to me, so I ask for his help.

"It's no good," he tells me, his long fingers flutter as tentacles at the end of his arm, trying to dismiss me. His fingers are relatively clean, for a mechanic.

"No good? This lorry *has* to work!"

"No," he shakes his head. "But you go on, and leave this bit of Jerry rubbish with me. I'll see what I can do." He smiles at me and something about his smile reminds me of that chap in Cairo, Elliot Westbrook.

"Who are you?" I ask and examine every bit of his uniform, only it is difficult to determine really who he is, and what regiment he comes from. We are all pretty much stripped to our shorts, boots and socks, and a beanie or a wide-brimmed hat to shade our heads.

"Don't worry about me. Worry about yourself. They're conducting another one of those venereal disease check ups. Very public and personal, don't you think?" His eyes shine bright and his brows jump up and down in a face that radiates puckish delight. "Trot along, I'll watch over your lorry!"

"No, no."

"No?" Undoubtedly, he expects me to obey his gruff dismissal. Even the threat of a medical check up fails to upset me, and that surprises him above all.

"Who are you?" I ask.

This mechanic's speech smacks of upper class staccato and bravado, sharply reminding me of Toc. And because every move this man makes brings to mind Elliot Westbrook, the man who pretended to be a Frenchman courting Madame Sukey, I stand steadfast.

"Where are your identifying disks?"

"Damn!" His fingers shoot to his neck.

186

"I mistook you for a mechanic. But I'll call you Dr. Leclerc."

His eyes rest on me, and there is none of that gleeful mischief in them now.

"Leclerc. Madame Sukey's beau, only you are no longer French nor are you as old and stooped as you appeared in Cairo. So perhaps you're not Dr. Leclerc."

"Certainly not," he says with cheerful negation.

"Westbrook, then. Elliot Westbrook."

"Listen here, are you going to drive away with that lorry of yours or not?"

"It's rubbish. What do you need it for?"

"Why is it that nothing in this camp works? I am trying to drive off with any number of vehicles and all I get for my troubles is burps and snorts in the face!"

"What do you need a vehicle for?"

"Transport," he replies.

"Transport? Look here, what are you doing?" I ask, alarmed, when he thrusts his head into my lorry and examines the controls. "What on earth?"

"Does it run? Why is it here? Looks operable."

"How far and how long?" I ask.

"Damn. I'm out of time. Where are the keys?"

"Westbrook, how far do you have to go?"

"I have two friends that I have to extricate."

"I go with you."

The man eyes me with a sardonic smile. "What, what, have we forgotten English? Back to caveman utterances? I go with you?"

"Fine. Have it your way, Westbrook, but if you take me with you, if you promise to take me with you, mind, I'll get you a lorry that runs, that runs well."

"And no one will be searching for you?"

I shake my head.

"Who are you?" he snaps. "I cannot have an entire camp chasing after me because I've just abducted one of its cubs. I'm in no position to take any such chances. Besides, you have the advantage of me. Who are you? What's your name? How d'you come to suspect that I'm Madame's Leclerc, whoever the hell he is, or Westbrook?"

"Jack Johnson. No one'll be looking for me. Not today - not until noon tomorrow. We're gearing up today, so it's mostly the mechanics who are busy at the moment."

Elliot casts a scornful glance at the dusty vehicles. "Really?"

"As you're well aware, most of us are at the parade ground or getting medical check ups. But as for you, I know very well who you are, Elliot Westbrook. And you were impersonating Leclerc, Dr. Leclerc, wooing Madame Sukey for her nightclub! For shame! She is a fine lady."

"Good Lord! Where did you hear such a load of tosh? Yes, I am Westbrook but not this Leclerc chap and not with Madame. She's in her late fifties! And has halitosis!"

"Maybe, but I'm certain that you were Dr. Leclerc earlier in June, after the Gazala Line disaster and before the First Battle. It was my friend who spoke to the Auk about you and brought attention to your talents, if I may call what you do to elderly women as such."

"Cheeky, aren't you?" Elliot speaks softly and steps close to trace an insouciant finger along my cheek. His tone is not friendly, and his stare bores into me.

I brush him off brusquely. "Fuck off!"

He only laughs.

"Look here," I insist. "I don't relish your company more than you do mine, but I know that you're up to something. I was injured and cannot man the anti-tank guns. I've got reconnaissance, patrol, report writing. Secretarial duties. I can't bear it. I'd rather help you. One could always use another set of helping hands."

"But you're injured. I don't need a set of injured hands."

"I'm well enough."

Elliot eyes me solemnly. "Get your kitbag."

"And Toc."

"Toc? What, must you bring your teddy bear?"

"May I bring Toc along then?"

"As you will."

"You said it was a teddy bear, not a fully grown man as black as a Moore!"

"He's tanned."

"Black!" Elliot spits.

"Sun burnt, actually, just look at all the blisters he has," I insist.

"His hair isn't sunburnt!"

"It's not much darker than yours!" I snap. I hate this man criticizing Toc.

"Are you two aware that I am standing right here?" asks Toc, his clipped, upper-class intonation pronounced. He is indignant. Has he taken offense? "There's no need for all the effusive compliments."

"And I suppose that you, too, are injured or convalescing or lonely, and seeking my company?"

Toc's eyes narrow, blue fire emanating outward with anger. "No. I'm here with Jack."

"Look, there's no room for a couple of pretty boys here. I'm not a nursemaid. I can't..." Elliot breaks off, recalling his promise. "Hop on," he says in resignation, pointing at the lorry. He opens the door and slides inside, his feet and hands busy with the pedals and gearbox.

Toc, brusque and matter of fact, still bristling at either being called 'black as a Moore' or 'pretty boy,' plunges in and asks, "Where're we going and what are the orders?"

"We're looking for a certain Bedouin tribe. We'll pay a social call on an Axis outpost. Not too far off the road and low on the ridge."

"If only the flies would fuck off my face," I snarl as a swarm converges on my sores and lands in my eyes.

"Help yourself." Elliot points to a tin full of insect powder, while Toc automatically reproves with, "Language, Jack."

Then the lorry bucks and lurches forward at alarming speed, and we careen out of camp with an eldritch screech at our wake.

Hours later, when we pass yet another dilapidated village and get more stones thrown at us, Toc complains, "This is not the first town that we drive through and a bunch of village boys hurtle stones at us for sport."

"Didn't you recognize the star painted on Jack's lorry?" asks Elliot.

"The Jewish Legion?"

"Yes."

"Damn!" Toc shoots a glance at me.

"It was the only one that was operable. Your friend, Mosenson, lent it to me."

"Who's Mosenson?" Elliot asks.

"Yesterday, Toc made friends with a Jewish chap from a kibbutz in Palestine. So, Mosenson, a driver, lent me a lorry from their company. For 24 hours."

"Hey, what's this?" Elliot calls out in surprise as a bundle of fur blinks up at him.

"Bandar!"

"He's a monkey," Toc explains as the monkey groggily climbs out of Toc's kitbag.

"Has he been sleeping all this time?" I ask.

"Bandar's been sleeping poorly at night," Toc admits. "His owner could not take care of him so we took him in."

Noticing Toc's sudden melancholy, I hurry to describe the fright Bandar gave Turner.

"We share a tent with two blokes. Turner, a giant Yorkshireman, is petrified of Bandar."

Toc breaks into a peal of laughter and Elliot looks at him.

This Elliot chap actually cares, I realize, so I continue my tale. "Bandar doesn't like to cuddle for too long at night, and Toc is a restless sleeper."

"It's the abominable rats!" Toc protests.

"Abominable rats?" Elliot asks.

"Yes, at our camp, the rats are 'abominable' and the fetor of unburied bodies is 'hateful,' blood and cordite stench is 'repulsive,' and that's that."

"Better than the unimaginative curse words you assail us with!" sniffs Toc, as I reach out and give his shoulder a punch.

"So, back to Bandar and the Pudding," Elliot prompts me.

"Well, Bandar left our friend's bed. Hold on, what pudding?"

"Yorkshire," Elliot replies, simplicity lacing his word.

Toc chokes, "Turner would kill you for that," and I smile.

"Bandar went to Toc's bed on our first night after the retreat. From Toc's bed, he ventured elsewhere. We forgot to tell the new tent-mate about the monkey and so when a furry bundle landed on the Yorkshireman's face, oh, God, he leapt out of bed and screamed, but what a shout."

"A booming squeal."

"Impossible," Elliot interrupts.

"What is?" I ask.

"Booming squeal."

"No it isn't. Then the man jumps out naked, a veritable giant."

"He wasn't completely naked, was he?" Toc crinkles his nose.

"I suppose there were two identity disks on his chest tied on that scratchy corded cotton string. Anyway, Turner danced and shouted."

"And spewing a flow of oaths I don't recall ever hearing before in my life!"

"Penchant for beasts," I recall Turner's comment and Toc is now shaking with laughter.

"Would you consider giving Bandar away?" Elliot asks, extending his hand to Bandar, caressing the sleek fur on top of his head.

Bandar eyes Elliot and tolerates the caresses.

Toc shakes his head in the negative.

As our drive goes on, Bandar nestles in Elliot's lap. We approach the shoreline when Elliot stops the engine and orders us to go swimming almost like an indulgent uncle.

"Where?" Before me is a vast extent of undulating desert mounds. Is Elliot all right? Is he seeing a mirage?

Elliot shoots out his hand, "Look there!"

Toc strips and runs to the blue patch of warm sea, eager to wash off the flies and dirt, and all that filth that sticks to one when water is scarce and any sanitary conditions are only dreamed of.

"Don't be long." Elliot remains by the lorry, cradling Bandar.

Toc screams in pain, then I do the same. But although the saltwater burns our sores, we dive in and play in the surf, pain is soon numbed, and the refreshing, Mediterranean water is delicious.

When we return, Elliot has a fire lit and is handing us bits of clothing. Toc grabs the clean underwear while I slip on well-tailored trousers.

"Yours?"

"Yes. And freshly laundered, too," he says. "And here is a razor."

"What for?"

"Shave. When you're finished, I have tea ready."

We shave with bad grace, cursing the man.

"Well, that's better." Elliot confesses, "I had to get you two out here. You smelled something dreadful."

"Water is scarce."

"Tea?" I ask.

Elliot points to two tin mugs.

"We've certainly driven long enough. What's the plan for today?" Toc demands.

Elliot mumbles, "Reconnaissance," when a cackle echoed by a soprano yoo-hoo rips the air.

Toc jumps up, looking for his uniform.

"It's about time!" Elliot shouts, standing up and waving to a dark mass coming over the ridge.

Scrambling about, Toc and I get into our smelly uniforms, feeling grateful for the few garments we have on from Elliot's wardrobe.

"What took you so long?"

"It's your camels, Westbrook! What wretched, obstinate beasts! Where the hell did you get these bastards from? The Cairo meat market?" A tall Australian man shouts, sputtering curses left and right as he struggles to pull two slow camels forward.

"I'm glad now that I actually flew into camp," Elliot chuckles. "Was it very unpleasant?"

"It's a good thing that my dear friend has a way with beasts. *Shukran chabibi!*" the Australian looks up at the wizened bundle of rags sitting on a camel and holding a flute in his gnarled hand.

The bundle inclines his head.

"Jeep's buried in the sand with a puncture not too far from here! We'll have to fix it before we venture any further."

I recognize the tall, cantankerous Australian as my kinsman. "Bill!"

"You know him?" Elliot asks.

"My cousin."

"What are you two doing here?" Tate asks as he draws me into an embrace.

"These two jokers busted me! Your pretty blond cousin here caught me borrowing a lorry."

I squawk in protest right as Toc growls, "Wait a bit!"

"What a lorry! Could you not find one with a brighter, perhaps larger, Jewish Star of David?" Tate hurries on. "Jerry'll have a sporting good time with *that!*"

"We've already been stoned by village boys all over this bit of desert. And how are you my dear?" At the end of his speech, Elliot's voice softens, and he extends his arm to a Bedouin woman, pulling her to him. "And how did my wily wombats treat you?"

"Wombats? Wily?" Tate booms. "Take it back, Westbrook. We took good care of your girl, and it was not an easy thing and that's a fact!"

"A mighty difficult task," grumbles a shorter Australian, emerging from behind a camel. "As we had half a mind to turn back and return the lady *home*, to *safety*."

"Tom Sullivan? You here too?" I exclaim.

"We really should do with some niceties and handshakes all round," Toc interrupts and clasps the short Australian's hand and then lets his own hand disappear in Tate's massive palm. "And who is the fair lady?" Toc asks, peeking at the vision covered in a black wool robe, a vision that obliviates from our minds the old man on camelback.

"Lady Jane," says Elliot as a lovely woman emerges from under her headdress and outer robe. She has an oval, rose-complected visage and lovely lips.

Toc groans, and I swallow in astonishment, pinned to the spot.

Bandar decides that this is a great moment to introduce himself. He leaps out of the lorry and lands neatly on top of Elliot's head. "And right on cue, here's Bandar."

Lady Jane smiles at Bandar, sending my heart thundering. I catch a glimpse of Toc and he, too, is affected by that smile.

"May I hold him?" Now her voice stuns me for a moment. It is mellifluous, smooth and silky and rather low.

With an effort, I reply, "Reach your hand out to him, first." I am doing my best to recover my wits only to be thrown off again when the woman rests her gaze on me and beams a radiant smile directly my way, her eyes sparkling with delight.

"Slowly," Toc warns her, and Lady Jane extends a slender hand out to the monkey who studies her with his dark eyes. Bandar edges toward her hand, gives it a little pat and scuttles back to Elliot's neck and shoulder.

"Our turn, I believe," Sullivan approaches and Tate not far behind him.

"Makes me home sick. I miss those koalas they bring round to school."

"Koalas?" Jane turns to the Australians.

"Koalas and what nots, but we are short on time and so we need to prepare," Elliot and Bandar give us their backs and head to the lorry.

"Prepare? What do you mean? What of reconnaissance!" Toc asks.

"Reconnaissance?" Elliot shakes his head. "We have done enough of that. And enough of infecting mud puddles, too! No, not today. Today, we have bottles full of bacteria that give the runs and the ague to anyone too close to them. And we have gloves for Sullivan who will be dispensing drinks. Our Sheik is Tate. You two, since you are both young and slim and rather pretty and best of all *tanned*, if I may comment on that, you two will put on robes and join the performance. Only try to appear less tall. Can you dance?"

"What?" Toc straightens up, bristling.

"Dance?" My voice catches.

"Johnson, we're going into the desert as a tribe of Bedouins."

"Bedouins don't dance!" Toc interjects.

"Jerries don't know that. Besides, our tribe does dance."

"A tribe is much larger!"

"We've an excuse, Toc. British boys shot our tribe down. So we like *Alman*."

"You cannot be serious!" Toc is incredulous. "No!"

"What Toc means is that it is one thing for him to point the barrel of a gun at the enemy and another to enter an enemy camp as a Bedouin, a dancing Bedouin."

Toc's voice sharpens as he exclaims, "But this is straight out of the One Thousand and One Nights tales of Ali Baba. Is Lady Jane to be the brave and resourceful Morgiana? First boiling thieves in hot oil and then dancing a sword dance and stabbing the leader?"

"Remarkable memory! I'd forgotten all about the hot oil," exclaims Elliot, awe brightening his features.

"I hate to bring this literary orgy to an end but let us get ready," Tate urges. "And there'll be no stabbing, my dear Toc, because Elliot vomits at the sight of blood."

"It's true," Elliot says. "We'll do our utmost to avoid bloodshed, on my account. Now, put on some smelly robes and leather-strap sandals."

"What? No glittery bras for us?" I ask only to receive a fulminating glare from Toc.

"Jack! Do you know how hairy my chest is? And, no, absolutely not. I am not shaving my chest!"

"Robes only, Toc. Jack, we won't exactly dance. Just play some music, and you can move your hips a bit, long enough to distract Jerry's attention from what Sullivan is doing," Tate consoles Toc.

But to our horror, Jane produces rouge and kohl. Then she darkens our eyelashes. The only pleasant aspect to the nightmare of being dressed as a woman is Lady Jane's proximity to our faces. It has been months since we were near a woman, and such an incredibly beautiful woman.

Once lips and eyes are nicely altered, Jane darkens my flaxen hair with something that smells a lot like shoe polish.

Toc whispers, "This stuff reeks! I'm certainly glad now that I'm black as a …" he falters.

Lady Jane is letting her hair down. It's like a waterfall of warm caramel flowing down her slender back. Toc cannot remove his eyes from her hair and neither can Sullivan.

As Tate pulls Jane's hair and applies the horrible black coloring, simultaneous cries from the old man on the camel, Toc, and Sullivan rip the silence.

Jane laughs. She turns to the man on the camel and says something in Arabic to him and he nods in resignation.

Whistling, seemingly unmoved, Tate continues to massacre the caramel tones with dark sludge.

"I can't bear it," Toc announces and walks away, busying himself cleaning his gun, running a rag over it with jerky motions.

The jeep is not far at all. We follow the tracks and in less than an hour we reach a jeep with a puncture, a lowly patch of scrub its only companion.

While Elliot and Tate take care of the jeep, Jane is practicing her dance.

It is the drumming or the dance for me, and I choose to paradiddle on a leather drum skin. To my surprise, the small drum is heavy. Together with the old man with the flute, we eventually reach some harmony and consistency. I find it odd that no one has introduced the old man yet.

Meanwhile, Toc glowers at me from under a heavy lining of kohl outlining his blue eyes. His scowl makes it hard to look at him. Nonetheless, his hips are moving and rather well despite Bandar's affectionate hold on his neck.

I call Bandar, but my hair offends him, either the color or the smell, and he wants nothing to do with me.

"Not bad," Elliot declares and waves his hands in a gesture we come to understand as a summons to the jeep and lorry. "Both the jeep and lorry stay behind. We walk from here. Pull the beasts along but, if we're spotted, hide behind the brutes. After all, I did get them at the meat market." He grins. "Toc speaks German and Italian. So Toc stays close to sheik Tate in the lead. Right then, Lady Jane, who also speaks German, walks in the middle, but I want utter silence from you," he levels a stare at Lady Jane.

"Arabic?" she asks.

"Not unless it's necessary. Your voice, you know," he trails off.

I turn to Toc. "What about her voice?"

"Silky," he replies barely above a whisper.

I stare at Toc, uncomprehending.

"Jack, Lady Jane's voice is not at all guttural. It's unusual. Also, it's a fact that women often remain silent in the company of men."

Then I hear Tate inquiring about my role. "What about Sullivan and my little cousin?"

"Little? Your cousin's almost as tall as you are," Elliot barks.

"I'm six inches shorter."

"And Jack has a round, baby face," adds Toc grimly. "Not angular and roughhewn as yours, Tate. Are you really related?"

"Why not draw his portrait then?" Tate retorts. "Until such time, what's Johnson's baby face going to do?"

"Navigate," Elliot replies. "Also, keep an eye on Jane at all times, Johnson, especially while you play the drum. You won't be able to hear much so use your eyes."

Toc shoots me a surprised look.

"Be ready for any sign of hostility," Elliot continues. "Sullivan, you stay close to Jane, too. Except when you brew up coffee and serve. Toc can work with you so he can alert you to anything they say about us and their intentions." He looks at Toc. "It's good to have linguists."

"You forgot me," Tate rasps and pulls out his pliers and a bundle of wires. "Sheik Tate. Master saboteur. Although, I must admit, Sullivan is just as good."

"And one more thing," Elliot looks up at the old man with a gentle smile. "Anyone who's injured, make sure that you see Joseph when we're out of danger. He'll set you to right."

How? I wonder and hear a murmur from Toc, "Whack us on the head with his flute?"

#

Approaching an enemy pillbox, I pray that they are not trigger happy and don't shoot us on sight! Has Elliot taken that possibility into account? Probably not, because he has not been out here as we have. He is a privileged entity dangling himself at GHQ every now and then and this is his war, his bit toward the war effort.

But as I watch him move and direct, I must admit that Elliot is good at what he does, and his scheme certainly has merit. An enemy pillbox handicapped with disease is a clear passage at least through that stretch of armored ridge line.

"Jack," growls Toc. "I'll get you for this adventure!" Kohl is smudged round his bloodshot eyes, his lips hidden behind a filthy black veil.

"Your eyes look dreadful. Do I look like you?"

"Worse! You're not as pretty," he says, trying to sound malicious, gives another growl then twitches his hip, belly dancer-like, only it is a hard maneuver for a man, especially a man who is marching covered in thick black robes, a water vase balanced on his head, and an automatic strapped to his thigh.

"Watch it," Tate slows down and glances at a jebel, looming above the scruffy terrain.

Quickly, Elliot, Toc, and I creep up the hillock and observe the activity on the jebel. The enemy is using the scruffy vegetation on a ridge for cover.

"Italians," Toc whispers.

An Italian soldier is climbing back up with his shovel.

"So, they too know about the shovel trot?"

Elliot looks at me, confused.

"We're all told to cover up our shit."

"We bury excrement to reduce fly infestation," Toc elaborates. "To avoid the spread of disease."

"It's more than likely that they already have the shits. Most of them, actually, most of us often have the runs," I say sotto voce as I edge close to Elliot.

"Yes. But it won't do to lose hope, and the contents of our cocktail are stronger stuff than just plain old dysentery. It packs in fever with a rash or some such thing, I cannot recall precisely what the scientist told me."

Toc pushes us both flat and hisses, "Look out. Here's another one. He looks to be of some rank."

I want to tell him to get off of me so I can peek, but Toc is motionless, taking shallow breaths. When his weight is lifted, he whispers, "Better join the others."

We carefully scramble back down when Toc says to Elliot, "I hope that your flute player will cooperate."

"He's an excellent musician. He'll behave himself, and notably too, because he's no coward. And his expertise, besides music, is precisely what we should hope to avoid. He taught my brothers how to suture horses and donkeys!"

"Horses and donkeys? So, if I'm injured, how will he administer to me?"

"It's a good question, Toc. Do you see yourself as a horse or a donkey?" Elliot asks.

"I'm a camel," I chime in.

They snort with laughter.

"That brother of mine, the little one, William, was forever collecting curs and tourists' camels or donkeys that had been so ill-treated it was a wonder that they had made it *that* far and *that* close to the pyramids! Fear not. Joseph worked for my grandfather. He's retired now, of course."

"Joseph?"

"Joseph. An Egyptian Copt. Joseph had the charge of my grandfather's stables. Now that he has retired, I asked him to play music at my club, Monnayeur's. It's better that way, you know, for older people to be kept busy. Keeps them alive, and happier."

"Well, in that case... It's just that I have not been impressed by natives."

Elliot glances at Toc, bemused.

On our return, Elliot summons our company and gives his final orders.

197

We fall into our respective places in silence. Joseph begins to play a slow, melancholy melody. I tap the drum to Joseph's tempo.

"*Yallah, yallah!*" Elliot shouts. And as Jane ululates a good long "*lulululu,*" I wonder how she has the breath to do so while walking behind a nasty camel that spits and grunts and urinates on its own hind legs disrespectfully.

An Italian soldier pops his head out then summons his comrades. One of them runs up with a gun in his hand but the others hold him off. They gesture for us to come round their high perched defense box on the ridge, pointing to an easier place to ascend with our gear and camels. One of them speaks a few words in Arabic.

Elliot glibly replies that we are the tribe's last survivors. "British attack!" he shouts, pulling his hair.

The Italians are inquisitive and try to ascertain precisely where had we run into British forces.

Elliot's reply is oriental at best, with the sense of direction worthy of a hobgoblin. "We have coffee with nice soldiers, then we go," he says in slow simple Arabic, hoping the soldiers will understand and agree to be entertained. "Cafe?" Elliot throws in a word that sounds like Italian for coffee.

Meanwhile, Tate, using his great height to advantage, scans the dugouts the Italians set up, memorizing such information as type and quantity of ammunition and type and location of communication gear. He edges close to the communication line and indicates to Toc to set up his cushions while Joseph plays a sharp tune that distracts the Italians momentarily.

Soon after, Toc is busily helping Sullivan brew up coffee, deftly hiding Sullivan from view as Sullivan taps the scientific cocktail over tin mugs.

Watching Lady Jane dance like a goddess as I beat the drum, I consider the effects of heat on the precious bacteria. But since it takes Toc and Sullivan an age to serve, I realize that they let the brew cool down sufficiently and I cannot but admire the simplicity of the plot. I cast a glance at the Italians watching Jane.

Lust and impatience register in their smiles.

Elliot catches my eye, and I rise. Banging on the drum louder, I edge close to the Italians, nudging Jane out of their reach.

Elliot watches the Italians then immediately returns his gaze to Jane then back to the Italians. He is on the lookout for any attempts on her. He looks at Tate, who is sitting regally on a wooly cushion. Tate claps, then Jane backs away and Joseph comes forward for a solo. There is a murmur of disagreement over this change but the sheik's orders are tolerated at least for the next minute or two as the coffee is served. The Italians eagerly bring the dark tepid liquid to their lips. One bloke downs it like a shot of whiskey.

Soon, discomfort registers on some of the soldiers' faces and Tate decides to stand up, magnificent in his great height, and declares, "*Yallah*, we go!"

The Italians protest. Some are holding their crotches, others are caressing their guns but our party is already packed and moving. I fear that the inevitable fight will erupt at any moment. What man stranded in the desert for months on end can resist a dancing woman who is protected by an old sheik, a couple of musicians, a weepy buffoon, and some women?

It is then that Toc wails like a woman in pain and vomits in violent cascades over the soldiers closest to him.

Events take shape rather rapidly and to our advantage.

The soiled soldiers cry out and yell at the ugly woman to go away, when one of the Italians gets up and grabs the shovel. He walks away quickly. But he never quite makes it out of sight of his comrades. A terrible smell and loud sounds attend his retreat. A volley of laughter erupts.

We slip away as the Italians are distracted with discomfort or pain or trying to get rid of Toc's vomit and their comrades' mess that for several moments we hear nothing but rapid fire Italian.

But as we rush down the ridge, we hear the first shot.

Tate halts. He pulls and releases a grenade, his long arm sending it off with a powerful thrust upward, where it lands only meters away from the enemy dugout. A wall of sand rises up as Toc and Sullivan release more grenades, and the salt-flat dust rises, lingering airborne, shielding our retreat.

Elliot looks ruefully at the camels. He wants to take them but cannot. They will only slow us down.

As he runs, although with some difficulty, Joseph casts a wistful look at the camels too and I wonder at him. Does Joseph lament the loss of the camels? Does he wish to ride one? Is he sorry to leave the beasts to their fate?

We run to the patch of scrub where we hid our jeep and lorry under a tarpaulin covered with dirt and branches.

Although curses and gun fire chase our dust cloud, none of us is hit. Delirious and exhausted, we pile into the lorry and jeep.

As the engines roar to life, we find ourselves smiling. Even Toc, who had taken Sullivan's Ipecac and is consequently weak and out of sorts, is grinning, shaking his head at our narrow escape, and holding tightly to Bandar as he whispers soothing words to the monkey who had to stay under the lorry in his cage while we attended to the Italians.

"What'd you leave behind?"

Tate grins innocently.

"Did you slip something into their communication box?" Elliot asks Tate.

"A valedictory gift. A bit of gelignite cocktail in a cylinder and some acid eating…" Tate's description is cut short.

An explosion sends a column of dust up in the air.

"Too much gelignite? It's all still in the experimental stage!" Tate shouts as he pushes down hard on the gas pedal. Driving at alarming speed, he continues, "But, they won't be making any telephone calls tonight."

That evening, we camp only a few miles away from Alexandria. And by the fire, Joseph gives a few short tunes on the flute, quietly, unobtrusively. Toc expresses his wish that we could have reached more than one camp. "I want to wreak havoc on more than one pillbox a day. I want do a lot more damage. And what's more," he adds darkly, "I don't want to run the risk of one pillbox warning the next of our arrival or of the results of drinking our coffee."

"Or worse," Tate says.

"Or, of us traveling with Lady Jane." At this, Toc looks into Elliot's eyes with a grave expression and Elliot inclines his head.

"A stroke of brilliance, Toc, that you vomited on the guns!" Sullivan breaks the tension.

A round of laughter ensues as we recall the wrathful expression on the soldiers' faces who were showered with the horrid stuff.

"I had to vomit on the guns. They all wanted, well, they all wanted one thing and were about to point their guns at us."

"I wish we could go on to other pillboxes but damn it having no camels makes it hard!" Tate interjects. "It isn't as convincing."

"I'll go into as many pillboxes or camps as you like, but without Lady Jane," Toc says resolutely, and even adds, "I can learn to dance so there would be only men on such expeditions."

"Toc, it's very kind of you. But I dance and I also speak Arabic."

"It is kind, isn't it. At the same time, it's nonsensical," Elliot retorts gruffly. "Have you tried to dance like that before? We tried it and nearly killed ourselves trying. Well, not Sullivan. He had a jolly good time."

"Shove off, Westbrook," Sullivan squawks.

"Besides, what makes you think they wanted only Jane?" Elliot taunts.

"They'll take any…" Tate begins but stops as Toc growls, "Ladies present."

"If you are set on learning the dance, I can teach you, Toc, though it requires a lot of practice." Jane directs a grateful smile at Toc which makes me feel like an ogre not to have voiced my thoughts on Jane's safety. And I notice Sullivan turning dark red and averting his eyes after Elliot shoots him a comical look, lifting his eyebrows, whispering something like 'Soad.'

Elliot admits in subdued tones, "The one bit about this whole operation that I dislike above all is exposing Lady Jane to the danger of rape."

Silence follows the utterance of the very word we want to block out. But the solemn silence that falls on the party as each one of us contemplates what could have befallen us, besides rape, is soon broken again by Sullivan. "What should we name our operation?"

"What do you mean?" Tate asks.

"You know, Jasper Maskelyne was allowed to form the Camouflage Experimental Unit or, as he calls it, the Magic Gang, in return for performing before the troops to raise morale. And the engineers working on the dummy tanks and lorries out in the desert named their operation: Bertram. What about our operation?"

"It's not common knowledge yet," Elliot reprimands Sullivan in hushed tones.

"And it's not just dummy tanks either," Toc adds. "We have trucks that are tanks and tanks that are trucks and many more decoys and misdirection plans for enemy intelligence."

"So, you know about that?"

"I do. Jack and I made a lot of noise that we needed decoys and we were put in possession of some facts. The Auk himself, in fact, led us to believe that such a plan was indeed in progress and one day we drove into the midst of such a group of tanks disguised as trucks," Toc explains. "I also spoke to the Auk about you, Westbrook."

Elliot shoots Toc a glance then transfers his steady gaze to me.

Still under Elliot's direct scrutiny, I say, "Sullivan, you want a name for our operation? Well, I have it. Let's call it, Operation Seven Veils! You know, after the Seven Veils Dance in Oscar Wilde's play!"

"Oh, God no!" exhales Elliot, thrusting his hands to cover his face. "I'll never live that one down in headquarters! And what will my brother say to that?"

"James or William?" Tate asks.

"The baby," Elliot grumbles. "William."

"Seven Veils Dance? You mean that horrid dance scene from Oscar Wilde's play, *Salome*? No, no, that's too much!" Toc shakes his head. "And besides, your memory betrays you, Jack. It's known as the Dance of the Seven Veils."

"Then just Operation Seven Veils," suggests Sullivan who, of all present, actually seems to approve of the name.

"How about operation Seven Shits?" suggests Elliot and a roar of laughter ensues.

"Operation Seven Shits it is, mate! And let's have no more arguing about it!" Tate agrees, and with Australian enthusiasm shakes hands first with Elliot then with each of us in turn.

"Sheik Tate and his Operation Seven Shits," gurgles Jane and as her lilting voice carries the offending words to our sand-filled ears we are doubled up again. Am I dreaming all this?

I am in the desert, never far from bodies and minefields and Stukas and Messerschmitts, with tears of mirth running down my cheeks as I cheer on Operation Seven Shits, and a monkey is doing back flips in excitement as the melody of a flute travels across the dunes.

#

Wednesday 16 September 1942
CAIRO, EGYPT

"Elliot Effendi!" Ali began then his hessian sack issued a most disturbing string of yowls.

"Ali, what the devil is in the sack? Release it at once! And in a wadi far, far away from here, away from my brother. Lord knows we have enough strays on our hands." Elliot's temper was not at all affable after a horrendous visit to the old tailor's shop. Elliot certainly despised having to stand in the sweltering workshop to be measured for his wedding suit. But it was more than that. The tailor was a nasty specimen who enjoyed pricking his wealthy patrons with both needle and tongue.

"Effendi, Elliot Effendi," gasped the fourteen year old Ali, struggling to control his rapidly changing vocal chords.

Elliot eyed the boy. He was not handsome by any means and, at his particular stage of the masculine life cycle and mutation from boy to man, Ali was far from being an engaging creature. But Elliot had known the boy all his life, and was willing even now in his current ill humor to be patient with Ali, bestowing a reluctant smile on him. "Ali, what is it?"

202

"The horrible cook!" he managed, then regretted his words as Elliot asserted that he was well aware that, "Cook's a devil!"

"Yes," Ali interjects Elliot's acidic remark along with some of the spicier swear words he had picked up in the suk.

"Well, what is it then?"

"I have a black cat for the devil."

Elliot paused. "A black cat you say?" A wicked smile altered Elliot's face only to change again as he thrust a hand into his pocket. "Here you are, my boy. Go to the best shop and get us a feast. Bring it back to William's room, at the guesthouse! Go!"

"Effendi?" Ali raised his noisy sack.

Elliot grabbed the mewing and yowling bundle and held it tightly. "Go. Meet me at William's room. In the guesthouse. *Yallah*!"

Watching Ali skip and stumble out of the estate and into the teeming streets of Cairo. Taxis and donkey carts and heavy foot traffic never slowed down the eager boy.

Elliot lit a cigarette and turned his attention to the kitchen. Outside the back door, a thin maid was sweeping rotten vegetable remains by the dustbins.

"Salomé!"

Salomé raised her head in surprise.

"Where's Cook?" Elliot growled. His ill humor lent his mannerism gruffness he rarely possessed.

She stepped back as she noticed Elliot's thunderous expression.

"Where's Cook? Inside?"

Salomé pointed to the servant quarters.

"Excellent. Shout if he comes near!" Elliot made to enter the kitchen when he felt a hand grab hold of his shirt. "What is it?"

Salomé stamped her foot. She then banged on the dustbin with her broom.

Elliot broke into a bark of laughter. "You can't shout, can you? Very well, my dear, you bang if that devil comes near here! Get it? Cook comes, you - bang, bang!"

For a moment though he stood still as his changed tones and laughter altered Salomé's own features. She had removed her veil to show him that she understood his request, radiating a smile that brightened her face. "Oh, now I see," he remarked, his own breathing quickened as he felt a flush come over him. "Now I understand." He backed away from the girl and stepped into the kitchen, noisy sack still in his hand, only his steps were slower and his bad temper gone. Elliot had finally understood what attracted his younger brother to Salomé, and why William had even taken the trouble to name the little creature and not leave her mute and anonymous and neglected on the estate. She was a radiant beauty when she smiled. "And clever, too," he admitted to himself.

Opening a cupboard at random, Elliot raised the bag and dumped its contents onto a shelf loaded with crockery.

"You'll have to forgive the insult, black beast!" He shut the door on the indignant cat, grateful that the cupboard doors were well-made and with strong clasps for closure.

Shielding his eyes from the sun, Elliot bumped into Salomé. "Steady on," he wrapped his arm round her shoulders. "Come along."

Elliot escorted Salomé into William's guesthouse with his arm round her.

"Afraid?" Elliot looked at her when she faltered at the threshold, reluctant to enter. "Come."

After offering Salomé a chair, which she refused, Elliot turned his back to the girl to rifle through his brother's desk, carelessly opening and shutting drawers. "Whiskey!" he called as he pulled out a bottle. He took a long pull and replaced the whiskey back in the desk right as Ali scampered in, ululating a nasal melody, his head moving side to side, no longer fearful or even out of breath. Ali had a heavy load in his arms, and yet he was smiling.

"Ali! Come in."

But when Ali's eyes fell on Salomé, he checked.

"Come in, Ali. She'll help you set the feast."

"But, Elliot Effendi! She's a girl!"

"What of it?"

"She's a girl!"

"Yes, a girl, not a leper, damn you. Come in and shut the door. Lay out the goods and be quick about it. We celebrate as soon as we hear the cat and Cook say hello to each other!"

"Yes Elliot Effendi." Ali, his hands flapping about, directed Salomé.

Elliot glanced at the girl.

Salomé was uneasy. She cast anxious looks out the window. What worried her?

"Here he is!" Elliot said rushing away from the window and out the guesthouse.

Into the estate, drove William. Creaking out of the motorcar, the young man hauled himself out, yawned, then stretched, wearily.

Bewildered, Ali and Salomé watched as Elliot dragged his brother to William's room and thrust him inside.

William too was rather shocked at the handling of his person and was about to tell his brother off when he clapped eyes on Salomé. William's color deepened and, with an effort, he turned his attention to Elliot.

Events moved rather fast because before Elliot had fully explained what was happening he took off. Sprinting to the kitchen back door, Elliot locked the horrible cook inside with the cat.

The superstitious cook was about to be terrified by seeing a black cat, a harbinger of misfortune, in his very own kitchen.

Elliot returned to the guesthouse like a typhoon. Excited and energetic, demanding whiskey and beer and food and applause and laughing all the while, showering Ali with compliments for picking up such a hell cat, Elliot managed to turn a simple act of revenge into an outright celebration.

CHAPTER 30

Wednesday 23 September 1942
WESTERN DESERT

ELLIOT SHOOTS JANE a reassuring smile. "We'll have an easy return trip."

"Easy?"

"We'll fly back to Cairo. I've arranged it."

"Elliot, you cannot mean to fly across the desert in that horrid contraption again? I had no notion of its terrible instability, rising and falling like a leaf in the wind!"

"You disapprove of the plane that saved us hours of languishing on the tarmac?"

"Elliot, if it's all the same to you, I'd rather return by car or by jeep, or, I would even go as far as accepting a ride on an equipment carrier. In fact, I'll walk."

Tate peeks round the tent. "Westbrook, what's your position this time?"

Elliot pulls a dark wad from his coat, flinging it loose. He wraps himself with the shawl, tittering and gyrating.

"Look here, Elliot, no one warned me of you joining us again, much less dancing for me!"

"Not for you, Sheik Tate. I'll watch over Jane. She'll distract the bastards. You will ensure that they're out of commission as soon as you can. I have no intention of fighting them off! The sight of blood…"

Tate's eyes brighten suddenly as he reveals a small cylinder. "No worries, mate! Some bloke from SAS gave me a little something."

"Who? What?"

"David Stirling."

"Oh, I know him. I know him well. And I wouldn't call the founder of the SAS 'some bloke.' But what is it? What did he give you?"

"Lewes bombs."

Elliot stares at Tate. "And what do you intend to do with *bombs*?"

"Each Lewes bomb is less than half a kilo. So I can easily carry several of them."

"And?"

"Elliot, the Lewes bomb is a timed explosive device with a pencil detonator. I'll set it to go off within half an hour once I attach it to the side of a Jerry vehicle, right over the fuel tank. They won't be able to follow us. After last time, I've been thinking. Retreat is a rather tricky business."

"And did Stirling or one of his hairy apostles train you on how to use it?"

"Yes."

"Very well." Elliot then points to Tate's hands. "You better go get more dirt into your fingernails and roll in some goat cheese. You smell too English."

"I'm Australian, mate!"

"Maybe," Elliot winks. "Where's the drummer?"

A squinty eyed Australian pops his head out, his shock of black hair that smells suspiciously of shoe polish bounces over his forehead.

"Good, Sullivan's here."

"Toc and Jack, too," Sullivan points to us, a couple of darkly robed women. Toc and I are pulling up our sleeves to show a collection of knives and revolvers, strapped to our arms. Toc goes as far as lifting his dress to reveal the contraptions attached to his legs. And I do the same, wondering what on earth Lady Jane is thinking of all this.

Elliot eyes Toc, and his eyes narrow. Then he says, "Oh, very well equipped! But paint your toenails and shave the hair on your toes!"

"What?" Toc cries out.

"Details are important. You are tall and hairy." Elliot's elocution is so similar to Toc.

"We managed the first time!"

"A risk I am unwilling to take again. Lady Jane? Let's have your toenail paint, if you please. Toc first."

Toc recites a passage in French that makes Elliot's face flame up.

"Watch it, Toc!" Elliot leans close to him. "Your quotations don't make your temper any more tolerable than…"

Tate intervenes, waving rotten fruit between the two. "Is this smelly enough, do you think?"

"Christ!"

"Rotten dates!" Tate's teeth appear, as wolfish as Elliot's.

"Let's squeeze the noxious little fruit. Bad odor makes for excellent people-repellent," Elliot grumbles. And as he and Tate draw sticky, smelly liquid they attract more flies.

"It turns my stomach," Sullivan complains, resembling a sulky child among giants.

"Never-mind! Rub it into your skin."

"Must I?" Sullivan wails again but a trace of an impish grin gives the lie to his protests.

"Authenticity," Elliot says.

"You forget, the peculiar scent might keep their amorous attentions at bay," Tate adds.

"I doubt that," Toc interjects with a darkling comment.

"You volunteered," Elliot reminds him, his tone none too friendly.

Lady Jane approaches Elliot and rests her exquisitely shaped palm on his arm.

Toc breaks into a smile and offers his hand to Elliot, unable to remain bad-tempered in the presence of the radiantly beautiful Jane. "And so I did. Here, let us have that toenail varnish and rotten fruit and anything else you'd like me to have. You'll have no more churlish remarks from me. Let us have camel dung as well! Why not?"

"That's it!" Elliot claps Toc's back.

Lady Jane and I, both relieved, begin helping Toc get into character.

#

In the gloaming, we approach an Axis pillbox. We are cautious, but soon suspect that something is wrong.

There is no movement.

All the signs that this is an Italian post are there: the lorries and the machine guns. But as we get closer, the sight that awaits us is beyond all horrors. The flies swarm and their buzz is something like a siren. The limbs in the box are indistinguishable because of heat, flies, rats and maggots and because the bodies they were once attached to are peppered with bullets.

Elliot turns away, and in short sharp bursts vomits over Toc's sandals. I take a step forward in anticipation for the confrontation. I expect Toc to take offense and begin an odd, posh-sounding exchange with Elliot, but Toc does nothing more than pull Elliot's sleeve. He drags him down the slope, giving the alarm to Sullivan and Tate to keep Lady Jane back.

I pick up one of the bullet shells and pocket it. I want to know who hit the box.

Lady Jane stares at Elliot's stricken face.

"Change of plan," Elliot groans, wiping his mouth on his filthy black sleeve. "Where's the next box?"

I am in charge of intelligence and navigation, something that never fails to buy sniggers from Toc, but not this time.

Elliot and Toc stand close together, stooped, and wait for me to come back with coordinates.

With only a few nods and grunts that puncture the mask of stoic silence, we agree to drop off supplies at a rendezvous point for the LRDG and SAS, then go on to our next destination, a German box, according to recent RAF reconnaissance.

Our jeeps were serviced before we left LRDG base camp, and so Elliot is driving rather fast, tenaciously pressing the pedal hard, only calling on me to switch gears when making a sharp turn. Toc and I are crammed together with Elliot while Lady Jane is squeezed between the two Australians in a separate jeep with an SAS Vickers' machine-gun looming above their heads. Our jeep, instead of a machine-gun, carries water, food, and medical rations to be dropped off at a rendezvous point.

"That was some box," I remark.

"Yes," Elliot replies, abrupt and distracted.

"The rendezvous isn't far from here. Slow down, Westbrook," Toc stiffens and scans the horizon which is cast in deep shadows.

"I can't see a thing," I complain.

"Look for signs of movement. Make a mental note of what you see, then look for anything that's changed."

"There's a rendezvous area near Bir Chalda. But we are not equipped to go that far. Our drop point is here, along the Qattara Depression, and with luck we might meet some of the LRDG men. They might need to communicate with HQ," I talk, my mouth dry, but I feel that I must talk because Elliot and Toc are pensive and the deadly stare in Elliot's eyes and Toc's intent scanning of the space ahead unnerve me.

"Here. Stop."

Elliot brings the jeep to a shuddering halt at Toc's command.

I turn to look at Tate's jeep and notice that Sullivan is manning the Vickers' gun, his eyes in a pronounced squint.

Engines are switched off, and the silence that ensues is almost deafening in its absoluteness. Even the dust our jeeps have kicked up is settling down.

Tate is first to jump out and walk about, searching the precise location to drop off the water jugs and rations.

Elliot follows him, dirty and shaken.

When the two find what they are looking for, Tate gives a cry of delight. But Sullivan remains by the Vickers, and I stay frozen, alert to a danger I can almost sense, one thigh against the gearbox, another against Toc's thigh and my hands holding a gun at the ready.

Elliot begins to unload. "Not you," he says gruffly to Lady Jane who makes to get up.

Sullivan hands Lady Jane field glasses like a toy offered to a scolded child by an indulgent, maiden aunt.

And it's then that we hear it.

The steady roar of approaching aircraft, two M.E. 110's, a couple of pale menaces flying into the setting sun, catching its last rays, sparkling silver for a moment, terrifies us. We scuttle out of the jeeps and into cracks and crevices in the wadi walls. We crouch motionless until the drone of the engines echoes in the distance, then dies down altogether. Elliot has Jane under him, his body covering her, pressing her into the gritty hard surface of the crevice none too gently. He recovers and steps back and reaches to steady Jane. With a handkerchief that he miraculously produces from his black robe, he wipes the dust off of her face.

Toc growls, "He covers her and I have to cover the nuisance," then shoots a withering glare at Bandar, who looks adoringly back at him.

"It's the shoe-polish. He won't come near me or any of us, because of the horrific smell."

Toc heads to the rations, briskly unloads and delivers the neat packets into a cache Tate had unearthed moments before the interruption.

"No sense in driving on tonight. It's too dark," Tate declares.

Toc breathes a sigh of relief and drops down against the wadi wall, closing his eyes.

"Check for scorpions," I say as I throw a blanket over Toc.

I drop heavily by his side.

Toc looks languidly all round him. Then he closes his eyes and falls asleep.

At day break, when the rising sun casts long shadows on the desert, we head toward a recently constructed German pillbox.

As we skirt along the Qattara Depression during the hottest part of the day, relying on the heat haze to obscure our tracks from enemy aircraft, I edge close to Elliot, trying to give the sleeping Toc more room.

"Westbrook, look ahead," I lean forward.

Elliot swears and swerves the jeep toward the cover of green scrub.

A rather prominent ridge comes into view.

"Wake Toc up! We could use his superhuman vision right now."

As Toc opens his eyes, his body is shivery and his stare confused, sweat pooled in the crook of his neck, and he wipes some drool from his mouth.

"Toc, look at that ridge. What d'you make of it?"

"Jerry," he says, his voice still sleepy which makes the pronouncement all the more frightening.

"Tate!" Elliot swivels to call the approaching Australian. "Jerry."

"Anyone there?" Tate leans close to Elliot. "Did they see us, do you think?"

"Only if they have someone like Toc," Elliot admits. "Someone with superhuman vision that can see through the heat haze."

Snapping out of exhausted sleep a drive in the desert can induce, Jane and Sullivan look owlishly about. Together, they scramble to our jeep.

Sullivan runs his hand over his forehead, mixing shoe polish dye and sweat across his face.

"Germans. Up on the ridge. I cannot see them now but when we were driving, exposed on the dunes, Jack saw movement and Toc determined that they were Germans," Tate explains.

"Well? We don't have camels and Joseph isn't here to play the flute, but we're here and I'd like to see my painted toenails put to good use," Toc drawls. "After all, I even shaved for the occasion!"

"We shaved yesterday," Sullivan complains.

"We go." Elliot's lips are a grim line. He jumps out, his robes billowing about his legs.

We stare at each other, rather somber.

"Stoop and shuffle this time," Elliot advises. "We will be victims of British cruelty. Jane, the only surviving daughter of Sheik Tate, will be assisted on by her maid or companion. No dancing, damn them, and no music. Lots of veils, cover our faces."

"I'll play the drum as we march. I want to give them the alert so they are not jumpy and trigger happy," I suggest.

Elliot glances at us.

Tate and Sullivan shrug.

"I'll support Lady Jane," Toc volunteers then looks at her. "Would you mind it terribly?"

"Your hand will not be free to pull the trigger, though. In case..."

"Can you shoot?" he asks her and she nods.

"I gave her lessons," Elliot admits. "Well, then, we march. Jane stumbles close to the foothills, and Toc gathers her close to him, in an affectation of feminine good will. We have just been ravaged by Englishmen by the shoreline."

"Toc's too tall," I observe. "Standing next to Lady Jane, his height alone makes him mannish."

Toc slews, glaring at me, but I persist, "Sullivan will make a more believable lady's maid, don't you think? We all stoop and shuffle but when close to a real woman, we don't stand a chance to pass ourselves off as women, least of all Toc."

"It's the way he moves," Tate agrees with me.

Elliot weighs my suggestion then consents while Toc raises his lip in a surly gesture.

"Lady Jane? Will Sullivan do?" Elliot looks at the beautiful woman, apparently impervious to the radiance of her looks which, to my surprise, have not diminished with dust and shoe polish.

Lady Jane shakes her head and smiles at Toc, "Too mannish," she repeats in flattering tones, then she turns to Sullivan and takes his proffered arm.

But Sullivan pauses. "But what of me? Surely, I am not womanly?"

"Just a better actor," Jane reassures him.

"*Yallah!*" Elliot calls us to hasten.

Now mirthless, we head for the ridge, ready to play our roles.

The glint of field glasses is the first sign that our presence is known to the enemy.

I bang on the drum, my heart beating fast. There is no telling what the men on the ridge will do. Shoot us for sport? Will they wait for us to get closer?

"*Salam!*" Tate booms and waves as he sees a German pointing his gun. He makes a show of fumbling for something then produces a filthy rag and waves it in the air. The rag is red so Elliot quickly replaces Tate's rag with a muddy white pair of ripped undergarments. Tate, with all the innocence of the East, waves the white rag with idiotic enthusiasm. I keep a steady beat. Toc holds onto Bandar because Toc is the only one without the sickening smell of the hair dye and so Toc has the undivided attention of our fastidious monkey.

"*Salam!*"

A German soldier scurries down the slope, many other comrades behind him, guns at the ready.

Elliot begins a rapid fire guttural Arabic explanation of all the misfortunes that have befallen his tribe complete with wails and hand gestures and spitting, often too close to the German's booted feet.

Understanding little of what Elliot is saying, the German nods patiently as he runs his eyes over our company, resting on Jane, but then elated to see Bandar.

"*Affe,*" he says and for a moment his guard is lowered. Looking like a schoolboy, he grins but only for a moment. He suspiciously looks about again, his glance darting from Elliot to Tate.

Elliot repeats the German's word for monkey, pointing at Bandar. "We go now, yes? No boom, boom?" Elliot gestures bombs exploding and even goes as far as placing a brown, dirty finger on the German's weapon.

But Bandar has other plans. Noticing that he's caught the man's attention and that the German might be an appreciative audience, Bandar scampers down Toc's robes, evades Toc's arms trying to grab him then begins a series of flips.

The German's face lights up. Soon, his comrades approach us, suspicious at first then captivated like children at the sight of the monkey, chittering and dancing, flipping this way and that.

One soldier kneels, summoning Bandar.

"*Yallah*, monkey, *yallah!*" Elliot calls out in Arabic and claps like an oaf, cheering Bandar on and I am grateful that he remembers not to use Bandar's name. Moss, Bandar's previous owner, loved Kipling's Jungle Book and so named Bandar using the Hindi word for monkey.

Toc quickly pulls out Bandar's ball. In swift motions, he grabs Sullivan's vial out of the kitchen utensil pouch, opens it and, with utter disregard to his own health, taps the contents of the vial on the ball then throws the ball to the German, but rather clumsily, like a woman, or rather, like Toc imagines a woman throws a ball. The kneeling German reaches out and grabs the ball which makes Bandar shriek and chatter, hands outstretched. Bandar flips and the German tosses the ball to the monkey, unsure whether that is the thing to do. He is rewarded with a shriek of delight and another flip and some clapping from Bandar before the ball returns to the German. The German and Bandar play catch.

The soldiers watch on, smiling, some laughing, some joining in, until a shout, then a crack of gunshot, rips the happy chittering sounds, and we fall silent, looking up the ridge. A volley of Germanic orders summons the soldiers up the ridge, some walking backwards, guns trained on us. But otherwise, we are left unmolested and are allowed to leave.

Elated at our good fortune of not running into any aggressive confrontation, we decide to check out one more Axis pillbox indicated on the map by RAF reconnaissance before returning back to base. Toc is congratulated for thinking of using the monkey as we use precious water and soap to disinfect Toc and Bandar.

#

"How many more outings like that can we pull off?" I ask.

Toc pours benzine into a sand-filled tin can. He lights the fuel and sets a pot of water to boil. "We're not far from camp. Tea?"

"Yes, please." Lady Jane smiles at him.

"According to my father, there's a major offensive planned for early autumn," Toc says.

"But we're to give offense, harassment, if you will. Fatigue the Panzerarmee. Our LRDG…"

"And SAS," Sullivan adds to Tate's lecture.

"We are to blow up aircraft, or any transport, supplies, and communication-lines. It's arrows against the lightning, but it just might save a few of our boys. Make a few mothers less miserable!"

"On both sides," Toc interjects.

"Maskelyn prepared dummy troops," Tate says.

"Dummy tanks, dummy water pipeline, dummy trucks, dummy men," Elliot grumbles. "But it was not only Maskelyn. He's been sacked, you know. It's Geoffrey Barkas and his engineers, his zoologists and stage mechanics and even actors. Barkas has been made Director of Camouflage at GHQ in Cairo. And Operation Bertram is more than just that. Besides phantom armies of dummy tanks, artillery and even men, his camouflage team manufactured dummy railheads and pipelines. They went as far as disguising real tanks as lorries."

"What a clever team!"

"They even thought about adding track marks, smoke from 'cooking,' and 'washing' hanging on lines where they staged their dummy troops. We, you and I and Toc, Jane, and the Australians are just an infinitesimal part of the operation, attached closer to the Long Range units rather than to the camouflage unit but we enjoy the support of both. Lucky us," Elliot explains.

"Lucky us? Lucky we have Sir Niles on our side. Few have jeeps and costumes!" Tate says.

Elliot's gaze falls on me, his eyes are tired. "Jack, I have not thanked you for saving my life today. I had no idea that that German boy in the second box had a gun. Only officers carry guns."

"But he was an officer!"

"So young?"

"They're running out of experienced, mature men just like we are."

"Well, I won't rush into a box like that again!"

CHAPTER 31

Wednesday 30 September 1942
CAIRO, EGYPT

WEDDING BELLS REVERBERATED in his head.

He did it for his country, but mostly for the boys in the desert. If he could save them from ending up in hospital or blown to bits, he was more than happy to do it. And the prospect of obtaining valuable information about the Bakers seemed promising. He had already collected enough information about Mr. Baker, Louisa's father. Marrying Louisa would allow him discrete, close scrutiny of the daughter's financial and social affairs. His lawyers had assured him that proper arrangements were made.

The Cairene street-noises assaulted Elliot's ears as he led his bride to his car under intense, mid-day sun. Motorcar horns blew and donkeys brayed, the bootblacks shouted and merchants haggled but the metallic music of the East dominated the clamor until the motorcars' engines were switched on and began to roar. The acrid smell of burnt petrol and rotting rubbish singed his nostrils. Behind him, a long procession of fancy motorcars followed to the Westbrook estate, obediently plodding through the hot and dusty streets.

While Louisa's chatter rang in his ears, Elliot drove fast and recklessly. He loved speeding across Cairo, and so he never hired a chauffeur. He relished the sight of his bride clutching to her seat, tightlipped, before resuming her noisy monologues.

After escorting Louisa into the house to freshen up, Elliot walked to the courtyard to greet the guests first to arrive but when he heard a loud crash and saw a woman escape out the gate to the street outside, Elliot made to chase after her.

William grabbed hold of his sleeve. "It's the general maid. Cook sent her packing."

"Oh, how I envy her," Elliot rumbled.

"Why? Cook's wrath is not at all the thing to envy!"

Elliot cast William a reproachful look. "Not Cook! I envy her freedom. I don't think that I can bear those tittering idiots."

"What idiots?"

"Bridesmaids."

"Yapping curs, Elliot. Malicious yapping curs."

Elliot grinned.

"Forget them. The orchestra is loud enough now. You can't hear a thing." William tugged at his brother's sleeve and urged him to hurry, as the wedding celebration was already drowning any other sounds that would normally drift into the secluded estate. "Elliot, you have to dance with your bride."

He grimaced. "Yes, well, I was afraid of that, too."

"There's more to wedding and marriage than just dancing, you know."

"Oh, I know. And there's always the switch."

"Switch?" William asked, confused and alarmed as bits of lurid imagination crept into his thoughts. "What switch?"

"Light switch," Elliot elucidated and added the hand motion.

#

Feeling trapped, Elliot prowled the hallways. His flippant remark to William about a light switch triggered a string of memories of Lady Jane. He missed her terribly and was sorry for the misery he was putting her through. But he had explained the situation to her. He had done so regardless of fear of what would happen should she fall into enemy hands.

"Elliot?"

"William!" Elliot turned round, pinning a smile on his face.

"What is this? A scarf round your neck? Or shall I call it a noose?"

Elliot was rather pleased with his choice of elaborate, old fashioned neck wear but was happy to use it to mask his ill humor. He complained of the horrific scent of garlic and cumin that clung to everything coming out of the tailor's shop. He sniffed, tilting his lips downward. His posture shifted somehow. His chest swelled and his bottom protruded out ostentatiously. "Curse that tailor." Then, with the slightest gesture, Elliot sent William into peals of laughter. "William, I have a surprise for you. Come outside."

Music and chatter filled the air. The piano plinked, flirting with a trumpet. Someone laughed immoderately and was soon hushed.

Elliot and William left the house and its gardens and patios and courtyards and headed to the main irrigation canal, stopping by the diversion where Elliot pulled out a flask of whiskey from the reeds.

"Why not have a table and chairs set up for us while you were at it?" William teased him, noticing Elliot's soiled suit. "It's ruined, you know. All this dark muck on your suit and the rips along the back and shoulder lines scratch you out of your own wedding party."

"Never-mind that. Cheers!"

Even though he enjoyed the smooth liquid snaking its way into his body, William made a token protest, "Elliot, you have to return to your guests."

"All in good time. I just hope that I can change before anyone spots me."

"Why did you marry Louisa?"

"She has beautiful legs."

"You are incorrigible."

"Legs are an excellent excuse."

"Father's excuse was more convincing. He choked something like 'a suitable match' then fell into a fit of coughing and gurgling noises."

"That too!" Elliot brightened. "Well, I better go dance with my suitable match and her fine legs. By the way, have you seen Mr. Baker?"

"The man's impossible! He skulks about like a stage villain, watching his girl from dark alcoves. Last I saw him, Elliot, he was edging toward the bandstand, his eyes flicking between you and Louisa. What's the matter with the man? You are marrying his daughter after all, why the funereal expression? Have you ever seen him smile?"

"No, I never saw him smile. Nervous habits, I suppose, or guilty conscience. He let it slip that he finds me roisterous and would have liked his daughter to ally herself with one of the Arab princes of the oil-rich lands of the East." Elliot rose, not at all steady.

"A prince? For Louisa?" William laughed.

With great effort, Elliot returned to the house, to change.

Standing by the canal, William regarded the retreating form of his older brother. The excuses for the marriage were all too casual and badly presented. William was sure that there was some other, more important, reason for the marriage and he was certain that it related to the war.

#

On the edge of the dance floor, Elliot scanned the crowd, as if looking for someone. He smiled when he saw Louisa and in a few unsteady steps was asking her to dance with him.

"So, have you resigned yourself to the fact that your husband would always have the smell of either whiskey or brandy on his breath?"

"Darling, are you going to tell me your plans for tonight? Or, where will we be spending our wedding night?"

"I'm afraid not."

"Secretive, aren't you?"

217

Elliot threw his head back with a laugh but found it difficult to keep his balance and he took a step back. "You'll love it." He brought his mouth down on hers and pulled her close to him. He had no intention of telling her that beyond a short stay at Shepheard's, he had no other plans and that her father insisted that they stay close to Cairo. The arrangement suited Elliot, and so he had made no objections. He doubted that Louisa would object.

Her next words confirmed this. "You know, you cannot carry me off too far from Cairo."

"I know. Your father made it quite clear," he lowered his voice.

For a moment, Louisa looked surprised and even confused but she soon regained her composure. "Yes, well, you know how it is. I am his only child and he is lonely."

"No doubt."

CHAPTER 32

An excerpt from Jack Johnson's Notes
Wednesday 30 September 1942
WESTERN DESERT

OUR JEEP IS coughing and spluttering as we motor across the desert to some point in a book of ever-changing coordinates given to us by our commanding officers and RAF intelligence. Although I often consult Sullivan as we navigate the vast sand seas together, today, I persevere on my own.

Tate and Sullivan are grieving.

The New Zealanders and Australians took heavy losses during the September offensives in the desert. Admiring the two formidable men, I notice that their flinty expressions are unyielding.

When we stop to brew up tea, we are silent. Sullivan stirs the pot with a long stick and Bandar rests sleepily in Toc's arms.

Our assignment is sabotage.

We are to get to fuel and ammunition dumps and arrange for massive explosions. The LRDG has more Lewes bombs, compliments of the SAS.

"Wish Elliot were here." Toc lowers the now sleeping Bandar to his lap.

"Nothing like watching him wave his arms about to cheer a fellow up," agrees Sullivan.

"Like the village idiot," Toc adds.

"Do we have biscuits? Jam?" Sullivan asks.

"And Jane," Tate growls as he riffles through our rations.

And I recall a comment Toc had once made about taking one look at Jane's beautiful face and the world is put to right.

"Is she really in Alexandria?"

"Probably already tight."

Tate nods. "Cecil Hotel."

"Does he have to marry that creature? Louisa Baker?" Toc pronounces the word creature in such tones that I almost mistake his dislike of Louisa for hauteur.

"Is she a creature?" Sullivan asks, his head tilts, his nose crinkling.

"Yes, but the less we know about it the better. Something to do with codes bouncing about into enemy hands. Information that should not leak out to Rommel. And supplies. But, my dear cousin, you never heard a thing, not a whisper, about it!" Tate looks at me, grimacing as he explains the absence of Elliot and Jane.

What terrible sacrifices people make!

"I cannot imagine a more perfect lady for Elliot than Jane but here he is at church with a creature."

"Worse. He's at church," Toc says, well aware of Elliot's religious sentiments, then he adds, "and getting married to an Axis supporter for there is no other reason for Elliot to have to marry a mousy nobody like Louisa Baker when Lady Jane is already his."

"A nobody? But Louisa is wealthy! She's the daughter of one of Cairo's wealthier merchants," Sullivan responds.

Toc only repeats, "Nobody."

So I whisper to Sullivan, "Not of the gentry or aristocracy." But as I say the words, a dark fear grips me. If I survive the war, what will happen to me? What will happen to Toc? Will we ever see each other again?

"Look, I don't know about you, but I cannot stomach the idea of Lady Jane on her own today, not today!" Tate rasps.

"Go and get her then," Toc suggests, his refined accent is rather harsh and challenging.

"I will." And Tate, good to his word, hops into his jeep, switches the engine on and to our great amazement, drives off toward Alexandria.

"Tate!" I leap up.

"Does he know where he's going?"

"One of us should be with him in case of an emergency!" I call out.

But today is not a day for precaution.

Tate has taken off so impetuously that we just watch the trail of dust his jeep kicks up as it disappears into the horizon.

"Don't fuss. We're not too far from Alexandria, not yet. And Tate is a capable navigator. But, he forgot his tea!"

#

"More grenades would be better, you know." Tate has his field glasses fixed on the jebel far ahead on the horizon. "They are guarding the supplies with everything they have!"

Toc shifts and asks, "Dogs?"

"Dogs, too."

"Jolly good."

"What?"

"It's a larger box than any of the other ones we have visited. We'll need a massive dust screen as we drive away," Toc agrees with Tate.

Sullivan emerges from under a jeep and approaches me. "Jeeps are all right, mechanically."

"Yes?" I stare at the maps, wrestling with coordinates to plan our quickest escape route.

"They're in excellent shape. Tires are good, and the engines purr."

"Even when Tate drives them? Does he always drive like that? Fast and with utter disregard to shifting gears?"

"He's used to farm equipment, and he can't resist speeding over dunes, doing a cool sixty, or more, and often in third gear," Sullivan replies, grinning as his headgear flaps in the hot desert wind. "One hand barely on the wheel and the other waving a cigarette about. It's really a wonder how he does that."

Lady Jane is by my side, too. "I am glad that he rescued me from the Cecil, however hair-raising our drive out of Alexandria was. And so dusty," she says quietly, her eyes are trained on the horizon, scanning for any movement.

"I'm glad that you're here," I say but as I glance at her, I almost regret my words.

Pain is etched into her face.

I am certain that she is thinking of Elliot. I place my hand on her back and she leans into my hand, seeking my touch for reassurance. I almost feel disloyal as the connection sends a shiver of excitement through me although disloyal towards whom I cannot tell, Lady Jane or Elliot, or someone or something else altogether. "Look, I'm sorry. I only meant that it is better that you are here with us, with friends."

"And busy!" Tate interjects. "He has to do what he has to do. And so do we. Now, let us get going!" he says though his intonation is somehow soft and quiet.

"Thank you for rescuing me from Alexandria," Lady Jane gives Tate's hand a squeeze.

"Hold off your thanks because we had no idea that this box is a rather large one. Panzerarmee infantrymen guarding a supply convoy."

"I'm not at all keen on the infantry," I blurt out. Over the past year, I have had several run-ins with Panzer infantry and I do not relish a close-up encounter. "I'm not a coward, I just don't like their firing range. Those 88mm anti-tank guns, you know. The shell pops out and doesn't stop until it hits something or someone."

Toc lowers his gaze, but I can tell that he is watching me. He, too, probably wants to turn back. Would Toc ever say so?

"If we drive away now, can they spot the dust our tires would be kicking up?" Lady Jane asks.

"Quite possibly. Driving through that dust storm earlier today popped us right here. We're close, very close to them. They never saw us coming," Tate replies, his field glasses glued to his eyes, watching the movements on the ridge.

"I couldn't see where I was going," I clarify.

"And I followed Johnson!" Sullivan chimes in.

"We can either make the best of it, or we can hang out here until either another dust storm comes along or night falls," Toc suggests. "But I need to blow something up. I don't care what. A supply convoy is a jolly good target and sounds like fun."

"Will there be another dust storm?" Lady Jane scans the horizon again.

"There always is!" Toc says.

Sullivan, watching Lady Jane's face, quickly adds, "Or we wait for nightfall."

Lowering his field glasses thoughtfully, Tate says, "I don't like the idea of sitting here, next to our jeeps and supplies. What if there is overhead activity?" He points upward, obliquely referring to either an Axis bomber or air patrol. "And what if they too send out scouts and patrol units just like Toc and Johnson here were doing in June when they were supposed to be convalescing?"

A long moment of silence settles on our oddly attired group. Somewhere inside me I feel bubbling laughter rise up. There's my cousin, the very tall Tate, dressed with all the elegance of a Bedouin sheik who has been through hell and back, having obtained his new costume from the theater production engineer working with Geoffrey Barkas. But studying Tate, one cannot mistake the good natured, guileless Australian face with his brown hair escaping his headgear. True, his matted beard hides a portion of his visage, and he has been in the habit of using henna to darken his dirty whiskers but his light brown eyes and fair lashes and light brown hair, poorly dyed, are harder to camouflage. Then there is Toc: Proper, almost stiff with good manners and posture. He is dressed as a Bedouin woman. His fingernails and toenails are painted bright red and the hair on his face, hands, and feet is shaven off. His eyes are rimmed with black kohl and his lips are slightly stained with beetroot from our rations of cans. Underneath his rather flamboyant robes are a knife and a Colt. Sullivan is a lowly servant, responsible for serving our sickening brews. He chooses to stain his flaxen hair and bristly beard with the horrid shoe polish dye because he's "damned if he will be a woman again and have to shave his face in the desert!" Lady Jane is a Bedouin woman, her face almost completely covered by her black veil. And I am ridiculously malodorous and dirty.

222

We none of us as we should be. The stench of rotting fruit and unwashed bodies intermingles with the spices of the desert, the garlic and sage and goat, fire pit smoke and dung. And I recall that Elliot had his costume dipped in camel dung, washed and dried by campfire smoke, then rolled in a salt marsh and let dry!

"Authenticity," I begin with a giggle that rises into convulsive laughter I dearly try to keep quiet, but I cannot.

The others regard me with confusion, then, as they look at each other, smiles appear on their faces and low sniggers and giggles cover up my unexpected mirth. Tate laughs but tries to shush us. His attempts are ineffective. We crouch low, letting the wave of laughter ride out but every time we raise our heads and catch each other's eyes, we choke up again.

Jane's laughter turns into hushed sobs before too long though, and Tate reaches out to her. Tate pulls her into his arms in an almost avuncular manner though he cannot be older than her by more than a year or two. We watch, still half buried in a shallow sandpit, like children watching grownups deal with problems beyond comprehension.

Then Sullivan's innocent comment, also child-like in itself, brings us round. "I don't know how she stays in his arms when he smells like a camel's arse!"

Toc swivels his attention to Sullivan and regards him for a moment. "Are you familiar with that particular scent?" Toc asks rather curious.

"What, the scent of a camel's arse?"

"Well, yes."

"Toc!" I shake my head, warning him to avoid such a discussion but it is no good. Sullivan is already squinting in contemplation. Is Sullivan recalling an incident when he had actually encountered such a scent? Or will he manufacture some fib that would satisfy Toc's curiosity?

But in the end, Sullivan shakes his head, "No, no, I cannot say that I have!"

"Whilst you settle the matter of scent and camels and arse, why not check the coordinates, figure out where we are and how far are we from our own people?" Tate's whispered words carry a tinge of admonition, but not really.

I nudge Toc. "What's the proper way to reply to a sheik?"

"Just do as he says, I suppose. I cannot recall if there are any formal words of acquiescence within tribal communities," Toc tries to help but when he looks at us, he frowns. "Well, what is it?"

I clap him on the back and crawl out of the sandpit to the back of the jeep, to study my instruments and maps. There's a hushed but heated discussion going on in the sandpit and I smile to myself, wishing I could hear Toc's replies, when a stray bullet whizzes by me, landing in the sand and setting the particles of sand into an upward dance.

"Down," I hiss as I drop and wriggle for cover behind the bush we have parked the jeeps under.

We wait for more bullets to follow but there are none following the first.

"We better go on with the show," growls Toc. "But I certainly wish we had more fireworks for the grand finale."

"Why aren't they shooting at us now?" I hear Sullivan squeak in bewilderment. "Why was there just the one bullet?"

"I don't know."

CHAPTER 33

Wednesday 30 September 1942
CAIRO, EGYPT

TORTURED BY GUILT, Elliot shuffled into Faraj's café. Sounds of wedding music still ringing in his ears like hell's bells, he clenched his fists, opened and shut them again. He had wanted to check in with Faraj before the day was over, so he took a taxi to the suk, letting his *wife* know that he'd return shortly.

Faraj fell silent when his eyes alighted on Elliot's stooped figure. His palm opened, letting his dice fall onto the board. Ponderously, Faraj moved toward Elliot, throwing careless apologies at his companions.

"*Mon ami,*" his baritone voice caressed the words as he whisked Elliot to the office.

Within the privacy of Faraj's sanctuary, Elliot's head fell, and he let Faraj gather him into an embrace, the older man's thick arms enveloping the young Englishman, his salt and pepper bristles rubbing against Elliot's soft brown curls. "So, you had to go through with it. I was afraid of that. You are not as cool a cucumber as you would like us all to believe! And that's why I did not accept your invitation, Elliot. Do you forgive me?"

"Yes, of course," Elliot's muffled voice replied into Faraj's shoulder. "Faraj," he choked.

"I was hoping for a sandstorm or even Axis invasion on your behalf. Can you believe how foolish I was?"

Faraj's comment made Elliot look up at Faraj, a grin fighting its way across his tears and worry lines. "Axis invasion?" Then the mirth was wiped out, and Elliot asked, "Faraj, do you know what they do to Jews? Do you know what the Nazis have been up to with regard to your people? Genocide's too gentle a word."

Faraj held Elliot's gaze. "Oh, I have a fairly good idea. I have been contributing financially to the Jewish resistance."

"A wedding is not such a bad thing after all, is it?"

"Elliot," Faraj rasped. "It's your wedding night. I suppose you just stopped by to say *à bientôt?*"

Elliot's expression sharpened. They were whispering, huddled together in Faraj's private office but one could never be too careful. "Jane? Where is she?"

Faraj indulged in a long sigh before replying. "My man tells me that she is with the big man."

"Tate?"

"My man followed her to Alexandria as you wished. Jane went to the Cecil, by the waterfront. He saw your hairy Australian friend enter the hotel about an hour later. Lady Jane and Tate left in a jeep. They were going in the direction of the desert road. He did not follow them."

Elliot choked miserably. "I love Jane."

"She understands more than is told."

"And you, Faraj? How much do you know?"

Thrown by the directness of Elliot's question, Faraj blinked. "A friend, a very good friend, knows more than is said to him in words. But as for Jane, she understands your position and your business. Her brother trained at Aldershot, and is now somewhere in Europe. She understands. Elliot, I want to tell you something."

"Faraj?"

Faraj lowered his gaze. "Remember, I was a friend of her father's. He was a British politician. He had no large property, no estates here in Cairo nor in England. He had enough, however, to buy him entry into the diplomatic circles. Well, then the Great War broke out. He became a military man. He served here in Egypt then returned to England when it was all over. But he remained a military man. A great man. And, a brave man. In 1940, he died in France almost as soon as he set foot there. Lady Jane came here to Cairo at her father's request. Her brother was supposed to join her as the old man wanted his two children out of England and as far away from Europe as possible. He had communicated his wishes years ago knowing very well that the Great War was not the war to end all wars. When war again broke out, I sent for both brother and sister. Only my Lady Jane showed up, in the springtime. Her younger brother joined your army."

"Why do you call her Lady Jane?"

"I had you boys fooled. You thought it was a term of endearment, but it is not just that. She is Lady Jane, you see. Her voice and talent for performance, she got that from her mother. But her father was an earl. A prominent English socialite, a politician, an aristocrat. He married outside his class. Nonetheless, Jane is Lady Jane. The first signs of trouble began during the Great War. Jane's maternal grandmother lost two boys. Jane's mother, a ballerina or some such dancer, if I remember correctly, married in haste, to leave the grief stricken household. The Earl, Jane's father, was a politician, as I said, but he decided to buy his commission in the army and he became an army man, a decorated soldier, in fact. He never did anything by halves. But, the first few months of this war carried him off."

"What of Jane's mother?"

"Jane's mother is terminally ill. She is in England, withering away. She, too, requested that Lady Jane come to me. As her health declined, she wanted privacy. Now Jane's younger brother has left Aldershot, and is shooting anything in sight in Europe. Not a very cheerful story. One of my worst yet!"

"Yes. And without the usual flair for oriental drama!" agreed Elliot.

"Well, you have to take the rough with the smooth as you say!"

"Do I?"

"You volunteered," Faraj imitated Elliot's words to Toc.

"Faraj, has that wretched old Joseph been regaling you with tales of my exploits?"

"Who else? But, no, this little bit of English insouciance I discovered from my Lady Jane. Joseph was not there."

"And I thought that I could count on the old ass!"

"The old ass being Joseph?"

"Why, yes."

"You can. He talks to me about your escapades, but to no one else. He is loyal to you and your family. You forget, he believes that he raised you boys. You spent more time in the stables than with your books. He is loyal, and you can trust Joseph, Elliot."

"How can you be so sure?"

"Joseph has no children of his own. How do you think he views you Westbrook boys? He won't risk blabbing. He would never betray you," replied Faraj with assurance.

CHAPTER 34

An excerpt from Jack Johnson's Notes
Wednesday 30 September 1942
WESTERN DESERT

"*YALLAH, YALLAH!*" TATE ululates, his arms in the air.

Sullivan is by Tate's side, then Toc and Lady Jane bring the rear. Lady Jane is not dancing. She is walking slowly, weary. At a sign from Tate, Jane raises her voice in a fairly good imitation of the "*lulululu*" cries of belly dancers and her fingers snap her cymbals.

Sitting far away from them in the jeep, I wonder at how loud such tiny metallic instruments can sound and sure enough I notice that the Jerries certainly spot my comrades. My field glasses are trained on the moving Bedouins, then shift to the soldiers above, and I pause for a moment to wonder how the hell we have made it this far? Here we are, alive, facing another regiment of the fierce Afrika Korps!

Heads pop over the ridge, and vegetative cover begins to shift and move.

The mouths of guns appear.

"*Yallah!*" Tate's deep booming voice carries across the desert, butting up against the enemy-infested ridge line.

I stay back with our jeeps under the low-lying bushes. Our tactics this time are a bit different. As soon as Tate manages to distract the Germans, I am to drive right into the convoy of parked lorries and their supplies, tape Lewes bombs to as many lorries as I can get to, then drive away.

The sun is still high in the sky, and my eyes sting with grime and sweat dripping down my forehead. I watch Sheik Tate, Sullivan, Toc, and Lady Jane walk to the ridge. Any moment now I expect them to be picked up by some soldier looking for sport. Jane stumbles then regains her undulating steps and Toc follows her, trying to match her hip motions and feminine ways. As my beard itches, I actually envy Toc. His face is freshly shaven.

"*Halt!*" I hear a shout from above. Then gunshot. My stomach clenches, and I find it hard to breath.

Tate stops in his tracks. He looks up in surprise then waves his hands frantically, almost like a half-wit, or a man happy to be rescued. "*Alman!*" he turns, telling the remainder of his tribe of the presence of Germans. "*Alman!*" he repeats the word with praises to *Allah*.

Lady Jane, of course, resumes her ululating celebratory cry and chinks her finger cymbals even louder while Sullivan gets a dirty rag and flaps it in the air.

The Germans on the ridge manage to locate a boy who speaks Arabic and they pull him forward, nudging him to walk down and meet with this motley procession of Bedouins.

Tate launches into a tirade he memorized under the tutelage of Elliot. Overwhelmed by rasping speech and hand gestures, spitting and clapping, shouts of laughter and shouts of anguish, the German boy looks round in silence while Sullivan and Toc unpack and give the impression of careless indifference. Sullivan actually goes as far as lighting a fire and pulling out a blackened coffee pot. The German boy casts anxious glances upward then waves his hand and his commanding officer begins to make his descent. Sullivan pours water into the little pot and spoons out coffee.

Lady Jane falls back, quietly watching over Bandar, holding out a rattle for his entertainment.

Meanwhile, Tate's complaints of the *Inglizi* continue in rapid fire never giving the blond boy a chance to reply.

The German officer and the boy look back up to the ridge and shout something that brings several helmeted heads up. Many soldiers emerge and scramble down.

Sullivan, stooping in reverence, brings a copper tray of three small coffee cups, each cup with a scant amount of coffee, mumbling curses of the English who spilled his coffee in rather good imitation of the Bedouin Arabic dialect.

The German officer does not hesitate and shoots his hand to the tray and downs the few sips of coffee, nods a *"danka,"* and calls out orders to his men. Sullivan's brew this time is rather innocuous. But the rims of the coffee cups have been laced with a rather wicked strain of influenza.

Tate is still driveling on when one of the Germans eyes Jane and Toc and Bandar. The German is rather small and brown, flies on his lips because he too suffers from heat or sun blisters. His eyes are riveted now on Toc. Lady Jane flutters her hands around Toc's back as if shooing her companion forward and accompanies the gesture with a demurely whispered *yallah*. With impish delight, Toc gyrates further away from the gathering soldiers while Bandar carelessly moves from Toc's broad shoulders to Lady Jane's head, back and forth.

This is my cue to drive into camp. Praying that I got the Jerry markings correctly painted on the American jeep, and that no one will notice the odd, foreign-looking vehicle among the German Volkswagen Kübelwagens, I check for the supply convoy once more.

Switching the engine on, I ease the jeep out of the rough scrub and drive along the back of the ridge, waving a casual hello to a German using a shovel to cover up his recent messy activity. The flies are horrendous, I notice, as I hop off the jeep and begin taping the bombs close to the Kübelwagens' petrol tanks. I work swiftly, expecting the worse at any moment.

Suddenly, I hear hurried steps and voices nearby, so I amble as casually as I can back to my jeep. I am in German uniform and, if caught, my punishment is immediate and lethal. Heart thumping, I jump into the jeep when I hear the sounds of altercation. I throw caution to the wind and plow into the camp and out the other side hoping to pick up my comrades as they make a run for it.

Safety lies northward, where, in the distance, the sea sparkles beneath sunlit cerulean sky.

I halt meters away from the impossible scene playing behind me. There is a sudden clatter of copper. I watch Bandar's charming flips as if it is all a part of some playful game. Bandar thrusts handfuls of sand into the soldiers' eyes, they back off and shout as one of them throws his leg to kick the monkey. But Lady Jane stoops quickly to Bandar, and he leaps up to her. She turns her back to the Germans and walks away, northward toward my jeep. Tate begins a volley of curses against infidels who kick monkeys and Sullivan launches the burning remains of his fire at the Germans who are still shouting and trying to rid their eyes of sand and now dodge bits of hot coal. Toc walks backward. He has a grenade and an automatic under his dark robes.

In great big strides, Tate and Sullivan head for the clumps of brush where my jeep is waiting for them and then continue to crawl on the ground as Toc releases a grenade and sprays ammunition into the wall of dust.

Next, Sullivan gets up to release a grenade then throws himself down on the sand, Tate, only a yard away from his friend, is in the prone position as he releases his grenade.

Hidden behind the wall of dust and confusion and shouting and screams of pain, the Australians and Toc now run to our jeep.

While they run, Tate pauses long enough to cast another grenade and the men drop on their bellies once more and crawl. The shots that were being fired in their direction are few but in a matter of minutes, afraid that the anti-tank guns will talk, they are back on their feet, running.

In the confusion, I forget to look for Lady Jane until I hear her calling Bandar. Cold fear grips me because her voice is far away.

Too far.

I slew my head round and spot a dark figure squatting, hands extended forward. Leaving the jeep's engine in idle, I jump out, sprinting to Lady Jane.

Lady Jane is crouched low, chirruping and calling and coaxing Bandar to come, but the animal is in one of his moods, refusing to go near her.

"Bandar," I call and give his command to come.

Almost sheepishly, the monkey chitters as he obeys.

Muttering impatiently under my breath, I send Bandar to the deepest, darkest places of Hades.

Bandar on my shoulders, I take hold of Jane's slender hand. It fits well in my palm, and I realize that I have not held a woman's hand in mine since war broke out. Together, we run back but suddenly I feel her slip from my grasp.

I turn to look.

Lady Jane's expression is one of shock, then pain and regret, and she collapses on the desert floor.

A bullet.

A single stray bullet has hit Lady Jane.

I stand confused, the monkey restless on my shoulders.

But Tate is not confused. Long, giant strides bring him to Lady Jane. He picks her up and sprints to the jeep.

And once again it is Toc who rescues me.

When Toc reaches the jeep, he sees that I am standing stock-still, rooted to the spot.

"Jack!"

I am motionless.

Toc springs out of the jeep, and runs to me. He savagely grabs my hand, pulling me along, dragging me at times, to the jeep through the veil of dust and smoke and noise. And Bandar tightens his grip on my neck, holding on, and even his screech fails to shake me out of my stupor, out of my shock.

CHAPTER 35

Tuesday 06 October 1942
CAIRO, EGYPT

"FATHER?"

"Here," Sir Niles replied, hoping that the howls of a rescued white mongrel outside would provide good background noise.

The study was dark, lit only by what little suffused light sneaked through the window.

"She's gone. Did you know?" rasped Elliot.

"Lady Jane? Yes. And you, how are you?"

"I got a message on my wedding night that she had been *injured*," Elliot squeaked, choking on remorse and pain. "After I had a couple of goes at Louisa, that dried up piece of…"

"Elliot! Do try to be…oh, but what's the use. Coarse and uncouth you are and coarse and uncouth you will always be. Who told you? How did it happen? How did they get Lady Jane? How did the word get back to you? And so soon?"

Elliot took a deep breath and with great effort barked, "Tate."

"Tate, the big Australian boy?"

"Yes."

"Well?"

"It is all so… Father, I've been such a careless, pompous fool."

"But you had another role to play," Sir Niles commented dryly, hoping that by keeping his frustration and grief for the brave woman at bay he was helping his son. He, too, admired Lady Jane's courageous ventures to the desert with little support and mercilessly exposed to the enemy. "So, she is dead then."

Elliot nodded, unable to say the words. "She was with our men, our Bedouin tribe, but the Germans got her."

"How?"

"Tate and company drove through a dust storm and parked close to a ridge peppered with German outposts and a fuel convoy in their midsts, too. Toc let the Germans play with Bandar, the monkey, who had a good dose of biological goods on him. Then they all scrammed for the coast line, running toward a hidden jeep."

"And did they not make it in time?"

"It was a German bullet. The absurdity of it is that the Germans had no idea who they were! Tate had some grenades. But, so do some Bedouin tribes. So, the

Germans were shooting at an unknown group of strangers, for sport! They did not know who they were, not at first, because Jack Johnson, the baby-faced one, taped Lewes bombs on their supplies lorries and set the bombs for fifteen minutes later. The soldiers were probably hoping to snag some women or camels. It's all the same to them, maybe they even prefer a camel willie up their…"

"Elliot."

"Jack Johnson carried her back to the jeep. No, it was Tate. Jack tried. Then afterwards, after they told me, I had to stop by here, to pick up some things. I drank coffee and William, oh, Father, William saw me."

"Elliot, you did not tell him!"

"No, of course not. But right away he was asking all sorts of questions, damn him, he always knows when I'm not myself!"

"Does he? Well? You did not tell him the whole thing about Lady Jane, I hope."

"No, no, of course not! There's the required secrecy but, oh, Father, what would William think of me? Dragging such a woman out to the desert like that. No, I fobbed him off with some nonsense about Louisa painting her legs instead of wearing stockings and that my sheets are dirty. He didn't like it, but I pushed off. That was that!"

"Painted legs?"

"Yes, some of the women paint their legs because of rationing and limits on stockings."

"But surely Louisa has no such pecuniary troubles. William is well aware of that!"

"He certainly is. He was. But, you know how he is. He's too polite, too well-bred to call me a damn liar to my face."

"Language, Elliot!"

"What is this infernal noise?"

"A mongrel."

"A dog?"

"William's latest charity specimen."

"Damn." Then Elliot put his head down between his knees, breathing and hoping that the pain would go away. That the emptiness would vanish and somehow the guilt, the immeasurable feeling of remorse would cease to gnaw at him. He wanted to howl, to scream. "Damn it, Father, I loved her. I asked her to marry me when it was all over."

"I know."

"Wait a bit," Elliot growled, anger replacing pain as he realized that there was one thing that he could do now. It would not bring Lady Jane back and neither would it help him with his grief and contrition. But he would march right into the Bakers' mansion. He was the horrid creature's husband after all. "Father, telephone Crumper. Tell him that I am going in."

"What? Elliot? What is this? Going in where?" alarmed, Sir Niles was asking questions but Elliot was already bounding down the stairs.

"Telephone him Father. It's important. Telephone him right away. I am going in."

With shaking hands, Sir Niles turned to his desk and picked up the telephone receiver, suddenly wishing that the dog would settle down and keep quiet, like Bruce, the rescued black cat now sleeping on a stack of papers on his desk.

#

Tuesday 06 October 1942
CAIRO, EGYPT

"My stars and garters!" Elliot's squeak of delight mimicked his Great Aunt Clara. He remembered his odd aunt arriving at the estate in Cairo. She had showed up with an ancient holdall fifteen years earlier. And until her death a year after her arrival, she had persistently creaked about his grandparents' Egyptian residence, finding endless delight in every modern refinement, especially hot running water and electricity. But why was he thinking of his odd great aunt at that very moment?

Elliot was at the Bakers' mansion, alone for a change. Wracked with guilt, he found the courage to walk right into the grand residence, pass the ornate iron gate and through the lush garden. Then, when the butler blinked warily at him holding the heavy front door open, Elliot simply barked at the man that he had to pick something up for his wife. His wife! A spasm of pain still wrenched his gut when he uttered those words, pain and anger and disgust. Elliot could not bring Lady Jane back to life but he was certainly going to do his best to honor her death by eliminating Louisa Baker and her dreadful father.

Now standing in a cramped office, his eyes scanned the room, taking in the unusual layout of the furniture.

On a previous visit to the mansion, he had spotted the locked door because the door knob was a glass door knob and the only such knob in a house that boasted solid brass knobs throughout. Crumper, too, had indeed confirmed that it was either a room or an office that was strictly private. And although the locking mechanism was a robust Yale, Elliot managed to get through the lock with a set of keys Crumper had given him.

Elliot stepped into the interior of the heavily carpeted room after throwing the latch back into the locked position on the knob. Quickly, he looked up at the ceiling.

How much time did he have?

His eyes moved from the unexceptional ceiling to the contents of the room, noticing the incongruity of the place. Why was a low side table so far away from the two chairs by the window? The chairs were certainly made of mahogany while the table resembled oak. Most offices kept low side tables by sofas or settees or next to wingback chairs. So, the positioning was odd and the fact that the threesome was not a set in a house full of carefully selected pieces of furniture and matching artwork was unusual. Also, why were the two bookcases in the office set so far apart? Bookcases were generally consigned to the back wall of offices, anchored to the wall, side by side.

Elliot decided to look into the side table first. Walking to the window, he began tapping on the oak table. The strangely hollow sound surprised him because the table gave the appearance of being very solid, heavy and unyielding. He nudged the table with his foot. The blasted thing was a lightweight-shell! And interestingly, a metal box was hidden under the shell.

Elliot paused. Did he imagine it or was there a sound coming from the hallway?

Quickly, he bent down and began jabbing the flimsy padlock with his knife. And when the padlock popped open and the lid fell back, Elliot whistled and squeaked, "My stars and garters!"

Elation at finally putting his hands on enough documentation, enough letters and even a book of accounts, to cast Louisa Baker and her father into the darkest of dungeons, or better, to Crumper's wishful firing squad, was making him giddy.

How easy it had all been after all! The arrogance of the Bakers struck him. They assumed that they were safe in a mansion in Cairo with only few security precautions. Did they think so highly of themselves as above suspicion or so little of the British government, or for that matter, of him that they barely bothered to conceal their documents and contacts? Everything was even carefully labeled. An office with an easy lock to pick and a shell of a side table placed over a metal box with a flimsy padlock were less than the bare minimum. Cook had more security measures in his kitchen, particularly now after the incident when a black cat had infiltrated his cupboards!

Elliot smiled to himself.

"What are you doing?" An accented, scratchy old voice cracked behind him, and Elliot froze. His stomach clenched.

How did he miss the sound of the key turning in the lock? How could he be so stupid, so careless?

"Reading, what does it look like I'm doing?" he replied, anger gripping his words. "Damn you, you startled me! And who the devil are you?" He turned to face the rather heavy-set woman who stood staring at him. "You smell like my Great Aunt Clara," he blurted out, surprising himself and the woman.

Her eyes raked him and settled on the papers. She moved forward, fast and nimble for her age and size.

On an impulse, Elliot turned to sweep the papers into an unruly mess in his left arm then shoved the woman forcefully further into the office. In three steps, he was at the door. Another well placed kick at the persistent old hag, and he slammed the door shut behind him, locking and cursing as he struggled with the key and the opposition on the other side, remarking how powerful the woman really was! How was she able to bump him, a six foot tall, well-built man, from the door, twice! In a flash, he opened the door, and aimed a swift, hard kick at the woman's head.

She reeled back, bumped into a box, and fell sprawled on the floor.

Elliot then forced the key in and twisted the mechanism, jamming it shut.

Was there any noise coming from inside the office? He did not have time to check!

Elliot took off at full speed down the hall, heading to the nearest window.

The Bakers' mansion was palatial. From the sizable width and length of the polished marble halls, to the spacious rooms and curving staircases, everything was grand. And so were the windows of the mansion, all overlooking exquisite gardens. There were also two-toned, long damask silk curtains hanging majestically above the apertures, barring the Egyptian sun from entering the cool interior.

Heartbeat thundering, legs stretched out in a sprint, Elliot had a mad idea to bundle his papers into his shirt and make his escape out the window as heavy footsteps pounded on the polished floor of the hall, only steps behind him.

The first shot missed him, making his hair stand on end and ice run in his veins.

Without looking back, Elliot lifted his leg and kicked the window, shattering the glass. He barely had time to think, to properly time his jump. Clutching the disorganized bundle of papers to his chest, he ejected himself out the window.

There was a moment of weightlessness, of almost euphoric joy. Is he leaping to his death? Is there an afterlife after-all where he might be reunited with Lady Jane?

Gunshots sounded from every direction and in the din his body chafed against some horrid sharp tangles, then collided with something hard. Momentary pain then oblivion as his eyes became heavy then shut.

When his treacherous eyes blinked open again and consciousness returned, Elliot was in agony.

Where was he? What were all the blinking lights and noises all around him?

Fear gripped him as a terrible thought that he was caught by the Bakers' small army popped into his head. He opened his eyes properly, wide and alert, and stared.

He was in a makeshift ambulance, the type that was used in the Western Desert by the Eighth Army. He twisted round, aware of throbbing pain in his back and head. He was anxious to be up, though. Pulling his long legs to his chest, he rolled up only to bang his head on the lorry's overhead metal bars. The juicy imprecation that escaped him, brought a blotchy and nervous-looking orderly into view.

Wasting no time, the orderly turned his head and shouted, "Sir, he's up, Sir. I can't believe it, but he's up, standing up."

Surprised voices erupted and Crumper appeared, hands extended to steady Elliot and help the orderly get Elliot out. And to his dismay, they propped him against the bumper of the lorry.

A shout of pain escaped his lips as Elliot felt thorns dig into the skin of his back.

"Hold him up!" Crumper shouted. "Where's that damn doctor?"

"Damn you, Crumper."

"Well, Westbrook, we had you down for dead but you got them." Crumper was rather direct, a treat never offered to Elliot before. "They certainly put up a fight, but military police have them now. And I managed to extract and collect all the papers you were holding so tightly before you took the leap into the rosebushes. An unfortunate choice, Westbrook."

"What?" Elliot asked, still dazed.

"Rosebushes, Elliot. You landed in the rose garden, on a rose bush, from a drop of a second story height. On the other side of the same hall are the coy ponds. Tst. I did provide you with the floor plan."

"What about the woman who smelled like Great Aunt Clara?"

"What? What great aunt? And who the devil is Clara?" Crumper was confused.

"Must be the shock, Sir," offered the orderly.

"Be a good chap and call for the doctor to examine him," Crumper dismissed the orderly with more tolerance than he would normally have exhibited.

"Elliot, what are you talking about? What woman?" Crumper's tone was urgent.

"She caught me going through the papers, in that office. I shoved her in, and locked the door behind me. I twisted the key in hard, jamming the mechanism. Most likely, she is one of them. She was so powerful, damn her."

"Good God! It's like kicking a hornets' nest." Crumper ran a hand across his forehead. "Is that where you found it all? That little room I'd marked private and unknown?"

"Yes. Go get her, Crumper. You'll have to force the door open, as I'd jammed the mechanism." Elliot tried to steady himself and retrace his steps back to the mansion but pain in his head and back seized him and he groaned, repeating, "Get her, Crumper. She must be one of them. She caught me off guard and fought like the devil. And see what you can learn about the bookcases."

"What bookcases?"

"The orientation of two of the bookcases and their set up was all wrong. Wrong layout. But the woman, Crumper, go get that Amazon!"

"Yes, of course. Our men are inside, scouring the place, but I'll go make sure they get into that office quickly and carefully. Did she have a gun?"

"Don't know. She fought me, pushed against the door with such strength. With luck, she's still unconscious and inside that office. I had to pull open the door to knock her out cold. She would have chased me with the rest of that little army if I let her be. She was powerful."

Quickly, Crumper had several of his men surrounding the office while a doctor examined Elliot, pulling out thorns, marveling at Elliot's luck after falling two stories to the ground.

Within minutes, Crumper's men appeared in the grounds of the estate, dragging a woman who was writhing and struggling against their tight hold.

Looking like an innocent school boy, undersized and clean-shaven, Crumper approached the woman, lifted up his revolver, and put it to her head. "Who are you?"

The woman fell silent, no longer kicking and screaming.

"Well, you'll talk later, Love." Crumper, his revolver still pointed at her, was staring with distaste at the heavy woman. Then he began calling out instructions. "Pack her up and send her with the other scum. Don't let her get away, no matter what. You have my permission to shoot her if necessary. And," he added, "it'll be perfectly legal." His last command he repeated in German and Italian. Then he gave a cheeky wink that carried more venom and hate than any scowl.

When Crumper finally returned to Elliot, he waved a book in his hand.

"What's this? Are you looting a novel for your perusal when all this is over?" Elliot asked.

"*Rebecca! Rebecca!*"

"What?"

"On 10 July, when the Australians captured the Afrika Korps' signal Company 621, they discovered a copy of *Rebecca* by Daphne Du Maurier."

"And? What's a novel about a sadistic dead wife to do with all this?" Elliot asked.

"Code. They use the book as a basis for their code and, damn, Elliot, you must have concussion, can't you see how incriminating this copy of the book is? And it was purchased in Portugal."

"Portugal? Portugal's spy city! But what of your *Rebecca?*"

"This book is a cipher book," Crumper explained, still waving *Rebecca* about. "Used by Axis agents. Good work, Westbrook."

"I recollect that my father rang you up? Did he alert you to my actions? Is that how I had sufficient coverage once out in the rose garden?"

Crumper bowed his head. "Yes. Sir Niles would have wrung my neck had he been next to me. Under no uncertain terms, he ordered me to storm the Bakers' mansion. 'Full force!' he'd said. He had no notion of keeping the operation clandestine. So, we came out in full force, as you can see. A very good thing as it turned out."

"There was such a ramshackle lot chasing me down the hall, you know."

"Guards in disguise," Crumper said.

"Yes. Appearances can be deceiving, because they materialized as a veritable army. I had to jump. Did you collect them all?"

"Yes. Although I haven't a clue where they came from!"

"Like a pack of terriers!" Elliot eased himself off of the bumper of the ambulance.

"Before you go, Westbrook, how the hell did you get in?"

"I walked in, damn it. I am…" Elliot grimaced and corrected himself. "I *was* the creature's husband after all. I walked in through the front door."

"Cheeky bastard! But at least the Eighth Army will head into battle with one less impediment. Did you see what you grabbed out of that office?"

"Book of accounts, correspondence…"

"Oh, much, much more than just that. If I am not mistaken, we now know who is in charge of providing supplies to the Axis forces in the Libyan desert."

Elliot whistled.

"Not bad. And we have *Rebecca*, too. Men are working on prying open those bookcases. I'll let you know what else pops up."

Elliot shakily clapped Crumper on the back then turned away.

He should be elated and proud of his achievement, but he felt nothing of the sort. He blindly walked away, marched on forward, and into seething darkness. Longing and remorse, his lonely life without Lady Jane stretched before him, a bleak desert.

CHAPTER 36

TOC AND I are back with our original regiment, recalled back because a major offensive is on the way. Of our original regiment, so few have survived.

Miraculously, Bandar is still by my side. Many of the other pets, even the Australians' kangaroo, have already perished or disappeared, but not our Bandar. He and I have been through so much for what seems to be a long time, but is only, in fact, a few months.

Nightfall brings the whistling wind into focus. I crawl under two army blankets and shiver.

Toc is lying in his bed, his odd muttering and twitching, always an amusement to me in the past, worry me now. How long will our run of luck hold? We are both now a part of the Long Range Desert Group. When we go away with Tate and Sullivan, we broadcast that we are on patrol duty. Sergeant grits his teeth but says nothing. He is well aware of Toc's lineage, and is rather afraid to have to report that Toc is again injured, or worse. What would Toc's father say or do should something else go wrong? He fears the wrath of an English lord. And one who resides so close to the battlefield, too, only miles away, in a sprawling mansion in Cairo.

But as the sun rises, a flurry of British bombers and fighters overhead reassures us that this time we have proper air coverage.

Toc's arm shoots out of his blanket, triumphant. "It's going to be splendid this time, Jack!" he delivers his words with his usual care. "RAF coverage!"

I remain silent, watching him, a miserable expression on my face.

Noting my reaction, Toc casts an anxious glance and asks, "Jane? Lady Jane?"

I have not been myself lately. I blame myself for letting Lady Jane slip from my grasp. I have held many dead men and crawled over bodies and fought in deadly engagements. But I never held the hand of a beautiful woman who, moments prior, was running and smiling by my side then, moments later, lifeless on the down slope of a sand dune.

My thoughts are shattered to bits when an RAF bomber flies over our camp. Then another one follows and more aircraft shoot across the sky.

241

Fully awake now, both Toc and Bandar are on my bed, chattering nonsense I cannot hear. Bandar reaches for my neck and holds onto me and I can sense his uneasiness. After all, he cannot much like the tremendous noise. Toc reaches for rum and we sit together, sharing our drink with a monkey, waiting for orders to come.

#

Thursday 22 October 1942
WESTERN DESERT

The desert has seasons of its own. There is bitter cold, blistering heat, and the constant companion, the dust storm. Now that the end of October approaches, the nights are colder.

The darkness smothers me, and I am cold as I have never been cold before. Mice are dancing on top of me. And I can only be thankful it is not a troupe of scorpions, although Sergeant tells me that it never is scorpions plural but a single specimen unless of course you run into a mother carrying her young on her back.

"A mother scorpion carries her young on her back? Good Lord, man, how many little ones are we talking about?"

"Let's just hope that you don't run into such a family," is the only answer I get.

Now, we are crawling forward in the dead of night. Toc is by my side, telling me about some of the soldiers, even middle aged ones, who have B or C health cards and demand to be re-examined, to be allowed to join us.

"Toc, what's going to happen?"

"They'll bring in a couple of medical officers to re-examine the men. You should have seen the commanding officers' faces. And the rookies' too! They were astounded by the men's desire to go to the front, again."

"What did you do with Bandar?" I ask.

"He's in his cage, though I cannot be easy on that score."

"Why not?"

"Jack, it's going to be hellish tonight! The sounds are frightening enough to an animal, and I can scarcely imagine what the flashes of light and the ground-shaking explosions are going to be like for him."

"But he has been through similar engagements before."

"Jack, this time it is different," Toc confides in measured tones. "We have heavy RAF coverage, record breaking coverage. Rommel, too, is putting forth all he has."

"Move it, Johnson! We have to get there by midnight," a low growl catches up with me, and Toc looks back.

"It's Sergeant."

"Pff," Toc puffs in reply. "Of course it is Sergeant! Move it, Johnson," he echoes, then helps me by pushing up on my boots.

#

Friday 23 October 1942
Second Battle of el Alamein

My ration of rum was scarcely enough to buy me courage. But I know that I will do my bit as best I can.

Our battalion has orders to march to the front, then advance toward the objective. What the commanding officers now call the Second Battle of el Alamein is underway.

Allied air operation, massive hammering from above and dog fights in the sky, set the stage.

A tremendous barrage follows.

The Eighth has waited for too long to retaliate after the retreat in June to el Alamein and the stalemate in July and August.

Toc and I are moving our equipment out of the dugout and onto carriers. And once equipment is loaded, we pile into a lorry and follow the engineers through Rommel's Devil's gardens.

The sappers' dangerous work of detecting mines is laborious and slow as they struggle through the minefields, making a path for us to pass without getting blown up.

"Hellfire," Toc croaks, his eyes trained on the horizon, as we wait for a path to clear.

"Will we have proper and sustained air support this time round?" I ask Toc.

"Probably."

I step out of the lorry, calling, "I'll be back in a moment."

In the clear night air, I watch bombs drop from a lone Axis Stuka, then German machine and mortar fire erupt, and I doubt the Allies' success.

I scan for any enemy sniper brave enough to crawl across the minefields to take potshots.

Then a heat wave follows after a petrol dump ignites and a wall of fire illuminates the desert. My body is thrust back. My face, warm and sweaty, feels like it is on fire.

"Jack," Toc screams.

I am on all fours, inching my way back.

"Where'd you go?"

"I wanted to see."

"See what?"

"The sky."

"Get in."

But as I scramble into the lorry, I see Toc's exhausted face. "I'll do the driving now."

"No, neither of you will do any more driving," Sergeant's pugnacious face plunges inside the cabin next to Toc, and he growls a string of commands that send us to the troop-carrying vehicle in the rear.

"This is taking ages!" Toc groans. "We'll never make it to our objective, and the ground is hard. How will we dig? How will we set up our artillery?"

"We'll use sand bags."

"Wish we were with that crazy Elliot Westbrook again. Dancing away and eliminating them one Jerry at a time!"

"He did not eliminate them, just gave them general discomfort. Toc, I will never forget the Italian who drank his coffee in one shot."

"He turned purple, didn't he?"

"Yes, and ran out of the mess tent, shitting all the way out and how those stupid bastards screamed and cursed!"

"That's when I took my dose of ipecac!" Mirth finally reaches his eyes, crinkling up his face.

"And those horrible camels!"

"I hate camels. Did you know that one of the camels urinated on Elliot's sandals?"

"Is that why he howled like a wounded animal?" I laugh until a sharp reproof brings us to order, and we pile out of the troop-carrying vehicle, grab our shovels and dig a hole to retreat into, just in case.

But it is not us retreating this time.

The night sky lights up again and the horrendous din now familiar yet hated keeps us going through a 'battle high.'

By sunrise, a number of enemy soldiers wander into our lines. They are unarmed and rather silly looking because the barrage ripped them of sense and they are shell-shocked or 'bomb-happy' as we prefer to say, because 'bomb-happy'

244

sounds cheery and 'shell-shocked' grim and none of us want to face that aspect of the war, not now, not ever.

We mark their appearance - youthful.

"I say, Toc, look at him! Are they bringing in kids now?"

"The Italians?"

"Yes, no, I mean, both, the Italians and even some of the Germans look child-like."

"We are not much older," whispers Toc as I point out an Italian so undersized and brown with ears that stick out, severe desert sores disfiguring his lips. The Italian seems to catch our attention and we stare at him and he stares back at us.

#
Saturday 24 October 1942
WESTERN DESERT

A crisis ensues when British tanks take a heavy hit. Morale sinks, and Toc comes under criticism as he loses patience with an older comrade.

"Scolded again by that uncouth fellow?" I ask.

Toc silently cleans his Bren gun. His head is bent over the task, ignoring me.

"He's on edge, that's all. We have to make it through more minefields today. Minefields with wooden mines made with the smallest possible bit of metal. Even our sappers with their metal detectors can barely detect them."

Toc raises his blue eyes to mine, his face filthy, streaked with black soot and cordite, grease, dust, and the runnels of sweat drawing an intricate map of dark rivers and streams.

My words do not miss the mark.

"It's not enough that the mines are wooden, some are interconnected. As soon as one mine is lit, a chain reaction erupts."

Toc's hands furiously rub the Bren gun, his identity disks bouncing on his chest, and I send a prayer that I will never have to remove the red one from Toc's chain.

CHAPTER 37

Thursday 29 October 1942
CAIRO, EGYPT

"WILLIAM! WE'RE IN the study."

Sir Niles handed the pale young man a tumbler of brandy when he entered.

"Well?" Elliot stood up and hurled an inquiry. He noticed William's extreme pallor, a telltale sign that his brother was worried.

The Eighth Army had been paying a heavy price for every inch it advanced beyond el Alamein.

Elliot wanted to distract his brother but with what? He had planned to tell him of the public meeting held back home in England between leading politicians and the clergy concerning the Nazi persecution of Jews but surely that could not be a more cheerful subject. He could tease him about Salomé or mention Madame Sukey or, curse him, the confounded cook or even Aziza the Beast but Elliot doubted that any of that would brighten William's wan face. What would? His thoughts raced and kept hitting on the subject of Salomé.

"Have you looked in on Salomé?" he asked.

Both his father and his brother leveled their almost reptilian eyes at him. What on earth had made Elliot mention the maid?

"No, why should I?"

"That cur hasn't stopped howling."

"Cur?" William asked.

"The dog!"

"She's a puppy. Puppies cry at night. Besides, her leg was broken. She cannot be very comfortable."

"Does it bother you?" Sir Niles asked.

"What?" Elliot wondered.

"Elliot, don't be stupid. We're talking about the dog, are we not? Does the dog bother you?"

"No, of course not. I am hardly ever here. And besides, she's a beauty, a rare beauty with white fur and upright ears and a sassy, twisty tail. Can't think of a lovelier creature."

William looked at Elliot with mounting impatience. "So why do you ask?"

"I thought that you'd do something about it."

"About what?"

"Now who is being stupid?" Elliot snapped.

Exasperated and tired, William walked out of the study, tumbler of brandy empty but still clutched in his hand.

Elliot edged to the window, watching his brother walk to the stables.

"You did that on purpose, didn't you?" his father commented, bemused.

"Someone had to do it for him. That lovely girl's the only one of us who cheers him up a bit. His work cannot be easy at the moment. The wounded from the front get sent back to Cairo and Alexandria by droves. I'm surprised Monty has any soldiers left, really. They're marching straight into heavy artillery. Marching into the 88mm's, bagpipes playing. The Black Guard is in shreds. Few survived, from what I understand."

"Still, I wish that you hadn't encouraged him to go to the stables," brooded Sir Niles.

"Why not?"

"Have you thought of her feelings, Elliot? It'd only end in disappointment, or worse."

"Worse?"

CHAPTER 38

An excerpt from Jack Johnson's Notes
Saturday 31 October 1942
WESTERN DESERT

"AREN'T THEY MARVELOUS?" Toc remarks.

"The engineers?" I ask.

"Their plows, if one may call the tanks they drive as such."

Plowing through Rommel's Devil's gardens, the engineers now use tanks with rotating metal arms attached at the front.

"Impressive," I reply, but my heart is not in this conversation. Watching the sappers work, I hold my breath.

Applying new techniques where the sappers suspect s-bombs (shrapnel bombs or bouncy betty) that explode at waist level, they now approach lying down, using a poker rather than the mine detector.

"When are you two jokers planning to leave?" Sergeant erupts between us.

"As soon as the jeeps arrive, Sir."

Sergeant growls, "I have the paperwork already turned in. LRDG, and even the SAS, wrote back, both happy to accommodate you two now that you have officially joined their ranks. They are merging, you know. An SAS detachment and fellows from the LRDG are already being sent to the north of Palestine and Syria for special training. We plan to push the Germans and Italians out of North Africa. Then we cross the Mediterranean to Europe, probably Italy. Will you be all right?"

"Yes, Sir," Toc replies.

"Look after yourselves." He clasps our hands.

CHAPTER 39

Sunday 01 November 1942
WESTERN DESERT

THE BOOTS WERE no longer black, but Elliot paid little attention to his footwear or anything else for that matter as he marched to the jeep. His Australian friends and their two English apostles were already waiting for him to join them on a last mission in the Libyan desert.

"Well?"

"Recci," Sullivan replied. "But there are railway and communication lines and possible fuel dumps just a bit further."

"We'll take a detour and, ah, explore in a more explosive way," Tate promised.

"A fuel dump would be nice," Elliot growled. "Makes for such great fun."

Toc and Johnson exchanged looks.

"Where's the monkey?" Elliot asked.

Toc's face darkened as he thrust his head in the direction of a cage strapped to one of the jeeps. "Asleep."

Elliot did not know what his feelings should be toward Bandar, as he now possessed the entire story, all the events leading to Lady Jane's death.

"We better get going or we'll be caught between the Jerries and the Eighth. Rommel's making a last stand at Alamein, and rumor has it that if it fails, the Jerries'll retreat," Tate said with a sad twist to his mouth. He blamed himself for driving to Alexandria to bring Lady Jane along with them on their disastrous excursion, nor could he forgive the monkey for his obstinate behavior that day.

Elliot trained his eyes on the shimmering horizon and found himself thinking of Lady Jane singing 'You Go to My Head' in the desert. A bitter lump choked his throat, and he was grateful for the driving goggles that caught his warm tears.

EPILOGUE

Friday 25 December 1943
NORTHERN PALESTINE

TOC, SULLIVAN, AND I stand still and stare at the rows of white crosses before us, cool mountain breeze tousling our hair.

"It's been over a year, but he never really got over losing Lady Jane," Sullivan's voice rides softly on the crisp, Carmel breeze.

"But he didn't lose her. I did," I say. "I lost her."

Toc looks up briefly at me and shakes his head. "Tate felt guilty for having brought Lady Jane along."

"But I lost her. I let her chase after Bandar." The monkey's name trickles uneasily out of my lips.

"Tate believed himself responsible. He drove her to the desert from Alexandria on the day of Elliot's wedding. Well," Toc grated at the rocky ground beneath our feet. "At least, Tate's here, and not over there," he jerks his head toward Egypt. "At least he's not in the Western Desert somewhere, unmarked, unidentified."

"Mountains were his thing," Sullivan agrees.

I feel an emptiness one feels in funerals when relatives and visitors alike begin building a shield of inane comments that hardly pertain to the harrowing pain wrenching their minds when thinking of the dead, of the loved ones they've just lost, never to see again. What a terrible loss!

Tate, dead now and all because of an accident during a drill on Mount Carmel.

"What will I tell his mother?" I turn aside and vomit as another searing thought hits me, *What will I tell my mother?*

"It's a good thing that Elliot isn't here," Toc says. "I don't think that I could stomach his convulsive retching, and the noise and smell. At least Jack's quiet about it," he concludes with his sophisticated accents becoming more acute.

"You spoke too soon, mate," Sullivan's Australian drawl reaches my ringing ears and I look up to see a tall, thin man in dusty, disheveled suit approach us.

"So, you're here," Toc throws his welcome at Elliot.

Elliot stares at the grave as his hand reaches into his jacket and he pulls out a tattered book, "Yours, I believe?"

Toc takes the paperback and nods, "Madame Sukey's choice, the Forsyte Saga."

There's a moment of silence then we snort with laughter, tears running down my cheeks and Elliot, too, is looking rather red in the eyes. Sullivan's mirth ends in dry heaves, and Toc launches into the foulest string of oaths ever to escape his lips as he pulls a bottle of brandy out of his jacket.

"Language, Toc," I manage and with the unaccountable resilience of youth, I choke on a salty, sour grin.

Acknowledgements

Both *Into Seething Darkness* and its sequel, *Sheol's Ransom*, blossomed out of a friendly request for more details about the puckish Elliot Westbrook and the military surgeon, James Westbrook. And, so, the second novel in the London to Cairo trilogy was born. I am therefore indebted to Bethany Kapusta for her fearlessness, her encouragement and support.

I thank my beloved family for their patience and help. Particularly, I am grateful for my husband and son who read this book out-loud, discussing scenes and characters by the fireside. Inspired, my son then created LEGO sets for such scenes or characters that suited his fancy.

Storytelling aside, this book, this trilogy, is dedicated to those who fought the Axis and to those who lived or died during such turbulent, merciless years.